AND SO IT BEGINS...

"What shall we do?" asked Laruhk.

"There is not much we can do. If we were to go down there now, we would be slaughtered along with the rest of Athelwald. No, we must wait and watch. With any luck, we shall be able to identify the attackers."

"Why? To seek revenge?" asked Laruhk.

"No," Kargen replied, "this is not our fight. To intervene would be to invite disaster for our own people."

"As usual, you are in the right, my friend. We shall let them kill each other, and then there will be fewer Humans to threaten us in the future."

"You misinterpret, Laruhk. We shall wait until the riders have left and then enter Athelwald. There may be survivors."

"I thought you said it was not our fight? The Orcs of the Red Hand have been left alone by the duke. Are we to change all that with our actions this day? Surely, if we interfere here, there will be repercussions?"

"I cannot stand by and do nothing," said Kargen. "We Orcs exist in a precarious position, surviving only so long as the Duke of Holstead does not see us as a threat. I would have thought the same of Athgar's people, but something has altered that relationship. Change is coming, whether we want it or not."

They watched the riders as they torched the village. The dead lay scattered about, while others, cut off by the horsemen, cowered before the display of weapons.

"They mean to take prisoners!" announced Laruhk.

A drop of rain fell, landing on Kargen's face. "Our ancestors weep," he observed. "Mark this day well, for something has started here that will have a great effect on our people, I can feel it."

"Surely you jest, Kargen. The Therengian's are a minor people. How could the loss of this one village affect our tribe?"

"Just as the loss of a single hunter can change the fortunes of the hunt, so too, can the loss of a single ally leave ripples in the lives of others. I do not know what has happened this day, but I feel it has changed our future."

ALSO BY PAUL J BENNETT

Heir to the Crown Series

Servant of the Crown

Sword of the Crown

Mercerian Tales: Stories of the Past

Heart of the Crown

Shadow of the Crown

Mercerian Tales: The Call of Magic

Fate of the Crown

Burden of the Crown

Mercerian Tales: The Making of a Man

Defender of the Crown

Fury of the Crown

Mercerian Tales: Honour Thy Ancestors

War of the Crown

Triumph of the Crown

Guardian of the Crown

The Frozen Flame Series

The Awakening/Into the Fire - Prequels

Ashes | Embers | Flames | Inferno | Maelstrom | Vortex Torrent | Cataclysm

Power Ascending Series

Tempered Steel: Prequel

Temple Knight | Warrior Knight

Temple Captain | Warrior Lord

Temple Commander |

The Chronicles of Cyric

Into the Maelstrom

Midwinter Murder

The Beast of Brunhausen

A Plague in Zeiderbruch

ASHES

THE FROZEN FLAME: BOOK ONE

PAUL J BENNETT

MAP OF THE CONTINENT

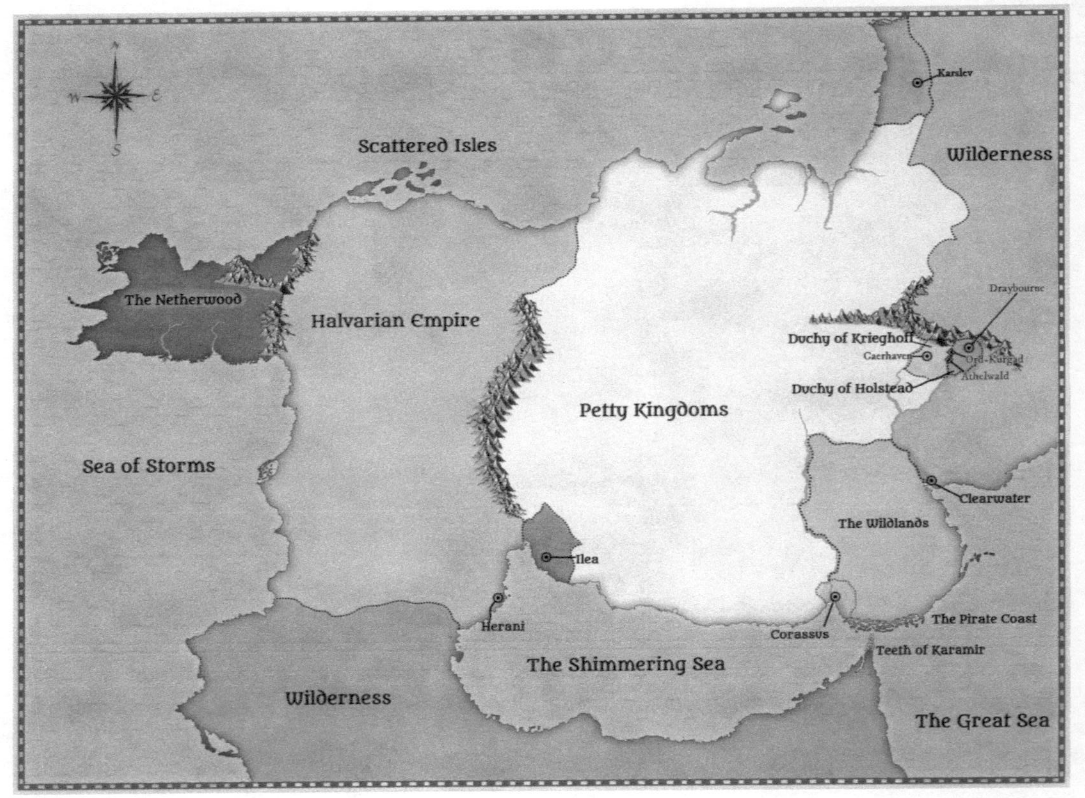

ASHES

FROM THE ASHES

SPRING 1102 SR* (SAINTS RECKONING)

(In the tongue of the Orcs)

An arrow sailed through the air, digging into a tree near a deer. Alarmed by the sound, the creature bolted, disappearing deeper into the woods.

A bellow of rage exploded from a nearby bush. Its occupant stood up, his green Orc skin blending in well with the surrounding forest. "I should have had him," he growled.

"There will be more," called out his Orc companion. "To be honest, Laruhk, I am surprised you got so close. I would have heard you at twice the distance."

"You mock me, Kargen," he replied. "My skills are just as good as yours."

"And yet the deer escaped," stated Kargen, his face breaking into a grin, "but it is of no consequence. We shall merely have to find another."

"Had you not given our last deer to Athgar, we might be back at our village, enjoying the smell of roast venison."

"He needed the kill," defended Kargen, "and we are sufficiently skilled that we shall not return empty-handed."

"Bah, you favour the Human too much. What is it about him that you find so interesting?"

"He is not like the rest," asserted Kargen. "He treats us with respect, and in turn, I offer the same to him."

"Athgar is not much of a hunter," observed Laruhk.

"Neither are you if your last arrow is any indication." Kargen wandered over to the tree, pulling the shot loose. "The tip is undamaged," he said, offering it back to his companion.

Laruhk tucked it into the quiver that hung from his belt. "Where shall we look next?"

Kargen didn't answer, he was too busy sniffing the air.

"What is it?" asked Laruhk.

"Something on the wind, smoke I think, coming from the west."

"A nearby hunter?"

"No," said Kargen. "It is too strong for a simple campfire. This is something bigger."

"An army camp, perhaps?"

"Here, in this part of the woods?" asked Kargen. "Humans know this is Orc territory. They would be fools to enter."

"And yet, it has not stopped them in the past," said Laruhk. "It is the reason we built a palisade around Ord-Kurgad, remember? I can think of no other explanation for the smoke, can you? The only other thing nearby is the village of Athelwald."

"Perhaps it is under attack?" suggested Kargen.

"Who would attack the Therengians?" asked Laruhk. "They form a buffer between the duke and us. Without them, there would be trouble on the border."

"Perhaps that is someone's intent?" supplied Kargen. "We know so little about the ways of Humans, but they are said to be devious."

"You think that outsiders mean to invade us?"

"It is a distinct possibility," said Kargen.

"And so Athgar's people, these Therengians, would they fight?"

"They would not fight us," replied Kargen, "for we are the only ones to trade with them, but they would, I suspect, fight to defend their village."

"If that is so, then what are we to do?" asked Laruhk.

"We must investigate further," his friend decided, "and try to discover what has befallen them. Let us see if we can solve this mystery."

They made their way upwind, following a westerly path until they emerged from the trees onto a slight rise, the Therengian village of Athelwald visible some distance off. Even from their current position, they could make out flames. Thick, black smoke poured from the dwellings, while horsemen rode about, torches in hand, their armour glinting in the sun.

"Your suspicions are correct, they are under attack!" called out Laruhk.

"Yes, but by who?" asked Kargen, shielding his eyes, straining to make out what details he could.

"Armoured riders on horseback, it would appear," said Laruhk.

"I can see that, but who are they? Mercenaries? Agents of the duke? Soldiers from Krieghoff? They wear heavy metal armour, perhaps a war has broken out, and Athgar's village has been caught in the middle?"

"What shall we do?" asked Laruhk.

"There is not much we can do. If we were to go down there now, we would be slaughtered along with the rest of Athelwald. No, we must wait and watch. With any luck, we shall be able to identify the attackers."

"Why? To seek revenge?" asked Laruhk.

"No," Kargen replied, "this is not our fight. To intervene would be to invite disaster for our own people."

"As usual, you are in the right, my friend. We shall let them kill each other, and then there will be fewer Humans to threaten us in the future."

"You misinterpret, Laruhk. We shall wait until the riders have left and then enter Athelwald. There may be survivors."

"I thought you said it was not our fight? The Orcs of the Red Hand have been left alone by the duke. Are we to change all that with our actions this day? Surely, if we interfere here, there will be repercussions?"

"I cannot stand by and do nothing," said Kargen. "We Orcs exist in a precarious position, surviving only so long as the Duke of Holstead does not see us as a threat. I would have thought the same of Athgar's people, but something has altered that relationship. Change is coming, whether we want it or not."

They watched the riders as they torched the village. The dead lay scattered about, while others, cut off by the horsemen, cowered before the display of weapons.

"They mean to take prisoners!" announced Laruhk.

A drop of rain fell, landing on Kargen's face. "Our ancestors weep," he observed. "Mark this day well, for something has started here that will have a great effect on our people, I can feel it."

"Surely you jest, Kargen. The Therengian's are a minor people. How could the loss of this one village affect our tribe?"

"Just as the loss of a single hunter can change the fortunes of the hunt, so too, can the loss of a single ally leave ripples in the lives of others. I do not know what has happened this day, but I feel it has changed our future."

They watched in silence, the raindrops increasing in frequency till they became a heavy rain, obscuring their view of Athelwald.

"Come," said Kargen, "it is time we approach."

They made their way down the hill. The rain had soaked the ground, yet smoke still poured forth from the buildings. As they drew closer, a quiet settled over the area, lending an eerie feeling to their journey. Arriving at the edge of the village, they paused, listening intently, trying to ascertain if the enemy horsemen remained.

"They are gone," announced Kargen, advancing.

Slowly, cautiously, they walked into the remains of Athelwald. The thatched roofs had, for the most part, been burned away, while little was left of the buildings save for some scorched timbers and mud.

Laruhk stopped, gazing down at the body of a villager. "This was no battle," he declared, "this was a massacre."

Kargen swept his gaze across the area, taking in the footprints that were yet to be washed away by the rain. "Yes," he finally said, "and yet I fear killing was not their objective."

"How can you say that? Look at all the bodies!"

In answer, Kargen ran forward, then paused, pointing at the ground. "There, you see? They were taken from here in a large group, herded, like the Humans herd cattle."

"But why would someone do such a thing?" asked Laruhk.

"There is only one reason I can think of," replied Kargen. "They were taken as slaves."

Laruhk made a face. "How barbaric," he spat out in disgust. "Have they no sense of decency?"

"No, they do not, whoever they were. I suspect these people fought back," he waved his hand to indicate the dead, "but they had little chance against armoured horsemen."

"Poor Athgar," said Laruhk, "I shall miss him."

"I doubt he was taken," offered Kargen. "He is not the type to surrender without a fight."

"Then he is likely dead," said Laruhk, "and yet I do not see his body."

"Let us look around some more, perhaps we will be able to find him, and let his spirit rest."

They poked their way through the burned-out huts, ignoring the rain. It was Kargen that finally found what he was looking for. "Over here," he called out.

Laruhk came running, "What is it?"

"This is what is left of Athgar's hut," said Kargen. "The rain must have extinguished the fire."

"Is he in there?"

"I do not know," Kargen replied. "The timbers that formed the roof have collapsed. Help me move them, and perhaps we can find his body."

They quickly got to work, hefting the timbers and tossing them to the side. As they moved yet another one, Kargen tripped on something, sending the wood toppling to the side. He looked down to see a boot, still attached to a leg.

"A body," he called out. "It must be Athgar, buried in the debris."

Laruhk moved forward, crouching to wipe ashes from the body, revealing Athgar, the human's brown hair framing a face with a patchy beard. The Orc pried open an eyelid to look into the human's grey eyes. "He is dead," he declared.

"No, he is not," said Kargen. "Note how the rain bubbles around his nose? Quickly, we must pull him free."

Kargen lifted the man's head, shielding him from the rain with his massive green body. "Grab his legs, let us pull him from the remains of this hut."

They dragged him out, laying him on the ground. As they did so, the rain slackened, then suddenly stopped. Kargen looked up at the sky in surprise, "The ancestors look kindly upon us."

"It is just rain," offered Laruhk, "not the ancestors."

"Do not be so sure to dismiss things," retorted his companion.

Laruhk looked over the body. "He seems to have taken a rather nasty hit to the head," he observed, "and there are several cuts to his arms, along with burns."

"Strange that he would have taken refuge in a burning hut," observed Kargen.

"I suspect he fought back, but something must have forced him into the hut. Perhaps he was driven back by a horseman?"

"Perhaps," said Kargen, "but we will not know for sure unless we can save him. He looks to have suffered quite a few burns."

"He is young, is he not?" asked Laruhk.

"He is," agreed Kargen. "Only twenty years of age, if I am not mistaken. Not even old enough to have a full beard, see how patchy it is?"

"Even more so with his burns," noted Laruhk. "It is a shame that Uhdrig is not here to heal him."

"Then we must transport him," said Kargen.

Laruhk turned to his companion with a look of surprise, "Are you suggesting we take him back to our village?"

"How else would we save him?"

"But we cannot," Laruhk objected. "A Human has never entered Ord-Kurgad."

"There is a first time for everything," stated Kargen, "and I will not leave him here to die, unless you have a better suggestion?"

"No, I do not," said Laruhk.

"Then, it is settled. Now, how do we move him?"

Laruhk swept his gaze around the remains of Athelwald. "We could carry him dangling from a pole?"

"Very well, let us bind his hands and feet, then slip a pole between them. We shall carry him back like a prize deer. It will allow us to move swiftly."

Kargen pulled strips of leather from his satchel and bound Athgar's arms and legs firmly while Laruhk dug around the ruins of the village, finally returning with a spear.

"How about this?" offered Laruhk.

"It will have to do," said Kargen, "for we have little else."

They threaded the pole between Athgar's arms and legs then hefted him into the air, each Orc bearing one end of the spear.

"He is lighter than I expected," said Laruhk.

"He is a Human," reminded Kargen. "They are slighter of frame than us. We must remember that he is not as hardy as an Orc, so try not to jostle him too much."

They began moving eastward, soon clearing the remains of Athelwald, and making their way towards home.

Sometime later, they came into view of the palisade that marked their home. They were spotted almost immediately, and Kargen recognized the two Orcs that ran out to meet them.

"What have we here?" asked Khorsune.

"It is a Therengian," declared Kargen. "We found him in the ruins of his village."

"Is he alive?" asked Durgash.

"He is," confirmed Laruhk, "though he is badly burned. He will need the healing touch of Uhdrig."

Khorsune stood still, looking at the Human suspended from the spear.

"What are you waiting for?" asked Kargen. "My arms are tired."

"We cannot take him into Ord-Kurgad," defended Durgash, "it is forbidden."

"This is Athgar of the Therengians," Kargen reminded him. "Have you forgotten the arrows he has made for you over the years?"

"No, but Gorlag will not be happy."

"Gorlag can kiss my ancestors."

"Kargen," Durgash admonished, "you cannot speak that way of our chieftain."

"Help or get out of our way," warned Kargen. "I shall take responsibility for everything."

"Very well," said Durgash. "Khorsune, grab the other end."

They transferred their burden, and then all four Orcs continued on. The palisade ran around the entire perimeter, save for a small gap. To cover this, a secondary wall had been constructed outside of the main wall, forcing everyone to walk parallel to the wall for some distance before entering.

They passed through quickly, revealing the village beyond. Huts made of wood and mud were built close to the palisade, leaving a large fire pit in the centre, much like the Therengians. The structures themselves, however, differed significantly. In place of the small dwelling of the Humans, Ord-Kurgad was more communal in nature, for the vast majority of the Orcs lived in longhouses that held anywhere from twenty to fifty hunters. Only the old Orcs, or those who had bonded, lived in smaller huts. The largest one of all was that of the chieftain, the mighty Gorlag, who was exiting the building, lured, no doubt, by the commotion.

"What is the meaning of this?" he called out.

"It is a Human," offered Laruhk, as the party halted.

"I can see that," replied the chieftain, "but what is he doing here? It is forbidden!"

"He is injured," defended Kargen, "and requires the help of our shaman. Where is Uhdrig?"

The old shamaness stepped out from behind Gorlag. "I am here," she said, moving towards Athgar. The Orcs carrying him lowered his body to the ground and removed the pole while she knelt by the Therengian, casting her eyes over his wounds.

The chieftain opened his mouth to speak but was forestalled by the shamaness, who raised her hands, taking the attention from him. "What happened here?" she asked.

"His village was attacked," explained Laruhk, "and we found him in the ashes."

"You say you found him in the ashes?" repeated Uhdrig.

"Yes," said Kargen, "that is right. Why? Is it important?"

In answer, she returned her attention to the Therengian. She pulled out a knife, slicing through the bonds that held his wrists and ankles together.

The chief, Gorlag, moved closer, his shadow falling across Athgar. "He must be taken from here immediately!" he ordered.

"No," objected Uhdrig, "he is marked by fire."

There was a collective gasp from the assembled Orcs.

"Surely you are mistaken," said Gorlag, "it cannot be!"

"Do you doubt my proclamation?" asked the shamaness.

"No, of course not," said the chieftain, "but he is a Human."

"Human or not, he has the mark." She pointed with her finger. "See how his burns already begin to heal?"

"But-"

"But nothing, Gorlag," she retorted. "You know our ways as well as I. We cannot refuse one who has been marked by flame, it is the very essence of our tribe."

"Those rules only apply to Orcs," objected Gorlag.

In answer, the shamaness raised Athgar's right hand. "Can you not see the blood-encrusted on his hand? He has been marked as a member of this tribe. Where is Artoch? He is the master of flame, he can tell us more."

"Very well," said Gorlag, turning to those behind him. "Go and fetch him, he will see the wisdom in my orders."

A couple of hunters ran off to locate the master of flame while the others turned back to the body before them.

"Will you heal him?" asked Kargen

"I shall," replied Uhdrig, "but it is not for me to decide whether we expel him. That will be the decision of the tribe."

"What have we found?" called out a voice. A relatively short Orc pushed his way forward, his light green skin in stark contrast to those around him.

"Master Artoch," said Uhdrig in greeting. "Come, tell us what you think of this... Human."

The master of flame knelt, lowering his head to examine the burns on Athgar. "He lives," he announced, "though he should, by all rights, be dead."

"He was found in ashes," offered the shamaness.

He looked to her in surprise, "Found in ashes, and yet alive. This is the mark of one touched by fire. Can you heal him?"

"I can," she admitted, "though it will take some time. The skin must be regenerated. It will take several days at the very least."

"We must first determine his fate," declared Gorlag.

"And so we shall," replied the master of flame, "but he must be fit to stand trial."

"Trial?" asked Kargen.

"Yes," said Artoch, "the tribe will sit in judgement to determine if he will stay or be banished."

"Very well," said Gorlag, "we shall let our... guest recover from his wounds. In three days, we will determine his fate. In the meantime, who will speak on his behalf?"

"I will," declared Kargen, meeting the chieftain's stare with a steely gaze.

"Very well," Gorlag replied, "and I shall speak against him. The will of the tribe will decide what is to be done with this Human."

. . .

The sword struck downward, cutting into the wood. Athgar felt the shudder as the bow absorbed the blow, narrowly missing his fingers. The rider's massive horse forced him back.

As his vision blurred, he saw his sister, Ethwyn, staggering forward, blood pouring from her forehead. Another rider loomed over her, striking her down with the flat of his blade.

Again a blur, and then he felt his chest tighten as the horse's hooves impacted, knocking him backward. When his enemy opened his visor and laughed, Athgar saw the man's face, one he would not soon forget; the long scar running down the left cheek, cutting through the thick black beard was forever seared into his memory. The Therengian staggered back as all turned dark.

Athgar opened his grey eyes. Everything around him was fuzzy, and out of focus, then a green face loomed over him. Sounds started coming to his ears, the language of Orcs.

"Where am I?" he asked, using their tongue.

"You are in Ord-Kurgad, our village," replied the face, finally coming into focus.

Its wrinkled countenance identified it as an elderly Orc, or at least that's what Athgar assumed. "My name is Uhdrig, I am the village healer," the Orc said.

"I am Athgar," he murmured, his voice weak. "What happened?"

"You were found in Athelwald, buried in the ashes," she replied. "What do you remember?"

The images once again came flooding back to him in a rush. "There was a battle, we were attacked. Men on horses burning the huts," he coughed out.

"You must rest," Uhdrig advised. "You were badly burned. I have used magic to heal you, but the burns will take longer for the spell to have an effect."

"How long has it been?" he asked.

"More than a day, why?"

"I must find the survivors," said Athgar, trying to sit up.

"There were no others," she said, pushing him back down. "Kargen told us you were the only one they found."

"They were all slain?"

"No, but Kargen will explain later. For now, you must rest and recover your strength. Once you are better, we have much to discuss."

Another Orc loomed over him. "How are you feeling?" the newcomer asked.

"Sore," replied Athgar, "and my skin feels like it's on fire."

"That is to be expected. I am Artoch, Master of Flame. Tell me, how long have you held the spark?"

"What spark? I don't know what you're talking about."

"You have an affinity for fire," continued Artoch. "You have been touched by it. With patience and training, you can be taught to harness that spark, to control the flame."

"I don't understand," said Athgar. "Are you saying I have the makings of a Fire Mage?"

"You have, as long as it does not consume you. This gift can be controlled, and even directed if you wish, but it will take great mental discipline."

"I don't understand," said Athgar, "if that was true, shouldn't I have shown some affinity for fire in the past?"

"The gift of fire can be a fickle thing," said Artoch. "While some show an aptitude as they grow, others only have their power unlocked through great suffering. I believe you fall into the latter."

"This is all too much for me," the Therengian replied. "I remember fighting the horseman, and then waking up here, and now you're telling me I'm a Fire Mage?"

"You have the potential to be one, yes," said Artoch

"Who found me?"

"Kargen and Laruhk. They were out hunting when they detected the smoke from your village. I am sorry to tell you it has been burned to the ground."

Athgar tried to sit up again, but firm hands pushed him back down. "You must rest and heal," said Uhdrig. "The time for questions will come later."

"But I have to track down the attackers," insisted Athgar.

"It is far too dangerous," said Artoch. "Without learning to control the fire within you, you would perish."

"I don't understand," said the Human.

"You have great magical potential," explained the Orc, "but you are untrained, making your days dangerous and numbered."

"Nonsense," objected Athgar, "I've never had that problem before."

"No," said Artoch, "I do not suppose you have, but it has been released now, and it can only grow, putting your own life in danger unless you learn to control it. And it is not just you that you must consider."

"What do you mean?" Athgar asked.

"You might find survivors, only to burn them to death in your sleep. Is that the fate they deserve?"

"No, it's not," Athgar agreed, "but I must begin my search before it's too late!"

"You may go if you wish," the elderly Orc replied, "but you would likely not live out the week."

"It's that dangerous?" asked the Therengian.

"It is," said Artoch. "If you would permit me, I would teach you, provided the tribe agrees to let you stay, of course."

"In any case," added Uhdrig, "it is too late. They are long gone, their tracks washed away by rain. One day, perhaps, you will find them, but the ancestors have clearly spoken, that day is not today."

Athgar closed his eyes, his head in turmoil, trying to make sense of everything, until sleep finally claimed him.

THE UNLEASHING

SPRING 1102 SR

Stanislav Voronsky entered the room, the child following as he took a seat, waiting for the inevitable greeter to arrive.

The door opened, revealing the wrinkled countenance of none other than Illiana Stormwind herself, Matriarch of the family.

"Mistress Illiana," said Stanislav, "I'm surprised to see you here. I thought you'd moved on to other things?"

"I have indeed," the old woman replied. "I am the matriarch of the family now, but I like to keep my eyes on our future leaders. I see you've brought us another candidate."

"I have," the mage hunter replied, "I found him near Caerhaven."

"A substantial journey," Illiana replied, "and what led you there?"

"Rumours of a witch, as usual," he replied. "Though in this case, they proved accurate. He displays the usual signs and should make a valuable addition to the Volstrum."

Illiana looked at the boy with a well-practiced eye. She had once been mistress of this academy, had trained many of the mages that passed through its halls, but then the family had called upon her to become matriarch, not an honour to be refused. It might be called a family, she thought, but the bitter in-fighting never seemed to cease.

She pushed the thought from her mind, returning her attention to the boy, though perhaps young man was a more accurate description. He appeared to be about thirteen, the usual age to start manifesting powers, and though he needed to be tested, she was confident enough in the mage hunter's abilities to agree with his assessment. "I'll see to him," she said, "you can leave."

"I'm actually staying," said Stanislav. "Natalia is going through her unleashing today, and I'd thought I'd offer my support."

"I'm surprised by your attachment to her," she remarked. "Out of all the people you have delivered here, why such an interest in her?"

"She is the youngest person I ever brought to the Volstrum," he said, "as you well know. She saved me from the treachery of Nikolai, and I always felt as though I owed her for that. What of yourself? It's obvious she holds a fascination for you, or why else would you be here today?"

"My interest is purely academic," Illiana replied. "Natalia shows strong potential, possibly the strongest I have ever seen, but if you tell her that, I will deny it."

Stanislav chuckled, "Very well, your secret is safe with me."

Marakhova Stormwind strode through the halls of the Volstrum, her feet gliding across the marble floor. For generations, the Stormwinds had trained the most powerful Water Mages in all the known lands, and this day, another group would officially be welcomed into the family. She paused at a mirror, examining herself, noting the ornate trappings of a Grand High Mage, the highest rank achievable in the family. She plucked at an imaginary thread and then resumed her walk.

Two female guards were standing by a set of elegantly decorated double doors which led to the ritual bathing pool as the Grand High Mage arrived. She was about to enter when a voice drew her attention.

"Marakhova," called out the familiar voice of Illiana Stormwind, the matriarch of the family.

"Illiana," she replied frostily, "you honour us with your presence. Have you come to see the unleashing?"

"You know full well I have," responded the old woman. "I've heard great things about them. How many girls are undergoing the ceremony today?"

"Seven," said Marakhova, fully aware that the matriarch already knew, "though only two are destined to become greater mages."

"Two? I thought there was only one high-born Stormwind among the candidates."

"While it's true there is only one high-born, there is, in fact, another that shows extraordinary promise, the young peasant girl, Natalia, but you knew that already."

"Indeed," admitted Illiana, smiling, "I've kept an eye on her since she arrived here. She's been doing well, I hear."

"She has," admitted Marakhova, "though I daresay she will find challenges to overcome moving forward."

"Your opposition to her being granted station as a greater mage is well documented," Illiana pointed out.

"As is your fascination with her," replied Marakhova. "You nominated me to be the Grand Mistress of the Volstrum when you left. You should leave me to run it as I see fit."

"I shouldn't have to remind you that I only left to take up the mantle of the matriarch of this family. In that capacity, I outrank you, along with everyone else. Do you question my authority?"

"No, Matriarch," said Marakhova, bowing her head respectfully, "but I wish you would see reason where this girl is concerned. I have reservations about her."

"As you have stated, multiple times, but the decision has been made. Now, where are we in terms of the ceremony?"

"They are being bathed now. Once they are done, they will be purified by smoke, and then the ceremony will commence."

"And you have made sure the magebane has been administered? It would be bad form for them to manifest powers in the middle of the ceremony."

"I have done this before, Matriarch," stated Marakhova, a hint of annoyance in her tone. "The magebane was administered with breakfast, the same as it always is. None of the initiates will be able to use their powers, and they'll receive their customary afternoon dose long before this morning's wears off. The ceremony will be completed by then."

"Excellent," said Illiana, nodding her head. "Shall we proceed?"

"By all means," said Marakhova, nodding at the two guards.

They opened the doors, revealing a stone bathing pool, built into the floor, with small steps leading into the steaming water. Even as they entered, a young woman stood within, waist-deep in the water, wearing only a cotton shift, though her hair was immaculately styled.

The initiate sat, letting the water come up to her neck only briefly, then stood again, stepping forward to climb out of the pool. Attendants wrapped a thick robe around her and fussed with her hair, making sure not a strand was out of place.

"That's Svetlana," said Marakhova, "she's the high-born I was telling you about."

As her name was mentioned, Svetlana turned, curtsying to the matriarch and the Grand Mistress of the Volstrum.

"You may proceed," commanded Illiana.

Servants opened a side door, revealing another chamber filled with smoke from braziers that lined the walls. Svetlana stepped forward, taking a deep breath before entering. The door closed behind her, and they waited a moment for the smoke to clear in the pool room.

"Send Natalia in next," commanded Illiana.

The servants hesitated, but Marakhova nodded her head in approval, a motion that was not lost on the old woman. It was rare for the matriarch to visit the Volstrum but even rarer for one to issue orders. Though she was the appointed head of the family, the reality was that control was held by many, of which the matriarch, though powerful, was only one.

A side door opened, admitting Natalia, a young woman of approximately twenty years, the typical age for this ceremony. She was of average height, but her jet black hair and pale countenance were an unusual combination in this area of the continent. She carried herself with style and grace, despite her peasant birth.

Nodding to the two powerful women, she stepped into the pool, the water quickly losing its steam.

Marakhova looked on in surprise, but Illiana simply smiled. "I see she's the same old Natalia, though I must say she carries herself well now."

"She's still a peasant," derided Marakhova. "There are some things that training cannot quite eliminate."

"You forget your history," said the matriarch, "for the founders of our line were not high-born."

"That was more than six hundred years ago," said Marakhova, "before we understood how proper breeding could produce such powerful mages."

"And yet, here is Natalia, the very antithesis of our theories. How can one of such low birth display such power?"

"It is a mystery I cannot explain," continued Marakhova, "but I shall keep my eye on her."

"As shall I," warned Illiana. "I've had an interest in her ever since she arrived at the Volstrum."

They fell into silence, watching as Natalia knelt in the water. The young woman rose, leaving ice crystals on the surface of the water as she stepped from the pool.

"Curious," observed Marakhova, turning to one of the servants. "Are you sure the magebane was administered?"

"It was, Mistress," the girl replied.

"And you made sure she drank it?"

"I did, Mistress," the girl stared at the floor, expecting to be rebuked.

Instead, Marakhova turned to the matriarch, "You have an explanation, I assume?"

"It is her power," the old woman replied. "Did I ever tell you about how she came here?"

"No," said Marakhova, "when I took over two years ago, you told me very little about her. I knew you took an interest, but you never told me why."

"Tell me," said Illiana, "how old are candidates when they first come to the Volstrum?"

"You know as well as I," she retorted.

"Humour me, if you will."

"Very well, candidates are typically thirteen when they first begin to manifest powers, why?"

"Natalia, here, was ten, and she may have manifested as early as six if rumours are to be believed."

"How is that even possible?" asked the Mistress of the Volstrum.

"I have no idea," said the matriarch, "but ignoring her would be a mistake. With this kind of potential, she may well become more powerful than us all." She pointed to the water, where small pieces of ice still floated. "I remind you that she is dosed with magebane, and yet look, she's not even conscious of doing it."

The door to the next room opened, letting the smoke drift in. Natalia stepped forward, foregoing the deep breath that Svetlana had taken. The two women watched as the doors closed.

"If what you say is true," said Marakhova, "then she will breed a powerful line."

"Yes," said Illiana, "but we must pair her carefully. No doubt her true father was a powerful mage, but we cannot identify who he was."

"We have time," said Marakhova, "and she must learn her spells first. She's proven to be adept at her studies, I expect she'll learn to cast quickly."

"You must take care," said the matriarch, "for when she unleashes her power, it will be strong. Might I suggest others are not present when she first casts."

Marakhova stared at the water, watching the ice slowly melt. "I think I am more than capable of deciding how her training should be conducted."

Natalia exited the smoke room, the heavy scent of incense clinging to her robes, into a short hallway where the senior students waited to guide her to her next location.

"Natalia," called out a young woman.

Moving towards the blonde-haired woman only slightly older than herself, Natalia called out, "That's me."

"Come along," her guide bid, taking her to the end of the hallway, where others stood waiting. Natalia watched Svetlana go through the doorway, disappearing into the room beyond.

"Past this door lies the great chamber," her guide explained. "Someone will knock lightly, and then I'll open it. You'll walk towards the front of the room to take up a position by the other initiates."

Natalia nodded her head in understanding, then looked around at the others waiting here. This was, by any measure, an auspicious day for them. Each was to be admitted into the Stormwind family, given the family name for all official purposes. The others shifted nervously, but Natalia stood perfectly still. She had come to the Volstrum as a girl, and now, ten years later, she was still here, eagerly awaiting admittance into the family.

A knock at the door grabbed Natalia's attention. She waited while her guide opened the door, revealing the great chamber beyond.

To her right, at the far end of the hall was a raised platform, upon which stood Lord Kelvin Stormwind, the Grand Master of the Volstrum, the male equivalent to Mistress Marakhova. Before him sat dozens of onlookers, here to witness the ceremony. The first of the candidates stood facing him, both men and women, and she walked down the aisle to take up her place at the end of the line. She had been witness to this part of the ceremony before, for all students were required to be present, but to be at the front was a new experience for her.

She looked to her left and noticed Svetlana nervously staring at Lord Kelvin. Natalia understood the other woman's apprehension, for induction into the Stormwinds was no small matter. Logically, she knew that it was just a formality, the family wouldn't go through this ceremony if they weren't sure of their students, but it was still nerve-wracking.

Soon, the other candidates took up positions to her right, each appearing more nervous than the last. She turned her gaze back to the front, where the Master of the Volstrum was readying himself to start his speech, organizing some papers on a lecturn.

Natalia watched with interest as Lord Kelvin spoke, repeating his speech from previous ceremonies. Finally, his litany complete, he called the first candidate to the stage. Mikhail walked up the steps, bowing his head as the master placed a wreath upon it, signifying his admittance into the family. Lord Kelvin pronounced him, Mikhail Stormwind, and then turned the young initiate to the audience to receive their applause.

One by one, the grand master intoned the names of the candidates, calling them up to the stage, garnering the same loud applause each time.

Finally, Natalia's name was called, and she moved up the stairs to the stage where Lord Kelvin waited. Bowing her head, he placed the wreath upon her immaculately coiffed hair.

"I pronounce you," he paused for a moment, "Natalia Stormwind." She turned to the audience but was greeted by only sporadic applause, with the exception of one man who stood, his cheers ringing loudly over the reticence of the others. She smiled as she saw him, Stanislav Voronsky, the mage hunter that had brought her to the Volstrum all those years ago.

She stepped from the stage, resuming her position in the line. The last few candidates advanced, one by one until all had received their reward and then the ceremony was complete.

Now was the time to mingle and receive the accolades of the adoring crowd, a task that most students relished, but which Natalia knew would be a lonely experience for her.

True enough, as the other new candidates were swamped with well-wishers, she stood off to the side, avoiding the press of people.

"Congratulations," said Stanislav, pushing his way past the crowd, "you've made it."

She smiled as she saw him, perhaps the closest thing to family she had left. He was getting old, grey hair starting to pepper the dark brown, but he still looked hale and hearty.

"I suppose I'll have to refer to you as Mistress Stormwind now," he said, grinning from ear to ear.

"Natalia will do fine," she said, though a smile managed to creep out.

"What happens now?" he asked.

"We stand around and mingle, and then food will be served."

"I knew I came here for a reason," Stanislav replied.

"Is that all you ever think of? Food?"

"What else in life do I need? I've got everything I want."

"How about a wife? You need someone to look after you."

"I tried that years ago," he said, "but I travel too much."

"Yes, where have you been these last few months? I haven't seen you around the Volstrum."

"I had to go all the way to Krieghoff, if you can believe, then back to Caerhaven."

"Any luck there?" Natalia asked.

"Not in Krieghoff," he admitted. "It turned out he was nothing more than a potential Earth Mage, but I hit gold with Caerhaven, brought that one in this morning."

"So you didn't bring the Earth Mage back?"

"Why would I?" Stanislav asked. "The family doesn't pay bounties for such folk. I did pass his name onto someone else though, and managed to pick up a few coins for my troubles."

"You should have someone help you, some assistants."

"No," he said, "I did that years ago, it didn't end well."

"Hey, now," she said, "you found me. I wouldn't say it ended badly."

"True," he said with a grin, "but I haven't taken an assistant since. You never know who you can trust."

"It must be lonely," Natalia suggested.

"I get along all right," he replied. "How are things going here? Still avoiding making friends?"

"I'm told they've picked me for training as a greater mage," she said, quickly changing the topic.

"Well, I never!" Stanislav said. "Little Natalia, a greater mage. Who would have thought? I suppose that means you'll be learning battle magic."

"In time, yes," she said, "though I have to master the basics of manipulating water first."

"You'll learn that quick enough," he said, "I know you. You froze Nikolai's arm when you were small, do you remember?"

"I do," she said. "Whatever happened to him?"

"He became a mage hunter," Stanislav replied, "though I wish I'd killed him when I had the chance."

"Why? Because he took over your job?"

"No, because he betrayed me. The man's ruthless." He grabbed her arm, steering her away from prying ears. "Do you remember much about the day I brought you here?"

"No," Natalia confessed, "I suppose I was in a state of shock. Why?"

"No particular reason," he admitted. "I just ran into Illiana earlier, and it reminded me. She seems to take an interest in your progress."

Natalia laughed, "You're seeing too much. She takes an interest in every student's progress."

"If you say so," he replied, "but if you see Nikolai, I'd advise you keep your distance."

"Why?" she asked.

"He and I don't get along, and he knows we're friends."

"You think I'm in danger?"

"I don't know," Stanislav confessed, "but it wouldn't hurt to be vigilant. I suppose I'm worrying over nothing. After all, you're safe here in the Volstrum."

"I'm a Stormwind now," said Natalia with pride, "he wouldn't dare try anything. I think you're just being paranoid."

"Maybe," he said, "but it's kept me alive all these years. A healthy dose of caution never killed anyone. Just be careful, all right?"

"I will," she promised. "Now, it's time for food."

"Just point me in the right direction and let me go," he pleaded.

"Through here," she said, laughter falling from her lips, "follow me, but we'd best get there before the high-borns eat everything."

JUDGEMENT

SPRING 1102 SR

(In the tongue of the Orcs)

Again the dream. This time, Athgar saw his sister running towards him, blood gushing from her forehead. He reached out to Ethwyn, grabbing her arm, but at his touch, she erupted into flame. She fell, screaming as her body turned to ash.

He awoke to the smell of smoke, lying on a bed of skins, the heat of a fire to his side. Tilting his head, he saw a small fire pit in the middle of the hut, a single dwelling by the looks of it. Its furnishings were sparse, little more than a few skins scattered about. Uhdrig tossed another log onto the fire while Artoch and someone else sat nearby.

"He is awake," spoke the master of flame.

The third Orc got to his feet, coming closer to reveal the features of Kargen. He stooped, grabbing something, then rose to hover over Athgar. "Here," he said, offering a small bowl, "have a drink."

Athgar drank thirstily, consuming the offering. "How long has it been this time?"

"You have been out of it for some time, my friend," offered the Orc. "For the past three days, you have been in and out of wakefulness, despite the best efforts of Uhdrig. She was afraid you would succumb to the fire."

"My burns were that bad?" asked the Human, lifting his arms to examine them. They looked perfectly normal, leaving him confused.

"They were," said Kargen, "but Uhdrig regenerated you. No, it was not your wounds that worried us, but your inner spark."

"Artoch spoke of the spark, I still don't understand."

"It is our name for the magical power that lies within you."

"But how do you know I have it?" Athgar asked.

"Artoch can sense such things," explained Kargen, "but now is not the time to talk of it, we must prepare you."

"For what?" asked Athgar.

"You are to be judged by the tribe this very day. If you pass, you will stay with us. Otherwise, you will be banished."

"I haven't had time to prepare," Athgar objected.

"Do not worry, my friend," said Kargen, "I have volunteered to speak in your defence. You need only be present. Now, let us get you to your feet, shall we?"

Athgar nodded his head, and Kargen took his hand, pulling him up into a sitting position. His head swam a little, then everything began to clear. He swivelled in his bed only to find his legs dangling. The furs on which he lay were placed upon a wooden shelf that lined the edge of the hut, half a leg above the dirt floor.

As his feet touched the ground, he felt the cool earth beneath him. "My clothes?" he asked.

"They were badly burned," responded Kargen, "but Shaluhk has made you a fine new set."

"Who is Shaluhk?" Athgar asked.

Kargen's face darkened a little, the telltale sign of an Orc blush. "She is Laruhk's sister," Kargen explained, "and has been helping to look after you. She is in training to be a shamaness."

Athgar looked down at the crude tunic that covered him, the sewing was coarse, but the skins were warm.

"We have boots for you as well," said Kargen, offering up a pair.

Athgar, once again looked down, this time at the soft heeled boots, admiring their sturdy construction. He pulled them onto his feet, surprised at their comfortable fit.

"If you are done admiring yourself," said Kargen, "it is time to go, the tribe awaits."

"Very well," said Athgar, "let us be off."

Kargen led Athgar through the doors of the great chieftain's hut, the largest in Ord-Kurgad, which housed a rectangular fire pit running the length of it.

Members of the tribe sat three deep around the burning fire. Athgar was used to seeing his own people gather, particularly after a hunt, but to have the entire village within this one structure was surprising. He had heard of buildings this large in faraway Human cities, but had never seen one of such size before.

Kargen guided him to a seat at the top end, near the chieftain, but along the side of the fire, rather than at its end. That position was reserved for the shamans, Uhdrig and Artoch, Kargen told him. Opposite them, across the fire, sat Gorlag, a look of displeasure evident on his face.

Kargen leaned in close to talk quietly to Athgar. "That is Gorlag, our chieftain. He will argue against you this day, while I argue for you."

"How is the winner chosen?" Athgar asked.

"It will be for the tribe to decide by a count of stones. The shamans act as the hosts. They are forbidden from voting and are to be impartial."

At the head of the fire pit, Uhdrig stood, causing all in the hut to fall silent. She waited until everyone's focus was on her before speaking.

"Orcs of the Red Hand, we are gathered here today to decide the fate of the Human, Athgar. Kargen will argue that he be allowed to stay," she indicated the Orc with a hand, "while arguments for banishment will be presented by our Chieftain, Gorlag. Are there any here today that wish to dispute the method we will use to resolve this issue?"

Athgar glanced around at the assembled crowd. They all looked at him briefly, then turned their gaze back to their shamaness.

"Very well," she continued, "then let the proceedings begin. We will first call on Gorlag, Chieftain of the Red Hand, to argue for banishment." She waited for him to rise, then sat down, allowing Gorlag to make his case.

"My fellow hunters," the chieftain began, "we of the Red Hand have a noble and ancient ancestry. Our forefathers founded this tribe more than a thousand years ago. Many other tribes have sprung from ours as Orcs spread throughout the land. We join our brothers, the Black Arrows, the Crimson Spears, and the Blue Hawks as one of the oldest clans. It is only through the stringent observation of our ways that we have managed to survive, while others have died off or been destroyed by our enemies. If we were to allow this... Human to live among us, it would be a gross violation of our beliefs. We must remain pure, free of the taint of Humanity if we are to survive."

He paused, staring around the room, meeting the eyes of as many as he could. "Humans are a greater threat than ever before. Our ancestors were driven from their homes by the filthy Elves, and now we are in danger of being forced out, once again, this time by the Humans. To invite one into our lives is to court disaster. It is true that Athgar's village was destroyed by his own kind, but I say that if he remains here, we may well face the same outcome. They came for his people once, what is to stop them from continuing the search for survivors? Let us be rid of him and keep the tribe safe."

The crowd was enthusiastic, and Athgar saw many of them pounding the dirt floor with their fists. He looked to Kargen for an explanation.

"They are showing their support for Gorlag," the Orc explained. "Hitting the ground shows approval."

"Like we clap, I suppose," offered Athgar.

"So I am led to believe."

Gorlag, having finished his speech, waited for the pounding to subside, then took his seat.

Uhdrig stood again, waiting once more for all eyes to focus on her. "I call on Kargen to argue for inclusion," she stated, waiting for the hunter to rise.

Kargen rose from his seat, then waited, respectfully, while the shamaness sat back down. "Orcs of the Red Hand," he began, "we are this day, standing at a crossroads. It has ever been our way to keep outsiders at bay, to safeguard our homes by keeping ourselves at arm's length from the outside world, but I say that it is time for a change. As our chief is fond of telling us, our traditions are everything, and yet, do not our traditions change over time? Do we still hunt with stone weapons? No, of course not. Do we only hunt with spears or live in caves? Again, no. We have changed with the times, and each time change has come, it has enriched our lives; our smiths work metal, our warriors wield bows and axes rather than spears. Our chieftain even wears a shirt of chain when we march to war. None of these would have been possible if we had held tight to our ancient traditions."

He paused to take a breath, and Athgar could see the rapt attention of the other Orcs.

"We have traded with Athgar for years," Kargen continued, "and his father before him. He has made bows and arrows used by many of our hunters. We have hunted with him, and," he paused for effect, "he has been blooded in the manner of our tribe." This drew considerable attention, in the form of pounding the dirt. He waited for it to finish before continuing, "Our ancient ancestors brought the gift of Fire Magic to our tribe, a tradition continued by our noble master of flame, Artoch." He bowed reverentially in the shaman's direction, "Please tell us, Master Artoch, what you found when you examined Athgar."

The master of flame stood, clearing his throat, "The Human, Athgar, has the spark within him. He has been marked by fire."

The assembled Orcs burst into discussion at the revelation.

"And in your expert opinion," asked Kargen, "what does this mean?"

"It means," said Artoch, "that, much like our ancestors, he is a naturally gifted wielder of fire."

"Then we should be rid of him," interrupted Gorlag, "the better to keep us safe."

"Tell me, Gorlag," said Kargen, "would you rather we have a fire wielder that is friend or foe?"

"You try to trick me," said the chieftain, "for this man is not trained. He is no threat to us at present, lest it be from his very presence here. Surely his enemies will come for him!"

"You have had your say, Gorlag," interrupted Uhdrig. "Kargen, you may continue."

"We have always traded with the Humans," continued Kargen, "some have even travelled as far away as the village of Cragmore, but the Therengian people, Athgar's people, have never reviled us as have others."

"Humans have brought nothing to us but misery," interrupted Gorlag. "They have hunted us, enslaved us, even made war against us. Bringing this Human in among us will cost us dearly."

"No," countered Kargen, "Athgar's people have suffered, just as we have. Like us, they were driven from their cities, centuries ago. We have few enough allies these days, let us embrace him as a friend."

The volume of noise grew considerably. Kargen waited for it to die down, then sat.

Uhdrig rose once again, "We have heard both sides, now it is time to hear from the tribe. Ask your questions that we might all hear the answers."

A number of Orcs stood. Uhdrig pointed at one, allowing him to speak.

"What threat have the Humans ever presented to us, and what are the potential risks?"

It was the Chieftain Gorlag that answered, rising to his feet. "Like the Elves before them, the Humans desire land. They will not rest until they have driven us from it!"

"That is not true," corrected Uhdrig. "Even as we speak word comes to us of a distant land where a group of Humans has come to our aid."

"What nonsense is this?" demanded Gorlag. "You are making that up."

"I have done no such thing," she replied. "Our brethren in the Great Netherwood tell us of a Human hero named Redblade who defeated our enemies with her friends."

"Lies," accused Gorlag, "the Humans have no female heroes."

"She speaks the truth," said Artoch, "or do you speak against the word of Uhdrig?"

The grumbling grew amongst the Orcs. The shamaness was beyond reproach in their opinion, and their chief's remarks did not sit well.

Uhdrig turned back to where the Orcs had stood, to see them all sitting. "You have no further questions?" she asked.

"No," one replied, "we are ready to decide."

"Very well," said the shamaness. "Let us cast our votes. Stones represent a vote to allow Athgar to stay, while the lack thereof is a vote to banish."

The master of flame stood, lifting an earthenware pot from behind him and handed it to a fellow Orc, who dropped a stone in and passed it on. In this manner, it moved down the hall, around the far end of the fire pit, and then back to Master Artoch, who stepped back, emptying the contents on the ground and began counting.

The Orcs sat in silence. Athgar leaned towards Kargen, whispering, "What is he doing?"

"Artoch knows the strength of the tribe, each vote in your favour is a stone. If he counts the stones and they number more than half, we have won."

They waited as the master of flame returned each stone to the pot. His work complete, he advanced, whispering to Uhdrig, who then stood, drawing everyone's attention.

"It is the decision of the Red Hands," she said at last, "that the Human, Athgar, be welcomed into the tribe."

The pounding resumed, echoing through the large hall.

Athgar glanced at Gorlag, and even he could see the Orc was not pleased. Athgar looked back to Kargen, "Will he accept it?"

"He has no choice," Kargen announced, "it is the will of the tribe."

"I don't know if I trust him," said Athgar.

"Do not let it trouble you, my friend. We are allowed to disagree, but once a decision is made, all must abide by it."

FIRST LESSONS

SPRING 1102 SR

Natalia rose from her bed. As a new Stormwind, she could now eat with the other members of the family, a room far removed from the one she had used for the last ten years. Before making her way to the dining hall, she straightened her bed; years of regular inspections had taught her the importance of following the rules.

The unleashing ceremony was conducted four times a year, but advanced training only commenced each spring, that meant that she could expect quite a few students to join her, and she looked forward to seeing who might be in her class.

The senior dining hall, as it was officially known, consisted of round tables lined up in rows. Natalia sat at one, far removed from the other students, and waited as a servant brought over some food. Looking around, she noticed Svetlana, another recent graduate and the only other woman to be selected for training as a greater mage. Svetlana sat with a group of senior students, high-borns no doubt, who were looking across the room to the young men sitting on the opposite side, a rare view not afforded to junior initiates. Naturally, everyone here was a Stormwind, though Natalia was the only low-born.

She finished her meal, wondering what the day might portend. The high-borns walked past her, turning their gaze purposefully away in a blatant snub. She rose, falling in behind them, knowing full well that since Svetlana was with them, they all had to go to the same room to begin their lessons.

They arrived at the door to a circular room. A woman Natalia didn't recognize stood before them, watching their approach.

"Greetings," the woman said as they drew closer. "I am Mistress Tatiana, and I'll be taking you through your first casting today. As you know, for the last several years you have been kept on a regular regimen of magebane, to prevent you from inadvertently casting magic. Now that you are Stormwinds, the morning dose has ceased, allowing your full power to be unlocked. Today, we hope to channel that power for the first time. Are there any questions?"

Svetlana raised her hand.

"Yes?" asked the mistress.

"What spell will we be starting with?"

"Let's get inside first, shall we?" she replied, turning to open the door. She stepped inside, beckoning the rest to follow. Natalia brought up the rear, walking into the circular room and closing the door behind her.

In the centre, sat a small stone pedestal with a bowl of water upon it, along with a silver stirring stick. The students all gathered around, watching and waiting.

"All of you here," began Mistress Tatiana, "have been chosen to become greater mages. Can anyone tell me what that means?"

Once more, Svetlana raised her hand.

"Yes?" asked the mistress.

"It means we are to learn battle magic," she said, with a rather smug look.

"That is correct," the mistress continued, "but battle magic is all about inflicting damage on the enemy. Before you can master such skills, you must learn the rudiments of casting, only then can you advance to the more difficult spells. Up until your unleashing ceremony, you have been kept on magebane. What does that do?"

"Suppresses magical ability," offered Oksana.

"Good, now you've all studied the magical alphabet and can recite the letters without aid. The next step is to string them together in complex arrangements to unleash the power within you. Any questions so far?"

Katrin raised her hand, "What spell are we to learn first?"

"We will begin with calm water," replied Mistress Tatiana. "Here, you see a bowl of water, rather a simple thing overall. I shall stir the water with this stick, creating waves and currents, and then still it with a spell. Now, watch as I demonstrate. Afterwards, I'll explain what I did."

She picked up the silver stick, using it to stir the water and create small waves. Quickly placing it back on the pedestal, she held her hand over the bowl, palm down as the words of magic came to her lips, and then the water went glassy smooth.

"You just heard me recite the magical words," she explained, "but you must form the correct image in your mind as well. Why is this important?"

"You must link your gestures to the image," said Katrin, "or the spell will fail."

"That's correct," she replied. "Now, who would like to go first?"

When no one volunteered, the mistress picked a student at random. "Oksana, let's have you begin."

The young woman stepped forward, placing her hand above the bowl. Mistress Tatiana stirred the water, then nodded her head. Oksana mumbled the words, making them difficult for the others to hear, but the effects were soon felt. First, the air buzzed, as it did whenever a spell was cast, and then the surface of the water went smooth.

"Very good," said the mistress, "you have taken the first step in casting. Soon, we'll have you firing ice shards down the ranges. Now, who's going to go next?"

Each took their turn, with Natalia waiting until the end. When it was her turn, she stepped up to the bowl.

"I bet she messes it up," someone said, though she didn't recognize the voice.

"Quiet!" commanded the mistress. "Go ahead, Natalia."

Natalia raised her arms, holding her hands out over the water. Mistress Tatiana put the silver stick into the water, but when she stirred, nothing happened, as if the water was a ghost. The stick simply passed through, without creating even a ripple.

Mistress Tatiana stared at the water in disbelief, repeating the gesture with no change in effect. "Put your hands down, girl," she said in annoyance.

Natalia did as she was bid, and then the instructor stirred the water, this time with noticeable effect.

"All right, girl, go ahead," the mistress said.

Natalia raised her hand a second time, this time merely facing her palm towards the water from where she stood. The water went instantly still. The whole class looked on in surprise.

"I don't understand," said Mistress Tatiana, "you didn't even say the magic words."

"I said them in my mind," said Natalia, rather defensively. She could feel the eyes of her classmates staring at her, making her feel uncomfortable.

Mistress Tatiana cleared her throat. "You have each demonstrated the ability to unleash a portion of your power today. You will now go to separate rooms where, under supervision, you will practice what you have learned this morning. When you have met the expectations of your tutors, you will proceed to your lecture rooms where you will be introduced to the theory of battle magic. Are there any questions?

Svetlana raised her hands, waiting for the mistress to nod her head before speaking, "When do we learn to destroy things?"

"That will come in time, child," the mistress patiently responded, "but there are many more mundane spells that must be mastered first. Remember, you each have a powerful force within you, and you must learn to unleash it to its full potential. Calming a small bowl is simple. Eventually, you will be able to calm the largest waves but to do that, you must first know how to harness your energy."

Natalia raised her hand, waiting for the nod. Mistress Tatiana looked about the room, avoiding Natalia's gaze, but when no other student raised a question, she turned reluctantly to the low-born. "Yes?" she said.

"Would it not be better to learn to control the power that flows through us?" she asked.

"No," corrected Mistress Tatiana, "you are being trained to be battle mages. On the field of battle, you must let loose with everything you have, or you may fail."

"But surely-"

"But nothing," the mistress angrily cut her off, "there will be no further discussion on this topic. Now off with you, I have other places to be."

It was easy for Natalia to become adept with her first spell. In fact, if truth be told, she had mastered it the moment she first cast it. She had manifested similar powers early in her childhood, and so it was a simple matter for her to unleash it now, in a more controlled environment. She thought back to her lesson, but something nagged at her. Surely, there were times that spells should be held back, for if one were always to unleash power at full force, they would quickly deplete their stores of energy. She resolved to bring up the topic the next chance she got.

That chance came just three days later when they were taken back to the bowl room, as the students had named it. This time, Mistress Tatiana chose not to use the stick.

"Before us, you see, once again, a simple bowl of water. Can anyone guess what we are to do to it today?"

"Freeze it?" offered Galina.

"Yes, very good. Now, ice takes more power than a simple, calm water spell, as well as a significant amount of concentration. You have to see the frozen water in your mind in order to create it. Visualization is the key, along with uttering the runes in the correct order, of course."

"Runes?" asked Svetlana.

"Yes, dear, the magical words of power. We often call them runes, that's how they're written. Remember, runes are universal, they are the same in every language."

"Even the language of the disgusting Orcs?" asked Galina.

"Yes, even them," said Mistress Tatiana, "though as a greater mage, you'll likely spend all your time at court. The chance of an Orc showing up there is ridiculously small."

"What about the Elves?" asked Katrin.

"Never mind them," said the mistress, "you must concentrate on forming the words yourself. Now, as before, I will demonstrate the technique. Pay close attention while I cast."

She held her hands in front of her face as she began the incantation. All could feel the familiar buzzing in the air, and then the mistress's fingers started to glow a pale blue colour. As she touched the water, the glow began to fade while a layer of ice crystals formed on its surface.

"You'll notice," she said, "that the power fades as the ice is formed. In time, you'll develop a higher power level that will allow you to freeze a larger area, but for now, we'll concentrate on just this small bowl. Let's have Svetlana go first, shall we?"

"Don't we have to wait for the ice to melt?" Katrin asked.

In answer, Mistress Tatiana waved her hand over the bowl, dispelling the effect, and removing the thin layer of ice. "If you can freeze water," she said, "you can also unfreeze it."

"What if someone else used a spell to freeze it?" asked Galina.

"Then it would merely take a little more energy to thaw it," the mistress replied. "Now concentrate, Svetlana, and try to visualize the ice in your mind as you call forth your power."

The young woman advanced to the bowl, holding out her hands as she had watched the mistress do. Next, she incanted the words, but nothing happened.

"Take your time," said the mistress, "and try controlled breaths between the words. If you rush it, the spell won't work."

Svetlana started again, and this time she was rewarded with a thin film of ice on the surface.

"Very good," said Mistress Tatiana, waving her hand to dispel the effects. "Now, who will go next?"

"Natalia should go next," said Katrin, "she's the show-off."

Natalia stayed silent, refusing to be baited.

"Go ahead," said the mistress, looking right at her, "unless you don't think you can?"

Natalia pointed her hands at the water bowl and uttered the words of power. They spilled from her lips quickly. Suddenly, there was a cracking sound, and then the room turned noticeably colder.

Mistress Tatiana turned her attention back to the bowl; the water in it had frozen solid, and the sudden change in temperature had cracked it. She held her hands over the ice to dispel it but looked on in surprise when it failed to melt. She turned to Natalia. "Dispel it," she ordered, "immediately!"

The young woman pointed at the bowl, uttering the words that would undo the effects. A moment later, the ice was gone, and water seeped through the cracks to pool on the floor.

"That's enough for today," proclaimed the mistress. "We shall have to see about replacing the bowl. Now, head along to your next class, girls. Mistress Dominique will be lecturing you about battle awareness."

They all began filing out, but Natalia, finding herself at the back of the line, felt a hand touch her arm.

"Not you, Natalia," said Mistress Tatiana.

She turned to her instructor, unsure of what to expect.

"How did you do that?" she asked

"Do what?" asked Natalia. "I simply did what you asked.

"Don't play games with me. Who put you up to this?"

"No one, I swear," she replied. "I let loose with everything I could, just as you said."

"You need to learn control," the mistress said.

"You're the one that told us to release the full fury of our powers," Natalia bit back, instantly regretting her temper.

"Don't argue with me," demanded Mistress Tatiana, "or you'll find yourself in front of the grand mistress. Do you understand?"

Natalia wanted to argue the point but was wise enough to hold her tongue. "Yes, Mistress," was all she could utter.

"Very well," said Tatiana, somewhat mollified. "Now be off with you, and don't cause any more problems."

Katrin sat down at the table, waiting while servants brought food. "She's nothing but a show-off," she griped.

Svetlana, eager to please, gulped down her food. "Yes," she agreed, "who does she think she is?"

"We were only supposed to create a thin layer of ice," said Katrin, "not freeze the whole bowl."

"Perhaps she's thick," offered Oksana.

"Thick?" said Svetlana.

"Yes, you know, not all there in the upper halls?"

"Well, she is a peasant."

"Once a peasant, always a peasant," Oksana said. "I heard Mistress Tatiana use that very phrase. Still, there's little we can do about it."

"I beg to differ," said Katrin.

"Oh?" asked Galina. "You have an idea?"

"Wouldn't it be fun if she was unable to cast?"

"Yes, it would," agreed Oksana, "but how would you do that?"

"That's easy," suggested Katrin, "just dose her with magebane."

"And where would I get that from?" asked Oksana. "You know they guard it well."

"Simple," she responded, "we give her ours."

"But we need ours," said Svetlana, "unless you are suggesting we go un-dosed?"

"No, it's simple," continued Katrin, "every time we sit to eat at lunch and dinner, they give us those little vials to drink. I'm not suggesting we don't drink them, just that we leave a little in the vials. After we eat, we can combine the leftovers to give us a full dosage."

"And how do we get Natalia to drink it?" asked Galina.

"We don't, we simply put it in her breakfast. It should be easy enough to convince a servant to allow it. After all, they're not going to argue with a Stormwind, are they?"

Svetlana clapped her hands in glee. "I like it. When shall we make our move?"

"Not till next week," suggested Katrin, "we have to wait until we're back in a casting room, and it has to be done where there are witnesses."

"Yes," agreed Svetlana, "that will make her humiliation complete."

"Serves her right for being born a peasant," added Oksana.

The mistress waited until all the students had arrived before speaking. "Greetings," she said, "I'm Mistress Nina, and I'll be teaching you the basics of battle casting. This room we are in is called the casting room, though some of you may have heard it referred to as the range. It is the longest room in the Volstrum, apart from the great hall, that is. In here, you will learn how to use your magic against opponents that are some distance away. Today, I will show you how to cast the most basic of battle magic spells, the spell of mist."

There were groans all around.

"I want to learn proper battle magic," whined Oksana.

"You cannot learn battle magic..."

"Till we master the basics," everyone intoned.

"Of what good is mist?" demanded Katrin. "Are we going to chill everyone into surrendering?"

"Mist," continued the mistress, "can be used in a variety of ways. It can be used to aid in an escape, for example."

"Stormwinds don't run," said Katrin, "surely you know that."

"Stormwinds might be powerful," said Mistress Nina, "but a mage is only part of an army. If the soldiers are defeated, you may find yourself having to withdraw. What else can mist be used for?"

She looked around the room, but all the students, save for one, had their eyes cast downward. "Natalia?"

"It can be used to obscure sight, for example, to block bowmen from loosing their arrows."

"Correct," said the mistress, smiling. "Can anyone think of anything else?"

"Confusing an enemy?" offered Oksana.

"Yes, a carefully placed mist could lead the enemy into an ambush or the wrong path."

"Wouldn't an ice shard be more effective?" asked Svetlana.

"I see someone's been reading ahead," said the mistress. "Ice shards are a powerful option, but only against one or two targets. If there are enough enemy combatants, even your most powerful spell cannot deal with them all."

"But Stormwinds are the most powerful mages on the continent," objected Katrin.

"True," agreed the mistress, "but even magic has its limits. A fully trained battle mage can destroy an individual, but spread that damage over an entire company of men, and the results are somewhat different. As you have learned in battle awareness training, a fight is an ever-shifting environment. You must learn to adapt to the situation at hand."

"But if there are only one or two opponents, wouldn't you just use ice shards?" asked Svetlana.

"You seem fixated on that one spell," observed Mistress Nina, who then looked about the room, meeting each student's gaze. "Can anyone here think of a reason why you might not want to use a shards spell?"

"There could be a hostage," offered Natalia.

"What?" said Katrin.

"A hostage," repeated Natalia. "You might not want to target your enemy for fear of hitting one of your own."

"What do we care for hostages?" asked Katrin. "Our job is to kill the enemy."

"Well," Natalia mused, "how about if you wanted to infiltrate an enemy position? Mist would be useful for that, surely?"

"Enough!" ordered Mistress Nina. "Natalia has made a valid point. Suffice it to say that sometimes a non-lethal option is needed. Now, to cast this spell, you need to visualize the mist. Luckily, we have a lot of experience with it in this part of the continent."

Svetlana raised her hand.

"Yes?" asked the mistress.

"Would you show us a demonstration first?"

"Of course," she replied, "now watch carefully. Mist is a very quick spell, it only requires stringing together three words of power. As such, it can be used when time is of the essence."

"Like when Natalia is running away," said Oksana.

"Quiet now," commanded the mistress, "and pay attention. I am going to cast in a moment, but unlike your previous spells, this one will be a ranged attack. If you look down at the far end, you will see a suit of armour. That represents an enemy. I shall cast the spell directly in front of him, engulfing him in the fog, allowing us to either leave or get closer for a more lethal attack. Just like the other spells you have learned, you can dispel this one at your own leisure."

"Does that mean," asked Katrin, "that you can dispel someone else's mist?"

"Yes, it does," she answered.

"But doesn't that make it useless if it is so easy to dispel?" asked Oksana.

"Dispelling someone else's mist would require expending energy greater than that which brought it into existence. There are few mages that could do that against a Stormwind. Now, that's enough questions, watch while I cast the spell."

The mistress turned to face the suit of armour and stepped forward, pushing her arms out in front of her quickly, and then uttering three words of power. A tiny shape flew through the area to strike the floor. The instant it hit a mist enveloped the far end of the room. A moment later, Mistress Nina used a wiping motion with her hand to dispel the effect, leaving the room, once again, free of the spell.

She turned again to face her students. "Now, who wants to go first?"

In answer, Svetlana stepped out in front of the others.

"Come up here," bid the mistress, "there's a faint line on the floor for you to stand behind. Take a moment to concentrate on the target before you release your magic."

Svetlana took up her place and stared downrange, taking a moment to judge the distance. She stepped forward, uttering the words of power and then a thin line of mist appeared halfway to her target.

"A good first attempt," declared Mistress Nina. "You'll get used to judging distance with further training. Go ahead and dispel it so we can give someone else a turn."

Svetlana waved her hand but failed to dispel the mist. She blushed profusely, then set her mind to it again, uttering the words to be rewarded with the desired effect.

"Who's next?" asked the mistress.

"Natalia," they all shouted.

"My goodness, you're popular today, Natalia. Come, stand on the line and prepare to cast."

"This ought to be good," whispered Katrin, "I can't wait to see her flub this one."

"Are you sure you gave her the magebane?" asked Oksana in a low voice.

"I put it on her food myself," Katrin replied, a smug look on her face.

Natalia stood behind the line, looking downrange. The suit of armour sat there unmoving, but she used her imagination to see it as an enemy soldier. Suddenly, she thrust out her right hand, palm forward. A single spot of white flew from her to sail across the intervening distance and land just in front of the target. As soon as it struck the floor, the entire room was engulfed in a thick mist, effectively blinding all present.

"Very impressive," came the voice of Mistress Nina, "now go ahead and dispel it."

Natalia uttered the words, and the mist evaporated, fading into nothingness almost as quickly as it appeared. She turned back to her schoolmates only to see Katrin staring at her with a look of shock.

"Now," said the mistress, "let's continue with the rest of you, shall we?"

Natalia sat down at the table, waiting for a servant to bring her lunch. For some reason, she was hungry, her morning's efforts leaving her feeling drained. A plate was placed in front of her, along with a fork, and she picked the implement up, ready to spear the meat when someone appeared opposite her. Raising her eyes, she saw Katrin standing there, looking down at her.

"What do you want?" asked Natalia.

"May I sit?" the young woman asked.

"Aren't you afraid of being seen with a low-born?"

"No," Katrin replied, "I mean I was, but I was wrong about everything."

"What's that supposed to mean?" asked Natalia.

"I've been raised as a high-born," Katrin said, "and for my entire life it's been ingrained in me that only a high-born can hold the most powerful of magic, but when I saw you cast that spell today, it proved all my upbringing was wrong."

"Because of the magebane?"

"You knew about that?" asked Katrin, a shocked look on her face.

"It has a rather distinct taste," Natalia replied.

"I take it you didn't eat it then?" prompted Katrin.

"I did, it just didn't have much of an effect."

"I don't understand," said Katrin, "it's supposed to suppress your power."

"I've been on magebane since I was ten," confessed Natalia. "Over the years, the Volstrum has increased my dosage. I have to take much more than a single vial to suppress my power."

"So you showed us today," remarked Katrin. "Anyway, I just wanted to apologize. You should have the same opportunities the rest of us take for granted. I've had my say, I'll leave you alone now if you wish."

"Sit down," said Natalia, pointing to the seat across from her, "as long as you don't mind sitting with a low-born."

HARNESSING THE FLAME

SPRING 1102 SR

(In the tongue of the Orcs)

Athgar held the arrow close to his eyes, examining the fletching. Satisfied with his work, he placed it with the others, picking up another shaft to begin the time-consuming process. He was interrupted by Kargen, who, seeing his friend at work, wandered over.

"I see you are keeping yourself busy," offered the Orc. "That is a fine batch of arrows."

"It's the least I could do," replied Athgar, "after all the tribe has done for me. What are you up to?"

"Laruhk and I are thinking of going hunting later. Would you care to join us?"

"I don't have my bow," said Athgar, "it was destroyed in the fire."

"A pity. You shall have to make another. I am sure we can get you the proper tools. Perhaps we could travel to Cragmore and trade for some. Your arrows would fetch a reasonable price."

"In time, perhaps, but I don't think I'm quite ready yet."

"It has been more than a week, Athgar. Surely you are not still suffering?"

"My body has healed," the Human replied, "but my heart is still damaged."

"I understand," offered Kargen, "it is not easy to lose a family, let alone

one's whole village. Perhaps we shall undertake the journey at some time in the future."

"You seem eager," said Athgar. "I rather suspect you have something specific in mind."

"I do," said the Orc. "I was remembering that fine bow you made before we went hunting."

"Yes, one of my best. It's too bad it burned in the fire."

"Indeed, but do you think you could create another," asked Kargen, "perhaps larger?"

"If I had the tools, certainly. Why?"

"The bow you made had a heavy draw for a Human, but Orcs are much stronger. Do you think you could make a bow that would test the strongest of Orcs?"

"I don't see why not," replied Athgar, "though I couldn't test it myself. What would be the purpose of such a bow, surely you wouldn't use it to hunt? It would be long, even for an Orc, and unwieldy to carry through the forest."

"True," admitted Kargen, "but it would likely be powerful enough to penetrate armour, would it not?"

"There's more to penetrating armour than just the pull of the bow. You'd need special arrowheads."

"See? I knew you would have the answer."

"Why would you want such a bow?"

"I was talking to Shaluhk the other day," offered Kargen.

"Laruhk's sister? Isn't she apprenticed to Uhdrig?"

"She is," confirmed Kargen, blushing slightly. "Our shamaness seems to think that a time of conflict is coming. I want our hunters armed with these bows of yours if it comes to that. It would help protect us from armoured soldiers."

"Like the ones that burned my village?"

"Yes, there is always the danger that they might come after us as well, and we must have protection."

"I'll give it some thought," said Athgar, "though I must admit the concept intrigues me. These war bows you speak of would take some trial and error."

"Warbows, I like that," said Kargen. "I shall be your assistant."

"I didn't know you could make bows," said Athgar.

"I cannot, but I can certainly use them. If you are going to be making these warbows, you will need someone who can pull them to their full draw, will you not?"

"I will," he admitted.

"Good, then it is decided."

"What is?" came a voice.

They both turned to see Artoch, the master of flame, walking towards them in his usual, quiet manner.

"We were just discussing making bows," explained Kargen.

"I am afraid I must interrupt," said Artoch, "for it is time that Athgar begin his training to harness the flame."

Kargen looked at Athgar and grinned, "He is all yours, Master Artoch, our business is concluded for the time being. I must be off anyway, Laruhk is expecting me."

"And his sister, no doubt," added Athgar. The smile on Kargen's face told him the remark had hit home. "Very well, be off with you, master hunter."

Kargen ran off, perhaps with a little more energy than was needed.

"Put down your work, Athgar, and walk with me," said Artoch, "we have much to discuss, you and I."

Athgar rose, looking down at his handiwork. "I shall just put all of this away first," he said.

"Do not bother," said Artoch, "it is safe where it lays."

"Someone could steal it," Athgar objected.

"No Orc would do such a thing," the master of flame replied. "Now come, we have work to do."

Athgar followed the pale Orc, who was in no hurry. The old master had the eyes of a hawk, and his penetrating gaze took in everything as they passed. Eventually, he halted before a small fire pit filled with kindling and wood in anticipation of the initial flame.

Artoch halted, then sat, cross-legged, indicating with a wave of his hand for the Human to do likewise. "A wielder of flame has an inner spark that he, or she, must learn to control. I will demonstrate the technique for you first, then show you how to conjure it forth from within. Do you understand?"

"I do, Master Artoch," replied Athgar, watching intently.

The Orc closed his eyes for a moment, reaching out his right hand towards the stack of wood. Athgar detected a momentary buzz in the air like a swarm of mosquitoes, and then a small amount of smoke issued from the tinder, finally bursting into flame a moment later. Soon, the entire bundle of sticks was alight, its warmth washing over them both.

"There, you see?" said Artoch. "I have used the spark within to ignite the kindling."

"What words were you uttering?" asked Athgar. "They didn't sound Orcish."

"They are not," replied the flame master, "they are words of power. They can only be invoked by one who has the power within. These words are universal."

"Meaning?"

"Meaning that Orcs, Humans, and even Dwarves would all use the same words to invoke the flame."

"And I can invoke them?"

"Once you are trained, yes," answered Artoch.

"This is powerful magic," said the Human.

"More powerful than you can imagine," the Orc replied. "Releasing the flame is a controlled action and must only be done when necessary. I have shown you how I created fire without flint and steel, and yet have you ever seen me use it before?"

"No, I can't say I have. Why is that?"

"To become a master of flame, you must learn to respect fire. If one is trivial with it, it will consume them. Although you will learn this spell, you will hardly ever use it."

"Then why teach it?"

"It is merely a stepping stone to greater things," answered the Orc. "Once you have learned to create fire, we can apply it elsewhere, such as to weapons, for example."

"A flaming weapon?"

"Why not?" said Artoch. "Can you imagine the damage such a weapon would inflict?"

"Would it not consume the weapon?"

"No, not at all. Though it is true the woodpile here feeds the flame, there is a more practised approach. You can harness the spark to feed the fire, creating fire without fuel."

"You could use that to enchant arrows," Athgar offered.

"Yes, or axes, spears, or whatnot. Eventually, you will learn to create a streak of fire that could strike at distances without a bow, but we must start with simpler steps."

"I understand," said Athgar, "just as I must have patience when making an arrow, so too, must I have patience learning to wield fire."

"You are wise, for a Human," said Artoch. "Many have been the Humans that were consumed by their attempts to control the flame, it only leads to madness."

"Where do I start? Must I learn all the magic words first?"

"No, you will learn each as we progress from spell to spell. You already show strength of will, or you would not have survived the devastation of your village. You must learn to apply that same will to the power within you."

"The spark?"

"Yes," agreed the master of flame.

"Do all mages have the spark?" Athgar asked.

"Only those that seek to master the flame. Human mages do not understand the spark, they seek only to unleash the power, not realizing that the flame can consume them."

"Consume them? Do they burst into flames?"

"Sometimes, but often they simply become obsessed with it. They think they are masters who can control the most powerful of nature's elements."

"Elements?" said Athgar.

"Yes, there are four, representing the primal forces of nature. Fire, water, earth and air, each of which can be mastered by one with the corresponding potential. All types of magic must be respected, but fire is the most destructive, for only fire can consume."

"But what of Uhdrig? Doesn't she control magic? What element does she control?"

"The elements are not the only types of magic," replied Artoch. "Uhdrig has the power of Life Magic, and some tribes have Enchanters, but the Red Hand has only passed down the tradition of life and fire. Now, are you ready to begin?"

"I am ready," responded Athgar. "What do you want me to do?"

"Gather wood and kindling," said Artoch, "for you cannot start a fire that already burns. Once you have stacked the wood and placed the kindling, I shall show you how to release the spark from within."

"Should I go to the woods?"

"No, there should be a sufficient amount by the woodpile against the north wall."

Athgar wandered off, leaving the flame wielder staring at the fire. It was the arrival of Gorlag that interrupted his thoughts.

"You are treading dangerous ground, Artoch," the chief declared.

Artoch turned his gaze to Gorlag, "He is ready, at least as ready as he will ever be. The time is right for him to learn."

"He will destroy us all."

"No," said the master of flame, "he will save us."

"Save us?" exclaimed Gorlag. "Surely, you jest? What is he to save us from?"

"Annihilation!" declared Artoch.

"What makes you say that?"

"Our race is already dying off," continued Artoch. "In a few generations, we will be gone like the ancient Saurians with whom our ancestors once traded."

"If you feel that way," asked Gorlag, "then why go through all this?" He pointed to the fire pit.

"We must bridge the divide that separates Humans from Orcs, or we will be wiped out. Athgar will be that bridge!"

"Surely you jest? There cannot be friendship between our two races."

"You are wrong," said Artoch, "I know it for a fact."

"How can you know such things?"

"Far to the west, others of our race thrive. Our brethren in the Netherwood have shown us the way. We must, like them, ally ourselves with the Humans to save our people. Athgar is the key to that!"

Athgar looked down on his handiwork, all the wood stacked with the kindling ready to be set alight. "Where do we start, Master Artoch?"

"Come," said the flame wielder, "sit before the wood as I do, your legs crossed, and prepare to clear your mind."

The Human sat, crossing his legs awkwardly, not used to the position.

"Close your eyes, Athgar," said Artoch, "and feel deep down inside you."

"All I see is darkness."

"Be patient, in time, it will come. A spark of light that appears to grow brighter when you concentrate on it."

They sat in silence for some time until, at last, Athgar spoke. "I see it," he said, "a tiny little light."

"Good, now concentrate on it. You must nurture it to allow it to grow. It is an ember, waiting to burst into flame. Picture yourself holding it in your palms."

"It's growing brighter," he proclaimed.

"Good," said Artoch. "Now you are ready to release it. You must open your eyes, but remember the flame, just as you have seen it. Concentrate on the stack of wood, and then release the flame by uttering the words of power."

"I can feel it growing stronger," said Athgar, his eyes still closed. "I feel its heat."

"Open your eyes," commanded the Orc, "or you will be consumed."

Athgar finally opened his eyes, looking directly at the stack of wood. "It's getting too hot!"

"Utter these words," said Artoch, "Cal, Exar, Ute, Fal

"I can't, it's too hot!"

"You must! Now concentrate, before it is too late."

Athgar was now sweating profusely, his face dripping. "Cal, Exar...," he took a deep breath, "Ute, Fal."

Suddenly, a breeze blew out of nowhere, and the wood burst into flame, not a tiny spark, but a large conflagration as if the fire had been burning for some time.

Athgar let out a huge rush of air, then took a fresh breath like a man who had nearly drowned. He looked at the fire in surprise. "It worked," he proclaimed.

"So it did," said Artoch, "though it very nearly consumed you."

"I felt like I was going to explode."

"That was the spark, growing out of control. In time, you will learn to harness it, but once you conjure it forth, you must release it quickly."

"It felt like a great weight was lifted from me when I uttered those words," said Athgar.

"Yes," agreed the Orc, "a feeling I know only too well. You very nearly caught fire. Remember, if you do not master the flame, the flame will master you."

"And if I did catch on fire?" he asked.

"You would die," said Artoch, "for not even a master of flame is immune to burning to death, and there is no Water Mage here to extinguish a magical flame."

"Magical flame? Isn't all fire the same?"

"Watch closely," said Artoch, holding his hand, palm upward before him. Words spilled from his tongue and the air buzzed with energy, then a small flame appeared, floating just above the Orc's outstretched hand.

"It's green," said Athgar in wonderment.

"Yes, it is magical fire in its purest form, though it changes colour as it grows in intensity."

"But there is no wood to burn," said the Human. "How does it sustain itself?"

"Just as fire consumes wood, so this flame consumes some of my internal energy."

"What happens if you run out of energy?" asked Athgar.

"Then it would consume my body."

"You would be consumed by the fire, that's what you meant earlier?"

"Yes, you must be careful to always keep energy in reserve, to fail to do so could cause death."

"Is that true of all mages?"

"To a limited extent," said Artoch. "Even a healer may run out of energy and consume a portion of their body. In those rare cases, you would notice, perhaps, spontaneous bruising or bleeding from the nose or ears. The damage heals in time, but for Fire Mages, the secondary effect can be ignition, causing the caster to erupt into flames. I would imagine it would be quite painful."

"How much energy do I have?"

"We will find out, in time. This first spell will only consume a little. By noon you will have recovered the expenditure of energy. Later on, as you use more powerful spells, you will learn to recognize the feeling as your energy is drained. It is hard to explain, yet easy to understand once you experience it."

"So do all mages have a limited supply of energy?"

"They do," said Artoch, "though it varies considerably between individuals. There are even ways to increase it, much as a hunter may increase their strength over time."

"I can see there's a lot I have to learn," said Athgar.

"We will take it in small doses," said Artoch. "Now, shall we have you try again?"

"Should I fetch new wood first?"

In answer, Artoch turned to the roaring fire, uttering more words. Moments later, the flames died out, becoming nothing more than a smoking pile of wood. "If you can create a fire," he said, "you can also extinguish one, though if it is not yours, it requires more energy to do so. Now, let us continue with the exercise..."

THE COMPETITION

SPRING 1103 SR

Natalia waited as Katrin finished tying her shoe. "How are you progressing?" she asked.

"Not so well," her friend answered. "I can get the spell cast, but I'm having difficulty with targeting. They often miss entirely, though I'm all right for those with no range."

"Well," offered Natalia, "isn't it good that we get time to practise?"

Her shoelace tied, Katrin rose from her seat. "Let's go, shall we. We don't have all day."

They made their way through the halls of the Volstrum, halting as they reached the casting range.

"Are you sure we're allowed to be here, unsupervised?" asked Katrin.

"I cleared it with Mistress Nina," Natalia replied. "Now, are you ready to begin?

"Where shall I start?"

"How about something simple? Let's go back to the mist spell, and we'll work on ice shards later. First, cast the spell with no range. I'd like to see your strength before continuing on to a distant target."

Natalia watched as Katrin incanted the words, the familiar buzz coming to her ears. A moment later, they were surrounded by mist.

"Not bad," said Natalia, waving her hands and uttering the words needed to dispel it. "Now, let's make it a bit more challenging."

"Challenging how, exactly?"

"Try to target a space halfway between us and the dummy down there," Natalia said, pointing.

Katrin cast the spell again, this time the mist appeared farther into the room, midway to the target.

"Again, a good casting, though your aim is off a bit, you're hitting to the left. Try to adjust your aiming point. Go ahead, do it again."

In answer, Katrin shook her hands to release tension. "Did you see the visitors today?" she asked.

"You mean the Sartellians?" asked Natalia. "What of them?"

"They were a handsome set," remarked Katrin.

"You should concentrate more on your studies," Natalia chided.

"They've come a long way to see us," her friend continued. "What do you think they're doing here?"

"I don't know," Natalia admitted, "but the Sartellians and the Stormwinds are two branches of the same tree. Where we master water, they master fire. What else is there to know? Now," she said, changing the subject, "are you ready to try once more?"

Katrin cast again, this time hitting closer to the target.

"You're getting there," said Natalia.

"I'm always getting there," fumed Katrin, "but never arriving. I'm never going to hit the target."

"You're tensing up too much," offered Natalia. "Remember, first you cast, you've got that part down, then you have to target. It's like letting loose with an arrow, you have to visualize hitting the mark."

"Easy for you to say," said Katrin, "you never miss."

"It'll come in time, I promise you. After all, you wouldn't expect someone who just picked up a bow to be a perfect shot, would you?"

"No," she admitted, "I suppose not."

"Well, there you go," said Natalia. "Now, try again."

Katrin dispelled the mist then tried again, this time landing the shot closer to the target. She dispelled it with an audible sigh, then turned back to her companion, returning to her previous conversation, "So why do you think they're here?"

"Perhaps they're only visiting relatives," said Natalia. "Just ignore the Sartellians and concentrate. Put all else from your mind."

"I can't, it's bothering me."

"Why would it bother you?"

"I have to know, don't you see?"

"No, I don't!" said Natalia. "What possible reason is there for you to be concerned about a bunch of visitors?"

"We live a life of total isolation from the rest of the world," explained Katrin. "Aren't you dying to know what's happening outside the walls of the Volstrum?"

"No," said Natalia, "but then again, I was very young when I started here. I don't remember much of my previous life."

"I don't know what to say, I just assumed you came at the same time as the rest of us."

"No, I was only ten when I arrived. They kept me separated from the rest of you until I turned thirteen."

"So you never knew your parents?" Katrin asked.

"I vaguely remember my mother," Natalia explained, "but my father is a blur. I don't think I spent much time with him. Stanislav tells me he was a farm labourer."

"Stanislav? The mage hunter? How would he know?"

"He's the one that brought me here, all those years ago. I still hear from him, and he tells me what's going on in the world. How is it for you?"

"I get letters from home," said Katrin. "After all, we might be Stormwinds, but we still have parents."

"It's different for you," said Natalia, "you're a high-born. You can trace your roots back to the founders of the line."

"True," she admitted, "but I wish I had their penchant for ranged magic. I can't seem to hit anything I aim for."

Natalia was about to say something, but the door suddenly opened, and a man wearing very ornate robes stepped in.

"What's this?" he asked. "I thought the casting range was empty."

"We were just practising," said Natalia. "We have permission from Mistress Nina. My name's Natalia, and this is Katrin. Might I ask who you are, sir?"

"I'm Gregori Stormwind," he answered. "I teach battle magic to the young men. I take it that's what you're practising?"

"We are," said Natalia. She glanced at Katrin, but the young woman seemed too petrified to speak. "Did you want the room right now, Master Gregori?"

"As a matter of fact, yes," he replied. "I'd like to warm up before class begins. Might I ask what it is that you're working on?"

"Katrin, here, has trouble targeting spells," she explained. "I was helping her."

"I see," he said, "and, in your opinion, what is the root of her problem?"

"Concentration."

"Let's take a look then, shall we? You cast first, Natalia. Let's see what you're made of."

Natalia turned suddenly, targeting the distant dummy with a blast of ice that struck the target dead centre.

"Impressive," he said. "I can see you're highly focused. Now you try, Katrin."

Katrin cast the spell, and ice shards flew forth, sailing down the room, narrowly missing the target.

"Almost had it," she said.

"'Almost' is not good enough for the battlefield," he said. "You do that in a real fight, and you'll be dead. Now try again, there's nothing like repetition to master a skill."

She cast again, this time hitting an arm.

"You're getting there," he said, "but I'm afraid we're out of time. My students will be coming shortly, and it would be better if you weren't here when they arrive."

"Thank you, Master Gregori," said Katrin.

"No thanks are needed," he replied, "but I'll tell you what. If you come here tomorrow at the same time, I'll give you some more pointers. How does that sound?"

"That would be wonderful," said Katrin.

"Yes, thank you," added Natalia.

"You're welcome," he said. "Now, be off with you before you ruin my reputation."

"Your reputation?" asked Natalia.

"Oh yes, didn't I mention it? I'm known as a hard taskmaster when it comes to instruction."

"Your secret's safe with us," said Katrin, opening the door.

"Yes," agreed Natalia, "and thanks again for all your help."

Natalia attempted to chew her food and then spat the mouthful back onto her plate. "The meat's a bit grisly today," she said.

Katrin, who had been waiting for her friend's opinion, simply poked hers with a fork. "I don't think I can eat it, it looks like it's still alive."

Natalia looked around the room. Others appeared to be enjoying their food, and she wondered if perhaps, someone had targeted them with the bad meal. Across the centre aisle, the young men were digging in with gusto, certainly not the sign that there was anything wrong with theirs. "It's just us," she whispered.

"The meat might be bad, but the rest of the meal looks fine," said Katrin.

The sound of doors opening reached their ears, and they both looked to see Marakhova Stormwind, Grand Mistress and Head of the Volstrum, enter, followed closely by Grand Master Kelvin and Mistress Tatiana. They proceeded to walk past the students to the other end of the hall, where the instructors would normally sit for formal dinners. Today, the space was cleared of all tables. Their entrance had drawn considerable interest, for the grand mistress seldom visited the dining hall.

Marakhova carried a staff, topped by a large blue crystal that pulsed with energy. Halting, she faced the students, and rapped the butt of it on the floor three times, the sound echoing off the walls. At the sound, the diners all fell silent.

"At the behest of the grand master," Marakhova announced, "it has been decided to hold a competition to determine the strongest students at the Volstrum. Each side, male and female, will choose their best three to compete in a display of battle magic. The winners shall receive a place of honour at the head table, along with the first pick of assignments once they leave these hallowed grounds."

The students immediately broke into lively conversation, for this was something unheard of, at least in recent memory. The volume of noise increased significantly until the grand mistress again rapped her staff on the floor, quieting the hall.

"The disposition of the teams," continued Marakhova, "shall be determined by the most senior instructors, and will be announced in the coming days. Good luck to you all, and may you uphold the honour of this institution." She turned, leaving the room, the others following along behind.

As soon as the door closed, those left in the room burst into conversation.

"Did you hear that?" asked Katrin. "You must try to be part of the team, we'd be sure to win."

"I have no interest in sitting at the head table," said Natalia, tapping her meat with her fork.

"Maybe not," replied Katrin, "but it would show everyone, once and for all, that you're worthy of being here." She looked down at her plate, "And maybe they'd stop messing with our meals!"

"I suppose," said Natalia. "Who do you think is picking the girls team?"

"My guess would be Mistress Tatiana. Why else would she have been standing there?"

"That's not good," said Natalia, "she doesn't like me."

"She doesn't have to like you, but she has to admit you're talented, perhaps the most powerful student here."

Natalia gazed across the aisle to where the men were deep in discussion. "They say men are more powerful mages," she said.

"Who says?" asked Katrin.

"Most of the instructors," said Natalia. "I overheard Mistress Nina saying so. This whole competition is just a colossal waste of time. They already know the men will win, they just want to soothe their egos."

"So are you going to participate or not?"

"Very well," said Natalia, "but only if you apply as well."

"I can't," her friend confessed, "I'm failing my courses."

"Failing? How can that be? Your aim is getting better."

"I've been practising a lot, that much is true, but at the expense of my other studies. I already have to retake two classes. If I fail another, I'll be removed."

"You're a high-born," Natalia reminded her. "They can't kick you out of the Volstrum, what would your parents say?"

"Not true," said Katrin, "it's been done before."

"You worry too much. Everything will work out fine, you wait and see." Katrin rose from her seat. "Come on," she urged, "hurry up."

"What's the rush?"

"We have to sign you up before the list is full."

Mistress Tatiana examined the target carefully before turning and walking back, remaining silent as she did. The students all held their breath in anticipation. Their instructor stopped, then looked each of them in the eyes before speaking. "An accurate shot, Yana," she said, singling out a blonde-haired woman, "but you need to put more energy into it. That would scarcely count as a wound."

The blonde's head fell, a look of utter failure darkening her features.

"Who's next?" called out the mistress.

Another student moved up, this time an auburn-haired young woman.

"Ah, Lydia," said Mistress Tatiana, "let's see how you make out, shall we? Go ahead and cast whenever you're ready."

The young woman began the incantation, firing off the spell. A large number of ice shards flew down the range, narrowly missing the target.

"Good power," said the mistress, "but you're going to need to hit the target if you want to be on the team." She cast her eyes about the remaining students, "I remind you we have one berth left to fill. Ordinarily, we would allow only students in their final term to participate, but it has been mutually agreed upon that at least one member of each team must not be so, however, if we cannot find someone who can hit the target with sufficient force, we shall have to disqualify ourselves from the competition."

"Here!" yelled Katrin, raising her hand.

"You want to try?" asked the mistress.

"No," she replied, "but Natalia does, she's the best shot here."

"Low-born," muttered Galina.

"Is there anyone else?" asked the mistress.

Hands popped up, and Mistress Tatiana scanned over them, all too familiar with their classroom progress, for she was their primary instructor.

"Natalia is powerful," persisted Katrin, "you should at least give her a chance. Or don't you want us to win?"

Mistress Tatiana, perhaps stung by the words, looked at the low-born peasant girl with a look of distaste on her face. "Very well, Natalia, let's see what you're capable of."

In answer, Natalia stepped forward, stood on the line, peering down-range at the dummy. Some of the other students mocked her, but she tuned them out, concentrating only on her target. Taking one step forward, she thrust out both hands, uttering the words of power. Ice shards leaped from her fingers to fly downrange and hit the target full in the chest, knocking it over. Lowering her hands, she turned to face the rest of the class, which had grown quiet with her demonstration.

"I think we just found the last member of our team," announced Mistress Tatiana.

Natalia watched as Matias let loose with his spell. Shards, dozens of them, erupted from his hands and flew downrange. At least half of them hit, striking the target's right arm and splattering the back wall with ice.

"A good shot," exclaimed Grand Master Kelvin. He was standing to the side, along with Mistress Dominique and Master Gregori, the judges of the competition, though there was little open to interpretation. All that counted here were the points earned. Much like an archery competition, the target was painted, but instead of a circle, it was a mannequin with coloured parts to indicate the value of a hit. The most points were rewarded for a head shot and the more shards that hit, the better the score.

Mistress Nina walked down to the target, and the watching students fell silent as she counted the hits. She returned to the judges, announcing the score, "Three arm hits for a total of nine points."

Natalia did the math in her head. Each arm hit was worth three, and now, with all three men having cast, they were ahead by more than twelve points. The women had done well, hitting the target every time, but so far, neither of them had been able to conjure more than two or three shards. It would take a massive score to make up the shortfall, and it fell to Natalia to accomplish it.

"Next," called out the grand master.

Natalia made her way to the casting line. She stared at the target, looking over its strange colours. A head shot was worth the most but was the smallest target. The body was next, covered by a breastplate, and was naturally the largest target of all, but a body shot wouldn't win them the competition. She focused on the head, closing her eyes to visualize it.

The room had grown quiet as she readied herself. Normally she would step forward to cast, as that was the accepted custom, but this time she stepped back with her left foot, bracing herself against the kickback of the spell. The words flowed from her lips, and then the spell was released.

Instead of a cluster of small shards of ice, a single giant spike flew down the range, striking the chest of the target dead centre, creating a noise like a gong and hurling the dummy to the floor.

Natalia looked on in annoyance. She had meant to hit the head, and now she had lost the competition. Her miscalculation had cost them the prize, and her classmates would not forgive her.

Mistress Nina walked back to the target. Natalia could hear the complaints already, starting as whispers that grew in intensity the longer they waited for results. She looked downrange where the mistress was lifting the target. Instead of replacing it, she carried it back towards the judges, tucking it awkwardly under one arm.

She held it before the judges, who looked at it closely, the grand master even poking it with a finger at one point. Natalia could only wonder what was so interesting, for Mistress Nina's back blocked her view. Natalia moved slightly, trying to get to a better vantage point, only to see a bemused look on the face of Master Gregori. A heated discussion was underway between the three judges, and then the grand master said something to Mistress Nina, nodding as he did so.

The mistress turned to the assembled crowd, showing the target to everyone. Natalia's shot had been a solid hit to the body, fewer points for accuracy than a head shot, but the ice shard had punched a hole clean through the breastplate, destroying the underlying chest of the mannequin.

Master Kelvin raised his hands to get their attention. "Though the chest hit is only worth five points," he said, "it is the opinion of the judges that the attack, this ice streak if you will, was the equivalent of ten ice shards. We award fifty points to the women's team."

The women in the room broke into spontaneous applause while the young men grumbled. Mistress Nina, having set the target down for everyone to examine, made her way towards Natalia. "You did well today," she called out.

"I should have done better," replied the young woman, "I was aiming for the head."

"It's as well you didn't hit where you were aiming then," the mistress said, "for had you, I have no doubt you would have knocked the head clean off the target."

"And that would be a bad thing?" said Natalia.

"Had you knocked it off, I doubt we would have been able to assess the damage as easily, and the force of your attack would have been mitigated. When you hit the chest, there was enough mass to resist the attack, making it easier to view the damage. You should be proud of yourself."

"I could feel the power getting away from me," complained Natalia. "I need more control."

"Nonsense, you did exactly as you should have. You'll make a fine addition to the cause when you graduate."

"The cause?"

"Yes, the family and its interests," explained Mistress Nina. "You made quite a name for yourself today. Now, go and celebrate, you've earned it."

Natalia turned, wandering through the rest of the students. They were shaking her hand, patting her on the back, all thoughts of her upbringing completely forgotten in the joy of victory. She looked for Katrin, but her friend was nowhere to be seen.

Natalia spotted Master Gregori coming towards her, a bemused look to his face.

"Congratulations," he said, "that was quite an accomplishment. I knew you had it in you."

"You knew we'd win?" she asked in surprise.

"Let's just say I rather suspected you would. I saw you casting, remember? Where's that friend of yours, Katrin?"

"I don't know, I was just looking for her."

"It is quite crowded in here, I suspect she's waiting outside in the hallway, maybe getting a breath of fresh air."

"I suppose so," said Natalia in disappointment.

"You'll have to excuse me," said Master Gregori, "I need to console the men's team on their loss. Good work today, Natalia, keep it up. You'll go far in the Stormwind family, I have no doubt of that."

"Thank you," she said, but the instructor had already started moving across the room.

She made her way to the hallway and turned to watch as the other students came out of the room, most on the way to the dining hall, where a celebratory feast waited. Natalia scanned the crowd, but still saw no sign of her friend.

Thinking that Katrin might have returned to her room, Natalia made her way to the dormitory. As she approached her friend's door, she noticed it was open. She slowed, then quietly moved forward, intent on a good scare. Jumping into the doorway, she was ready to yell surprise, only to be met with an empty room. She saw naught but a bed, devoid of blankets, and a dresser, its drawers half pulled out.

Natalia looked again at the door, half convinced that she had picked the wrong room, but the number that stared back at her confirmed it was Katrin's. She asked a few of the students wandering about the dormitory, but none of them knew anything of Katrin's whereabouts.

Next, she sought out Mistress Tatiana. The woman was in the dining hall, overseeing the celebration from a corner of the room. Natalia approached cautiously, waiting for her presence to be noticed.

Mistress Tatiana looked at her, a smile crossing her face. "Natalia, why the long face? You did well today, you should be proud. Is something wrong?"

"I was wondering if you'd seen Katrin?" she asked.

"She is gone," the mistress replied, with no further explanation.

"What do you mean, gone?" asked Natalia.

"She was showing insufficient advancement in her studies."

"I don't understand?"

"She failed too many classes," the mistress explained.

"But she's a high-born," Natalia argued, "from one of the founding families."

"High-born or low, it matters little if they can't master what they are taught."

"So she's gone? Just like that?"

"It should come as no surprise," said Mistress Tatiana, "after all, you've been tutoring her for months now. You, of all people, should have realized how badly she was doing."

"How do I get in touch with her?"

"You don't," the mistress replied. "She has been removed from the Volstrum, you are no longer to have any contact with her."

"But Mistress-"

"No excuses," interrupted the mistress, "and no more talk of Katrin. Celebrate your victory today, and be glad of your success, you have earned it." The mistress walked off, leaving Natalia with her thoughts. Here she stood, in a room full of students, but to Natalia, she was once again all alone.

MASTER OF FLAME

SUMMER 1103 SR

(In the tongue of the Orcs)

Athgar and Kargen entered the palisade followed by the hunting party. The Orcs of Ord-Kurgad rushed forth to take the game from their arms, freeing up the hunters to greet their loved ones.

Shaluhk waited until the crowd dispersed before stepping forward, hugging Athgar, and then turning to embrace Kargen tightly.

Athgar looked at Kargen's bondmate. "How much longer until you deliver?" he asked. "I'd swear you're not even twelve weeks along."

"A few more weeks yet," she said, with a grin, "and then we shall have small green feet running around our hut."

"That soon?" asked Athgar.

"Soon?" said Kargen. "Why would you say that? Few Orc's carry their young for more than five months."

"Human's take nine," explained Athgar, "or so I'm led to believe."

"Such a long time," observed Shaluhk, "I do not know how they bear it." She rubbed her belly, "This mighty hunter wants out as soon as possible."

"How long till a Human matures?" asked Kargen.

"Individuals differ," said Athgar, "but we reckon most will mature between sixteen and twenty years. Why? When do Orcs mature?"

"They are fully formed by fourteen," said Shaluhk.

"Yes," agreed Kargen, "though they often toughen up more as they age, becoming stronger with each successive hunt. Even I was not born with these muscles."

"I hope our son has muscles like you," added Shaluhk.

"How do you know it won't be a female?" asked Athgar.

"We do not," she replied, "but it matters not. Apart from carrying young, there is little difference between males and females in our society. Was it not so with your people, Athgar?"

"To a certain extent," he replied, "both could hunt or fight. In fact, we underwent the same rite of passage to adulthood."

"Oh yes, I remember now," said Kargen, "we had to help you get your first kill on a hunt."

Athgar blushed, for it was true. If it hadn't been for Kargen and Laruhk, he might still be an un-blooded Therengian.

"Stop teasing him," said Shaluhk, "you know that it was not his fault."

"It is true," Kargen replied, "he is blameless in this. Now, let us retire to our hut, I have need to feel our little hunter kick again. Will you join us, Athgar?"

"Yes," added Shaluhk, "please do, you know you are always welcome."

"Thank you for the offer," said Athgar, "but I'm very tired. I haven't the stamina of your race, and the hunt was a long one."

"Indeed," remarked Kargen, "it was a hunt that shall be spoken of for years. Now come, my little shamaness, and let us retire to our hut." He placed his arm around Shaluhk's shoulder and led her off towards their home.

Athgar looked around at the villagers, already cutting apart the day's bounty. His feet were sore, and his muscles ached from the strain of drawing his bow so frequently. It had indeed been a successful hunt, and the village would be well-stocked with food for weeks to come.

He finally convinced his legs to carry him home. As a wielder of flame, he warranted his own hut, as was typical of a spellcaster, though the Orcs preferred the term 'Shaman'. He halted at his door, a simple animal skin that hung to form a curtain, and pushed it aside, stepping inside.

His bed was built into the framework which formed the walls, a wooden shelf that extended out over the floor, its surface littered with furs. He sat, removing his boots, and looked around his small space, taking in the bows that lay stacked against the far wall. In the last year or so, he had been working on the great warbows that Kargen had suggested. It had taken months to come up with a design that worked for the Orcs, and now, his planning complete, he had begun fabrication of them in larger numbers. Twenty such weapons lined his wall, finished and ready to use, while another eight were in various stages of construction. So powerful were they, that the Orc chieftain, Gorlag, had proclaimed them too dangerous for the hunt and so they stood in Athgar's hut, ready for use should the need arise.

He lay down on his bed, taking a deep breath, and was soon asleep.

Kargen sat back, gulping down a drink from the small pot while Shaluhk roasted some meat over the fire that sat in the centre of their hut, its aroma tempting his nostrils.

"Are you hungry?" she asked.

"I am," he replied, "though I would gladly forgo food just to be here. I cannot have enough of you."

She laughed, causing him to smile. "You have picked up Athgar's habits," she said, "and you use a lot of his phrases."

Kargen screwed up his face, "He said he cannot have enough of you?"

"No," she admitted, "but he said the same thing about the stew I prepared yesterday."

"Well," he said, "it was very good."

"You should go and get him," she said. "You know he is terrible at cooking, the poor man would starve if not for us."

"He is likely sleeping."

"Go and get him," she persisted, "you know he is like family."

"Oh, very well," Kargen said, with an exaggerated expression as he stood. "I shall go and fetch my Human friend."

"Now that is the Orc I am bonded to," she said, her eyes twinkling in the light of the fire.

He paused at the doorway, the curtain held ready to fling aside, looking back at her a moment.

"Will you miss me?" he asked.

"Every time you are out of my sight," she replied.

He grinned, "Well, you will have to excuse me a moment if I am to drag that Therengian back here."

"You are excused," she said, "but be quick about it, the food is almost ready."

Kargen stepped into the sunlight, letting his eyes adjust a moment before continuing. The village was busy, as it always was after a successful hunt. He made his way past the other huts, his mind looking forward to the reward his stomach would soon enjoy.

Athgar's hut was situated on the west side of the village, among the other shamans and their apprentices. Kargen halted at the Human's door, ready to knock on the framework, then stopped himself. Thinking it would be far more fun to surprise his friend, he pushed the hide curtain to the side, preparing to enter as quietly as he could.

To his surprise, he saw Gorlag, the chieftain, standing over Athgar, axe in hand, ready to strike the sleeping Human. Kargen leaped into action, tackling the chieftain and driving them both to the floor. The axe, knocked from the assailant's hand, flew through the air, landing on the dirt floor across the unlit fire pit.

Gorlag struck back, punching Kargen in the side, causing him to roll to avoid further injury. Now separated, they both rose, glaring across the tiny hut at each other.

The chieftain spat blood from his mouth as he pulled a knife from his belt. "He must die, do you not see?"

Kargen stared back. He had divested himself of weapons when he had returned from the hunt and now stood, unarmed, waiting for Gorlag to make the next move.

Athgar was awoken by a loud noise. He snapped his eyes open and sat up, his pulse quickening. Before him were two Orcs, facing each other, and in the dim light, he soon recognized them as Kargen and Gorlag. Even as he watched, the chieftain drew a knife, and then lunged, jabbing Kargen in the stomach, driving the blade deep, until only the handle remained exposed.

Kargen fell to the ground, the great chieftain on top of him, now withdrawing the blade and raising it for another strike.

Athgar acted instinctively, summoning forth his arcane powers, and released a streak of flame that raced across the room to hit Gorlag in the side, knocking him off of Kargen. The chieftain quickly stood up, the side of his body burned, his clothes still smouldering.

Athgar rose, preparing to cast another spell, but the sight of Kargen lying in a pool of black blood changed his mind. Instead, he ran forward, ignoring the attacker in a vain attempt to save his friend's life.

Athgar lifted Kargen's head. Beneath him, a pool of blood grew at an alarming rate, the Orc's face pale and unresponsive. He tried to stem the flow, placing his hands over the injury, but the wound was deep, and the black ichor flowed freely through his fingers. There was yelling outside, and while Athgar was concentrating on trying to help, he didn't even hear others entering the hut.

Moments later, two Orcs seized Athgar, pulling him from Kargen's body.

"That is him," snarled Gorlag, "he has finally shown his true colours and murdered one of our own."

Athgar tried to argue the point, but all he could think of was the body and the ever-widening pool of blood.

It was Laruhk who broke his stupor. He had entered the hut with the rest and was kneeling beside his friend. "He is dying!" he proclaimed. "Send for Uhdrig!"

"She is not here," replied another Orc, the hunter Khorsune. "She is visiting another village."

"Then send for my sister, she is skilled in the arts of healing."

Khorsune rushed from the hut, impelled by the anguish in Laruhk's voice.

"You will die for this!" proclaimed Gorlag. He had been watching, along with the other Orcs, and now stood in the doorway, gloating at the Human who was held tight. "Bring the interloper out for execution," he ordered, triumphantly stepping out into the sunlight.

The Orcs pushed Athgar forward but halted as once again the door hanging was pushed aside, this time to reveal the countenance of Shaluhk.

"Kargen!" she called out, dropping to his side. Blood was everywhere, blackening the ground. She looked closely into her patient's eyes, then turned her attention to his wound.

"The Human tried to kill him," announced Khorsune.

"Do not be ridiculous," she shot back, "Athgar would never do such a thing." She closed her eyes and began drawing forth her power. The air buzzed and her hands glowed bright yellow with magical energy. She placed them on her bondmate's wound, and the flesh began to knit itself back together.

Kargen's eyes fluttered open.

"What happened?" asked Shaluhk.

"It was Gorlag," he replied huskily, "he was trying to kill Athgar while he slept, but I stopped him."

"Is this true?" she asked, looking to the Therengian.

"I don't know," the Human replied, "I woke to them fighting."

"Only the ancestors will know the truth of it," offered Laruhk. "It is Gorlag's word against that of Kargen."

"I saw Gorlag stab him with the knife," said Athgar, "that's when I burned him."

"But you did not see what started it?" asked Laruhk.

"No," he admitted, "but isn't it obvious?"

"Not according to our laws," Laruhk responded.

"So what will happen?" asked Athgar.

Laruhk thought a moment before responding, "The tribe will have to sit in judgement."

"There is another way," offered Shaluhk. "Athgar can demand it be settled by combat."

"Gorlag is an accomplished warrior," said her brother, "he would cut Athgar to pieces."

"No," she replied, "Athgar can call upon the flame."

"But Gorlag cannot fight a shaman, it is forbidden."

"You forget," said Shaluhk, "while Athgar is considered a member of the tribe, as a Human, he cannot be recognized as a shaman, only Orcs have that right. As a friend of Kargen, though, he can still make the challenge."

"But Gorlag is the chief."

"The chief is not beyond the law," she reminded him.

"Would you have Athgar slain?" asked Laruhk in surprise.

It was Athgar himself who settled the argument. "I'll do it," he announced.

"Release him," ordered Shaluhk.

The Orcs released their hold, and Athgar pushed his way out of the hut, Laruhk following while Shaluhk saw to Kargen.

Gorlag was standing just outside, deep in conversation with some of his followers.

"I challenge you!" called out the Therengian.

"What is this?" responded the chieftain.

"You tried to kill Kargen," accused Athgar. "It is the right of a tribe member to challenge the attacker if the offence is dire."

"You are no tribe member," swore Gorlag.

"But he is," said Laruhk. "Did he not stand with Kargen when he was bonded to my sister? You, yourself, bore witness if I am not mistaken. Surely only a member of the tribe can have that honour."

"It is true," came a voice, startling everyone, "he has that right." They all turned to see Artoch, the master of flame.

Gorlag stared at Athgar, a look of fear in his eyes. "Very well," he finally acquiesced, "but I claim the choice of weapons."

"Agreed," said Artoch. "Now, see to your wounds, Gorlag, you cannot fight with those burns. The fight shall be three days hence."

"Shaluhk must heal me first," demanded the chieftain, "for Uhdrig is not here."

Laruhk laughed, "If you are waiting for my sister to heal you, you will wait a long time. You have struck her bondmate, she will have no sympathy for you. Three days, Gorlag, that is more than enough time for Uhdrig to return and heal you. Feel your burns and count your last days while you can."

Gorlag snarled, then turned, heading to his hut, his advisors following.

Laruhk turned his attention back to Athgar, "That was risky, my friend, he is deadly with an axe."

"Not as risky as you might think," suggested Artoch.

"What do you mean?" asked Athgar.

"The rules of combat are simple," the master of flame continued, "you may only fight with what you take with you into the circle."

"Yes," said Laruhk, "but Gorlag has the choice of weapons."

"Agreed," said Artoch, "but does not Athgar step into the ring with his magic?"

"Is that allowed?" asked Laruhk.

"It is not disallowed," responded the shaman.

"I thought shamans were supposed to be neutral in disputes?" said Athgar.

"And so we are," replied Artoch, "I am merely informing the contestants of the rules."

Three days passed in the blink of an eye, and before he knew it, the day of the duel arrived. Athgar made his way through the village, accompanied by Kargen and Shaluhk.

Kargen was in fine form as they approached the entrance to the palisade. "The circle will be outside," he said, "and will be nice and large. You should have ample space to use your magic."

"I'm nervous," said Athgar. "Gorlag is an experienced fighter, what if he gets in close?"

"Do not worry about it," said Kargen, "you will be able to roast him before he can close the distance, and being nervous will keep you alert. We can hardly have you falling asleep during the fight, now can we?"

"Leave him be, Kargen," said Shaluhk, "he must have time to concentrate on the task at hand. Do you feel you are ready, Athgar?"

The Human glanced at her quickly, "I'd feel better if Gorlag didn't have all that chainmail."

"You need not worry about that," she replied, "your fire will penetrate it easily enough."

"My fire is not as powerful as you might think," said Athgar. "I let loose with everything I had back in my hut, and it only singed him a little."

"It did more than that," said Shaluhk. "According to Uhdrig, he was badly burned beneath his armour. I think you underestimate your power."

"It is the way of Humans," added Kargen, "to denigrate one's own skill. You should be proud of your power, Athgar, you are a mighty wielder of flame."

"Pay no attention to my bondmate," she added, "he is too full of himself this day. He would not be so smug if he were facing Gorlag himself."

Athgar looked to his friend, "Is this true?"

"Sadly, yes," admitted Kargen, "for he is the mightiest fighter in the tribe, and I lack your power over fire. If I were to face him with weapons, he would surely defeat me."

"You're not making this any easier for me," said the Therengian.

They exited the village. To the south, in a clear field, they saw the assembled witnesses. More than half the Ord-Kurgad had emptied onto the field of combat to witness the fight, for such a thing was very rare indeed.

The crowd parted as they approached, and Athgar made his way to the circle that had been marked on the ground in ash. He stared down at the grey dust for a moment, thinking back to the loss of his village. Finally, bringing his eyes up from the ground, he spotted Gorlag. The mighty Orc chieftain was standing opposite him, across a circle that was a spear's throw away.

Kargen and Shaluhk remained at the edge of the circle as Athgar moved forward. Uhdrig stood at the centre, waiting for the combatants to join her, then raised her hand as they stood facing each other, with only the shamaness between them.

Athgar stood with axe and shield, while Gorlag held two axes and wore his chainmail armour, complete with helmet.

Uhdrig raised both hands in the air and waited for the witnesses to quiet.

"Life," she began, "that which we hold most sacred has been threatened and accusations made. It is the word of one against that of another, and so, in accordance with our ancient laws, a challenge has been issued to decide the truth of it. In the tradition of our ancestors, combat will be until one submits, or is driven from the ring, or till one breathes no more. Do you both understand these conditions?"

She looked to Athgar and then to Gorlag, and they both nodded their agreement. "Very well," she said, "then our ancestors will determine your fate. Return to the edge of the ring, and the fight will commence."

Athgar turned, making his way to the perimeter.

"Good luck, my friend," said Kargen, "and may your ancestors watch over you."

"Be wary of Gorlag," warned Shaluhk, "for he is like a snake preparing to strike."

Athgar nodded, then turned to face the centre. Gorlag had already started running across the battleground, his axes swinging from either side, forming a whirlwind of steel. Athgar knew he would have scant time to cast a spell, so he advanced to meet the Orc, his shield held upright.

Gorlag's axes dug into the wood, sending splinters flying from its rim. Surprised by the ferocity of the attack, Athgar staggered back, almost touching the edge of the circle, then ducked and rolled, coming up behind the great Orc, whose momentum had almost carried him too far.

The chieftain turned quickly, taking the Therengian by surprise. Athgar put up his shield just in time, feeling the press of the Orc's axes numbing his arm. A chunk of wood flew from his shield, removing a section the size of his fist. Athgar backed up, trying to remember a spell, but the attack was too ferocious, and he had little time to think.

After a whirlwind of slashes, Gorlag backed up, his face growing more confident. "I shall enjoy this," he boasted.

Athgar dug deep, bringing a spell to his mind. He pointed his weapon hand at the chieftain, sending a streak of fire towards the Orc.

Gorlag dodged, and the shot sailed past him, narrowly missing a group of spectators. The crowd backed up, suddenly aware of the close confines, and wishing more room betwixt them and this fight.

The Orc chieftain launched another attack, closing the range rapidly, and then driving the Therengian back with a flurry of blows. Athgar stumbled, his feet slipping, and he crashed to the ground, onto his back. Gorlag towered over him, striking down with an axe but the Human managed to block with his own weapon. Their axes struck one another, sending sparks flying, and still, the Orc bore down with all his strength, pushing the weapons ever closer to the Therengian. They were almost face to face now, the fetid breath of the chieftain close enough to smell.

Athgar uttered a magical phrase, and the head of his axe burst into flames. Gorlag pulled his face back to avoid the fire, and then the Therengian bent his knees and used his legs to shove the Orc away from him. As the chieftain staggered back and tried to gain his footing, Athgar hurled his axe. It dug into Gorlag's left shoulder, causing him to yell out in pain, and drop one of his axes. The edge had buried itself into the chieftain's armour, and now the Orc let out a bellow of pain as the padding beneath started smouldering.

Gorlag pulled the weapon from his wound, tossing it to the side while Athgar used the time to rise to his feet. The Therengian uttered the words of power and a streak of flame shot from his fingertips. This time, Gorlag was unable to dodge, and it hit him full in the chest, knocking him from his feet and sending him to the ground.

Athgar dropped his shield and rushed forward to stand above the Orc, his hands held ready to cast again.

"I yield!" called out Gorlag.

After a surprised gasp from the spectators, the field went quiet. Athgar recognized fear in the chieftain's eyes, but also loathing. He wanted to finish the Orc off and be rid of him, but he knew that would result in his own banishment, for the ways of the tribe must be followed; Gorlag had yielded, and the Therengian's task was now done. He was the victor, but he stood still as if caught in the moment, unable to move.

He felt a hand on his shoulder. "It is done, my friend," said Kargen quietly, "you have won."

Athgar lowered his hands and backed away from Gorlag.

Uhdrig entered the circle and raised her hand, waiting for everyone's attention. "Our ancestors have seen fit to grant victory to the Therengian, Athgar, this day," she proclaimed. She turned her attention to the defeated chieftain. "Gorlag, you are banished from this land for your actions. Let it be known that no Orc of the Red Hand shall give you shelter, nor any Orc give you aid. Three days food will you receive, enough to see you to our borders. Do not return here upon pain of death. Are there any here who would contest this decision?" She looked around at the crowd, but no one spoke up. "Very well, then let the rest retire to the grand hut where we must choose a new chieftain and wipe the stain of Gorlag from our memories, and that of our ancestors."

THE TRUTH

SUMMER 1103 SR

Natalia was sitting on her bed, reading, when she heard a knock. She rose, crossing the small space to open the door, revealing the countenance of the grand mistress herself, Marakhova Stormwind.

"Yes, Mistress?" said Natalia.

"There is a new arrival," the grand mistress said in her punctual tone. "It is your time to act as greeter. You know how to get to the stables?"

"Yes, Mistress," she replied.

"Good, make your way there quickly, you're expected." The grand mistress turned suddenly and departed, leaving Natalia to watch as she marched down the hall.

Natalia returned her book to the table, then looked in the small mirror, fixing her hair. The Volstrum always stressed the importance of making one's self presentable, likely due to the family's presence at royal courts throughout the continent.

Satisfied with her appearance, she made her way to her dresser, digging through her clothes to retrieve the letter she had written some time ago. It was sealed with wax and sat waiting for the opportunity to be delivered, an opportunity that, until this day, had not been available. She tucked it into her skirts, then left, making her way through the huge complex towards the waiting stables.

The students at the Volstrum were not allowed outside, but the staff and servants suffered no such restriction. In addition, a myriad of merchants and other suppliers brought goods to the structure, necessitating a place of business. Though referred to as the stables, it was more than just that, as it also doubled as a loading dock, and on occasions such as this, as a receiving area. It was towards this very place that Natalia now strode.

It was rare that a potential student was brought through the stables and when it did occur, it was usually for one reason, and one reason only; the applicant was being brought in by a mage hunter. High-borns used the front entrance, but low-borns were typically brought in the back, as she had been. She hoped she might see Stanislav, for he was one of the more successful mage hunters, but there were others who showed up from time to time.

Rounding the corner to the stables, the smell of horses drifted into Natalia's nose. Moments later, she entered the busy room where merchants were unloading a couple of wagons of food near a group of male instructors who waited while servants brought them mounts. She passed them, nodding her head to show the requisite respect, and then made her way to the waiting room. This was a small chamber beside the stables where hopeful candidates were held until they could be processed.

She opened the door to see a young lad sitting on a chair, his back to the wall, casting his eyes about trying to take it all in. Opposite him sat a man, and her face broke into a smile as she recognized him.

"Stanislav," Natalia said, "so good to see you. How have you been?"

"I've been well," he replied, likewise grinning. "My, but you've grown. You look like a proper lady now."

"Who's this you've brought us?" she asked.

The mage hunter looked at the young lad. "His name's Pyotr," he said, "and I brought him back from Kasdar."

"Never heard of it," she said.

"I'm surprised," he replied, "it's only a couple of days from here. I take it you're to greet the new initiate?"

"I have that honour, yes," she said, then remembered the letter. "Stanislav, can you linger for a moment? There's something I'd like to talk to you about, but I have to see to Pyotr here, first."

"Of course," he said, "but before you do, I do need you to sign my contract so I can get my catcher's fee."

"By all means," she said, holding out her hand, "give it to me and then you can collect the coins."

He fished through his overcoat, withdrawing a carefully folded piece of paper.

Natalia took it and placed it upon the table that sat nearby. After scanning over it quickly, she signed her name neatly at the bottom. She lifted it to her lips, blowing on it till the ink dried. "Here you go," she said, "all neat and proper."

"Thank you," he replied, taking it back. "I'll just go and collect my fee. Shall we meet back here? I shouldn't be too long."

"Sounds perfect," she said, then remembered the note she had brought with her. She pulled it from the waist of her skirt. "Hold onto this for me, won't you?"

"What is it?" he asked.

"A letter I'd like you to deliver, I'll tell you about it when I get back."

"Very well, then."

She returned her attention to the youngster, "Come along, Pyotr, it's time I took you inside."

They made their way through the back halls of the Volstrum until Natalia found the room she was looking for. They were called interview rooms and were used for a variety of purposes. Today, this room would be used to assess the potential of young Master Pyotr.

She opened the door, revealing a table inside with two chairs, facing each other.

"Have a seat," Natalia said, "and someone will be along shortly."

The young lad sat down, his eyes wandering about the sparsely decorated room. It reminded Natalia of her first visit, a lifetime ago. She closed the door, but remained in the hallway, waiting.

Shortly thereafter, she spied Mistress Voltana, one of the senior instructors.

"Is he in there?" the mistress asked.

"Yes, Mistress," Natalia replied.

The newcomer halted before entering. "What do you make of him?"

"He's underfed," she said, "and could do with a good wash, but his eyes are bright."

"A good sign," the woman replied, "and as for the rest, well, we can take care of that easily enough."

Natalia opened the door, allowing the mistress to enter. "Will there be further need of me, Mistress?" she asked.

"No," the woman replied, "you may leave us. The servants will take him to the dormitory when required."

"Very well," she said, curtsying slightly. Natalia made her way back to the waiting room. Stanislav, having collected his coins, was sitting in a chair awaiting her return. He stood as she entered.

"This letter," he said, "who's it for?"

"Didn't you read the name on the front?" she asked.

"I did," he replied, "but I don't know anyone named Katrin, and there's no last name."

"Her name's Katrin Stormwind," she said, "and she's a friend of mine."

"Isn't everyone here a Stormwind?" he asked.

"Yes, but she was born a Stormwind."

"Do you realize how many people with that name live here in Karslev?" Stanislav said. "Don't you have an address?"

"I'm afraid not," Natalia answered, "she left without telling me."

"Left? You mean she quit?"

"No, she actually failed the training. They shipped her out before I could say goodbye. I hope it's not an imposition, but I thought you might be able to deliver that letter. I've been worried about her."

"I've got a few days between contracts," remarked Stanislav, "I'll see what I can do."

"You might try the hall of records," suggested Natalia. "I understand wealthy families record all their births and deaths there."

"They do," he agreed. "It's how they keep inheritances straight. Her birth would be registered, and from there, it should be easy to locate her parents."

"I'm afraid I can't pay you," she said, "I don't have access to any funds until I graduate."

"That's all right," he returned, "one of these days you'll be at some court and can do me a favour in return."

"With pleasure," Natalia said, "though I'd do it regardless."

He looked down at the letter, deep in thought. "There's something else I need to tell you."

"What is it?" she asked.

"Do you remember when I warned you about Nikolai?" Stanislav asked.

"Yes, what of it?"

"There's more to the story, much more if I'm being truthful. You'd better sit."

Natalia took a seat, a look of worry creasing her brow. "What is it?"

"Where do I start?" he pondered.

"How about at the beginning? Has this got something to do with my coming here?"

"Yes," he finally admitted. "You see, when we found you, your mother was living in squalor. She was happy to know you'd be properly cared for, and also I gave her funds to release her out of servitude."

"I have a vague memory of it," said Natalia, "but what of it? It has little bearing on my current situation."

"I'm not done," continued Stanislav. "When we retrieved you, as I said, I gave your mother some coins. Nikolai later returned to steal them. He also murdered your mother."

Natalia was shocked. She had always wondered why her mother had never visited her, but to hear first-hand of her death shook her to her core. "Why would Nikolai do that?"

"He was under orders, orders I knew nothing about."

"Who ordered it?" she asked. "Do you know?"

"A man named Dagor Sartellian," he replied.

"And who is this Dagor person, to so callously order the death of my mother?"

"In those days he worked for the Volstrum, and reported directly to Illiana Stormwind."

"The matriarch?" asked Natalia.

"The very same," replied Stanislav, "but she wasn't the matriarch in those days, she was the head of the Volstrum."

"And so the matriarch ordered my mother killed?" she asked.

"No," said the mage hunter, "I don't think she did."

"What do you mean?"

"I think there was some sort of power play going on, though I can't, for the life of me, figure out what it was. Illiana took an interest in you, insisting I bring you directly to the Volstrum. That was rare in those days."

"Then how is this Dagor Sartellian involved?" asked Natalia.

"He's the one that sent me to investigate you. I was tasked with evaluating the rumours surrounding your powers."

"But why kill my mother?" she asked. "It makes no sense."

"We discovered that the man that lived with your mother was not your father," Stanislav said. "I rather suspect they wanted to hide your true father's identity. Your mother was likely the only person that knew."

"That can't be true," she said.

"How so?" he asked.

"Someone else must have known, or how would they know to kill her?"

"A valid point," he confessed, "and one which hadn't occurred to me."

"Tell me," she continued, "why tell me this now, after so many years?"

"I just wanted you to know the facts," he offered. "Nikolai also wanted a share of your bounty, but I refused. He's borne a grudge ever since."

"But isn't he a mage hunter now?" she asked.

"He is," Stanislav confessed, "and now that you're a senior, you may have to interact with him."

"Thank you for telling me," she said, "I know it must have been hard."

"Well," he said, "I suppose I'd best get going. With any luck, I can locate Katrin's birth record before the bell tolls for dinner."

"Very well," she said, "I'll leave you to it. Good luck, Stanislav, and look after yourself."

"I always do," he said with a chuckle.

He left the room, exiting back to the stables, leaving Natalia deep in thought. Hopefully, she would hear back in a couple of days and could resume her friendship with Katrin.

Stanislav looked down at the paper in his hand, the address was correct. He stood, gazing at the entrance, taking in the ornate stonework and worked metal gate. A servant, alert to his presence, came towards him from the mansion that lay beyond. The man stopped just out of reach on the other side.

"Who are you," the servant asked, "and what is your business here?"

"My name is Stanislav Voronsky," the mage hunter answered, "and I'm looking for Katrin Stormwind. Do I have the correct address?"

"There's no one here by that name," the servant replied, rather indignantly.

"This is the house of Lord Kolyak Stormwind, is it not?"

"It is," the servant replied, "what of it?"

"According to birth records his wife bore a girl at this very house. They named her Katrin."

"I know of no such thing, you've obviously made a huge mistake."

"I think not," said Stanislav. "I'm a mage hunter, and I work for the Volstrum."

The servant's eyes bulged ever so slightly. "Well," he huffed, "you should have mentioned that immediately. Please, come in, and I'll show you to the sitting room where you can wait for Lord Kolyak."

"Thank you," Stanislav replied, "I should be delighted." He waited while the servant opened the gate, admitting him.

"It's right this way," the man said, "if you'll follow me."

Stanislav was led down a winding path that culminated at a stately wooden door. Pausing a moment, he glanced at the symbols carved into it. They looked like runes of some sort, but he didn't recognize them. Following the servant inside, he entered a comfortable looking sitting room decorated with plush chairs around the perimeter, while in the centre was an imposing statue. It looked odd to see the marble artwork here, in this otherwise homey room, and he leaned in closer to examine it in more detail. It depicted a mermaid, coiled around an anchor, no doubt inspired by some sort of legend.

His examination was disrupted by the arrival of a well-dressed man who looked to be in his fifties, with carefully trimmed hair and sideburns, but otherwise devoid of facial hair.

"You are Lord Kolyak Stormwind?" the mage hunter asked.

"I am," the man replied, "though I fear you have me at a disadvantage. I'm told your name is Stanislav Voronsky, but I'm afraid I'm not familiar with you. Should I be?"

"I don't believe our paths have ever crossed," the mage hunter replied, "but I do work for the Volstrum, on occasion."

Stanislav recognized a flicker of irritation on the lord's face but made no remark.

"I'm a very busy man," declared Lord Kolyak. "What is the purpose of your visit?"

"I'm looking for someone," he replied cryptically, "and was told you might have some information."

"Who is it you're looking for?"

"A young lady by the name of Katrin Stormwind." Again, Stanislav saw the barest flicker of emotion on the man's face.

The lord cleared his throat. "There is no one here by that name," he stated.

"You were married to Helene Sartellian, were you not?"

"We were bonded, that is true, though it wasn't what you would call a marriage."

"Pardon me, but the hall of records registered the birth of a girl named Katrin. Both of you were named the parents."

"And so we were," he said, "but Helene died years ago."

"Oh, I'm sorry to hear that," said Stanislav. "Might I ask how?"

"She was consumed," replied Lord Kolyak, "by fire."

"I take it she was a Fire Mage?"

"Of course, she would scarcely have the name Sartellian otherwise."

"And what of your daughter?"

"There is nothing to tell," he replied. "She was sent to the Volstrum and failed. She is of no further interest to me."

"I beg your pardon?" Stanislav burst out. "Do you mean to say you disowned her?"

"I wouldn't expect you to understand," the lord continued, "you are obviously not of our line."

"Have you no word of her at all?"

"No, I have heard nothing other than her failure, and I shall hear of nothing else. Is there any other subject on which you would care to speak?"

"I don't think there's anything else to say," said Stanislav, extending his hand. "Thank you for the assistance, I will show myself out."

A servant rushed forward to open the door, and the mage hunter stepped through, eventually making his way to the front door.

"I told you so," said the servant, a smug look on his face.

Stanislav ignored the man's comment, following him out and back down to the path to the street. There, he waited while the gate was opened, allowing him to leave. He turned as the door was shut behind him. "You know," Stanislav said, "you should be careful how you treat people, it might come back to haunt you one day."

The servant sneered at him and retreated to the mansion, leaving Stanislav alone. His search for Natalia's friend had dead-ended, and he hated to be the bearer of bad news, but it looked like Katrin would remain missing for the foreseeable future. He wondered if the girl was not alone in her situation, for surely, after all the years of operation, there had been others who had failed. Perhaps, if he found one, he might find more. He turned back towards the Volstrum and strode off, intent on making at least some sort of progress.

Natalia stood on the casting line, eyeing the target before her, a wooden frame holding a door, standing freely downrange, not more than a dozen arm lengths' away. She looked back to her tutor, the only other person in the room.

"You may cast when ready," said Mistress Tatiana.

Natalia uttered the words of command and ice formed around the handle of the door, spreading across the frame until the entire door was encased.

"Very nicely done, Natalia," her mentor praised, "you pick these spells up so quickly. It's refreshing to see one of such skill."

"Thank you, Mistress," she replied. "Shall I dispel?"

"Yes, dear," the mistress responded.

Natalia waved her hand, uttering the counterspell. The ice began to vanish, just as the door to the room opened.

"Am I interrupting?" asked Mistress Dominique, poking her head inside.

"Not at all," said Mistress Tatiana. "Natalia was just trying her hand at a frozen portal spell."

"I hate to be a bother," Mistress Dominique continued, "but there's a visitor here to see your student."

"Now? She's in the middle of being tutored."

"Yes, now. The man has a letter from the matriarch herself."

"The matriarch?" said Mistress Tatiana. "Then we mustn't keep him waiting." She turned to Natalia, "Well, don't just stand there, girl, off with you to the visiting rooms."

"Follow me," said Mistress Dominique, leading the way.

They threaded their way through the grand edifice of the Volstrum to a sitting room where Natalia was told her visitor awaited her arrival. The mistress headed off, back to her own business, leaving the young woman standing alone before the door.

Natalia opened the door. Inside was an elegant room with luxurious furniture. Sitting on a rather comfortable looking chair was none other than Stanislav Voronsky, the mage hunter, holding a glass of wine, sniffing its bouquet. He made a face and downed the drink in one gulp, then set the glass down.

"Stanislav?" she said in greeting.

"You were expecting someone else?" he said.

"But I was told it was someone with a note from Illiana Stormwind."

"Oh, you mean this?" he asked, brandishing a letter. "She wrote this years ago. I find the seal on it to be of particular use from time to time, though very few have read its contents."

"It didn't take you long to return to the Volstrum," Natalia said. "Does that mean you found something?"

"Something, yes, but not what you were hoping for, I'm afraid."

"Meaning?"

"Meaning, I found Katrin's father, but I'm afraid it wasn't good news. It sounds like he's disowned her. There's no trace of her at their estate."

"Disowned her? She's his daughter, for Saint's sake."

"The Stormwinds are different people from you and me," Stanislav explained.

"I'll remind you I'm a Stormwind, now," she protested.

"Yes, but you know what I mean. To them, everything is about appearance and power. Prestige, if you will. A failure in the family would bring disgrace to his line. I imagine he's trying to distance himself from her as much as possible."

"What about her mother?"

"She died years ago," he said, "apparently burned to death."

"I'm told that's common for Fire Mages," said Natalia. "Tell me, was she a Sartellian?"

"She was, how did you know?"

"They're the most powerful of Fire Mages, it only stands to reason."

"I'm still not sure how a Fire Mage burns to death. Aren't they immune to fire?"

"No," she replied, "no more so than the rest of us, and fire consumes."

"I'm not sure I understand," Stanislav said.

"Mages fuel their magic by their innate energy," Natalia explained. "Power is consumed as spells are cast. It regenerates over time, of course, but if you use too much at once, you can run out."

"Then what happens? Do your spells just fizzle out?"

"No," she said, "it starts to destroy your body. In most mages, it might manifest as a nosebleed or bleeding ears or eyes, but in a Fire Mage, it can manifest as flames. Unfortunately, there's no such thing as fireproof robes, and a fire like that is very difficult to extinguish."

"Aren't fire and water magic opposites?" Stanislav asked.

"They are, why?"

"Wouldn't they cancel each other out? What I mean to say is, wouldn't the child of a Fire and Water Mage union be powerless?"

"You'd think so, wouldn't you?" offered Natalia. "And yet, the Sartellians and Stormwinds have been doing it for generations, and they're the most powerful of mages."

"And yet," added Stanislav, "it doesn't always work, hence Katrin, who couldn't master her magic."

"I suppose nothing is guaranteed in life," mused Natalia.

"I'm sorry I didn't bring better news," he said, "though I did make some further enquiries. Unfortunately, they didn't pan out either."

"What kind of enquiries?" Natalia asked.

"It occurred to me that other students must have failed over the years. I looked into it and discovered a few names, but none of them were ever seen again, though of course, they could have changed their names."

"A pity you couldn't learn more," she said. "I'm afraid we'll have to give up trying to find Katrin. I only hope she's doing all right, wherever she is."

"Is there anything else I can help you with?" he asked.

"No," she said, "you've done all you can for now."

He watched her a moment, deep in thought.

"Something's troubling you," he said, "something other than Katrin's disappearance. What is it?"

"I don't know," Natalia confessed, "but I'm beginning to get the feeling my time here is drawing short."

"That's only natural," he said, "you'll be graduating soon."

"No, you don't understand. There's something about this place that's been gnawing at me. I don't know how much longer I can remain."

"You think you're in danger?" Stanislav asked.

"No, but I can't help but feel I'm being groomed for something. Something over which I shall have little choice. I'd rather have the freedom to make my own decisions."

"I can understand that," he said, "but after all they've given you, you can't say it comes as a surprise. When you first arrived here, you were a young peasant girl, and now you're likely to graduate as the single most powerful mage to pass through these halls."

"I haven't graduated yet," Natalia reminded him.

"You know what I mean."

"Yes, I do," she said. "And I appreciate that my life has improved substantially, but I'm still concerned."

"If you need help, I'm always willing to lend a hand," he said, "no matter what."

"Thank you," she said, "that means a lot to me. There's nothing more you can do right now, but there may come a time in the future that I might take you up on the offer."

"I'll be there when you need, me," he said, "I promise."

FAREWELL

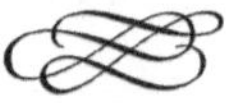

AUTUMN 1103 SR

(In the tongue of the Orcs)

Athgar entered the great hut to be greeted by Kargen. In the background, echoing throughout the structure, he heard the cry of a young Orc.

"Your son sounds hungry," he said.

"Constantly," replied Kargen. "We have been waiting for you, the rest have already arrived."

"The rest? Am I late?"

"No, but they were eager, so they arrived early," Kargen laughed his typical deep-throated roar.

"I thought we were just eating a meal together?"

"And so we are, but others have joined us," explained his friend. "It is good we only have one child, or the entire village would have been invited. As it is, it is a little cramped in our chambers."

Kargen led them past the great fire pit to one end of the longhouse. There, a doorway led into the chieftain's private quarters. They entered, to reveal those assembled.

Shaluhk was here, of course, with the newest member of the tribe held tightly in her arms. To her right sat her brother, Laruhk, while to her left was the shamaness.

"It is good to see you well," said Uhdrig.

"And you," replied Athgar, "though I'm surprised to see you here."

"I am here for the naming ceremony," said the shamaness, "did Kargen not tell you?"

Athgar looked to his Orcish friend, who merely shrugged, a very Human expression.

"I may have lured you here under false pretences," Kargen replied, standing to the left of his bondmate.

"Come, sit," offered Shaluhk. "Uhdrig will say the blessing, and then the ancestors will speak, and a name will be given."

"We'll hear the ancestors?" asked Athgar, taking his seat.

"No," corrected Kargen, "only Uhdrig has that power."

"Sit down, Kargen," said Shaluhk, "and then the ceremony can begin."

The great Orc sat, and Laruhk burst into laughter.

"What is so funny?" Kargen asked.

"Only my sister would dare order around the chieftain," said Laruhk, between laughs.

Shaluhk gave him a withering stare, and his laughter subsided.

"Shall we begin?" asked Uhdrig.

"Yes," said Shaluhk.

"Since long ago," began the shamaness, "our ancestors have watched over us, to guide and offer us wisdom. Many have been the Orcs that have trod this land, and their blessings have seen fit to enrich our lives, granting us bountiful hunts and bestowing the gifts of love and life to bondmates."

Athgar saw Shaluhk look at Kargen, and the great Orc blushed.

"Today," Uhdrig continued, "we offer this sacrifice that we might beseech you, our glorious ancestors, for your wisdom once more." She held up a pot of liquid then took a small sip, passing it around the circle, each taking a measure in their mouths, and then passing it on. It returned to her, and she placed it aside, closing her eyes.

Athgar could feel the anticipation. The room was quiet, save for the sounds of the village that penetrated the walls.

Uhdrig soon started speaking very quietly, the words tumbling from her mouth like a stream. He recognized them as words of power, though he had no idea what their effect might be. There was the familiar buzzing in the air, and then the hair on the back of his neck stood on end.

"What name will you choose?" asked Uhdrig.

Athgar was confused. Who was she asking? He looked to Shaluhk, but the younger shamaness merely put her finger to her lips, silencing him.

Uhdrig nodded her head in agreement, though no sound could be heard. "A good name for a strong hunter," she said. The shamaness opened her eyes, looking at each visitor in turn, saying nothing until her observation was complete. "The ancestors have spoken."

"And by what name shall my son be known?" asked Kargen.

"His name shall be Agar," proclaimed Uhdrig.

"A good strong name," said Shaluhk, "does it please you, Kargen?"

"It does," the chieftain replied, letting out a chuckle.

"What's so funny?" asked Athgar.

"It seems our ancestors have seen fit to name my son after you, dear friend," said Kargen, "for Agar is your name in our language."

"Nonsense," objected the Therengian, "you've always called me Athgar, not Agar."

"Ah, but we use your language for your name, as is only proper. Athgar means 'he who is strong', does it not?"

"It does," admitted the Therengian, "though I've never felt I was particularly strong."

"Strength is not always physical," offered Uhdrig, "there is also strength of will, and you have demonstrated that in abundance."

"Yes," admitted Kargen, "and Agar means the same thing in Orcish, 'one who is strong.' It is a powerful name, and he shall be proud to bear it, like his uncle, Athgar."

Athgar blushed, "I'm humbled."

"And so you should be," said Kargen with a smile, "for one day Agar shall grow to be chieftain of this tribe, just you wait and see."

Athgar, seeing cups had been laid before them, raised his into the air. "In the manner of my own people, I should like to offer a toast."

They mimicked his actions, though they had to wait while Laruhk refilled his cup.

"To Agar, son of Kargen and Shaluhk," started the Human, "may he have the prowess of his father and the wisdom of his mother."

They all cheered, then downed the drinks in one gulp.

Kargen let out a burp, then smiled. "Now," he said, "it is time to feast." He clapped his hands, and a moment later, Durgash appeared at the doorway.

"What news?" asked the newcomer.

"I have a son," said Kargen, "and his name shall be Agar!"

"The ancestors have truly blessed you," replied Durgash. "Will you come now and feast with your tribe? They wish to celebrate the blessing of our ancestors."

Kargen rose from his seat, signalling the others to do likewise. "Let us join the tribe," he said. "Shaluhk shall lead the way with our son."

They followed her into the great hall where, much to Athgar's surprise, the fire pit was alight, and the entire village crowded around it. Meat now roasted over the fire, where only a short time ago, the room had been empty. He looked to the far end of the fire pit to see Artoch.

The master of flame had a sheepish look to his face and nodded as their eyes met.

They took their seats, and the celebration began.

It was dark by the time Kargen stepped out for some air. The sounds of merriment would, no doubt, continue well into the early hours of the morning, but the smoke from the great fire pit had started to burn his eyes.

He took a deep breath, relishing the cool breeze as it blew across his face. Turning about to re-enter the hut, he noticed Athgar leaning against the outside wall of the hut, his eyes staring into the night sky above.

"Something troubling you, my friend?" Kargen asked.

Athgar lowered his head, looking to his comrade. "It's time for me to leave," he announced.

Kargen moved closer, nodding his head. "I knew this day would come," he said. "I take it you are ready to find those that destroyed your village?"

"I am," he confirmed, "and somewhere out there, I have a sister that's still alive, for Uhdrig assures me she has not joined my ancestors."

"Where will you start?"

"In Draybourne," he said. "I don't believe the Duke of Holstead was responsible, but I have to start somewhere. You can't just cart off scores of people with no one taking notice."

"How much of the attack do you remember?" Kargen asked.

"Not much, I'm afraid. I remember the horses and the heavy armour, but there was something else."

"What?" asked the Orc.

"A man, one of the riders. He had a black beard and a scar that ran down his left cheek, all the way to his jaw. He wore a dark grey tabard, they all did actually, maybe even black, with a symbol of a sword on them."

"From your description, they sound like knights, my friend."

"Knights?"

"Yes, heavily armoured warriors who constantly train for warfare. They are dangerous opponents, you'd best tread carefully. Perhaps I should go with you."

"No," said Athgar, "though I appreciate the offer, you are needed here. You're chieftain of this tribe now, you have responsibilities here."

"There must be something I can do to help, you have done so much for us. Let me at least send some coin with you. We certainly have little use for it here, and maybe some goods for barter in the city."

"I would appreciate that," said Athgar.

"Will you come back to us, one day?"

"Of course," he replied, "this is my home now, though I have no idea how long it will be before I return."

"Perhaps you will return to us with a bondmate," offered Kargen, "and then you can settle down and raise a family."

"Maybe, one day, but such thoughts are far from my mind, at present. I have a difficult task ahead of me, and it will require my full concentration."

"Then I ask only one thing," said Kargen.

"Name it, my friend," said Athgar.

"Let us see you off on your journey. You are treading a long, and perhaps, perilous path. It would only be right to invoke the protection of our ancestors to safeguard you. When do you plan to leave?"

"In two days. I should like to finish the last of those bows for you before I go."

"Very well," said Kargen, "then two days hence we shall see you safely on your way. I know there are many that would wish you well, though your leaving will be bittersweet. Now, will you come back into the long house and drink to my son?"

"Of course," said Athgar, "lead on."

Athgar gathered the last of his things, slinging the bag over his shoulder. He carried a bow, an axe, and a knife for protection, and wore the tunic that Shaluhk had fashioned for him, along with the comfortable boots.

Stepping into the early morning sun, he took in the sight of the village before him, likely the last time he would view it for a long while. The Orcs of the tribe had all risen early, and now formed a corridor for him to walk through. Making his way forward, he first saw Kargen and Shaluhk with tiny Agar clutched to his mother's chest. Beside them were Laruhk, Uhdrig, and the master of fire himself, Artoch. Athgar halted before Kargen, at a loss for words. It was the chieftain that spoke first.

"Long have you been my friend," began Kargen, "and that of the tribe as well. I bathed your hand in blood on your first successful hunt, as befits a member of the Red Hand, and you responded with loyalty and honour. As you go forward on your quest, it is only fitting that we give you a gift to remember our friendship."

He turned slightly, and Uhdrig handed him something. Turning back to face Athgar, Kargen revealed a torc, fashioned as a large ring, open at the front to allow it to be worn around the neck. It was carved of gold in the pattern of rope, but the ends, where the gap was, were fashioned in the likeness of Orc heads, with red stones set in their mouths.

"This torc marks you a friend of the Orcs," Kargen proclaimed. "Wherever you go, should you find yourself in the company of our race, they will know you as friend and tribe mate."

Kargen leaned forward, placing it around Athgar's throat. It hung loosely, and though it was large, it was quite comfortable to wear.

"Thank you," said Athgar.

"There is more," said Kargen, "for Uhdrig and Artoch have seen fit to use their powers on it."

"It's magical?" asked the Therengian, in surprise.

"Yes," said Artoch, "those are fire stones you see at the ends, and they will help you when you use your magic, enhancing your power."

"I don't know what to say," said Athgar, "this is truly a great gift."

"Remember your training," said Artoch, "and remember to always respect the flame."

"I will," he said, "I promise. You have all been so generous."

"It is you that have been generous to us," said Shaluhk. "You have given us warbows to protect ourselves, and you have enriched us by your presence. Though we are sad to see you go, we wish you well. Farewell, Athgar, and may the blessing of our ancestors go with you."

She stepped forward, hugging him. Agar, as if sensing the moment, reached out with his tiny fingers, copying his mother's actions.

Each of them stepped forward, Laruhk, Artoch, even Uhdrig, embracing him in the Human fashion. At last, he stood before Kargen once more.

"Safe travels, my friend," said the chieftain, placing his hands upon the Human's shoulders. "And know that where you go, so goes the tribe."

Athgar nodded his thanks, too overwhelmed to speak. Turning to leave, he saw the rest of the village arrayed before him, lining the pathway to the edge of the palisade. Taking the first steps on his journey felt like the hardest thing he had ever done, and yet he knew it was time. He moved forward, travelling through the village with his head held high. As he walked, a noise started, and he looked on in amazement to see the Orcs clapping, a purely Human action, and he smiled.

Athgar reached the gate and halted, looking back one last time at his friends, his family. He nodded at them, then turned once more to the path he was now to tread, towards his future.

ULTIMATUM

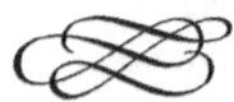

AUTUMN 1103 SR

Natalia gazed out the window of the tower she occupied. There were six of them at the Volstrum, every one topped by a copper dome. They were often used by full mages to practice their arts, but today they were being used for the final assessments of the graduating students. She waited patiently, staring out at the cold, wet weather that was so common this far north, wondering what tomorrow's dawn might bring, for today was to be her last day as a student. Her reverie was cut short when the door opened, revealing none other than the matriarch herself, Illiana Stormwind.

"Greetings, Natalia," she said, "I hope you are well?"

"I am, Mistress, thank you. And yourself?"

"As well as can be expected for someone of my advanced years," she said, sweeping her gaze over the young woman. "You look surprised?"

"I wasn't expecting you, Matriarch. I thought it would be one of the instructors here to present me with my final test."

"Final test? There is no such thing for you. I have watched your progress since the day you first came to us, Natalia. I had high hopes for you then, and you have not disappointed. You graduate the Volstrum as the most powerful of all casters, for your age."

"Surely not, Mistress," she replied. "There must be many with more power than I?"

"There are indeed," Illiana said, "but none were so powerful at such a young age. Your skill will mature as you do, lifting you higher within the family, perhaps even to its pinnacle one day, many years from now."

"I live to serve."

The matriarch looked slightly disappointed. "I doubt that," she said.

"When I was your age, all I wanted to do was see the world. Has youth changed so much since that time?"

Natalia blushed, "No, I suppose not, Mistress."

"It is the custom," continued the matriarch, "that when you graduate, you be given an article of jewellery containing a special crystal. Are you familiar with it?"

"Magerite?" Natalia asked.

"Yes indeed, and do you know the properties of magerite?"

"I believe it can be used to indicate magical power, can it not?"

"It can, but it is much more than that. Each member of the family wears magerite somewhere upon their person. It may be a ring, a necklace, even a brooch. As a Stormwind, you shall have a blue magerite, while Sartellians use red. The depth of the colour varies with the power of the wearer." Grand Mistress Illiana held up her own hand, revealing a ring with a dark blue crystal. "There, you see?"

"It's beautiful!" exclaimed Natalia.

The matriarch held it up before her own eyes, "I suppose it is, though my eyesight is not what it used to be; there are some things that even magic cannot help."

"You must be powerful, indeed, to colour the gem so deeply."

"Yes," the matriarch replied, "though, in my youth, it was much paler. As we grow older, our body withers, but our magical power increases. By the time you reach my age, you'll probably be the most powerful mage on the continent, provided you live that long."

"You think I might not?" she asked, intrigued.

"You have a target on you, Natalia," Illiana stated. "I have tried to lessen it, but there are members of the family that do not like a low-born becoming a battle mage. Even as we speak, there are those who work against you."

"Who? Which people?"

"No one that you would currently know," the grand matriarch replied. "Suffice it to say that they fear your power. You will always have to look over your shoulder."

"Do you have any advice?" asked Natalia.

"Pick your friends carefully," she advised, "and try to make some that are not mages, you can never fully trust those with magic."

"I'm surprised to hear you say that, Mistress. I would have thought, as head of the Stormwinds, you would prefer to trust mages."

"My experience tells me otherwise, my dear. I cling to the top of the family by a tenuous thread, at best. Those around me are constantly fighting for influence. Soon, I will be too old and feeble to continue my reign, and someone else will take over my duties."

"Why are you telling me this, Matriarch?"

"Because I want you to succeed," Illiana said. "This family, both families, have become corrupt with power and greed, and I don't mean just magical. The Stormwinds and the Sartellians have their fingers in courts all across the continent. It is time you realize the full extent of our influence."

"Is there something you want me to do?" asked Natalia.

"Do?" the old woman mused. "No, at least not specifically. I want you to use your own wits. Be mindful of those around you, everything at court is a play for power or influence. As a graduate, especially a powerful one, you will have your pick of assignments. You will arrive at someone's court and be apprenticed under a Sartellian, or a Stormwind. Remember that to them, you are a pawn, but you must be mistress of your own destiny, do you understand?"

"I think so, Matriarch."

"Good, then I shall say no more on the matter. Now, you must pass the final test."

"I thought you said there was no final test?" questioned Natalia.

"Well, we have to give you something to talk about with the others, don't we now?"

"Then what shall I cast?"

In answer, the matriarch pointed to the door. "Freeze that portal closed," she bid.

Natalia took a small step forward, extending her arms. Without uttering a word, there was the familiar tingle, and then a thick covering of ice sealed the door. "Shall I dispel it?" she asked.

"Not yet," said the grand matriarch, "for there is more I must speak of." She reached into her voluminous robes, withdrawing a pouch and handing it to Natalia. "Take this," she said.

Natalia grasped the pouch, "What is it?"

"Some gems," Illiana said. "Guard them well, for one day they may prove useful."

"For what? Are they magical?"

"No, of course not, but they are worth many coins."

"I thank you, Mistress, but I am hardly in need of it. As a graduate, I will be receiving a stipend, will I not?"

"You will," she replied, "as long as you are in service to the family. Now, we must return to our previous topic."

"Which is?" asked Natalia.

"The magerite. Tell me, how would you like the stone set?"

"A ring, I think," she replied, "much like yours."

Illiana Stormwind looked long and hard into Natalia's eyes, eyes which did not flinch. "Very well," she said, seeming to make a decision. "Now, there is one more thing about magerite that you need to know. When meeting another member of the family, always look for their gem. The darker the colour, the higher up in the family they will be. You should always show deference to one of more power. You'll also note that men will typically offer a handshake by holding out their hand with the palm down, allowing you to see their ring, or if they are bowing, they will hold their ring hand before them, displaying their power to those that know how to read the magerite."

"I will remember, Matriarch," said Natalia.

"Good, now I think we are done here. You may dispel the frozen portal spell."

"Is that it?" she asked. "Am I a graduate now?"

"There's still the little formality of the actual ceremony, of course, but for all intents and purposes, yes, you are now officially MISTRESS Natalia Stormwind."

Natalia curtsied. "Thank you, Matriarch, for everything."

"I know I have been hard on you over the years, Natalia, but I see a bright future for you, whatever path you tread." She turned to leave, opening the door but then pausing as she turned her head to gaze back at the young woman, "We will not meet again, my dear, but know that my hopes and dreams go with you, whatever you do."

Grand Matriarch Illiana left the room, leaving Natalia to ponder this strange turn of events, the pouch clutched tightly in her hands.

Three days later, Natalia stood in line. She was there with twelve other students, each waiting to be officially recognized as a graduate of the Volstrum. Turning her head, she perused the considerable crowd that had gathered. In addition to the entire student body, dignitaries and influential members of the family had come together to witness the day's proceedings, and it reminded her of the matriarch's words of warning.

The sound of Grand Mistress Marakhova Stormwind calling Natalia's name interrupted her musings, and she stepped forward.

"With this ring," began Marakhova, "I do proclaim Natalia Stormwind a Mistress of the Volstrum, and full battle mage."

The students in the crowd cheered loudly, her victory at the competition last spring still fresh in their minds.

"Hold out your hand," commanded Marakhova.

Natalia held out her right hand, waiting.

Marakhova turned to Mistress Voltana, who had advanced with a pillow on which sat a familiar looking ring.

"This can't be right," said Marakhova, "surely there's some mistake?"

"It is correct, Grand Mistress," said Voltana. "It is the ring of Matriarch Illiana herself."

Marakhova lifted the ring reverentially from the pillow, its gem a pale blue. "You receive a great gift this day," she uttered, just loud enough for Natalia to hear. "I hope you don't dishonour it."

"I shall do my best not to," Natalia answered, bowing her head slightly.

Marakhova placed the ring on Natalia's middle finger, and the gem immediately turned black. The grand mistress gasped, then looked to Natalia's eyes, which were staring straight ahead.

It only took a moment for the older woman to recover, and then she straightened her back, announcing, "Welcome, Mistress Natalia."

Natalia stepped back in line, and the ceremony continued. She remained still, keeping her eyes straight ahead until the last graduate was welcomed and the ceremony complete. It wasn't until the festivities were announced that she finally looked down to examine the ring in more detail. The magerite looked black, but as she held it to the light, she could see just a hint of blue, denoting her water magic. There could be no doubt it was the matriarch's ring, and Natalia wondered why she had seen fit to gift it to her. Was the matriarch trying to tell her something? Illiana's words in the tower came back to Natalia, and she realized her life was about to get much more complicated.

It didn't take long for the realization to become a reality, for the very next day she was summoned to the office of Grand Mistress Marakhova. Sitting next to her in the waiting room was Vasily Stormwind, another recent graduate, and she wondered what might bring them both here at the same time.

In answer to her internal questions, Vasily's name was called first, and she had to wait while his business with the grand mistress, whatever it was, was conducted. He exited sometime later, a smile on his face and a spring to his step. Her name was called next, and she rose, straightening her dress, then making her way to the open door.

"Mistress Natalia," the servant announced as she entered.

Grand Mistress Marakhova sat behind a large wooden desk, her hands steepled in front of her.

"Come in, Natalia," she beckoned, "and have a seat."

Sitting down in the chair, Natalia waited as the servant closed the door, leaving her alone with the head of the Volstrum.

"You are a graduate of this institution now," Marakhova began, "and as such you are to be assigned duties commensurate with your skills. You have demonstrated great power during your time here, a fact that has not gone unnoticed by numerous people of influence."

"Thank you, Grand Mistress," Natalia responded.

"You now have a stipend," Marakhova continued, "and greater freedom to walk the city, though you will always be accompanied by guards."

"Is that necessary, Mistress?"

"It is for your own protection, Natalia, always remember that. We've spent a lot of time and effort training you, we shouldn't like to see that investment go to waste."

"I understand."

"Now, on to other things. I have a list of names for you to look over."

"Names?"

"Yes, potential couplings."

Natalia wasn't sure she had heard correctly, "Couplings?"

"You are a powerful caster, Natalia. We can't let that gift go to waste. You must have a child to pass it on. A proper pairing could produce a child with exceptional capabilities."

"But I'm not ready to marry," she objected.

"And I wouldn't expect you to," Marakhova replied. "We're simply asking you to birth a child, not raise one. We have plenty of volunteers for that."

"Have I no say in the matter?"

"Of course, that's why we have supplied you with names. We can't let you couple with just anyone, your mate has to be carefully selected. A Sartellian with an impeccable pedigree and a demonstration of a suitable power level will be a good match for you."

"And these Sartellians," Natalia asked, panic starting to set in, "are they here, at the Volstrum?"

"Not yet," Marakhova answered "though they are on their way, I have word they left Korascajan weeks ago. We've been keeping an eye out for suitable candidates for you for some time. These three gentlemen have been thoroughly vetted."

"Vetted?"

"Yes, we have checked the history of their lines carefully. You're likely the offspring of a Stormwind yourself, and we can't have you coupling with a cousin, that just wouldn't do. I assure you we have done all we could to find the most suitable matches."

Natalia sat in stunned silence, her mind struggling to come to grips with her present situation.

"Come now," Markhova continued, "surely you don't think we'd invest all this time and effort in you, and then let it go to waste? The family has been breeding powerful mages for generations."

"I'd always known there was a connection between the Sartellians and the Stormwinds," said Natalia, "but I've never really understood the reason."

"You can thank our ancestors for that," said the grand mistress. "They were the ones that discovered that pairing a Water Mage with a Fire Mage could produce a child with exceptional potential."

"I would have thought they'd cancel each other out," said Natalia. "After all, they're opposite schools of magic."

"Yes," agreed Markhova, "and yet we cannot argue with their success. Ultimately, we are one big, extended family. When a child shows an aptitude for magic, they become either a Stormwind or Sartellian, depending on their gifts. We train the Stormwinds here, at the Volstrum, as you well know, but the Sartellians are trained in Korascajan. It is important that you understand how imperative our breeding program is to the future of the family."

"I shall need some time to consider things," said Natalia. "This has come as rather a shock to me."

"Of course," Marakhova said, "there's no hurry. Once they arrive, you can take a suitable amount of time to make a decision, or, if you like, I can give you their information, and you can decide before they arrive."

"And when am I to birth this child?"

"Sometime in the next year, before you take up your courtly duties."

"Courtly duties?" Natalia asked, feeling overwhelmed.

"Of course," explained the grand mistress, "we can't have you hidden away here forever. We need you out there, supporting the family's agenda."

"And what agenda is that?"

"The family is both powerful and wealthy. As such, it is always seeking new ways to extend its reach. At court, you will work to strengthen existing ties and expand our influence whenever possible."

"I see," Natalia said.

"So," continued Marakhova, "shall you take the list or wait until the men arrive?"

"Yes, I'll take the list. I would think it best if I was to consider what I'm looking for before I meet them, that way I can make a more dispassionate decision."

"An excellent way of looking at things, and entirely logical," said

Marakhova. "I applaud your decision." She lifted a piece of paper from the desk, handing it to Natalia.

"Will that be all, Grand Mistress?"

"It will, Natalia. You may go now. I will inform you when they arrive."

"Thank you, Mistress," Natalia replied, rising to her feet. She bowed, then left the room, her mind in turmoil. She thought back to her conversation with Illiana, was this what the matriarch had tried to warn her about?

By the time the door had closed behind her, Natalia knew what she had to do.

The halls were dark as Natalia made her way through the Volstrum, her candle throwing long black shadows against the walls. She paused at the door, then looked around to make sure she wasn't being observed before opening it.

Inside, the scent of horses met her nose. She was in the stables, heading towards the same room that she had been brought to all those years ago. It had taken a lot of effort to get a note to Stanislav, and now she risked it all by skulking through the Volstrum on this mad errand.

She approached the room to see the door open, a flickering light throwing shadows out into the hall. Moving closer, she peered in to see Stanislav, a lantern in hand.

"Natalia, is that you?" he called out softly.

"Yes," she said, moving into the room and closing the door behind her. "I'm glad to see you made it."

"I came as soon as I could, but it wasn't easy," he said. "The guards asked me a lot of questions. I had to use Illiana's letter to bluff my way through."

"I'm glad you're here," she said.

"What is it that's so important that I had to come in the middle of the night?" Stanislav asked.

"You once told me you'd be willing to do whatever it took to help me. Do you still stand by those words?"

"Of course, why?"

"I have to get away from here!" Natalia burst out.

"Surely you have the freedom to leave the Volstrum whenever you wish?" he asked.

"No, you don't understand. I want to get away from the Volstrum, the city, the whole country, in fact. I need to run away."

"Why? What's happened?" Stanislav asked, a look of concern creasing his features.

"They're going to breed me," she said.

"Breed you? You mean they want you to have children?"

"Yes, they want to expand the Stormwind line, give them more power. They've even picked out potential partners for me."

"Can't you just say no?" he asked. "After all, they can't take your baby without your consent, can they?"

"Consent has nothing to do with it," Natalia announced. "They expect me to bear them a child. I've been given no choice in the matter, other than picking the father."

"How long do you have?" he asked.

"Not long. They've sent for three prospective fathers from Korascajan, and they left weeks ago."

"How MANY weeks ago, do you know?"

"Several, I've been told, why?" she asked.

"I've been looking into Korascajan ever since I found out about those failed students. It lies far to the south, in an area of hot sun and dry lands. I think it would take a month or more to get here from there, maybe even two. We may still have time yet. If they do arrive, how long do you think you can keep them guessing?"

"Perhaps a week or two, nothing more. The grand mistress is intent on having me give birth sometime in the next year."

"Then we'll need to move swiftly," Stanislav said.

"I have a plan," she said, "but it will require you to do the bulk of the work. They're watching me whenever I leave the Volstrum."

"Tell me what you have in mind," he said.

Natalia handed the pouch over to him. "I received this from the matriarch, herself," she said. "It's full of gems."

"Why would she give you this?" he asked.

"I don't know, but I suspect she secretly wanted me to run away. Can you sell them for me? I need coins. You can take half of whatever you can get for them in payment."

"I'll do what I can, but it will likely take a few days to get a good price. What happens after that?"

"I'm not sure," she confessed. "I hadn't thought that far ahead."

"I have an idea," Stanislav said, "but it's best I don't burden you with details."

"Good," Natalia said, "make what arrangements you need but don't tell me about them. That way, I can honestly say I know nothing of an escape attempt if I should be confronted."

"You think that likely?"

"No, but I was warned there are those out to destroy me."

"How shall I contact you once everything is in place?" Stanislav asked.

"Do you think you would be done by next week?" she asked.

"I should think so, yes, why?"

"I'll come and visit you. There'll be guards, but we'll choose our words carefully."

"A good idea," he agreed, "and I shall refer to the date of your escape as my birthday. We'll act as though I'm throwing a party. That should confuse them."

"My guards will be from the Volstrum," Natalia reminded him, "might they not know your true birthday?"

"I doubt it," he answered, "even I don't know my birthday."

"I suppose it's safe, then. I'll see you in a week."

"Hold on, how many guards are you likely to have."

"Two," Natalia answered, "I understand it's the common practice. Is there anything else you need to know?"

"No, I have everything I need. Wait a moment," the mage hunter said, fishing out a paper from his jacket, "here's my address. I'll head out now, but you should wait a while before leaving this room, in case anyone takes notice."

"Very well, I will," she promised. "Good luck, Stanislav, I don't know how I'll ever repay you."

The carriage pulled up in front of a rather nondescript looking house. Natalia checked the address against the folded paper and then waited while a guard opened the door. She stepped down from the carriage, taking care that her dress did not catch in the doorway. Nodding her head to the guard, she made her way to the entrance, two armed men following. Pausing at the door, she glanced back. The carriage remained where it was, with two more armed guards present at its back. She turned her attention, once again, to the house before her and knocked.

The echo of footsteps on wood drew closer, and then the door opened, revealing the countenance of Stanislav Voronksy.

"Natalia," he said, "it's so good to see you." He looked at the carriage outside, taking note of the guards that were present. "Won't you come inside?"

She entered the house, pausing only a moment as she wiped her feet. "I thought I might drop by to offer my congratulations on your upcoming birthday celebration."

"Why thank you," he said, then looked at the two guards that had followed here. "And are these two gentlemen coming in with you?"

"I'm afraid they are," she replied. "I hope it's not too much of an imposition?"

"Not at all," he responded, "the more, the merrier. Come this way, we shall sit down and have a chat." Stanislav led them all to a sparsely decorated living room. "I'm afraid I must apologize for the furniture," he said, making his way to a side table, "but I seldom have guests. I'm away from home most of the time, you see, hunting down mages and whatnot."

"I understand," she replied. "Tell me, are you having a party?"

"A party?"

"Yes, for your birthday?"

"I am," he said, "in fact, I have something rather special in mind for the happy day."

"Remind me," she urged, "when was the happy day?"

"Why, today," he replied.

"Today?" Natalia burst out in alarm.

"Yes, didn't I tell you?"

She struggled to recover from the surprise, "No, you most decidedly did not. I feel awful, I didn't get you a gift."

"Your presence is gift enough for me," he said graciously. "Let me get drinks. Can I offer you gentlemen anything?"

This last remark was directed at the two guards. The taller man, a dark-haired individual, scowled at the suggestion. "We're on duty," he simply said.

"Come now," urged Natalia, "you must. We wouldn't want to appear discourteous to our host."

The tall guard looked like he was about to object but then changed his mind. "Very well," he said, "just a little."

"Excellent," said Stanislav, pouring a decanter into two cups. He carried them to the guards, holding them out for acceptance.

"You first," said the tall guard, his companion looking on in annoyance at the delay.

"By all means," said Stanislav, downing half a cup. "Will that suffice?"

"It will," said the guard, taking the other cup.

The mage hunter returned to the side table, pouring a cup for the second guard. "Here you go," he said at last. He sat down opposite Natalia but handed her no drink.

She looked at him for a moment, her eyes going to the two guards, a quizzical look to her face.

"Now, where are my manners," he continued. "How have things been at the Volstrum?"

"They have been much as expected," she replied, "though I must admit that time has seemed to drag on over the last week."

"I'm sorry to hear you say that," the mage hunter responded. "I, for one, have been quite busy. Did I mention the gift that my uncle gave me?"

"No, you didn't."

"How remiss of me," he said, "let me show you." He rose from his seat, returning to the side table.

Natalia looked at the two guards, the shorter of the two had drained his drink almost immediately, while his taller dark-haired companion had been lightly sipping his own.

"Here it is," Stanislav said, producing a small bag and handing it to her. "Now, don't take it out, I don't want it getting dirty."

She opened it carefully, gazing within to see the golden coins it held.

"What do you make of it?" he asked. "Is it not fine?"

"It is," she responded, "but it looks expensive. I hope your uncle didn't pay too much for it?"

"No, not at all. In fact, he told me it was quite the bargain." He glanced over at the shorter guard, whose eyes had closed. The other, halfway through his cup, was looking relaxed, but then quickly snapped his eyes open.

"What treachery is this?" the guard demanded.

"Whatever are you talking about," said Stanislav.

"Guards!" the man yelled at the top of his lungs, then stood to his feet unsteadily, reaching for his weapon.

Stanislav lunged forward, tackling the man and sending them both tumbling to the floor. "Natalia, the door!" he cried out.

She reacted instinctively, thrusting her hands out in front of her and uttering the words of power. There was a sudden chill to the air as ice began to form, encasing the door in its frozen embrace.

The short guard, woken by the commotion, stumbled to his feet, trying to make out what had happened.

"Take the coins," yelled Stanislav. "There's a carriage waiting for you out back."

"Come with me," she pleaded.

"I can't," he said, his voice starting to slur. "Don't you see, I drank the wine."

The other guard drew his sword and stabbed forward, driving the tip into the mage hunter's leg. Stanislav let out a scream of pain as he yelled, "Run, Natalia, run!"

Indecision wracked Natalia. She knew this was her only chance of escape, but Stanislav was bleeding and drugged. The short guard was drawing back for another strike, and she let loose with an ice shard spell. The frozen darts flew across the tiny space, striking the man in the left arm and sending him tumbling backward. He hit the wall and slid to the floor, clutching his wounds.

Guards were banging on the outside of the door, but the ice held the portal tight.

"Hurry," Stanislav told her, "before they get wise and try the back door."

She turned, rushing from the room, her heart thumping in her chest. In her panic, the house became a maze and, for a moment, she struggled to make sense of it. Turning, she ran for the back door which loomed nearby.

Outside she went, to see a plain looking carriage, the driver upon the seat, whip at the ready. She piled into the back seat, and it immediately lurched forward, the driver's whip stirring the horses on. They careened down the back street, and Natalia sat up, peering out of the window to see one of her guards coming down the side of the house, a crossbow in hand. She let loose with a spell of ice shards, narrowly missing the man, but forcing him to dive for cover.

The carriage finally reached the end of the street, and then turned into the heavier traffic of the main road, disappearing into the streets of Karslev.

DRAYBOURNE

AUTUMN 1103 SR

Athgar had travelled six days to get this far, and he wondered, not for the last time, whether his destination would supply the answers he sought. Exiting the tree line, he could see the road beyond, a meandering path that led, inexorably, towards the great city of Draybourne, its dark stones standing in stark contrast to the green fields of the farms that surrounded it.

He made his way down the hill to join those already heading north, likely making their way to the city's markets. There were all sorts here, from farmers bringing their crops to town, to merchants from distant lands, eager to sell their wares. Athgar passed a cart, heavily laden with straw, that looked as if it might tip over at the slightest bump in the road. As they drew closer to the gatehouse, the traffic slowed.

Two immense towers loomed overhead, one on either side of the gate, far larger than any other building Athgar had ever seen. He stopped, staring up at them, wondering how they were constructed, until he felt someone push him gently, urging him forward.

The ground here felt unusually springy, and he looked down to see he was crossing a wooden drawbridge. At the far end, two guards stood about casually, while a third examined all who sought entrance into the city. Athgar looked up to see others manning the walls, seemingly peering out over the countryside, without a care in the world. No one was in a hurry. Indeed, it appeared they prided themselves on the casual manner in which they operated.

Directly in front of Athgar, a mounted man, wearing a long blue cape, paused, exchanged words with the guard for a moment, and then there was the barest flicker of gold as a coin changed hands. The guard waved the man forward, and his horse trotted beneath the portcullis to enter the city itself.

Athgar stepped forward, waiting as the guard looked him over.

"What's your name?" he was asked.

"Athgar, son of Rothgar," he replied.

The guard looked at him in surprise, taking in his distinctive grey eyes, "A Therengian?"

"Yes," said Athgar.

"What's your business in Draybourne?" the guard enquired.

"I am here seeking someone," Athgar replied. "A warrior with a scar on his left cheek. Do you know of him?"

"Can't say that I do," the guard replied. "Why do you seek this man?"

"He's a murderer!" said the Therengian. "He and his men attacked my village."

The guard studied him intensely before speaking again. "When did this happen? Why haven't I heard of it?" the guard finally asked.

"It was last year," said Athgar, "in the spring."

"And you're just looking into it now?"

"Yes," he replied, "I'm afraid I wasn't in any condition to investigate it any sooner."

"Good luck finding him," said the guard. "I doubt you'll discover much by this late date."

"Should I report it to the duke?" Athgar asked.

"It likely won't do any good," the guard replied. "If this fellow was here, he's probably long gone by now, but you might try the Badger."

"What's that?" Athgar asked.

"It's a tavern. If anyone has heard of this man, there's a good chance it will be someone at the Badger, it's full of less reputable people. You should be careful, though, the wrong words can get you into a lot of trouble."

"I'll bear that in mind. Thank you."

"Go ahead, you can enter the city," said the guard, "and good luck on your search."

Athgar walked beneath the portcullis, then through the stone tunnel that opened into the city itself. As soon as he cleared the gatehouse, he was struck by the sheer amount of bustling humanity walking in all directions, overwhelming him with their numbers. He paused, trying to take it all in. This street alone likely held more people than his entire village, and he couldn't wholly absorb the concept that buildings could be multiple storeys. These structures were primarily made of stone, and he wondered if the cities of Therengia had been so immense.

A statue down the street drew his attention, and he made his way towards it, quickly noticing that it was situated in the middle of a cross-roads. Many people strolled about the stone circle, and he joined them, taking in the figure, a warrior astride a rearing horse. Looking closer, Athgar saw that beneath the figure's mount, trampled into the ground, was a man who, he was surprised to see, was dressed much like the people of his own village.

A young boy stood in front of the statue, reading from a plaque, "'598 SR'. What happened then, Father?"

"Never mind, son," his father replied, "we must be on our way."

Athgar immediately recognized the date. It was when the final battle of the Therengian Kingdom occurred, the year his people had failed in their efforts to stem the invaders.

He stepped back, shaken by the revelation; if the people here celebrated the defeat of the Therengians, then he would likely find little help. Devastated, he turned from the scene and continued down the street, following the general flow of citizens. Athgar quickly discovered where they were all headed, for the road soon opened into a vast area filled with market stalls. Many of those wandering about were examining wares or watching entertainers. A man walking on wooden stilts passed by with a horde of children following while a woman entertained passers-by with a dog that danced on its hind legs.

Athgar was struck by the cacophony of sound; dogs barking, hawkers selling their wares, children laughing, all melding together into continuous waves that assaulted his ears.

He stopped at a merchant's stall and snatched up an apple. "Do you know where I can find a place called the Badger?" Athgar asked, tossing the man a coin.

The man snatched it from the air. "Two blocks that way," he said, pointing, "you'll see a red sign on the northern side of the street."

"Thank you," said Athgar.

"No, thank YOU," the man said, doffing his hat in reply.

Deciding he'd had enough of the crowd, Athgar made his way westward, down the street the merchant had suggested. The road here was narrower, but, to his mind, still packed with people. His progress was slow, but he soon spotted the sign, a wooden placard with its namesake on it.

The place was busy, a noisy, raucous room that filled his ears with the chatter of its many patrons. He squeezed his way through the crowd that seemed impossibly dense, to make his way to the bar. Finally finding a spot, he raised his hand to get the barkeep's attention.

The tall, heavyset man behind the bar moved to his location. "What can I getcha?" he asked.

"I'm looking for someone," Athgar yelled, trying to be heard over the noise of the crowd.

"That's nice," the barkeep replied, "but you'll have to buy a drink first. I don't offer free information."

"Very well," said the Therengian, "I'll have an ale."

"Good choice," the barkeep replied, moving back down the bar, only to return shortly with a large tankard. "Here you go. Now, who's this man you're looking for?"

Athgar decided to drop some coins on the table before speaking. "I don't know his name, but he has black hair, a beard, and a scar on his left cheek that goes all the way to his chin."

"That's a very distinctive look," offered the barkeep, a slightly nervous tick to his face, "but I'm afraid I can't help you."

"Can't," asked Athgar, "or won't?"

"There's no one here that matches that description," the man replied. "I'd like to help you further, but I have to see to my customers." He disappeared back down the bar.

Athgar, suspecting there was more to it, followed him, pushing himself between two men to once again capture the barkeep's attention. "He would have been wearing a grey tabard," Athgar persisted, "with a sword on it."

This time the man paled. "Stop asking these questions," the barkeep said. "Trust me, it'll get you nowhere. I told you I ain't seen the man. Now, get out of here and leave me alone."

The men Athgar had pushed aside gave him a dirty look, and he decided it was time to leave. He forced his way back through the crowd to emerge into the open air. The sun was obscured by clouds, and he looked skyward to see if rain loomed. So taken had he been with this new experience that he had wasted away the better part of the day, for the sun was lowering in the west, indicating that evening would soon be approaching.

It occurred to him that he needed a place to stay for the night, and so he resolved to find one as soon as he could. Looking about, he spotted a man selling loaves of bread from a cart. Athgar made his way towards the merchant, waiting as another customer completed their purchase.

"I'll take a loaf," Athgar said, offering up a silver.

The man nodded his head, handing over the bread and taking the coin.

"Tell me," continued Athgar, "can you recommend a place to stay for a weary traveller?"

The man looked at the Therengian's clothing, noting the rough-looking tunic. "I'd say the Drake is your best option," he offered, "as long as you don't mind a communal sleeping area."

"Communal?"

"Yes," the merchant continued, "you share the room with the other guests. It's not the nicest of places, mind you, but it is the cheapest."

"Thank you," said Athgar, "that will do nicely. Can you direct me to it?"

"Yes," the merchant responded, walking around to the front of the cart. He pointed down the street. "You follow this road," he said, "until it bends to the right. On the left, you'll see a side street, that's Harcourt. Two blocks down on Harcourt, you'll see the Drake on the left. There'll be a sign over the door, a wooden one that hangs from above."

"Perfect," said Athgar, trying to sound as polite as possible, "you've been very helpful."

"No trouble at all," the man responded.

Athgar resumed his journey, now with a destination in mind.

The Drake turned out to be a very run-down place. He pushed open the door, the hinges squeaking noisily as he did. Just inside was a rather small room, with a narrow set of stairs to one side. A woman sat at a table, a man beside her. She looked up in expectation as Athgar entered while her companion eyed him warily.

Athgar halted before them, taking notice of the cudgel leaning against the man's chair. "I was told you rent rooms for the night?"

"We do," the woman responded, "how many nights?"

"Just the one will do," responded the Therengian.

"We have only one room," she continued, the speech well practised. "You share with everyone else. You pay upfront then go up the stairs and turn right. Pick out a mat, each comes with a single woollen blanket. You have to be out by first light. Do you understand?"

"How much?" Athgar asked.

"Three silvers," she responded, "and you look after your own food."

"Fair enough," he agreed, brandishing his loaf, "I have my own food anyway. I'll take it."

The woman put out her hand, palm up, leaving Athgar to wonder why. She sighed before she spoke, "You pay in advance, remember?"

"Oh, of course," he said, counting out the coins and dropping them into her palm. "Is there anything else?"

"Yes," she said, tucking the coins into her purse, "you're responsible for your own belongings. If anything goes missing, it's your loss."

"Very well," Athgar said, putting away the rest of his coins.

The man gave him a suspicious stare. "Off you go then," he said.

As Athgar made his way up the stairs, he noticed the paint peeling on the walls, and how the steps groaned with every footfall. Reaching the top, he turned to see the door on the right, the boards warped and the lock damaged, likely from someone kicking it in. He pushed the door open to reveal a room, not large, perhaps not even as big as his Orc hut, with bare wooden planks for a floor, heavily used and stained with who knows what. Upon this lay at least a dozen mats, most occupied by slumbering individuals.

Not wanting to wake the sleepers, he walked softly, choosing the closest available mat and dropped his bag at the foot. Picking up the blanket that lay at its head, he immediately felt the coarse wool it was made of and shook it out to examine it in more detail, noting its threadbare nature and the holes that were in evidence. Apparently, three silvers did not get you much in Draybourne!

He lay down and pulled the blanket over him, using his right arm to cradle his head. Despite the surroundings, Athgar was soon in a deep sleep.

The man with the scar struck down with his sword. It sliced into the Therengian's bow, cutting the string and biting into the wood, narrowly missing Athgar's fingers.

He awoke with a start, eyes wide open, his breath ragged. Taking a deep inhalation, he tried to calm his beating heart, when a sound by his feet caught his attention. The room was dark, lit only by a smattering of moonlight that trickled through the damaged shutters, but still, he saw something. In a moment of panic, he wondered if perhaps the scarred man had found him? Shaking his head, he cast his eyes back to the end of the mat to find someone stooped over his bag.

"Halt!" he cried out.

Whoever it was, gave him only a cursory glance, then made a dash across the room, Athgar's bag in hand.

"That's mine!" he yelled out, jumping to his feet.

His axe lay on the floor, left behind by the thief, and Athgar snapped it up, hurling it across the room. It missed the target, and instead dug into the wall beside the door.

The Therengian rushed in pursuit, tripping over another sleeper, sending him tumbling to the floor in the dark, face first. Striking the floor with his entire weight, he felt his nose hit wood, blood pouring forth as he struggled to stand back up.

Others in the room began yelling, awoken by all the commotion. Athgar looked to the door, but the perpetrator was long gone, all his belongings now lost to him. Stumbling to the door, still dizzy from his fall, the room felt slanted, and he had to reach out, steadying himself against the wall.

"What's going on here?" came a cry from the hallway.

Athgar looked over to see the man from the entranceway, his cudgel held in his right hand, the head tapping against his left palm.

"Someone stole my bag," the Therengian managed to spit out.

"What's that?" the man asked, pointing to the axe, still embedded in the wall.

"My axe," responded Athgar, "I was trying to stop him."

"By killing him? That's attempted murder!"

"He was taking my things!" Athgar objected.

"Out!" the man shouted. "And don't set foot here again, or I'll call the guard."

"But it wasn't my fault!"

"I don't care whose fault it was," the man ranted. "I'll not have a customer of mine damaging the building. Now, get out!"

Athgar took a deep breath, trying to steady himself. He tugged on the axe, pulling it from the wall, along with stray bits of plaster that flew everywhere.

He made his way out of the room and down the stairs, his head swimming. There was a push on his back as he reached ground level, propelling him through the door and flat onto his face. The door slammed shut behind him, leaving him lying on the ground.

Sitting up, he took stock of his surroundings. It was the middle of the night, the street deserted, a far cry from the heavy traffic he had witnessed earlier. Wiping the blood from his face, he rose, tucking the axe firmly into his belt. Feeling a drop of water hit his face, he swore as more followed in rapid succession. Casting his eyes about, he spied an alleyway where the roofs of the adjoining buildings overhung enough to provide some cover. He stood unsteadily, waiting for his head to clear, and then staggered towards the alley, making his way slowly as the street appeared to lurch. Moments later, he was there, beneath the eaves, his tunic wet from rain, but not quite soaked through.

Athgar leaned his back against the wall and closed his eyes, listening as the rain pelted down. His legs began to shake, and he slowly slid down to land, still upright, but now sitting on the ground. Struggling to stay conscious, he tried to think through his situation, but all his mind could focus on was the rhythmic drumming of the rain. Sleep soon claimed him.

. . .

Athgar awoke with a start. His head throbbed mercilessly, his legs stiff and sore. He glanced about, realizing he was still in the alleyway. In fear, he checked his belt, but the reassuring shape of his axe was still present.

What was he to do, he wondered, then decided to take stock of his situation. His possessions included only the clothes on his back, an axe, and his torc, but little else. All of his coins had been in the bag, along with the trade items the Orcs had supplied. Should he return to the Orc village? He knew he would be welcome, but the very thought of returning in failure brought bile to his throat.

He looked to the sky, in an effort to gauge the time of day. The sun was well past its zenith, telling him he had been unconscious for an inordinate amount of time. Surely someone would have seen him, he thought, but then he remembered the statue he had observed the day before; no one here would care about a Therengian lying in an alleyway. Anyone who saw him probably thought him a vagrant.

Finally, he rose to his feet unsteadily, using a hand to brace himself against the wall. Moving back towards the street, he spotted a puddle of water. As he passed, his eyes were drawn to it, and he saw his reflection, dried blood caked everywhere. Dropping to his knees, he splashed his face, doing his best to wipe away the gore.

Somewhat refreshed, Athgar stood back up. Expecting dizziness, he was pleasantly surprised to find the alleyway remained stationary, though his head still throbbed. Making his way out to the street, he looked about, trying to decide on a course of action.

Knowing that the market was nearby, he began retracing his steps of the day before. Perhaps, he thought, he might be able to sell his axe, for he had little use of it, and his stomach would need some encouragement if he were to persist in his search for the scarred rider.

A young woman walked by him, her dress the colour of the morning sky. Having never seen such clothing before, he watched in interest as she turned down an alleyway. This, in itself, was not so strange, but a moment later, a man pushed past him, running after her.

"She's down this way," the stranger yelled, "cut her off!"

"I've got her," called another, deeper voice from farther up the street. Athgar was instantly struck by the idea that someone was hunting this woman. His mind raced, and then he remembered how he was not able to help his sister in her time of need.

'Not again!' he thought. He pulled his axe and charged into the alleyway in hot pursuit of the stranger.

THE CITY

AUTUMN 1103 SR

Natalia stepped from the carriage, only to have her feet sink into the mud. She glanced down at the thick brown muck as it covered her toes, then lifted her foot, flinging the mud loose as best she could. In answer, her shoe, which admittedly was ill-suited to this type of terrain, flew across the intervening distance, to land in a puddle that lay more than an arm's length away.

She sighed in resignation. The trip from Karslev had been long and tedious, with constant changing of carriages to avoid being followed. Now, weeks later and hundreds of miles from her start, she finally felt a modicum of safety, only to be met with a torrential rainstorm that had flooded the roads.

Pondering her situation for but a moment, she decided there was little she could do but stand, and so she put her bare foot down, feeling the mud squish between her toes. The fugitive shoe lay just beyond her reach, taunting her with its delicate blue laces. In a thrice, she had made up her mind and leaned against the carriage, removing her other shoe. Now completely bare of foot, she tenderly crossed the distance, holding up her dress as the muck clung to her feet.

She bent down, retrieving her lost shoe and then straightened. "Are all the streets like this?" she called out.

"No," responded the carriage driver, "the richer parts have cobblestones, but you asked to be dropped at the gates of Draybourne. I can take you to an inn within the city, but it'll cost you more."

"Never mind," she replied, cognizant of her limited funds, "I'll find it myself."

"As you will," the driver responded, flicking his reins. The carriage rolled off, leaving Natalia staring at the intimidating city walls beyond. It was warm here, much warmer than back home. The air was thick with damp, most likely a result of the heavy rain that so recently had fallen. The gates of the city were close by, clearly visible beyond the drawbridge.

She struggled to walk through the mud. It clung to her legs, and she felt as though the very ground was resisting her efforts to move. Slowly, she made progress, hampered by the shoes in one hand and the hem of her dress in the other, desperate to avoid the same fate as her footwear.

Finally, Natalia felt the wood of the drawbridge beneath her feet and let her hem fall. She had been watching the ground carefully as she moved, but now, her footing secure, she glanced up to see a guard at the other end. He nodded at her in greeting and waved her through, a wry smile on his face as he spotted her muddy shoes in hand.

She moved through the archway to enter the city itself, the feel of cold stones beneath her feet a welcome change from the clinging mud. She made her way down the street, her eyes glancing briefly back to the gate, still nervous that she might be followed. The guards there had turned their attention to others, and she mentally scolded herself that she was being paranoid.

The streets of Draybourne were very similar to Karslev, lined by multi-storied buildings with thatched or tiled roofs. The majority here were built of brick or stone, but the occasional wooden construction could be seen, a rarity back home. The main difference was the width of the streets, for, in Karslev, they were much broader. The narrow streets of Draybourne, in contrast, felt constricting, causing her a sense of unease.

One of her fellow travellers on the last coach ride had recommended a place to stay called the Green Leaves. Looking for directions, she stopped briefly at a baker's, and they were most accommodating. Shortly thereafter, she found herself in front of a respectable-looking inn.

She entered to see a well-appointed dining area where several customers sat at tables, eating their mid-day meals and filling the room with their quiet conversations. As she stood, taking it all in, a young woman approached her, obviously one of the servers.

"May I help you, Miss?" she politely enquired.

"Yes," replied Natalia, "I am seeking lodgings and you were recommended to me. Do you have any rooms available?"

"We do, Miss. Would you like to see?"

"Might I enquire as to the rates?" asked Natalia.

"Two crowns a night, Miss, including breakfast and dinner. We also offer longer-term accommodations. Are you new to Draybourne?"

"I am," admitted Natalia, "and I've travelled rather a long way to get here."

"Then let's get you settled in, shall we?" the girl said. "If you'll follow me, I'll show you to your room."

Natalia followed the girl through the common room, into a hallway at the back of the building. It was a single storey affair, with tall ceilings to draw away the heat in summer and polished wooden flooring that felt warm to the touch.

The girl opened a door, revealing a scene inviting to Natalia's purse; a simple single room, although it was nicely furnished with a relatively large bed, nightstand, table and chairs, along with a vanity topped by a mirror. Servants had left out a jug of water and a washbasin with towels, which she could not wait to use.

"Is the room to your liking?" the girl asked.

"Yes," said Natalia, "this will do nicely, thank you."

"Here is your key," the girl said, handing it over. "Morning meals are served between sun up and noon. Dinner is served any time after the bell tolls three. If you have any other requirements, feel free to contact us at the front." The girl gave a little curtsy and left, leaving Natalia to wander into the room.

She made her way to the bed, sitting on it to examine her shoes in more detail. The elegant footwear was little more than a pair of slippers, an excellent choice for navigating the marble floors of the Volstrum, but evidently not the most suitable attire for a city such as Draybourne. The mud had finally dried, that much was clear, and it didn't look as though it would take too much effort to clean them, but better shoes would have to be found. First, however, she must clean the filth from her feet, a task made all the easier by the washbasin and jug nearby.

It didn't take long for Natalia to clean up, and then she sat back on the bed, thinking about her limited funds. She pulled out her purse, spilling out the contents. The coins had taken her this far, but she was fully aware they would not last forever. Beyond escaping her fate, she had given her flight little thought, but now, the end of the trip upon her, she must decide on what her next course of action should be.

The mirror caught her attention, and she moved before it, intent on checking how she looked. Natalia's dress was of the finest materials, but she couldn't help noticing its somewhat bedraggled appearance. It might pass for well-to-do here, but back in Karslev, it would be seen as scandalous to appear like this. Not having had a chance to purchase a change of clothes, she decided that perhaps that was the best place to start. Rather than bring a dressmaker to her, she resolved to save a bit and go in search of one.

. . .

Natalia's first trip out of the Green Leaves was pleasant enough, for the inn lay within a district known for its cobblers and dressmakers. No more than half a block away she found a suitable shop, and she spent some time with the proprietor, deciding on what to order. Having rarely set foot outside the Volstrum, her knowledge of clothing was limited. Only the finest of clothes were good enough for the Stormwinds, a habit, she soon realized, that could be excessively expensive.

She decided that a mage seeking employment would need well-made garments, the better to portray success and power, but her day to day activities would preclude the more ornate outfits common to mages of the court. At the dressmaker's suggestion, she ordered a few for everyday use and three more elaborate pieces that would present the image of a prosperous individual. With promises they would be completed later in the week, Natalia set off looking for more appropriate footwear.

She stopped in front of a cobbler's, trying to peer in as someone worked inside. The glare from the late morning sun reflected off the window, and she had to stand on her tiptoes to see through, her hand shading her eyes. An old man sat inside, sewing leather, while two more, slightly younger men, sat at a work table, cutting leather or cloth.

Natalia, moving towards the door intent on entering, caught a reflection in the window. Swearing she had seen a man looking at her, she turned to view her observer who was leaning against the building across the street. He tipped his hat to her, making a kissing motion with his lips. Her face turned crimson at the attention, and she quickly entered the shop, eager to be away from him.

She wondered, briefly, if the man had been following her? She was suddenly struck with fear! Had the family found her, even here, hundreds of miles from Karslev? Pausing in the doorway, Natalia looked over her shoulder again, but the unwelcome man had moved on. Perhaps she was overthinking things, she thought to herself. It was probably just a young man taking notice of her. She was, after all, wearing an elegant dress.

Her thoughts were interrupted by the old man who, having noticed her entering, had risen from his seat and was now enquiring about her needs. She had thought to visit a cordwainer, a person who made shoes for the rich and influential but had been told such a craftsman was unavailable in Draybourne. The cobbler, however, knew his business and was soon measuring her feet. By the time noon had arrived, Natalia's order was complete. He would make three pairs of shoes for her, varying in height and style, though he was so busy, it would take him a week or more.

She left him payment in advance and wandered out into the street, this time eyeing the crowd, looking for anyone that might be watching her. After stopping for a brief meal, she meandered about the town, taking in the sights. Several times she turned suddenly, cutting down a side street or alleyway, always on the alert, lest she was being followed, but nothing came of it.

By late afternoon, Natalia returned to the Green Leaves, feeling her coins had been well spent.

The next few days passed quickly, and before long, her dresses arrived at the inn. She was pleased with the finished products and took great delight in finally shedding her court dress, hanging it carefully in the wardrobe. It required a good cleaning, but she could see to that later, for, with her day dress on, she felt much less encumbered and was eager to get out of her rooms.

The weather was unseasonably warm, the sun on her face making her feel alive as she stepped from the inn. She looked about at the passing city folk, no one paying attention to her, and fell into the general flow of traffic, resolving to make her way to the cobbler's to see if her shoes were ready.

Vladimir Kurzak sat in the Lucky Weasel, by the window, the shutters open wide to clear the stale air out of the place. He was lifting a tankard to his lips when he spotted her. She was a vision in blue, her pale skin standing in stark contrast to her black hair.

He quickly put down his drink, fishing around in his pouch for a selection of crumpled papers. He skimmed over them, finding the one he was looking for. Unfolding it carefully, he searched through the words. It described a pale woman, of average height and black hair. Could this be one and the same? He read on to note she was last seen in Karslev and it mentioned a rather distinctive looking ring.

Vladimir's eyes flew back to the window, but the woman had moved farther down the street. He hurriedly got to his feet, tossing a coin on the table as he left. Out the door he went, casting his eyes about, desperate to find the young woman, for if she was the one the letter described, the bounty would be far more than he was used to earning.

A bobbing dark head in the crowd captured his attention, and he made his way towards it, soon sure it was her. He dropped back, keeping her in sight, but getting no closer. She was meandering about, visiting different stalls, and then he saw his chance. Manoeuvring his way ahead of her, he picked a fruit stand, then stood beside it, examining the vendor's produce. Soon, the black-haired beauty came into view, stopping to taste a strawberry. He saw the hand extend out with the ring on her finger, and knew instantly he had identified her. Shifting his attention to the vendor, he negotiated the sale and then left, dropping back in the crowd to follow the woman as best he could.

She seemed to be constantly on the lookout, and he wondered at first if she had seen him, but years of being a bounty hunter had honed his skills, and he came to the conclusion that she was just being cautious, a reasonable action considering the bounty on her head.

It took her all day to make her way back to her place of lodging, but Kurzak didn't mind for he would gladly spend a week following her if he could secure the reward. She entered the Green Leaves, making her way through to the back of the common room. It only took a few coins to ferret out her information. She had booked in for a further week, he was told, and that suited his plans perfectly. He left the inn, intent on finding his associates.

Natalia awoke in the middle of the night to the noise of thunder. It rolled in from the east, a forbidding sound that sent shivers down her spine. She rose from the bed, moving to the window where the rain lashed against the glass. A bolt of lightning lit the sky, illuminating the shadowy city beneath it. She had a strange sense of foreboding as if the Volstrum was seeking her out. Moving to the door, she checked the bolt, making sure it was secure. Her task complete, she returned to the comfort of her bed, pulling the thick blanket tightly around her, drifting into a fitful sleep.

The next morning proved to be sunny, despite the previous night's storm. Natalia made her way down the street, the weather clear, but the ground still wet. Pausing at an apple cart, she picked one out, passing a coin to the vendor, then turned, ready to resume her stroll. As she bit into the succulent fruit, she spotted a man across the street, standing in a doorway, looking off in a different direction, but he had a familiar face, and she was certain she had seen him before.

Stanislav had once told her that mage hunters often employ bounty hunters, men who typically looked for escaped criminals, but who would, for the right reward, search for virtually anyone. He had found it expedient to hire them on occasion, and the family had a network of them spread throughout the continent.

Natalia tried to place the man's face, and then it sank in, he had been at the fruit stand she had visited the day before. Now convinced that she was being tailed, she resumed her walk, intent on not revealing her newfound knowledge.

What was she to do, she wondered? She was alone in a foreign city, hunted by the family, and now it appeared that their long reach extended even to here. Her flight from the Volstrum had been swift and unexpected and yet somehow they had found her. No matter where she went, she realized, they would be hunting her. She must remain on the move, perhaps for the rest of her life. This insight hit her hard, and she paused in her stroll, suddenly overcome with emotion. Was she destined to spend the remainder of her life running, always in fear of capture?

Natalia hardened her heart, the family must not be allowed to control her life this way! The magic in her was strong, this much she knew, and she swore to fight back. If bounty hunters were seeking her, then she would allow them to find her, and they would pay the price for their folly. If the family wanted her, they would have to come in force!

A sense of calmness came to her at that moment, a knowledge that she had the advantage on her pursuers. They could do nothing in the open, not with all these witnesses, for Natalia had committed no crime here in Draybourne. No, these men would try to take her when she was least expecting it. They would look for an opportunity to strike when she appeared most vulnerable, and she realized that if she provided them with that opportunity, they would make their move.

She knew the family wanted her alive, for they coveted her power, if only for breeding purposes. That made capture their objective, rather than death. She, on the other hand, had no such limitation, though she must be careful not to have herself arrested for murder. A woman forced to defend herself, she was sure, was sufficient justification for a killing blow if necessary, but she preferred only to injure them if possible, sending the word back that she was a difficult target.

The problem, from her point of view, was that she was a powerful spellcaster. Natalia had been taught, from her earliest days at the Volstrum, to release her full power, a skill she had mastered. Now, however, she saw the wisdom of holding back her capabilities, though she had no idea how that might be accomplished.

Continuing down the street, she stopped to look into a jeweller's window, using the reflection in the glass to spot her pursuer. He was still there, occasionally looking to another individual. She entered the store, pretending to be shopping, but glanced out the window from time to time. The man's accomplice was easily spotted, and she suspected there might be others. How many opponents must she deal with, she wondered?

Stanislav had told Natalia stories of rogue mages. They were often improperly trained, at least according to the Volstrum, and had to be removed from the streets for the safety of the common folk. Early in his career, the old mage hunter had made a living from this work, in addition to finding new potential mages, like herself, but he had employed a team to assist him. How many people would they send to capture her? She was a powerful caster, and they would doubtless be armed with magebane, and yet how many would there be? The obvious answer, to her mind, was no more than three or four, for she felt any more would draw too much attention.

Could magebane be administered through a tipped arrow or crossbow bolt? Natalia had no idea, but decided that if she saw such an attacker, he should take priority. In her mind, she worked through various scenarios and then decided that it was time for action. She would face down the bounty hunters on her own terms, not theirs.

She had taken several shortcuts before, darting between buildings to cross to another street, and now she kept her eyes out for just such an opportunity. Spotting the cobblers, she made her choice. There was an alley that led down the right side of his shop, then turned, cutting across the back. It provided only one path, one that she could depend on, and yet allowed her to use the corner to her advantage.

She slowed her steps, approaching the alley to view it before making her move. Seeing it empty, Natalia entered, taking her time, walking as if in doubt. Halfway down, she paused to straighten her dress, killing time to make sure she was still being followed.

Sure enough, the man appeared behind her, at the entrance, and, as soon as their eyes met, he yelled out. "She's down here, cut her off."

She resumed her journey, more hurriedly this time.

"I've got her," someone called out, the voice echoing from in front of her.

The back corner of the cobblers drew closer, and then she rounded it, ready for action. Two men approached, the first armed with a crossbow, the weapon carried at the ready, but not yet aimed. Behind him came the second, with sword drawn.

The words of power sprang quickly to her lips, and then a wall of ice appeared between Natalia and her two new adversaries. The crossbowman gave a cry of alarm and skidded to a halt and then was obscured by the icy wall, only a rough outline visible through its surface.

She turned her attention back to the man behind her. He was halfway down the alleyway, another behind him, axe in hand.

She readied her spell, intending to let loose with ice shards, but as she cast, the axeman grabbed her pursuer by the arm in an apparent effort to stop him.

"Leave her alone!" the second man called out.

The shards of ice flew towards them but Natalia's target, pulled by the arm, twisted just before they struck, saving him from the full force of her attack, his arm taking only a few shards. Unfortunately, that left the bulk of her spell to fly past him into the chest of the axeman, tumbling him to the ground. Her pursuer, now free of the downed man's grasp, turned and ran from the alley.

She thought of casting another spell his way, but her attention was pulled back to the other two as the swordsman had moved forward and was using the hilt of his sword to chip away at the wall of ice. Cracks began to appear on its smooth surface, and so she readied herself. A loud thud signified the final strike, then the ice gave way, sending pieces flying.

As Natalia cast another spell, she could feel the power surge through her; it felt almost out of control as a solid bolt of ice flew forth, striking the hapless swordsman in the head. There was a spurt of red as the spike carried through and then the headless body dropped to the alleyway. It took her a moment to react, so stunned was she by the effect, and then she saw the crossbowman retreating around the far corner of the cobblers.

The swordsman was obviously dead, but the man with the axe, the one that had tried to stop them, lay there, unmoving. She approached cautiously, crouching down to examine him. He was clothed in a rough cut tunic with large stitching, and wore heavy-looking boots, quite unlike the others that had attacked her. His face showed a thin beard, his hair long and unkempt, unlike most of the townsfolk hereabouts. Reaching out, she checked for a pulse to find he still lived. His chest was bloody, the ice shards having punched clean through his tunic, but while his breathing was shallow, he had not yet made the journey to join the Saints.

WOUNDED

AUTUMN 1103 SR

Athgar awoke with a start. He was in a room, lying in a large bed, unlike any he had ever slept in before. It was comfortable, with thick blankets to ward off the chill of morning. Looking around, he realized he was in a spacious room, far bigger than the tiny hut he had lived in for most of his life. It was richly appointed, with rugs on the floor to keep the cold at bay and curtains hanging by a window that boasted glass, allowing light to filter through.

He sat up and immediately regretted his decision as his chest exploded in pain, feeling like a red hot poker had been thrust into him. Suddenly, the room swirled before him, and he lay back down. Closing his eyes, he took a deep breath, trying to calm himself and breathe through the agony of his wounds. Slowly, he opened eyes again and gazed about the room, looking for any sign of where he was, or how he got here.

He vaguely remembered hearing a cry for help and then entering an alleyway, only to be met with some type of ranged attack. It had felt like being hit by a volley of knives, all thrown in succession, pushing him back against a wall. Someone had loomed over him, and he recalled staggering along with help, but the rest was a complete blur. Somehow, he had ended up here, though for what purpose he couldn't say.

He gingerly probed his chest to find it covered in bandages; whoever had brought him here had decided to keep him alive for the time being. Lifting the blankets, he swung his legs over the side of the bed to feel a soft rug beneath his feet. His boots were on the floor, still covered in dirt, and his axe lay on a nearby table. No one would hold a prisoner and leave their weapon so close at hand, and so he breathed a sigh of relief.

Trying to stand, he felt another pain in his chest, and he reached out to steady himself against the frame of the bed. Doubled over, he took a deep breath, resolving to stand upright as soon as he could. He held his breath and forced himself up, releasing an audible groan as his back straightened. The action had pulled on his wounds, and he felt a fresh wave of agony.

A strange wooden box, his height, sat against the wall and he stumbled his way over to it. There were two doors on the front, and he pulled them open, unsure of what to expect. Inside, clothes hung on a pole that stretched from side to side. He rummaged through them only to discover they were all dresses. It appeared his benefactor was a woman! Athgar tried again to recall what had happened to him, but it remained jumbled in his mind.

A noise at the door drew his attention, and he turned, his mind racing with fear. The knob rotated, and then the door swung into the room to reveal a young woman, elegantly dressed in a blue outfit, the skirts reaching almost to the floor, with impossibly expensive-looking shoes poking out beneath. The most striking feature, however, was her face, a pale complexion framed by black hair, which had been braided into a convoluted style.

"You're up," she said, her voice tinged with some sort of accent he couldn't identify.

"I am," he said, defensively. "Who are you? How did I get here? What do you want?"

She raised her hand to forestall him. "I know you have questions, but I think you should sit down first."

"I'm not going anywhere till you answer me," he said defiantly.

"You're bleeding," she said, moving towards him.

He backed up, finding himself pressed against the foot of the bed. His hand sought his bandages, and he felt the dampness as blood soaked through.

"Let's get you back to bed," she soothed, "and then I'll explain everything." She reached out, lightly grasping his arm and guiding him around to the side of the bed.

He surrendered himself, climbing in, and lay down while she covered him with the blanket.

"Shortly, someone will be coming to take a look at you," she said.

"A healer?" he asked.

"Yes, a Brother of Saint Mathew."

"Whose brother?" he asked.

"A Holy Brother, of the Order of Saint Mathew," she said in surprise. "How can you not be familiar with the Church?"

"I'm a Therengian," he said stubbornly.

"I don't know what that is," she said, "but perhaps we're getting off on the wrong foot. Let me introduce myself, my name is Natalia St-" She cut herself off suddenly, then continued after pausing, "Well, you can just call me Natalia. What's your name?"

"Athgar," he said, "I'm a Therengian."

"So you just said," she replied. "Now what is a Therengian? I'm afraid I'm not from around here."

"We are...were an ancient people. We lived in this land long before the duke came along, but we've been reduced to mere vassals by force of arms."

"Are you saying you are a conquered people?"

"Yes, but that was many generations ago. Now, we live in a small village, minding our own business, or at least we did."

"Did?"

"Yes, soldiers attacked our village and took my people. I came here to Draybourne to find them."

"When you say someone 'took' your people, what do you mean?"

"I mean they were taken as captives. Carted off in chains, as far as I can tell. I was left for dead."

"That's terrible!" she said. "When did this happen?"

"A year and a half ago," he replied, "but I need to keep looking."

"I'm afraid you're not going anywhere with those wounds," she said. "You need to rest, for a few days at least. If your people were taken that long ago, another few days won't make much difference."

"I appreciate all you've done for me," he said, "but I don't understand why?"

"Do you remember anything about how you were injured?" she asked.

"Not much," he replied. "I remember hearing a fight in an alleyway, and I thought I heard a woman's voice."

"That was me, I'm afraid. I think you tried to come to my aid. It was very gallant of you but quite unnecessary."

"You were being attacked!"

"Someone was trying to abduct me if you must know, but I dealt with them."

"How?" he asked, looking at her clothing. "Are you a warrior? You certainly don't look like it."

She smiled, "I'll take that as a compliment. And to answer your question, no, I'm not a warrior, but I am a mage. Are you familiar with magic?"

He looked at her with a newfound respect. "I am," he said, declining to say more. "So you dealt with your attackers, I take it?"

"Yes," she replied, "but I'm sorry to say you blundered into the middle of the fight. You grabbed one of my assailants and twisted him, causing my spell to hit you instead."

His hands went instinctively to his chest, "That was quite the spell. Might I enquire what it was?"

"Ice shards," she said, "a particular favourite of mine."

"Does that make you an Ice Mage?" he asked.

She laughed, making him feel more at ease. "No, I'm a Water Mage, though that does include ice and snow, on occasion."

"Where are you from?" he asked. "You have an accent that I don't recognize."

"Somewhere far from here," she revealed, "but I doubt you'd be familiar with it. So tell me, Athgar, what is it you do? Apart from searching for slavers, that is."

"I'm a bowyer and a fletcher," he replied. "What is it you do?"

"You might say I'm a professional mage," she said, "though I'm not under contract at the present time."

"You're used to a finer life," he commented.

She looked at him in shock, "How do you know that?"

"Your clothes are a dead giveaway," he said. "No one wears those kinds of dresses around here. From what I hear, the only place where those would fit in would be at a Duke's Court somewhere."

"You're very knowledgeable for someone who lives in a small village," she mused. "I suspect you've travelled a little."

"Not as much as you might think," he said.

"How is it," she asked, "that you wear such crude clothing and yet have gold around your neck?"

He instinctively reached for his torc to find it missing. "Where is it?" he asked in a moment of panic.

"Don't worry," she said, "it's right here on the dresser. I took it off to make it easier to bandage you."

"You bandaged me? I thought a healer did."

"No, he hasn't arrived yet, he had other patients to visit first. I also took the liberty of acquiring you some new clothes, I'm sorry to say my spell badly damaged your old ones." She took his tunic from the back of the chair, holding it up before him. The holes in the chest were clearly visible.

He looked at them in wonder, "I'm lucky to be alive."

"I noticed you carry an axe," she said. "A strange weapon to carry in a city, isn't it? I thought most men carried swords."

"Not where I'm from," he said, "we use axes and spears."

"A sword is more lethal," she noted.

"Yes, but an axe is more versatile, you can't very well chop wood with a sword."

"Can't you?" she said. "I wouldn't know, I've never had to chop wood. I suppose it makes sense, though."

"What doesn't make sense," offered Athgar, "are those shoes you're wearing. They won't last long around here."

She looked down at the dress shoes that adorned her feet. "I suppose you're right," she said, "but I left my last place in a bit of a rush. I'm waiting for a few new pairs to be made."

A knock at the door drew their attention.

"It's Brother Ambrose," called a voice. "You sent for a healer?"

"Yes," replied Natalia, "just a moment." She turned her attention back to Athgar. "Now, you just lie still and please don't tell him I did that to you, it might prove troublesome to both of us. The town guard is already upset with me for killing one of my attackers."

She moved to the door, opening it to reveal a Holy Brother in the customary brown cassock of his order.

"Please, Father, come in."

"I am a Brother," he replied, quickly looking about the room, "not a Holy Father, but the mistake is forgivable. Is this the patient?"

"It is," she said. "This is Athgar, an acquaintance of mine."

"Good morning, Athgar," the brother intoned, "let's have a look at you, shall we?" He sat on the side of the bed and bent down to look at the chest bandages. "This bleeding looks fresh," he observed.

"I tried to stand," said Athgar.

"I should like to remove the bandages," said Ambrose, "though I must say that whoever placed them was quite adept."

"That was me," offered Natalia, "it was part of my training."

"Oh?" the holy brother remarked. "Did you spend time with the sisters of the order?"

"No," she said, "but I was trained as a battle mage, and that included helping the wounded."

"A battle mage? I'm surprised to see you here then, I didn't know the duke employed them."

"He doesn't," she said, "I'm just passing through."

"Lucky for Athgar here," he offered. "Now sit up please, I have to unwind these to look at your wounds." He offered his hand, which Athgar took, pulling himself to a sitting position. Brother Ambrose then stood, the better to unwind the bandages. Soon, the bloody cloths were on the table, while the Holy Brother lowered his head to examine the wounds in more detail.

"It appears you have been hit with multiple small objects," he observed, "knives by the look of it. Did you see your attacker?"

"It was dark," Athgar said, "and it all happened so fast." He looked at Natalia, wondering why he had gone along with protecting her.

"Normally I'd prescribe a poultice, but the wounds appear clean and free of corruption," Brother Ambrose said. "I should think rest is the only thing you need worry about now. Change the bandages each day if you can. You'd be surprised how many warriors get gangrene from dirty bandages, it simply staggers the mind."

"Thank you, Brother Ambrose," said Natalia.

"You're quite welcome," he replied, "though I'm a little surprised you called on me. You appear to have the situation well in hand."

"I only recently completed my training," she explained, "and though I studied hard, I've never actually treated a live patient before."

"Well," continued the brother, "you've done an excellent job of looking after him. Would you like me to check back in a few days?"

"No, that's quite all right," she said. "I'll contact you if there's any further developments."

"Very well," the Holy Brother replied, "then I'll leave you to it." He was about to depart when he stopped himself. "I should redress the wound," he said.

"Don't trouble yourself," she said, "I'll see to it."

"Very well," he replied. "The saints be with you, Madame."

"And you, Brother Ambrose."

He left the room, his footsteps echoing down the hall.

"Now that you have me at your mercy," said Athgar, "what is it you intend to do with me?"

Natalia blushed, "I hadn't intended to do anything with you, other than see you recovered from your wounds. What is it you'd like to do, once you're better?"

"I'm trying to track down my sister," he said.

"Along with the rest of your villagers?" she asked.

"I'm convinced they've all been sold into slavery. I'll start with my sister and go from there."

"Perhaps I can help," she said, "I know how to cast a spell or two."

"I don't think a Water Mage is what I need, I'm more likely to need someone who can fight."

"I might remind you I took on three opponents and won, four if you include yourself in the mix."

"A good point," Athgar said, "but I have no coins to hire you. I'm afraid the rest of my possessions were stolen."

"Don't fear on that point," she replied, "I can cover expenses. I'll make you a deal, I'll help you in your search, and you can travel with me once we're done."

"Why would you want me travelling with you?" he asked.

"I could use a bodyguard, and you're more familiar with the area," she said. "Besides, I don't want to be ambushed again."

"You think those people are still looking for you?"

"I know they are," Natalia said, a grim look settling over her face.

"And who are they, exactly?"

"I suppose you'd have to call them family."

"Family?"

"Well, not those men in particular, but my family hired them. I ran away from home, you see, and they want me back."

"They've gone to extraordinary lengths to get you if what you say is true."

"I'm not lying," she bristled.

"I'm not suggesting you are," Athgar said, "and yet I can't help but feel you're not telling the entire truth."

"And you are?" she accused.

"A fair point," he said, "but we've only just met. We don't know each other well enough to trust one another yet."

"I suppose you're right. You're very astute. You come across as a rustic fellow, but underneath, you have a sharp mind."

"I'll take that as a compliment, I suppose," he replied.

"And well you should," Natalia said, "I meant no disrespect. It wasn't so long ago that I was in a similar state."

"Meaning?"

"Meaning that I wasn't born to the high life. My parents were humble peasants."

"How does a peasant child end up like you?" Athgar asked. "Not that there's anything wrong with you, you're quite attractive." He blushed furiously. "I didn't mean that," he added.

"So you don't think I'm attractive?"

"Well, I do, but it's not my place to say."

"And why wouldn't it be?" she asked. "I'm not a noble, you know."

"Maybe not," Athgar defended, "but you've obviously been raised as a proper lady."

"And what of it? Does that make me unattractive?"

He could feel his face burning with embarrassment. "No, obviously not. Look, I'm sorry if I slighted you, it was certainly not my intent."

"I don't feel slighted in the least," Natalia said, warming to the conversation. "But I think I finally saw the real you, peeking out from beneath that rough exterior."

Athgar felt confounded. He didn't know how to behave in this situation. Back in Athelwald he simply would have married the girl his father had arranged for him and be done with it, but then he remembered that his life had fallen apart when he had failed to become a hunter.

Seeing the look of despondency on his face, she moved closer to him, placing her hand upon his. "I'm sorry," she said, "it was not my intention to embarrass you. Let's get you recovered first, the rest we can discuss later."

"Yes," he agreed, "that's probably for the best."

Athgar awoke in the middle of the night, opening his eyes to a room filled with moonlight. Gentle breathing came to his ears, and he looked about, trying to find its source. Glancing to the floor, he spotted Natalia, lying on the rug, a folded up dress acting as a pillow.

Athgar rose from his bed, stripping off the blanket and carrying it over to her. He gazed down at her as she slept, then placed it over her to keep her warm. She stirred as he did so and he froze in place, worried she might awaken to him standing over her, but all she did was shift her position slightly, and he breathed a sigh of relief. He returned to his bed, treading as quietly as he could.

"What are you doing?" she asked in a quiet voice.

"Nothing," he whispered.

"You put a blanket on me," she said.

"You looked cold."

"I didn't expect you to give up a blanket for me, but thank you."

"You should let me sleep on the floor," he said, "I'm not used to sleeping in a bed."

Natalia sat up, her outline visible in the gloom. "You didn't sleep in a bed?"

"I did, but not a bed like this," he clarified. "I've always slept on the ground, except in the Orc hut, their beds are more like shelves."

"Orc hut? What are you talking about?"

"Don't let it trouble you," Athgar said, "go back to sleep."

"Well I can't go back to sleep now, you have me intrigued."

"Is that a dangerous thing?"

"If you have to ask that," she said, "you don't know me very well."

"It's true, I don't," he replied.

"Don't what?"

"Know you very well. All I know is that you're from a rich family that wants you back, and you can use water magic. Oh, and you ran away from home. I imagine there's a lot more to know about you, but you don't seem the sharing type."

"I take exception to that," she said, "I like to share."

"Oh, really?" He asked. "Then tell me something about yourself."

"There's nothing to tell, and you're trying to change the subject," Natalia said. "You were the one that brought up Orcs. Were you held prisoner by them?"

"Prisoner? Where would you get that idea?"

"Orcs are a bloodthirsty race, I just assumed they must have captured you."

"Orcs are not bloodthirsty!" he defended. "In fact, they are quite welcoming. They took me in after my village was decimated."

"All right, you don't have to get all defensive on me."

"Sorry," he said, "it just annoys me when people make assumptions."

They fell into silence, and just as Athgar was about to fall asleep, her voice drifted up to him again, "So what was it like? Living with the Orcs, I mean?"

"They were very good to me," he replied, thinking back. "I'd known Kargen for years, of course, he's their chieftain, though that came later."

"How did you speak to them? Do they speak our language?"

"Some do, but I speak Orcish, I learned it years ago. Our people have traded with them for as long as I can remember."

"Is that where you learned your craft as a bow maker?"

"You mean bowyer," he corrected, "and no, I learned that from my father, but he traded with the Orcs."

"And that necklace thing?" she said.

"The torc?"

"Yes, the torc," Natalia continued, "it looks like someone put a great deal of work into it."

"It was a gift, from the tribe," he said. "It marks me as an Orc friend."

"Is that something worthwhile?" she asked. "I only ask because I've travelled hundreds of miles and I have yet to see an Orc. Are they common here in Holstead?"

"Outside of their ancestral homes, they're rare, but other tribes are scattered throughout the Petty Kingdoms."

"Petty Kingdoms?" she said. "What are those?"

"It's the term used to describe the various princes, kings, and dukes that hold lands between here and the great empire to the west."

"You mean the Halvarian Empire?" she asked.

"Is there another? I'm surprised you wouldn't know all this, you sound well educated."

"My studies have been quite focused," she said, "but I'm always eager to learn more."

"So am I," Athgar said, yawning.

"I suppose it is quite late," she said, "maybe we should get some sleep."

"Yes," he admitted, "but you should take the bed."

"Nonsense, you're the injured one."

"True, but I can't sleep on it anyway. Whether you want to or not, I'm sleeping on the floor."

He climbed out on the other side of the bed, his wounds still aching.

Natalia listened carefully to his efforts, then stood. "Very well," she said, "if you're not going to take the bed, I will."

He heard her get into bed and then all fell quiet. Moments later, her rhythmic breathing filled the room, and Athgar finally settled himself in to sleep.

It took five days before he was feeling well enough to leave the room, and then only for short walks. Natalia went with him, holding onto his arm to offer him some support. They were given quite a few stares as they walked through the city, he the rough-looking fellow with the scruffy beard, and she in her elegant dress. It was actually Athgar's idea for her to buy a more fitting garment, and so on their third day out together they managed to find a dressmaker, this time someone far more used to making commoners clothes.

The woman who ran the place was most polite. Natalia's blatant display of wealth was enticing as a client, and so they soon became the focus of her attention, despite other women in the shop.

"Might I ask what style you were looking for, my lady?" the woman preened.

"Something for travelling," offered Athgar, looking about. "She has elegant clothing, for special occasions, but needs something for walking about."

"Have you a preference for cloth?" asked the proprietor.

"Something that wears well," interjected Athgar again.

"I always wear dresses well," said Natalia, looking a little miffed.

"No, I mean something that is rugged."

"Oh, yes, I see what you mean. He's right," Natalia admitted, "I'll need something rugged."

The woman looked to Athgar, "Does she have a preference for colour?" she asked.

"Blue," said Natalia, causing the attendant to turn in her direction once again. "What do you think, Athgar?"

The Therengian was staring at bolts of cloth that were sitting on a table. He lifted one, examining its colour. "This cloth here," he asked, "this dark grey one, has anyone ordered any of this in quantity in the last few years?"

"Saints, no," the storekeeper replied, "we only get that in for the Temple Knights, even though they're rare, they do pay well."

"What's a Temple Knight?" he asked.

"That's the Order of Saint Cunar," offered Natalia, "they're one of the six saintly orders, I thought you would have known that."

"Sorry, no. My people worship the old Gods."

The look of revulsion on the proprietor's face was noticeable.

"Something wrong?" asked Natalia.

"Sorry, my lady, I didn't know he was a heathen."

"Correct me if I'm wrong," offered Natalia, "but isn't the Church founded on the principle of getting along with others?"

"I suppose, my lady, among other things."

"Then I think you should be more charitable towards others, don't you agree?"

"Of course, my lady," the woman said, eager for the sale. She continued taking Natalia's measurements as Athgar studied the material.

"It's a rather strange colour," he observed, "I don't think I've seen anyone in town wearing it."

"It's only the Temple Knights of Cunar that wear it," offered the woman. "The lay brothers wear simple brown habits."

"Like the Brothers of Saint Mathew?" he asked.

"You learn fast," said Natalia.

"I think we need to visit Brother Ambrose when we are done here," he said.

"Is it your wounds?"

"No, I have questions for him."

"Very well," she said, "but let's wrap things up here first."

It took till noon to finish at the shop, and they left with the promise that the clothes would be completed by the end of the week. They stepped out into the sun just as a knight rode past. Athgar instinctively jumped back, his hand going to his axe.

"Relax," said Natalia, "have you never seen a horse before?"

"Before I came here, I had only seen them once, and that was when my village was attacked."

"Then I can understand your nervousness, but you'll have to get used to them. They're all over the place. Now come along, we have to find the Church of Saint Mathew."

Their objective was easy enough to find, for it lay at the intersection of two major roads. They entered to find Brother Ambrose kneeling at the altar. Natalia suggested they wait and so they sat in the pews until such time as his vigil ended.

The Holy Brother rose from the altar and was about to leave when he spotted them. Changing direction, he drew closer, until he was standing before them.

"Ah, the patient is looking much fitter, I see."

"I am, thank you," said Athgar.

"It is the will of Saint Mathew," he said, "he watches over us all."

"Blessed are we to be under his gaze," said Natalia, "but we are not here to talk of the Saints, at least not Mathew."

"You have me intrigued," said Brother Ambrose. "If not Mathew, then who? There are only six in total, you know, unless you count the lesser saints.

"Tell me about these saints," said Athgar, "I'm having some difficulty keeping them straight."

"Well," began Brother Ambrose, "the Church recognizes six sects within its structure."

"Sects?" asked the Therengian.

"Yes, orders if you will. Each has a different calling within the church. Take the Brothers of Saint Mathew, for instance, our main purpose is to help the sick and poor."

"That's why you helped me," said Athgar, "though I understand it involved a donation on Natalia's part."

"Yes," continued Ambrose, "although we provide for the sick and poor, we still need donations to keep our missions going."

"And what about these other sects?" Athgar pressed.

"Well, we have the Sisters of Saint Agnes, they primarily concern themselves with the well-being of women. Our own order often works closely with them."

"And the Cunars?" pressed the Therengian.

"They are the fighting arm of the Church," explained Ambrose.

"I'm confused," said Athgar, "don't the other orders have Temple Knights?"

"They do, but their normal responsibility is to safeguard the houses of their respective orders. Thus a Temple Knight of Saint Mathew would guard the church that bears our blessed saviour's name."

"And, I assume," said Athgar, "that the sisters look after any temple to Saint Agnes?"

"Yes," confirmed Brother Ambrose, "but don't confuse the Temple Knights with lay brothers and sisters. Like me, they don't generally bear arms in defense of the order."

"And are there other orders?"

"There are, but you are unlikely to run across them, they confine their efforts to internal matters."

"These Cunars, you say they make up the army of the Church. What does that mean, exactly?"

"It means," said Ambrose, "that should the Church go to war, it is the Temple Knights of Saint Cunar that will fight the battles."

"Surely all knights would fight?" added Natalia.

"Well, yes," confessed Ambrose, "but the Cunars are trained in large scale battles. Command of a Holy Army would naturally fall to such men."

"And these Cunars take slaves?" asked Athgar.

"Saints, no," the Holy Brother responded, "that would be against the most basic tenets of the Church."

"My village was attacked by armed horsemen wearing dark grey cloth over their armour. Their leader had a scar on his left cheek."

"It's true that the Cunars wear black or grey," the brother responded, "but they would never attack a village for no reason. The man you describe doesn't sound like a Temple Knight, are you sure it wasn't someone else simply dressed in grey?"

"They had a sword emblazoned on their tunics," Athgar added.

"That's their symbol," confirmed Ambrose, his eyes growing wider by the moment, "but someone must have been masquerading as them. No Temple Knight would do such a thing!"

"Are you sure?" Athgar pressed.

"As sure as you are standing before me," the Holy Brother swore. "I'm afraid you've been the victim of a ruse of some type. No doubt, they wore that garb to put people off the trail; the Cunars haven't had a presence in Draybourne for more than twenty years. The only ones to pass through here would be those heading from the crusades in the east to their fortress in the south. I suggest you find them and report the situation, they'll want to know."

"Where is their closest chapter?" asked Natalia.

"You'd have to go all the way to Corassus," said Ambrose.

"Where's that?" asked Athgar.

"You'd have to travel downriver to the Great Sea," replied the brother, "and then west, along the Tylerian coast. Corassus is a great city-state and a major stronghold for their order."

"We must go there," declared Athgar, "if only to put my mind at rest. I know it's unlikely, but I have to see them, perhaps they'll know more of this scarred man."

"Perhaps," said Natalia, "but I have to admit it coincides with my plans nicely."

"What plans are those?" Athgar asked.

"I wanted to make for the south coast, I believe I can make a living there as a Water Mage. What do you say we travel together?"

"I would like that," he admitted, "though I must confess I have no coins."

"I knew that already," she said, "I had to undress you if you recall. Don't worry, I'll cover the expenses."

Brother Ambrose turned red with embarrassment. "Good luck to you, my children. You must excuse me, for I have other things to attend to."

"What got into him?" asked Natalia.

"I think it was you talking of undressing me," Athgar responded, "though I can't think why."

"Shall we look into finding passage downriver?" she asked.

"We shall," he agreed.

ON THE RIVER

AUTUMN 1103 SR

The riverbank appeared to sail by as they stood on the deck. The Marianne was a small boat by most standards, but big enough to sail downriver with a cargo of iron ore. The captain had been more than happy to have a Water Mage aboard, though he was less excited for the inclusion of the Therengian. A mage could help protect the ship should danger lurk, but Athgar was just another mouth to feed, and Captain Howe saw little usefulness in the axe wielder.

Athgar spent the whole time on deck, even sleeping there, for the close confines of the hull did little to comfort him. He stood, staring eastward, watching as the vast forests rolled by.

"They say it's all wilderness," announced Natalia.

"I doubt that," he responded, "there's bound to be much that lives there, a rich country like that!"

"Many have tried," she claimed. "Captain Howe tells me that more than five hundred adventurous souls have tried to tame the eastern bank over the last few years."

"No doubt an old wives tale meant to frighten people away. I bet there's Elves out there somewhere, maybe even Orcs."

"Orcs? What makes you say that?"

"They're a scattered people," Athgar said. "According to legend, there was a great war where all their cities were destroyed."

"The Orcs had cities?"

"Yes, why? Does that surprise you?"

"I never really thought of them as civilized. How long ago was this?"

"Many, many generations ago. I don't know exactly, but I'm guessing it was two thousand years ago, maybe more."

"I didn't think Humans had been around that long," she said.

"It wasn't the Humans that destroyed them, it was the Elves."

"Really? Or are you just pulling my leg? I find it hard to believe the Elves had anything to do with it."

"Why?"

"They're said to be so isolationist, having little to do with Humans."

"No doubt because we outnumber them so much," he replied. "Can you imagine what would happen if we declared war on them? It would be a short one for sure."

"I think you're wrong," said Natalia. "They have been working with magic far longer than we have."

"You think them more powerful?"

"I think their mages might be," she said. "Humans take a lifetime to become masters, but an Elf lives much longer. Think of how much more powerful they could become."

"If that's true, why don't they rule the land?"

"I don't know," she confessed, "I've never met one. But we learned about them at the Volstrum."

"The Volstrum? What's that?"

Natalia blushed, fearful she had revealed her secret. "Just a school I went to. We learned battle magic, and the subject of Elves always came up when we were talking about magic and warfare. Did you know that it was the Elves that first gave magic to Humans."

"How do you know that?" Athgar asked. "Surely, no one kept records that long ago."

"Well, that's the legend," she said.

"I think that Humans stole magic from the Elves," he suggested, "don't you think that's more likely?"

"I don't think you can steal magic," she said, "it's not a thing you can just take."

"I know, but it bears consideration. I mean, if Elves taught Humans magic, who taught the Elves? Someone had to discover it originally, didn't they?"

"I suppose so," she said, "I never really gave it much thought."

They lapsed into silence, watching the river bank as they floated by. It was peaceful here, and it lacked the overall stench of the city.

"Did you get a chance to try that bow I bought you?" she asked.

"No, not yet," he replied, "though I did string it, just to test the pull. I haven't had an opportunity to do any target practice yet."

"You should try it on the boat," Natalia suggested.

"I don't think Captain Howe would appreciate me shooting arrows at his mast."

"You could shoot at the trees as we sail past."

"And lose my arrows? No, thank you. I'll wait until we anchor for the night."

"We've been on this boat for five days," she scolded, "and you haven't found any time at all to practice."

"I can't help it," he said, "it's usually dark by the time we anchor. I can't very well practice in the dark, now can I? What about you?"

"What about me?" she asked.

"Shouldn't you practice casting your spells?"

In answer, she pointed at a distant tree, uttering the words to release her power. A familiar buzzing filled the air and then shards of ice flew from her hands, striking her target. The sound of the impact reverberated through the forest as bark flew everywhere, scattering birds in all directions.

The woods grew quiet for a moment, and then a creaking sound reached their ears as the tree trunk, no longer able to bear its burden, began to tilt. It crashed to the ground in a tremendous explosion of wood, sending pine needles everywhere.

"Impressive," said Athgar, "but don't you think you overdid it a little?"

"What do you mean?" she asked. "I hit the target, didn't I?"

"Yes," he replied, "but did you need to make it so powerful? You could have hit the target with half the power."

"If we had been in battle, that tree would be dead!" Natalia proclaimed.

"True," he said, "but you're overdoing it. You don't need that much strength to kill someone, you're burning through your energy at a high rate when you cast like that."

"Since when have you been an expert in magic?" she asked.

"I'm not, it was merely a suggestion."

"In my defence, magic doesn't work that way."

"Now it's my turn not to understand," he said.

"We learned many things at the Volstrum," she explained, "and one of the principles of magic is that when you release it, it must be unleashed in one big effort. A battle mage can't afford to hold back."

"But aren't you afraid of the magic consuming you?" Athgar asked.

Natalia was struck dumb by his remark, a look that didn't go unnoticed.

"What's the matter?" he asked. "Did I say something wrong?"

"No, it's just that sometimes I have that same feeling, as if I'm about to lose control. It happened back in Draybourne, in the alleyway. What made you use that phrase, about consuming you?"

She waited for Athgar's response, but there was nothing. Tearing her eyes from the trees to look at him, she hoped that he was merely mulling things over, but he was staring at the eastern bank of the river, his hands gripping the railing tightly. "What is it?" she asked.

"Somethings moving," he said. "I'd better get my bow." He ran towards the bow of the boat, where their belongings were piled, meagre as they were.

"Captain?" called out Natalia. "Athgar has spotted something."

Captain Howe moved to the railing. "I don't see anything," he called back.

Athgar, having retrieved his bow, was now in the process of stringing it. "Rygaurs!" he said.

"What, in the name of the Saints, is a rygaur?" asked the captain.

As if in answer, a terrible keening emanated from the woods, echoing across the river, sending shivers down everyone's spine.

The Therengian, arrow notched, stood ready, scanning the distant tree line. "They're hideous creatures," he explained. "The Orcs describe them as goblin-like."

"Goblins? But they're small," said Howe, "hardly a threat to the Marianne."

"Small, yes, but these fly, and they have razor-sharp teeth. Prepare yourselves, they tend to attack in groups."

An eruption of leaves flew into the air as the strange creatures emerged from their perches. There were at least a dozen of them, their distinct screeching pealing across the water. Hovering in place for but a moment, they came at the boat in a swarm.

Athgar took aim, watching as they drew closer. He had never seen one in person, but the Orcs feared them, and that was enough for him. He let fly with his arrow, but the range was too far, the shot falling harmlessly into the water. Natalia blasted one with an ice shard, hitting the creature's wing. It fell to the ground, twirling as it plummeted.

As they drew closer, Athgar could finally see the dog-like face and the serrated teeth that lined their sizable mouths as they screeched. The crew of the Marianne ran about, seeking shelter as the horde descended.

One rygaur flew too low and became entangled in the rigging. As it struggled, its claws ripped and cut, severing the ropes that held it. Athgar sent an arrow into its torso, causing it to fall to the deck, but as it did so, it flailed about, ripping the sail as it descended.

A scream from the aft end of the boat alerted them that the sailor who manned the tiller was under attack, a creature's claws ripping his arms as he tried in vain to fend off the monster. Natalia sent ice hurtling towards the rygaur, striking it and knocking it back against the aft railing, but the spell was so powerful that the rudder man also took a portion of the damage, falling to the deck, unconscious or dead.

Another flew by, snapping ropes with its teeth as it passed. The main mast wobbled, its stabilizing lines no longer in place. With the tiller now unattended, the boat began to drift towards the river bank. There was a scraping sound as the hull hit the riverbed, and then the ship lurched, coming to a complete halt.

Athgar tumbled to the deck, the bow flying from his hands. A rygaur hovered over him, no longer constricted by the severed ropes. Athgar rolled onto his back, sending a jet of flame in the direction of the creature, striking it dead centre and knocking it back. No longer able to fly, it plummeted into the water, leaving a greasy smoke trail in the air.

Natalia, rushing forward to look after the injured tillerman, fell into the view of another creature. It swooped in low to the deck, intent on its prey. She spoke quickly, bringing forth the words of power and then suddenly a wall of ice appeared in front of her. The rygaur struck it full-on, breaking its neck, sending chunks of ice scattering across the deck.

Natalia spotted another creature preparing to attack, its eyes focused solely on its target. "Athgar!" she called out in alarm.

He rose to his feet, searching the sky as he did so. When his nemesis began its descent, he fired off another streak of flame, once again hitting dead centre. The creature fell, its body alight until it splashed into the river. Athgar tore his gaze from his target, frantically looking about, but the battle was over. The rygaurs, dissuaded from their meal, had turned and were flying off to the east.

"Where in the Saints did those things come from?" asked Captain Howe.

"According to the Orcs, they usually live much further to the east," offered Athgar. "Something must have driven them westward, and then Natalia's spell caught their attention."

"Never mind that," called out Natalia. She was staring at Athgar. "Where did you learn to do that?"

"Do what?" he asked.

"Throw fire," she accused, "you never said you were a pyromancer."

"I'm not," he defended, "I'm a master of flame."

"It's the same thing," she accused, her temper flaring. "Who sent you?" She raised her hands as if to cast a spell.

"Slow down," he said, trying to soothe her.

"Are you from Korascajan?" she asked.

"Kasca-who?' he said.

"Korascajan, the home of the Sartellians. Did they send you to bring me back?"

"Nobody sent me," he said. "The Orcs taught me. I was touched by fire. That's how they found me."

"Touched by fire? What's that supposed to mean?"

"I told you my village was attacked," he said, trying to soothe her, "but I didn't tell you the whole story. The truth is, it was burned to the ground. Kargen and Laruhk found me buried in ashes, barely alive. They were the ones that took me back to Ord-Kurgad, the Orc village. It was Artoch, a shaman, that taught me to harness the spark."

"What spark?" she asked. "Is that a spell?"

"No," he continued, "now put your arms down and let me explain. I don't know what this Korascajan place is, nor do I know anyone called Sarnellian."

"Sartellian," she corrected.

"Whoever they are," he said, "they didn't send me. I was taught to harness fire by Artoch, an Orc."

She lowered her arms, "If you're a master of flame, why didn't you simply incinerate all those rygaurs?"

"And burn down the ship? We only had to drive them off, not utterly destroy them. Using fire is about control."

"Control?" she accused. "In battle, you need to let loose with everything you have."

"I disagree. I saw you hit the rygaur near the tiller. The spell was so powerful you injured a crewman with the splash."

"Casualty of war," she declared.

"But it doesn't have to be that way, don't you see? Look, you said you sometimes have the feeling you're losing control, didn't you?"

"Yes," she admitted, "but holding back on a spell reduces its effects."

"Precisely," he said. "If I wanted to light a candle with my magic, I wouldn't want to set the whole house on fire. It's the same in battle. You don't always swing an axe with full power, doing so would leave you vulnerable. Tell me, in battle, how many spells would you be able to cast?"

"I'm not sure," she revealed. "I've never been in battle, at least not one with armies. Why?"

"When you blasted that tree earlier, it must have consumed a significant amount of energy. How many times could you cast that in a day?"

"Not many," she confessed.

"You're a powerful spellcaster, Natalia," he continued, "of that, I have no doubt, but you would be more effective by holding back a little. There is such a thing as overkill."

"Overkill? I don't think I've run across that word before," she mused.

"Yes, inflicting too much damage. Beyond a certain point, you're just wasting your energy."

"That makes sense," she said, "but how do I learn to control it? I've been taught, throughout my training, to use full power whenever possible."

"I learned to control my inner spark," he said, "it's what gives Fire Mages their power. I don't know if the same is true of Water Mages, but perhaps some of the techniques Artoch taught me might work for you?"

"It's worth a try," she said. "I have to admit I graduated the Volstrum with a sense of superiority as far as magic is concerned, but having just fought those rygaurs I can see your reasoning. Where shall we start?"

"You mean WHEN," he corrected.

"No, I mean where. I see no reason not to start immediately."

"Are you always this intense?" he asked. "We've only just finished fighting these creatures."

"There's no better time to learn than right away," she declared, "it's what made me a top student at the Volstrum."

"But what about the boat?" he asked. "We still have to make repairs and get it moving. Can't your magic do something?"

"I can't move a grounded boat," she said. "That's a job for the sailors, and besides, if we're practising magic, we're already prepared should those creatures return."

Repairing the ship had proven easier than expected, but getting it off the riverbed was something else. They had to lighten the load, and that meant unloading a portion of its cargo. After hours of labour, the boat finally floated free, and they hauled it to mid-river using the anchor, a process called kedging, which involved using the boat's skiff to take the heavy weight across the river, then dropping it. Pulling on the anchor rope would then move the boat towards the anchor, which was caught on the underlying riverbed.

Athgar breathed a sigh of relief as the Marianne floated free, but then there was more back-breaking labour as the cargo was loaded back up. This was made all the more difficult by the fact that they could only load it in small quantities at a time thanks to the limited capacity of the boat's skiff.

It took two days before they were underway again, two days of constant surveillance of the sky, lest the rygaurs return. Natalia had pleaded with him to begin her lessons, but he insisted on helping the crew complete repairs. It was with some relief that he finally sat down on deck exhausted, his muscles sore from his efforts.

Natalia, who had been standing guard the entire time was less so, a fact that was made all the more evident by her line of questioning.

"Shall we begin?" she asked.

He looked up at her with a defeated look to his face. "You can't possibly mean right now?" he said.

"Why not?" she said. "The ship's underway and your labour is done, is it not?"

"It is," he replied, "but I'm aching all over. All I want to do is lie down and sleep for several days."

"Which makes it the best time to start," she said. "You'll have no distractions." She was smiling at him, a fact that didn't escape his notice.

He finally caved in. "Very well," he said, "come and sit before me, cross-legged."

She sat, spreading her dress carefully as she did so. "Now what?"

"Close your eyes and look deep within you," Athgar commanded.

"How do I do that?" Natalia asked. "Is it some type of meditation?"

"In a sense, yes, but it's more than that. You have to find your inner spark. I suppose, in your case, it would be an inner pool? To be frank, I'm not quite sure what you'll be looking for."

"What is this spark of yours like?" she asked.

"I see it as a small flame. The first time I tried this, it took me some time to see it. You have to stare into the darkness."

"The darkness? Is that your evil side?"

"No, I mean the black you see when your eyes are closed. Try to imagine the flame within you. Eventually, it should flare to life. You're already capable of casting, so I imagine it will appear quickly."

She closed her eyes, concentrating. It felt as though she was staring into the abyss, an endless pool of night. She didn't see anything but suddenly felt as though she had been bathed in water, luxuriating in its embrace. "I found it," she said. "Now what?"

Natalia waited for Athgar to respond, but when no words were forthcoming, she opened her eyes to see him sitting opposite, his head bowed and a gentle snoring sound issuing from his mouth.

She leaned forward to look closer into his face. "Sleep well, my friend," she said, then kissed him tenderly on the forehead.

CLEARWATER

AUTUMN 1103 SR

The Marianne hit the pier with a bump. Natalia and Athgar stood by as the crew leaped into action, tying the vessel off. Captain Howe, his attention no longer required, walked down the length of the deck to where his passengers waited.

"You've done a great job," he declared, "and you're welcome aboard my ship anytime."

"Thank you, Captain," said Natalia. "You've been most gracious."

"What will you do now?" he asked.

"We'll look for a vessel sailing to Corassus," she replied.

"You'll have to be vigilant if you're sailing those waters," he said, "it's a dangerous route."

"Dangerous?" piped up Athgar.

"Yes, you'll have to sail through the Teeth of Karamir."

"That doesn't sound too appetizing," replied the Therengian.

"That's not the half of it," offered the captain. "To get to Corassus, you'll also have to sail past the pirate coast."

"That sounds even worse," said Natalia.

"Why doesn't someone hunt down the pirates?" asked Athgar.

"Many have tried," said Captain Howe, "but the coastline is full of cliffs and small inlets, providing the perfect cover for sea bandits."

"Surely ships can just outrun them," suggested Athgar.

"You would think that would be so, but the fact is the pirate coast is notorious for winds that die down with little warning, leaving a ship becalmed."

"I imagine that would leave you ripe for the plucking?" said Athgar.

"It would," agreed the captain, "and it's one of the reasons I stay on the river. Besides, the Marianne isn't built for the sea, she's a shallow draft vessel, she'd wallow in any large waves."

"If there's no wind," asked Athgar, "how do the pirates attack?"

"They use galleys. They can be swift in calm seas and surprisingly agile when needed. The last thing a captain wants to see is a swarm of those vessels coming after him." He saw a look of confusion on Athgar's face. "Galleys are rowed ships," he explained.

Athgar nodded in understanding.

"We'll keep your information in mind," said Natalia. "What will you do now?"

"We'll unload the Marianne and then buy up some timber to ship back north."

"Timber?" said Athgar. "They have lots of trees in Holstead."

"Yes, but not shadowbark," he offered.

"Never heard of it," said the Therengian.

"I have," said Natalia. "It's a very hard wood. Ideal for siege engines, I've heard."

"Yes," agreed the captain, "though it's far more commonly used in furniture, especially amongst the rich. It fetches a hefty profit. I'll likely make more from that than I did on the trip down here."

"What about the rygaurs?" asked Natalia.

"I doubt they'll attack again," the captain responded. "We've sailed this river for years, and that was the first time we've seen them. Besides, you two gave them quite a drubbing, I doubt they'll be eager to try again."

"I hope you're right," said Athgar, "but you still might want to invest in some bows."

"I will, don't you worry."

"Good luck, Captain," said Natalia, "or should I say smooth sailing?"

"Either will do," the captain replied, "and good luck to the two of you. I hope you find what you're looking for. Now, I must get back to work, there's a lot of iron ore in my hold, and it won't unload itself."

He wandered off, bellowing orders to his men.

"Where to now?" asked Athgar.

"I don't know about you," said Natalia, "but I could use a bath."

"What about Corassus?"

"It will still be there in the morning," she replied, then noticed the look of distaste on his face. "What's the matter, don't you like the idea of bathing?"

"I understand the concept of washing," he said, "but immersing yourself in water to get clean? Wouldn't a simple bowl suffice?"

"I'm a Water Mage, remember?" she replied. "Bathing was a regular ritual for us. You might say it's the core of our being. Didn't you have any rituals?"

"Rituals?" he mused. "I suppose we did, now that you mention it."

"What were they?" she asked, her curiosity peaked.

"Creating a fire to cook meat," he replied with a grin.

"That's not what I meant."

"I know, I'm just teasing. If you want a bath, then far be it for me to deny it to you. Lead on, Mistress Natalia."

"Please don't do that," she asked.

"Do what?" he replied.

"Don't call me Mistress Natalia, it has some rather unpleasant memories associated with it. I'd much rather you just call me Natalia."

He bowed in an exaggerated manner, "As you wish, Natalia."

They stepped onto the pier, the crew scampering about them as they prepared to begin the unloading process. The two threaded their way through them, making their way north, to where the town itself lay behind a wooden palisade.

"We are truly on the frontier," noted Natalia. "I'm surprised to see only walls of wood protecting the town. I was expecting something more impressive?"

"I doubt there's sufficient stone around here to build walls," offered Athgar. "I rather suspect we'll see lots of wooden buildings once we enter."

They made their way to an opening in the palisade, a gap that allowed traffic from the docks to enter freely. There were wooden doors here, but they were swung wide open, and judging by the accumulation of weeds, had seldom been shut.

True to his guess, the town consisted of wooden structures, mostly of cut timbers, giving it a woodsy smell, and Athgar half expected a deer to wander out from between buildings. It reminded him of his own village, Athelwald, though the general shape of the buildings varied considerably, much more so than he was used to seeing.

They halted on what appeared to be the main street, taking in the view and trying to spot an inn that might suit their purposes.

"That looks promising," said Natalia, pointing at a rather large building. She turned to Athgar, but he was looking eastward, down the street to where a group of horsemen rode through the gate, their mounts covered in dust and dirt.

"Temple Knights," said Natalia.

"Saint Mathew?" he asked.

"Very good," she said in response, "you're learning."

"They look like they've had a tough time of it."

"Perhaps," she mused, "but it is of no concern of ours. We need to be on our way."

"To where?" he asked. "We haven't found an inn yet?"

"Yes we have," she said. "I was just telling you about it when you were distracted by those knights."

"Oh, sorry," Athgar turned his gaze where she pointed. "I suppose it looks as good as any other."

"Come along, then," she said, leading the way towards the inn. It had a placard outside that proclaimed it as the White Coaster, along with a painting of a bird. They entered to find a large common area, for the inn also doubled as a tavern. It was not as ornate as their lodgings in Draybourne, but it had a comfortable feel to it.

Natalia wandered off to find the innkeeper while Athgar looked around at the customers. It was easy to identify the sailors among the group, for their deeply tanned skin gave them away. The locals, on the other hand, were dressed in the sturdy clothing that marked them as woodsmen, and they tended to keep to their own kind, sharing drinks with friends, but the atmosphere here was pleasant and inviting.

His observations were interrupted by Natalia.

"I have the key," she said. "It's all taken care of."

"Don't we each get one?" he asked.

"I'm afraid there was only one room available," she explained. "I hope you don't mind."

"Are there two beds?" he asked.

"Only one," she explained, "but I thought you preferred to sleep on the floor?"

"I did say that, didn't I," he replied. "Let's go and see it, shall we?"

Making their way upstairs, Athgar paused at the top, looking out the window in the hallway only to spot a bathing pool below. It was a large wooden construction with a half dozen people in it, wearing naught but their underclothes. He turned away as he heard Natalia unlocking a door.

She stood in the doorway, examining the interior. "This looks reasonable enough," she said. "What do you think?"

Athgar moved up beside Natalia, peering into the room. He could feel her presence beside him, smell the faint scent of the perfume she insisted on wearing. He tried to ignore the distraction. "It looks quite nice," he said. "I assume you're going outside to bathe?"

"No," she stated, "I've arranged for them to bring a tub up here for me."

He looked at her in surprise, "Bring one up?"

"Well, I'm not going to bathe in the outdoor one like a commoner," she said.

"Why not?" he asked. "Everyone else does."

She blushed deeply. "I don't intend to bathe with my clothes on," she said.

He looked at her in stunned silence.

"Don't look at me like that," she responded, "it's perfectly normal."

"Normal is stripping down to your underclothes like regular people," he said.

"Well, I don't," she said. "I like to be clean, not bathed in other people's dirt, and I certainly don't want to bathe in front of strangers."

"So the innkeeper has to haul a big tub up here just for you?"

"He said they had one," she argued, "and it doubles as a laundry tub."

"It must weigh quite a bit," offered Athgar, "and then all those trips just to fill it with water."

"They don't have to fill it," she said.

"Oh? Does it fill itself?"

"No, Athgar, I'm a Water Mage. I shall fill it myself."

"Wait," he said in disbelief, "you mean you're going to traipse up and down stairs with buckets?"

"No, of course not. I can create water using my magic."

"You can?"

"Don't look so surprised," she said, "you can create fire, can't you? Why is it so surprising that I can create water?"

"To be honest, I never thought about it."

"It was one of the first spells I was taught," she said. "After all, what is an ice shard if not simply frozen water."

"That makes a lot of sense," he agreed. "Can you create enough to fill a tub?"

"Yes, though admittedly it will take several castings. Ideally, I'd like to warm it up, but you can't have everything."

"I can heat water," he said with a smile.

"You can?"

"Yes, of course. It's really just an application of fire."

Her face betrayed her joy. "I think I love you," she said, then blushed furiously. "That is to say, I love that you can warm water."

Now it was his time to blush. "Well, I'd best take a stroll and give you your privacy if you're going to bathe."

"The bath isn't even up here yet," she said, "and once I've filled it, I'll need you to warm it up."

"Of course," he agreed, "but when I've done that I'll take a walk. I can't very well be here while you're bathing."

"Why not?" she asked

"You'll be naked," he said, his face crimson.

"So?" she asked. "Am I so frightening?"

"No, but..." his voice trailed off.

"But what? Are you afraid of the female form?"

"No," he defended, "but I thought you'd want your privacy. Surely you don't want a strange man watching you bathe?"

"No, of course not," she said. "Why? Are you strange?"

"No, but..." once again he was left at a loss for words.

"But nothing," she said. "You'll remain, I insist on it. It will allow us to talk about things."

"I don't understand you," he said. "Earlier you indicated you didn't want to bathe in front of others, and now you're going to strip naked and climb into a tub right before my eyes?"

"Of course," she said. "I may need you to warm up the water. You can't do that if you're wandering off through the town."

"Trust me," he responded, "the water will remain warm for some time."

"It's not just that," she said, "I must admit to feeling safer when you're around."

"Is that all?" he asked.

"No, it's much more than that," she confessed. "I've never felt this way about someone before. The truth is, I want you near me."

She moved closer to him until their faces were almost touching. Her breathing was shallow, and he realized she was as nervous as he. They stared at each other for what felt like an eternity, and yet, to Athgar's mind, it wasn't nearly long enough. Slowly, their lips touched, and he kissed her. She responded with a passionate embrace.

Awakening early the next morning, Athgar rolled over to see the sleeping form of Natalia beside him. Gazing at her, he took in her beauty, a smile coming unbidden to his lips.

She opened her eyes to see him and broke into a smile herself. "Well," she said, "what do you think of bathing now?"

He blushed, despite his smile. "We should do it more often," he said.

She moved over towards him, kissing him tenderly. "Much as I'd love to spend all day here with you," she said, "we need to find a ship."

"Yes," he agreed, "I suppose we should be up and on the way."

"Perhaps we can linger just a while longer," she whispered, wrapping her arms around his neck.

· · ·

The docks were busy, as usual. The seabirds flocked about, trying to steal fishermen's catches while men loaded and unloaded goods. Making their way down the pier, enquiring about destinations as they went, Natalia did all the talking while Athgar was content just to be in her presence. He watched the sailors working, wondering about what distant ports they might call home. A Temple Knight stood further down the pier, in discussion with what Athgar could only assume was a ship's captain.

"No luck here," said Natalia, returning to his side. "This ship's heading south, towards the Dark Coast."

"That sounds ominous," he said, "but I think I may have found us a ship. The Temple Knights have a fortress in Corassus, do they not?"

"I'm not sure fortress is the right word," she countered, "but yes, I believe they do, why?"

"There's a Temple Knight down there, at the end of the pier. I'd wager that ship's on church business. Do the orders cooperate with each other?"

"They're all part of the same church," she said, eyeing the distant warrior. "Shall we go and introduce ourselves?"

Athgar smiled, "I believe we should. Would you like to lead, or shall I?"

"You're in a good mood," she said. "Would it have anything to do with our stay at the inn?"

"Of course," he said. "I feel...invigorated. Full of life and ready to face whatever the day might bring."

"I feel the same way," she said, "though I must admit it's a strange feeling."

"Strange?"

"Yes," Natalia admitted, "it's not something I've done before. At the Volstrum we were all segregated. We weren't allowed to interact with men."

"Oh?" he said. "So you've never..."

"No, not before last night."

"I hope it was everything you wanted," he said.

She turned and kissed him.

He blushed. "Aren't you afraid someone might see?" he asked.

"I don't care," she said, "it's what I want to do."

"You've certainly changed from the young woman I met in Draybourne."

"I suppose I have," she said, taking his hand. "Now, let us go and talk to this Temple Knight."

They drew closer, slowing to allow their target to finish his conversation before they spoke with him.

"Excuse me," said Athgar.

The knight turned. He had closely cropped hair the colour of sand and sported a neatly trimmed beard, shaved near to his face. He was fitted out in chainmail armour, a brown tabard worn over it, displaying the holy symbol of his order, a common axe.

"Yes?" said the Temple Knight.

"My name is Athgar, and this is Natalia," the Therengian said in greeting.

"How do you do," replied the man. "I am Brother Cyric of the Order of Saint Mathew. Is there something I can assist you with?"

"Yes, there is," said Natalia. "We are seeking passage to Corassus. Have you heard of it?"

"I have," he revealed. "As a matter of fact, I'm travelling there myself, aboard this very ship. What takes you to the great city-state if I might be so bold as to ask?"

"I am seeking information," responded Athgar. "We have travelled all the way from the Duchy of Holstead."

"Then you have travelled some distance," the Mathewite said, "though I wonder what information would bring you so far. Are you seeking the Archives of Corassus?"

"The Archives?" said Athgar. "I'm afraid I've never heard of them. What, precisely, are they?"

"A great repository of knowledge," offered Natalia, "unless I miss my guess."

"They are, indeed," said Cyric.

"Is that where you're bound," asked Athgar, "to The Archives?"

"Alas, no," the Temple Knight responded, "though I might visit them once I'm there. No, I have been reassigned. The Church has seen fit to move me to a new location where I can do the Saints work."

"Is that common?" asked Natalia.

"Common enough," he replied. "I've been in Clearwater for some years now. It's only natural that they should move me."

"Do you know the captain of this vessel?" Natalia asked. "We would like to talk to him about passage."

Cyric laughed, "You might say that. The truth is Captain Runell works for the Church."

"He's a knight?" she asked.

"No, a merchant," corrected Cyric, "but he carries cargo under the auspices of the order, or at least he does now that he's under contract to us. He's a hard man to pin down, he's been sailing the world. I can introduce you, if you like?"

"If you would be so kind," said Natalia.

"Harnen," called out Cyric, "there's a couple of people here who want to talk to you!"

A man on deck came closer. He was heavily tanned and had a weather-beaten look to him. His unkempt hair was tucked beneath a ragged-looking cap. "And who might you two be?" he asked.

"My name is Natalia," she said, "and this is Athgar."

"Unusual names," he commented. "I take it you're not from around here?"

"No," she replied, "we're from up north, near Draybourne, have you heard of it?"

"'Fraid not," Harnen replied, "but there's many the land I have yet to sail to."

"Not from what I've heard," said Cyric. "From the stories he tells, you'd think he's been everywhere."

"Are you here on business?" asked the captain.

"We are seeking passage to Corassus," said Natalia.

"I have room aboard if you have the coin," he replied.

"We have coins, but I was rather hoping you'd pay us to travel with you."

He looked at her in surprise, "And why would I do that?"

"I'm a Water Mage," she said.

"Experienced?" the captain asked, suddenly intrigued.

"I have a wide variety of spells that could prove useful. I can calm seas, bring favourable currents, that sort of thing."

He nodded his head as he stroked his chin. "I'm definitely interested. The sea voyage to Corassus is dangerous, and having a Water Mage along would be quite useful." He turned to Athgar. "Are you a Water Mage as well?"

"No," he admitted, "I'm a master of flame."

Harnen Runell looked taken aback, "I don't want a pyro aboard my ship, it's too dangerous."

"We come as a package," said Natalia, "and I'd offer you a discount on my services. You wouldn't have to worry about Athgar, he's very disciplined."

"He would have to be if he wants to board my ship."

"I don't understand," said Athgar, "I would have thought you'd want a Fire Mage aboard to fight off pirates."

"Most Fire Mages have tempers," offered Natalia, "and they can get very full of themselves. There's something about working with fire that gives them a superior feeling."

"I can guarantee you, Captain," said Athgar, "that I won't be a burden."

"Very well," relented Captain Runell, "we sail on the first tide. You can stow your gear now if you like."

"Thank you, Captain," said Natalia, "you won't regret it."

"See that I don't," he warned, "and welcome aboard the Swift, fastest ship on the Great Sea."

The captain returned to his work, leaving the others at the pier. "Well," mused Cyric, "it seems you've made an impression. I don't believe I've met a mage couple before. How long have you two been married?"

"Oh, we're not married," said Athgar.

"Not yet, anyway," added Natalia, "but we are travelling together."

"When is the first tide?" asked the Therengian.

"Whenever I'm ready to step aboard," said Cyric, "he's just giving you a hard time. You'll have to excuse Harnen's attitude, he just got back from sailing across the Sea of Storms."

"I have no idea where that is," admitted Athgar. "Is it far?"

"It's about as far away as you can get, clear over the other side of the continent, to the west."

"When do you plan to embark?" Natalia asked Brother Cyric.

"I had planned to leave first thing tomorrow morning. Where are you staying?"

"I suppose we'll have to spend another night at the White Coaster," she said.

"How about if I meet you there at first light? We can all walk down to the Swift together and be on our way?"

"An excellent suggestion," said Natalia.

"Yes," agreed Athgar, "it will allow us to bathe one last time."

Natalia blushed, but it escaped the notice of Brother Cyric. Either that or he chose to ignore it.

"Very well," said the Temple Knight, "until tomorrow morning then."

THE STORM

AUTUMN 1103 SR

A thgar stood at the rail, watching the shore pass by slowly as the Swift made its way inexorably southwest. Rocky cliffs towered over them, dwarfing the ship, but the Therengian was more interested in the swarm of birds that appeared to favour the area. They nested on the cliffs, that much was quite evident, but occasionally they would sail out over the water, carried on currents of air invisible to the eye. He watched one coast overhead as it made a gentle arc, then returned shoreward, its head craning down as it watched the water below. Suddenly, it folded its wings, plunging down through the air to dive into the water, emerging a moment later with a fish in its mouth.

He felt a soft hand placed over his on the railing and turned his eyes to see Natalia. She smiled as their eyes met, sending a warmth through him.

"Enjoying the view?" she asked.

"I am now," he replied, smiling openly. Athgar leaned forward, kissing her tenderly.

"What was that for?" she asked.

"Luck," he responded.

"You think we'll need it?"

"One can always use luck," he said. "You never know when it might prove useful."

"How are you finding the sea?"

"I was a little unsteady at first," Athgar responded, "but once you get used to the gentle rolling, it's not so bad. It's quite a bit different from being on the river, though."

"I'd have to agree with you there," she said.

"I take it you've sailed before?"

"No, never," she confessed. "I spent all my time in training. Until we boarded the Marianne, I'd never set foot on a boat."

"Ship," he corrected. "I don't think Captain Runell would appreciate you calling the Swift a boat. He's particular about those things."

She moved closer to him, then took his hand, passing it around her back. "There," Natalia remarked, "that's better."

"You're trembling," he said. "Is that the effect I have on you?"

She leaned her head onto his shoulder. "It is," she said, "but that's not why I'm trembling. I'm quite nervous."

"Why?"

"I let the captain believe I was an experienced mage."

"You ARE quite powerful," he reminded her.

"Yes, but I've never done this sort of work before. I'm afraid he's going to discover how little I truly know."

"You worry too much," Athgar said. "The sailing has been smooth, and before you know it, we'll be in Corassus with all of this behind us."

"I suppose you're right," she replied. "After all, the captain has sailed all over the world, and he doesn't seem worried."

They heard the sound of a hatch opening and turned to see Brother Cyric coming on deck. The Temple Knight had eschewed his usual armour and now wore only the simple brown cassock of his order.

"Good morning, Brother Cyric," said Athgar in greeting. "How are you feeling?"

"Much better than yesterday," Cyric replied. "Is it just my imagination, or is the deck more steady today?"

"I think you've just found your sea legs," offered Natalia.

The Holy Brother made his way to the railing, taking up a position to Athgar's left, gazing out at the distant cliffs. "Anything interesting happening?"

"It depends on your definition of interesting," said Athgar, turning his gaze to Natalia. "I find the view here to be quite nice, but other than the odd bird sailing overhead, it's been quiet."

"We should enjoy it while we can," suggested Cyric. "I hear things will get worse as we approach the Teeth."

"What are the Teeth, precisely?" asked Natalia.

"Rocks, mostly," said the knight, "that jut out of the water."

"Just like that?" asked Athgar. "Why would there be rocks in the middle of nowhere?"

"They're a continuation of the southern continent. The land juts out, cutting off the Shimmering Sea from the Great Sea. There's a channel at its northern tip that's free of rocks, but the winds can be tremendous, making navigating the gap difficult."

"Has the captain sailed the gap before?" asked Natalia.

"Yes, many times. The Swift is an agile craft, I doubt he'll have much trouble, but the weather can often change unexpectedly around here. The sky looks clear at the moment, but winds from the south can blow up clouds in no time, or so I'm led to believe. Personally, I'd have rather ridden overland to Corassus, but the Church wants me there as soon as possible."

"Trouble?" asked Athgar, his curiosity peaked.

"None that I'm aware of, but my predecessor has moved on to other things, and they are in need of an administrator."

"So you'll be in charge?" asked Natalia.

"More or less," the knight confessed, "though I'd say more of a junior administrator. I'll still report to someone higher up."

"Would that be a Cunar?" asked Athgar.

"No," said Cyric, "each order has its own hierarchy. I'll be the first to admit it's all rather confusing."

"Care to explain?"

"The church consists of six orders," Cyric explained.

"Yes, I know that," said Athgar in annoyance.

"Please," begged Cyric, "let me finish, then I can answer any questions you might have."

"Very well," replied Athgar.

"At the very top of the church is what is referred to as the Council of Peers. It consists of representatives from each of the six sects. They vote one of their members to become the Primus, the person in charge."

"Is that for life?"

"No, a five-year term," continued Cyric, "but the peers are only the representatives of each sect. The real power lies with the Patriarchs, of which there is one of each order, in my case, Saint Mathew. Beneath the Patriarch of each order are two rival organizations. One is the lay brothers, led in each region by an Archprior, the other is the order of Temple Knights, they report to a Grand Master, rather than an Archprior."

"But surely they're the same church?"

"You would think so, wouldn't you," offered Cyric, "and you'd be right, up to a point. The fact is they still follow the same doctrine, but the Temple Knights must deal with protecting their flock, rather than seeing to their spiritual needs."

"So the lay brothers preach," said Athgar, "while the Temple Knights protect."

"A very succinct, but accurate description," agreed Cyric.

"Then what is the difference between the Mathews and the Cunars?" asked Athgar.

"My order looks after the poor and injured," offered Cyric, "while the Cunars form the Holy Army."

"Holy Army, I've heard that before."

"Yes, the might of the Church, if you will."

"I thought the Saints preached peace between the races?"

"We do," the brother responded, "but people are still people. It is one thing to say that peace should reign, but quite another for people to actively choose that path. The Church plays the role of peacemaker, stopping the Petty Kingdoms from devolving into war. Think of us as arbitrators, if you like."

"I'm curious," said Natalia. "We were told that the Cunars maintain a large presence in Corassus. Why is that? Surely there are no enemies there?"

Cyric smiled, "In addition to forming the army, they command the fleet. Its main purpose is to ensure the safety of those travelling to the birthplace of our order."

"Your religion confuses me," confessed Athgar. "My people worship the old Gods, and it's much easier to understand. What is this birthplace you speak of?"

"Herani," replied Cyric, "said to be the birthplace of humankind. No one really knows if that's true, of course, but it was definitely where our Church originated. I, for one, would certainly like to see it one day, but I doubt that will happen."

"Why not?" asked Natalia. "Will your order not let you visit?"

A shadow seemed to cross the Temple Knight's face. "It lies in the hands of our enemy," he said at last.

"I didn't think the Church had any enemies," said Natalia.

"Officially, it doesn't," Cyric responded, "though we've been at odds with the Halvarian Empire for years. I fear it won't be long before war erupts once again."

"Again?" said Athgar. "When was the last conflict?"

"Conflicts are happening all the time," said Cyric, "but the Church likes to keep things quiet. Every decade or so, the Empire decides it's time to expand its borders. They stir up trouble in the neighbouring states, dividing their loyalties, then, when things are as chaotic as possible, they move in."

"They invade?" asked Natalia.

"Sometimes, but often as not, they'll put their own people into influential positions and then seek intervention for the sake of peace. It is an old game that they play so well."

"How do you stop them?" she asked.

"War?" suggested Athgar.

"That would require all the Petty Kingdoms to work together," said Cyric, "and even then I suspect the Empire would have the upper hand."

"What makes them so powerful?" asked the Therengian.

"Mostly their size," said Cyric. "You see, their army is massive."

"But surely, if they are as big as you say, their border is equally as large," suggested Athgar.

"It is, but their neighbours are incapable of banding together. The Petty Kingdoms are so consumed by internal squabbles that they fail to see the threat."

"They banded together to defeat Therengia," offered Athgar, perhaps with a little more venom than he intended.

"That's true, they did," agreed Cyric, "though I daresay it worked against them."

"How so?" asked Natalia.

"If Therengia remained today, it would, perhaps, be the only kingdom capable of facing the Empire in open battle."

"All this talk of war makes me uncomfortable," said Natalia. "I would rather the land be at peace, it would be better for everyone that way. Few profit from war."

"Wise words," offered Cyric. "I wish more felt as you did."

They stood in silence for a moment, watching the cliffs as they sailed past. A splash in the water caught their attention as something broke the surface. The strange creature rolled onto its back, a flipper in the air, then dove back below the surface.

"What was that?" asked Athgar, his hand instinctively going to his axe.

"A seal," said Natalia, "likely after some fish." She looked at Athgar, the poor man appearing ready to enter a fight, and she let out a laugh. "What are you going to do, challenge it?

Athgar looked at her, ready to argue the point, but her smile disarmed him. He grinned sheepishly, "No, I suppose not. Rather silly of me to react that way."

"Don't apologize for a warrior's instinct," offered Cyric, "it's kept me safe more times than I can count. It might be misplaced here, but you never know when danger will threaten."

"I'll keep that in mind," said Athgar.

"You never really told me why you're going to Corassus," remarked

Cyric, "though I vaguely remember you mentioning something about finding information."

Athgar swept his gaze over the deck of the Swift, making sure no one else was in earshot. "I'm seeking information about a man," he said, watching Cyric's eyes for a response. "A Cunar Knight."

"Oh?" said Cyric. "You have me intrigued. Who is this man you seek?"

"I don't know his name," continued Athgar, "but he has black hair and a scar that runs down his left cheek to his jaw, giving his beard a rather lopsided look."

"How do you know he's a Temple Knight?" asked Cyric.

"He and his people wear grey surcoats, with a white sword on them. That's the Cunar symbol, isn't it?"

"It is indeed," replied Cyric. "Tell me, what is this man to you?"

"He and his fellow knights attacked my village and took prisoners, among them, my sister. I was left for dead, and if it hadn't been for the Orcs, I'd have died there like many others."

"These are serious charges," remarked the knight. "How do you plan to proceed?"

"We hadn't thought that part through yet," offered Natalia. "Athgar is all for charging in and demanding answers, but I suspect that will prove fruitless."

"I would have to agree," said Cyric. "If these people are in Corassus, you'll alert them to your presence. I would suggest a subtler approach."

"Such as?" asked Athgar.

"I'd have to give it some thought, but you intrigue me with your story. I should like to offer my assistance if you would take it."

"We would be grateful," said Natalia. "Perhaps, as a member of the Church, you could make some discreet enquiries?"

"I shall do what I can," said Cyric, "though my order has little to do with the Cunars."

"That doesn't sound promising," said Athgar, feeling a gloominess descend on him. It was all so frustrating, these men seemed to be above reproach.

"You must give me time," suggested Cyric. "I have some experience with investigations."

"I thought it was the Temple Knights of Saint Ansgar that did the investigating for the Church?" said Natalia.

Cyric grinned, "Usually it is, but sometimes they are not available, and we must make do with who we have on hand."

"Well," said Natalia, "we would be grateful for any assistance." She squeezed Athgar's hand, causing him to look at her. "It'll be all right, Athgar," she said, "we'll get to the bottom of this."

A smile creased the Therengian's face. It was hard to stay in a sour mood with Natalia's eyes focused on him. "Very well," he finally acquiesced.

The ship heaved, sending Athgar tumbling from the bed. He struck the wooden planking with a groan and Natalia called out, "Athgar, are you all right?"

"Yes," he replied, "I just fell out of bed. The deck's pitching, can't you feel it?"

"I was fast asleep," she explained, "but now that you mention it, it's quite noticeable. I must get above!"

"Don't be foolish!" he said. "Can't you hear the storm raging outside?"

"Precisely why I must be on deck. I can calm the waves, or at least reduce them, but I must see them to work my magic."

She rose from the bed, taking a moment to judge the swaying of the ship before moving towards the steps.

"I'm coming with you," Athgar announced.

"Are you sure?" she asked. "It's likely to be rough out there."

"Someone has to keep you safe," he said.

"I can look after myself," she bristled, then softened her tone. "Sorry, I didn't mean that. I welcome your presence, but I'm not sure what help you'll be up there."

She halted at the steps, looking up the ladder, a steep angle to climb, but the planks were wide, making it more sure-footed. Stepping up, she grabbed the hatch handle above, bracing herself for what was to come.

Athgar thought her absurd to go out in this weather but withheld his comments. He watched as she pushed the hatch upward and a wash of water cascaded down, drenching her. At least the water in these parts was warm.

Natalia gasped for air, her breath briefly taken from her. The ship pitched, and she held onto the ladder with a vice-like grip, waiting for it to right itself once again. Taking another breath, she then climbed up, the rain lashing down, stinging her with its force as she staggered across the deck, heading for the mainmast.

The bow drove into an immense wave, pitching the nose upward. Rising on the crest, it peaked, then suddenly dipped, throwing Natalia from her feet as the deck dropped from beneath her. She rose a foot or two, then crashed down, her limbs askew, only to be pushed across the deck as more water rushed from the port side when another wave crashed against the hull. She grabbed the railing in desperation as the water tried to carry her out into the sea.

Athgar was now halfway out of the hatch and clinging on for dear life. A giant wave loomed nearby, threatening to smash the Swift to pieces, but the ship rose as it approached, riding upward once again. He could see Natalia clutching the rail, drenched through and through and knew, in this weather, she would be incapable of casting while her hands were engaged.

As he waited for the giant wave, he felt the heave, that feeling of being lifted into the air. The Swift rode the crest for a moment and then the inevitable plunging as the tiny vessel rushed for the trough. Athgar moved out, his bare feet planted firmly on deck, gripping as best they could. He rushed for the railing, grabbing it just as another wave swept over them, the cruel sea trying to pluck them from their precarious position.

Natalia was yelling something to him, but the wind and rain carried it away. He edged closer, going hand over hand along the railing until he was beside her. She grabbed his hand, yelling above the roar of the sea.

"I have to cast," she called out, "but I need to hang on to something."

"Wait a moment!" he yelled back, scanning the ship, looking for anything that might be of use. The mainmast was held in place by ropes, rigging as the captain had called it, and he could see where one such rope had been tied off, leaving an excess that thrashed about on the deck. He pointed to it, Natalia following his gesture. It was forward of their position, and he must first get around her, so he grabbed her by the waist, steadying himself as he went. Once past, he inched along the railing, pausing as another wave rolled across the deck. Natalia mimicked his actions, and soon, the loose rope was between them.

Athgar waited until the ship hit yet another trough, and then grabbed the end of the rope, looping it about his right forearm. He then turned to Natalia, beckoning her forward.

She took a step, closing the distance, and he put his left arm around her waist, holding her close to him. They were face to face now, the rain nearly blinding them with its ferocity.

"Turn around," he yelled, "and I'll hold you in place!"

She nodded her understanding and then pivoted somewhat awkwardly. She was now standing, her back to Athgar, secure with his strong arm around her. Closing her eyes, she tried to block out the storm, but as the words flowed from her mouth, an unexpected wave hit the side of the ship, sending a tremendous rush of water over them. She choked, gasping for air.

"Take your time," he called out, "and try to gauge the waves."

Natalia took a breath, watching as the ship heaved once more. On the downward wave, she cast, the words of power flowing freely. There was no visible sign of the spell letting loose, no flash of light or buzzing of the air, but the motion of the waves seemed to lessen a moment later. The rain still drove down on them, but the little ship appeared calmer as if the sea was not heaving beneath them. It was a strange sensation, thought Athgar, for just beyond the railing, he saw the massive waves, rising like cliffs outside their reach, and yet the water around the Swift rose and fell no more than a man's height.

He placed his mouth close to her ear, the better to be heard. "Can you do something about this rain?" he called out.

"I'm afraid not," she replied. "There are some things that even magic can't do."

"How long will your spell last?"

In answer, she turned herself around so that they were again, face to face. "A good while yet," she said, "though I'll have to cast it once more before daybreak."

She placed her arms around his neck, pulling herself closer to him. "Thank you," she said, "I couldn't have done this without you." She moved her face to his, intent on kissing him. Their lips met, but a sudden squall seemed to have other ideas, sending a sheet of water down upon their heads.

Athgar sputtered, gasping for breath, but Natalia was laughing, seeing the whole situation as absurd.

"We need to get you below," he said at last.

"I should remain here," she said, "though I don't need to be by the railing, I don't think."

"You can come back later," he insisted. "You need to change, you're still in your nightclothes."

She looked down to see the wet nightshirt, clinging to her and even in the storm, Athgar noticed her blush.

"Come along," he urged, "let's get you below."

They made their way across the ship, holding hands to keep together. The deck was much easier to navigate now, the heaving waves no longer pitching them at precarious angles.

Finally making it to the hatch, they stood aside as the crew started coming on deck, alerted by the change in the ship's rolling. Athgar stood to Natalia's front, gallantly blocking the view of her as the sailors filed past, then helped her through the hatch. Moments later, they were below deck, their soaked nightshirts leaving a rather large puddle where they stood.

"Let's get you out of those clothes," said Athgar, leading her back towards their quarters.

She paused a moment, causing him to turn back to her. "You know," she said, "you men are all the same, wanting to get women out of their clothes."

"No," he said, "I meant..."

In answer, she moved forward, finally able to kiss him. Their lips met, their bodies pressed close together, and then she withdrew briefly. "I know what you meant," she whispered.

THE TEETH OF KARAMIR

AUTUMN 1103 SR

Athgar was the first to spot the dreaded Teeth; they jutted out of the water like giant spikes, the bases occasionally obscured by the waves, while their peaks were visible through the light rain. About them, the waves foamed, the clear water of the Shimmering Sea mixing with the dark waters of the Great Sea.

"An impressive sight," said Cyric, "though I'm glad it's some distance off. I'd hate to be out in that water."

Athgar looked at him. "Why?" he asked. "What makes it so dangerous? Surely a ship can keep out of range of the rocks."

"You might think so," offered Cyric, "but the currents here can be treacherous. Ships have found themselves sucked towards the Teeth with little warning."

"I expect that's the Shimmering Sea," offered Natalia. "They say it shifts its height throughout the day. One moment, the water is draining into the Great Sea, the next it flows in the opposite direction."

"It shouldn't bother us," said Cyric, "we've lots of spare room. Captain Runell won't get any closer than our current position. With any luck, we should be clear of the Teeth by mid-afternoon."

Athgar returned his gaze to the rocks. There was something about the foaming water that demanded his attention, and he strained to make out what it was. "I see movement," he finally said.

"Not unusual, I'm told," said Cyric. "Debris from shipwrecks has a way of accumulating along the Teeth."

"It's more than that," Athgar said, shifting slightly in the vain hope that his sight would improve. "I think there are people out there."

Cyric and Natalia both moved to the port side railing, the better to view the distant Teeth.

"Are you sure?" asked Natalia. "I don't see anyone."

"I do," said Cyric, "by that tall spire, the one with the forked peak, do you see?"

"Yes, now I can," she agreed. "It looks like a boat."

"It is," said Athgar, "and it looks to be in trouble."

As they watched, the small ship came into view. Before, it had been blocked by the Teeth, but now the current carried it out between two of the giant spires. The vessel sat at a strange angle, it's bow pointing upward, its deck partly awash with water.

"They're in distress!" called out Athgar. "We must do something!"

"I'll get the captain," said Cyric, moving off the foredeck.

Athgar felt helpless. The forlorn boat was taking a pounding by waves, it's crew striving to board a rowboat. Even as he watched, water sluiced across the ship's deck, washing two men overboard. They disappeared into the foaming water, failing to resurface.

"What can we do?" he asked, turning to Natalia. "Can you calm the water as you did for the Swift?"

"No," she said, "they're too far away."

They watched the drama unfolding before them, gripping the handrail tightly in their concern.

It was Captain Runell that broke the silence. "We're launching the skiff," he announced, looking to Natalia, "and I'd like you on it. You can calm the seas around it, can you not?"

"I can," she said, "but it won't help the currents, only the waves."

"Can't you use a spell to control the currents?" he asked.

"I can," she said, "but currents of this magnitude will be hard to control. I doubt my magic would make much of a difference."

"We'll do what we can," said the captain, "but if we can't get close enough, we'll have to abandon the attempt."

"Very well," she replied, then climbed down from the foredeck. The crew had pulled the canvas from atop the skiff, and now they were releasing it, while others rigged up the block and tackle that would lower it over the side.

Natalia waited until it was in the water, then clambered down the side of the ship. A few crew members climbed in after her, taking up oars and then she spotted Athgar, bending his back to row. She waited until they pushed off to begin the spell that would calm the waters around this little vessel.

Athgar strained at his oar, putting his back into it, as did the others. He watched the Swift behind them, slowly getting farther and farther away as they rowed.

"Can you see them?" he asked.

Natalia nodded, "Yes, they're clambering into a rowboat, but the waves are making it difficult."

The boatswain, a senior crewman, was counting out the strokes, keeping the men rowing in unison. His voice droned on and on until it just became background noise.

A tug at the skiff was felt by all, and suddenly it turned, angling its nose off target by a right angle.

"What was that?" called out Athgar.

"A current," yelled back a crewman. "We're in the grip of it now, hold on!"

The boat swivelled again, causing one man to lose the grip on his oar. His mistake threw off the rhythm, but he soon took it up once again, waiting for the proper count to resume.

A loud cracking noise echoed across the water.

"Their boat's breaking up," called out Natalia. "The mast just snapped."

Athgar turned his head, but his position, with his back towards the front, made it difficult to see anything. "Are they all in the boat, yet?" he asked.

"Almost," she called back.

The skiff rose suddenly, throwing off the strokes.

"The water's rising and falling too quickly for my spell to hold," she warned, "it's going to get much rougher."

"We can't go much farther," yelled a crewman, "it's getting too difficult to control."

"Agreed," called out the boatswain, "prepare to turn and maintain this position."

The skiff came about, turning parallel to the distressed vessel. It was still some distance off, but now Athgar had a much better view.

"There's a woman helping people board the rowboat," he called out. Even as he finished his sentence, a wave rushed down the deck, catching the woman in its path, Athgar watching helplessly as she was swept overboard. "We have to help," he said, standing in his seat.

"Sit down!" yelled the boatswain. "There's nothing you can do."

"Perhaps there is," called out Natalia. "Athgar, can you swim?"

He looked across the intervening waves, "Yes, but I'd never make it through those waves, I'd drown."

"Hold on," she said, waving her arms about.

Athgar felt a tingle as if his hair was standing on end. "What was that?" he asked.

"A water breathing spell. Now tie that rope around your waist."

"It won't work," called out the boatswain, "they don't even know we're here."

"I can take care of that," said Athgar. He looked skyward as they tied a rope around him. It took him only a moment to bring forth his magic, and then a streak of flame shot into the air, a beacon to the distressed vessel.

"They've seen us," someone called out. "Their boat's struggling to come towards us."

"The rope's secure," the boatswain announced.

"Wish me luck," said Athgar.

"Always," said Natalia. "Now, be careful."

He dove overboard, the crew letting out the rope behind him. The Therengian disappeared beneath the waves to appear a moment later, several arm's lengths away. He began swimming, gasping for air, and then he realized the effect the spell had on him, for as his head disappeared beneath the next wave, his speed improved significantly.

The tiny boat of refugees was barely moving towards them now, wallowing in the waves, its rowers making scant progress. Athgar drew closer to them, water splashing over him every now and again as a wave intervened, blocking their view.

Activity exploded on the far boat as the occupants spotted him in the water. Moments later, they were hauling him aboard. Someone untied him and secured the rope to the bow of their boat.

"Haul away," called the Swift's boatswain, and the crew began reeling in the rope, drawing them inexorably closer.

Natalia breathed a sigh of relief, content that Athgar was safe, but then, all of a sudden, Athgar stood up among the survivors, looking to their rear, and then he dove back into the water.

"No!" she cried out, her heart leaping into her mouth.

Someone grabbed her, lest she upset the skiff, and pulled her back down to a sitting position. She held her breath, unable to even speak, watching in horror as Athgar disappeared beneath the waves.

The ship's boat drew closer, and someone pulled it alongside, allowing the occupants to scramble aboard. The boatswain ordered the damaged vessel pushed off and the rowers bent to the task of returning to the Swift.

Natalia, her eyes glued to the surface, suddenly called out, "I see him!"

Athgar had surfaced, floating on his back, trying to get to them while pulling something, or someone along with him. It was an awkward and cumbersome task, made all the more difficult by the rolling waves.

Natalia moved to a kneeling position, planting herself firmly on the bottom of the skiff. She cast her spell. It was a strange sensation, for it was designed to target a boat, but instead, she chose Athgar as the point of impact. He bobbed unexpectedly, no doubt feeling the effects as the spell hit, and then the water around him calmed considerably.

She could still see him struggling with his burden, his progress impeded by the extra weight, but now he had a fighting chance at success. Closer, he inched, until she could make out his features as he turned, the better to gauge his progress, but his face was gaunt, and she could tell he was near the end of his strength.

"Stop rowing!" she commanded, once again searching through her repertoire of spells. Her mind made up, she lowered her hands over the side of the skiff, dipping them into the sea. Ice crystals formed as she spoke the words and then a sheet of ice began to materialize, snaking its way across the water. She drew on all the power she could, unleashing the full fury of her inner magic. The ice grew farther, a thin sheet that cracked and popped as the waves hit it. She felt blood on her lip and knew she had exceeded her reserves, but still, she fuelled her spell. The ice thickened, and then everything went black.

Athgar thrashed about, desperate to keep the woman alive. Her head was just barely above the water, but the waves kept engulfing them, and she could not breathe in the water like him. He felt the water turn cold all of a sudden and turned, once again, to briefly look at the skiff that lay just out of reach.

He blinked in disbelief when he saw ice floating there as if ice in the middle of the sea was completely normal. He reached out, grabbing the edge of it and clung on, his hands turning cold from its touch. Somehow, he managed to get an arm over it, then used his remaining strength to drag the woman up onto the ice with him. It sank slightly with their weight, but now he could catch his breath.

Glancing back towards the Swift's skiff, he saw where the ice had broken up, the waves doing their best to destroy the frozen bridge, but Natalia's spell had given them enough to climb to safety, a small iceberg in the middle of a tossing sea.

Athgar lay back, his eyes skyward, the woman lying still beside him, his grip secure on the back of her dress. Shouting drew closer, and he turned his gaze to see the skiff approaching. As they pulled up alongside of him, he dragged her over to the skiff, the ice cracking beneath them. He realized the ice was melting quickly, and when it shifted suddenly, he dove for the skiff, his arms catching the side even as the ice sank beneath his weight.

The rowers pulled him aboard, and he lay in the bottom, too exhausted to even speak. The rhythmic rowing continued as the skiff began the long trek back to the Swift.

Athgar forced himself to sit upright, looking for Natalia. It took him to a moment to note her absence, and then he spotted her, lying, like him, in the bottom of the skiff, her face covered in blood that still flowed from her nose. He crawled towards her, heedless of the rowers, to sit beside her, cradling her head in his hands, wiping the blood away as best he could.

He could hear the creak of the oars as they rowed, pulling them closer to the Swift and worried that it might already be too late for the pale woman who lay at death's door.

"Stay with me!" he urged, though whether she heard him or not, he couldn't say. Finally, the oars were shipped, and the skiff nudged up against the side of the Swift.

The survivors climbed up to the deck, helped by a knotted rope that was lowered from above. Once safely aboard, they turned their attention to Natalia. They had thought to somehow lift her to the deck, but, unsure of her condition, they felt it wiser not to. Instead, they attached ropes and raised the skiff. Athgar remained in the tiny boat as they did so, feeling the swaying motion as the ropes hauled them aboard. Once there, it was a relatively simple matter to get her below, to bed.

Natalia's eyes finally fluttered open.

"She's awake," came Athgar's voice.

A face loomed over her, and she felt fingers force her eyes open farther. "She looks much better," came Brother Cyric's voice.

She felt the warmth of a hand on hers, a caressing touch. She glanced over to see the Therengian, a look of concern on his face.

"You had us worried," Athgar said. "We were afraid you'd overdone it."

"That was a remarkable feat," said Cyric. "I would never have thought it possible."

Natalia squeezed the hand. "I'm so happy you're safe, Athgar," she said, "I was terrified for you."

"It appears I was the one that should have been worried. You scared me to death, Natalia. I told you to have more control over your magic."

"Thank the Saints she didn't," observed Cyric, "or you might not be here to scold her."

The Temple Knight felt her forehead.

"How is she?" asked Athgar.

"She'll make a full recovery," he pronounced, "but she'll need a day or two of rest." He sat back. "Remarkable, the both of you. I've never seen such a display of bravery. You truly are sent by the Saints."

Athgar snorted, "Don't you mean the Gods?"

Cyric grinned. "Whichever way you like," he said, "I will not argue the specifics. Where did you learn to swim? I didn't take you as someone who liked the water."

"We swam in the river back home all the time, though I must admit that's my first time in the sea."

"And how did you like it?" asked Cyric.

"Let's just say I'm not in a hurry to repeat the experience," said Athgar.

Cyric laughed, "I can't say I disagree with you. Now," he turned back to Natalia, "I'll let you get some rest, though I rather suspect it will be hard to get this Therengian to leave your side."

Natalia smiled, even though she was weak, "Nor would I want him to. He's my Therengian, and I prefer him close." She squeezed his hand again for reassurance.

Cyric rose, banging his head on the deck overhead. "Saint's sake!" he called out.

Athgar burst out laughing as the knight turned to look at him in disbelief. "I'm sorry, Brother Cyric," the Therengian said, "but the look on your face was priceless."

Cyric rubbed the top of his head. "I must remember to wear my helmet when below decks," he said, "these damned ships are far too cramped for me. Are all the crewmen short?"

Natalia laughed, Athgar's mirth infectious. "Sorry, Brother Cyric," she said at last, "we mean no disrespect."

"None taken," the Temple Knight replied. "Now, after all we've been through, I think you can just call me Cyric. How does that sound?"

"Agreed," said Athgar, extending his hand. "Thank you, Cyric."

"You're quite welcome, my pyromantic friend."

"Where did you learn your healing?" asked Athgar. "You seem to know your business."

"It's part of my training. All the Brothers of Saint Mathew are competent in the healing arts. It would be handy if we could use magic, but alas, there is little of it to go around."

"Do you know Brother Ambrose?" asked Athgar. "I only ask because he helped me after I was injured in Draybourne."

"The name is not familiar, but we are a large order," said Cyric. "Though, if I ever do run across him, I'll be sure to give him your regards. Now, I think it's time I went up on deck, I certainly don't want to hit my head again. You two come and see me when Natalia here, is feeling better. I've been thinking about this search of yours, and I may have some ideas."

Natalia sat up, suddenly regretting her impulse. Her head ached as if someone was hitting her with a club, and she quickly lay back down.

Athgar smiled, even as Natalia grimaced. "Yes," he said, "we'll come and see you once our Water Mage has followed your advice and rested."

Cyric turned to leave but was halted by Natalia's next words.

"Wait," she called out, "what happened to the woman that Athgar pulled from the sea?"

"She's resting," replied Cyric, "only a little the worse for wear. She was exhausted, much like Athgar here. I suspect she'll sleep the night away, though I'm sure she'll want to thank the two of you come morning."

"Who is she?" Natalia asked.

"I have no idea," the knight replied. "She had passed out by the time you returned in the skiff, but her clothes would appear to indicate someone of means. It seems this voyage has just become even more interesting."

"You're enjoying this far too much," observed Athgar.

"Perhaps I am," the brother confessed, "but life in the order can often become dull and repetitive."

"Is that why you like to investigate things?" asked the Therengian.

Cyric grinned. "I go where I'm needed," he said, "and if that happens to allow me to learn new things, so much the better. Now, I'd best be off and allow you two to rest."

He made his way to the ladder, climbing up to the deck above.

Natalia was determined to get some fresh air. She opened the hatch to see a clear sky above, the distant sound of birds coming to her ears. Climbing up, she felt the warm planks on her bare feet, a sure sign that the sun had been out for some time.

Athgar was on the starboard side, looking out across the water, standing beside the woman he had plucked from the sea.

Natalia made her way over to them, walking slowly to avoid any sudden movements for the sake of her head.

At the sound of her footfalls, Athgar turned, a smile coming to his lips. "Good to see you up and around," he said. "How's the head?"

"Still a little sore," she confessed, "though much better than yesterday."

"Good morning," the woman said, "I don't think we've been introduced, my name is Arabel Calderra."

"Pleased to meet you. My name's Natalia, and I assume you've met Athgar?"

"I have," the woman confessed. "If it hadn't been for him, I'd have drowned."

"It was Natalia that allowed me to help," admitted the Therengian. "If it hadn't been for her magic, I'd have drowned alongside you."

"You're a mage?" asked Arabel.

"I am," Natalia replied. "You're lucky we were passing by."

"You must let me thank you," said the woman. "I'm told you're travelling to Corassus, you must allow me to host you. I've an estate that I think you'd enjoy."

"That's most gracious of you," said Natalia, then cast her eyes to Athgar, who merely nodded slightly, "we'd be delighted. How did you come to be on the Teeth?"

"We were on our way back to Corassus," the woman replied, "when the wind shifted rather unexpectedly, pushing us near to the Teeth. I'm afraid our captain wasn't the most competent of sailors, and once we were close, the current took us, pulling us into the rocks."

"Unfortunate," said Natalia. "Was the captain among the survivors?"

"I'm afraid not," Arabel responded. "He was washed overboard, much like me." She swept her gaze over the side of the ship to watch the surface of the water as they sailed past, lapsing into silence.

"You mentioned an estate," remarked Natalia. "I take it your family is influential?"

"You might say that," the woman responded. "I hold a seat on the ruling council."

"Ruling council?" said Athgar. "I assume they advise the duke?"

"No," Arabel replied, "there is no duke, in fact, there's no nobility at all, in the traditional sense. The city is ruled by a council of influential people."

"A strange system, from the sounds of it," offered Athgar. "How does that work?"

"The city was founded by merchants," she began, "the most powerful of which make the decisions that govern the city. It's a city-state, much like Ilea to the west."

"Never heard of that place, either," confessed Athgar, "though I must admit to not having travelled much."

"And yet you make the long trip to Corassus," said Arabel. "I rather suspect you have a good reason for travelling there, to pull you so far from your home."

"Has Athgar not told you already?" asked Natalia.

"No," Arabel replied, "he has not. In fact, he's been remarkably close-mouthed on the subject."

"That's my fault, I'm afraid," said Natalia, "the truth is we're travelling there to consult the Great Archives. I'm looking for my family."

"Well, that's fascinating," said Arabel. "What's your family name? Perhaps I've heard of them."

"I doubt it," said Natalia, "they weren't anyone of import, as far as I'm aware." She could sense the woman's interest and decided it was best to abandon the conversation. "Athgar, would you help me? I think I need to go and lie down again, my head is throbbing."

"Of course," he replied. Taking Natalia's arm, he escorted her to the hatch and then climbed down ahead of her. Pausing at the bottom, he guided her down, then walked her to their room.

"What was that all about?" he asked.

"Something tells me we shouldn't mention the Cunars to her," she said.

"Why not?"

"If she's a member of this ruling council she spoke of, it's likely she has close connections with the Church."

"I don't see your logic," he said.

"Well," Natalia mused, "I doubt a Cunar fortress could exist without the approval of the ruling council, do you?"

"I suppose I can see what you mean," he confessed, "best if we keep off the topic in future. I'll have a word with Cyric."

"Good idea," she said. "In the meantime, we'll stay nice and friendly with her, she might prove to be a valuable source of information."

"All right," Athgar agreed. "Now, you should lie down if your head is bothering you."

She looked at him with a smile that soon turned into a wicked grin, "My head is fine. I just needed an excuse to get you alone."

His look of concern was wiped from his face, to immediately be replaced with a smile. "You never need an excuse to get me alone."

"I was hoping you'd say that," she said.

PIRATES

AUTUMN 1103 SR

A thgar looked across the deck to Captain Runell. The old sailor was using a peculiar, brass coloured instrument to look skyward, no doubt plotting their position. The Therengian, wondering what strange magic the object might possess, decided to wander over and make an enquiry.

"Are we close to Corassus?" Athgar asked.

The captain, his observations complete, lowered the instrument. "Indeed we are," he said. "At this rate, we'll be anchored in the bay in another two days. Have you been to Corassus before?"

"No," replied Athgar, "never. Why do you ask?"

"The city can be a tricky place to navigate," the captain explained. "The streets are convoluted and can be dangerous at night."

"Surely they have guards patrolling?"

In answer, Captain Runell barked out a laugh, "That would cost money, and the city council is far more concerned with generating profit."

"What happens when there's trouble?" asked Athgar.

"That's simple," the captain responded, "they rely on the Temple Knights to keep the peace, but they're usually only around during daylight hours when the merchants are open. Corassus is not a place to wander in the dark, I'm afraid."

"I'll keep that in mind," said the Therengian.

Captain Runell looked back towards the aft end of the ship, then took a finger, wet it in his mouth, held it before him, cursing.

"What's the matter?" asked Athgar.

"It's this damn wind, it's waning. We're about to have a dry spell."

"Meaning?"

"Meaning the wind will die to nothing," said Runell, "and the Swift will find itself becalmed."

"Surely it will pick up again?" said Athgar.

"Eventually," the captain assured him, "but we could be like this for quite a while, perhaps even till nightfall. This part of the world is notorious for its fickle winds."

"What can we do about it?" asked Athgar.

"You can go and fetch that Water Mage of yours," replied the captain. "With any luck, she'll be able to keep us moving."

"I didn't know Water Mages could call the wind," said the Therengian.

"They can't, but she should be able to manipulate the currents, at least that way we won't be sitting here, helpless."

"You're worried about pirates, aren't you?" said Athgar.

"I am," acknowledged the captain. "They're common in this area. They lair in the cliffs, you see."

Athgar looked at him in surprise. "How do they lair in the cliffs?"

"The shoreline actually consists of numerous inlets and caves," answered Runell. "They hide in them, moving out to attack unwary travellers."

"Like us?"

"Yes, if we stand still."

"I'll go and fetch Natalia," said Athgar, making his way to the hatch. He disappeared below decks, emerging sometime later with the Water Mage just behind him.

She walked to the port side of the ship, looking over the railing at the water below. Moments later, she repeated the action, this time on the starboard side.

"What are you doing?" asked Athgar. "Can't you just use your spell to move us?"

"It's not as simple as that," she responded. "There must be room on either side."

"Room for what?" he asked.

"For the currents," she replied, moving back to the centre of the boat.

"I thought the currents just pushed us along?"

"And where, do you suppose, these currents would come from?" Natalia asked.

"I assume from behind us," he responded, "where else?"

"I can't just pull currents from the middle of nowhere," she explained. "When water moves, other water fills in behind. I'd have to affect water for hundreds of miles to make that work."

"Then where does it come from?" Athgar asked.

"Either side of the ship," she said. "If you imagine a whirlpool and then you drop a stick into the outside of it, what would happen?"

"The stick would be pushed along the outside of the whirlpool, wouldn't it?"

"Precisely," she continued. "So what happens is that I create two small whirlpools, moving in opposite directions to each other, placed so that our ship is directly between them. The edge of each will push us forward, but the displaced water will be replaced by the other water swirling around each pool."

"So if anyone was on the other side of the whirlpools, they'd be pushed backward?"

"Relative to us, yes," Natalia agreed. "But don't expect to see an actual whirlpool, it's really just a swirling current."

"I assume those circular currents will move along with us?" he asked.

"Of course, or else they'd be next to useless."

"Just how fast will it move us?" asked Athgar.

"I can't say for sure," she explained. "There are too many variables, that's where experience would come in handy. The smaller the ship, the faster I would be able to propel it. With a ship the size of the Swift, I rather expect we'll be moving at a sedate pace."

"Sedate?" he asked.

"Yes," she replied, "about the speed of a slow walk."

"Will that be enough to keep the pirates at bay?" Athgar asked.

"I doubt it," she replied, "so keep your eyes open for danger."

"How much energy are you going to need?" Athgar said. "I only ask because last time you exerted yourself, you ran into problems."

"It'll take more than calming a storm," she said, "but my energy has returned, I should be fine."

"Should be?" he balked. "You're not filling me with confidence."

Natalia smiled, trying to lessen his concern. "I'll be fine," she assured him, then looked along the deck, waiting for the captain to acknowledge her presence. "You should lower the sail," she said to him, "or it will hamper our progress."

Captain Runell barked out orders, and the crew scrambled up the rigging. After years of sailing together, they were quite efficient. Soon, the long canvas was rolled up and stowed along the yardarm.

"Whenever you're ready," called out the captain.

Natalia nodded, placing herself just in front of the mainmast, facing the bow of the ship. She started the incantation, and the hair on the back of Athgar's neck stood on end briefly. As her litany halted, Athgar looked at her, noting the perspiration on her forehead.

"It's done," she announced.

"Are you sure it's working?" he asked. "I don't notice any difference." He moved to the aft end of the ship, peering down to see the small wake they were leaving behind them. "It worked," he remarked.

"Naturally," she said, "did you doubt it would?"

"A useful spell," observed Athgar, "far more useful, it seems, than my fire. Perhaps I learned the wrong school of magic."

"It might seem that way at present," she said, "but the sea is my element. No doubt once we're in Corassus, it'll be your magic that sees more use."

"I somehow doubt that," he observed, "it's not like I'll be wandering about the city starting fires."

The day wore on without a change in the wind, the Swift only managing a slow forward motion even with Natalia's magic, but at least it was progress.

Athgar peered south, across the Inner Sea, but naught could be seen of any distant shore, just gently rolling waves and the reflection of the bright sunlight as it bounced off the occasional crest.

A cry from the crow's nest caught his attention. Looking up, he saw the crewman pointing northwest along the distant shoreline.

Athgar rushed across the deck, the better to clear his field of view, and spied the target off in the distance, two galleys, their oars out, ploughing through the waves with synchronized precision. They were still quite some distance away, but there could be no doubt that they would catch the Swift, hampered as she was in this sea bereft of wind.

Athgar made his way below decks, retrieving his axe and waking Natalia, who had taken a nap in the afternoon. The drain of casting her spell over and over, to keep them moving, was wearing her out, though she stoically refuted the allegation.

She opened her eyes as he was tucking the axe into his belt.

"What is it?" she asked.

"Pirates," he replied, "though they're some distance off at the moment. They won't be in range for some time yet."

"I'm coming up on deck," Natalia said, "I may be needed." She rose, throwing on a dress.

Athgar waited, watching as she tied her footwear. "I can't understand your fascination with shoes," he said, "surely boots are better suited to travel."

"Never underestimate the value of a comfortable pair of shoes," she said in her defence, "and anyway, we're aboard a ship, not traipsing through the wilderness. Can you honestly tell me boots are better here?"

"I hadn't thought of it like that," he replied, "but I suppose you're right. Are you ready to go up on deck?"

"As ready as I'll ever be," she responded. "And you?"

"All set," he said.

They made their way up, to find Brother Cyric already present, fully armed and armoured.

Athgar marvelled at the Temple Knight's mail. "Impressive armour, Cyric," he said.

"Thank you," said the Temple Knight, "though to be honest, it's quite archaic."

"Archaic?" said Athgar. "Why would you say that?"

"Full plate armour is all the rage these days."

"Then I'm surprised that's not what you're wearing," stated Natalia.

"My order wears chainmail to symbolize its humility," the brother said, "but the other orders all wear plate." Cyric turned to the captain, "What do you see, Harnen?"

"Two galleys," the man responded. "Now that they're closer, we've a better idea of what we're up against. They're ahead of us, on an intercept course."

"Can we outrun them?" asked Cyric.

"'Fraid not," said Runell. "Their rowing is faster than our Water Mage's spell, but it will take some time for them to get close enough to threaten us."

"How will they attack?" asked Athgar.

"If you look closely at their ships," said Runell, "you'll see a ballista mounted on each of their foredecks. They'll likely fire a grappling hook at us when they're close enough, then winch us in tight to them. Once they've done that, it'll be hand to hand. They'll want the ship intact so they can make off with its cargo."

"What is our cargo?" asked Natalia.

"Aside from you," said the captain, "just grain intended for the Temple Knights' horses in Corassus."

"Meagre pickings for pirates," mused Athgar.

"Hey now," said Natalia, "I resent that."

"Well," corrected the Therengian, "aside from you, there's little of value."

"Thank you, that's much better," she added.

"You've sailed these waters before, Harnen," said Cyric. "What kind of numbers are you expecting?"

In answer, Captain Runell looked to the enemy vessels that were drawing closer. "I would think no more than two dozen per ship, each eager for plunder."

"I would have said more," offered Athgar. "It must take close to a hundred men just to crew those oars."

"More like fifty," said Cyric, "but they'll be slaves, not pirates. These ships are not unlike those of the Temple fleet in Corassus."

"Are you suggesting they've captured church ships?" asked Natalia.

"No," said Cyric, "but the design is similar. In the temple fleet, each oar is manned by a Temple Knight. Be thankful that is not the case here."

"How are you at fighting?" asked Harnen, looking to Brother Cyric.

"I'm a Temple Knight," he responded, "trained to fight."

"And you?" asked the captain, looking at Athgar.

"I was trained in the Fyrd," the Therengian replied.

"What's a Fyrd?" asked Runell.

"A local militia," Athgar replied. "It dates back to the last years of Therengia. Every man and woman of age had to train in axe and spear. It's a tradition that was handed down to us. How about your own men?"

"They can handle themselves in a brawl," said the captain, "but they'll be sorely outmatched by those pirates."

"Then we'll have to stop them before they can grapple us," suggested Natalia.

"How do you propose we do that?" asked Runell. "They're faster than us by a significant degree."

Natalia smiled, "I have a few ideas, but they'll have to come within my casting range to carry them out."

"I don't know what your casting range is," offered the captain, "but they'll likely have bows."

The Water Mage's face fell slightly at the news. "That's bad," she remarked, "I can't cast if they're shooting at me."

"I'll just have to keep them distracted for you," said Athgar. "I'm pretty sure they'll ignore you if I'm lobbing fire at them."

"Yes," agreed the captain, "fire is the biggest fear of any sailor."

The afternoon stretched on, the two pirate galleys approaching unhurriedly as if the entire battle would unfold in slow motion. As evening began to fall, they could finally make out the man working the ballista, readying the weapon for use by loading up a giant grappling hook, a thin rope coiled on the deck attached to its head. Even as they watched, he completed his task, then swivelled the weapon, aiming it at the Swift.

"He won't fire yet," offered Runell, "they're still out of range, but their archers are starting to take up positions."

The Swift was set to meet the enemy head-on. Athgar stood on the foredeck, watching their approach. "Time to get their attention, I should say," he offered. He reached deep inside, bringing forth his inner flame. As he gesticulated, a streak of fire raced across the gap, falling just short of the enemy galley, striking the surface of the water to cause a jet of steam to erupt, quickly dissipating into the air.

In answer, the enemy vessels changed course slightly, the archers rushing to the bow.

"Any moment now," said Runell.

Natalia, standing to the right of Athgar, began her spell. The air crackled, and then a sudden chill surrounded her as she unleashed her power, a faint blue light racing across the distance, hitting the water directly in front of the lead galley.

The pirate crew jeered at the apparent miss, but where the light had impacted, ice began to form, starting as a thin layer of frost and then expanding to thicken and harden, growing more opaque as it widened. Soon, there was a man-sized chunk of ice, the majority of it below the surface, but it kept spreading, gradually expanding till it was easily twice as large as the galley.

Athgar was reminded of the ice that had saved him near the Teeth, but this time she had concentrated in one area, directly in front of the first vessel.

The Swift was close enough that they could hear yelling as the pirate crew began to realize the danger they were in. The prow of the ship struck the ice, emitting a crunching and scraping noise that echoed across the intervening water. Athgar watched as many of the pirates on the enemy deck flew forward, and at least one of the archers fell overboard, landing heavily onto the ice.

The second galley, following behind the first, but off to one side, now moved into the lead, its rowers working in unison. Runell barked out a command, and his crew leaped to the ropes. The Swift began a slow turn, from northwest to southwest, turning its flanks to the approaching enemy.

The catapult on this new enemy looked different, and Athgar watched as someone lit the end of the giant bolt. A moment later, there was a twang, and the projectile sailed through the air, ripping through the Swift's sail, setting it alight. The boatswain called out in alarm, but Athgar moved swiftly, invoking his magic to extinguish the flame.

Natalia repeated her spell, but her aim was off. Ice formed on the surface of the water, but the nimble enemy adjusted their direction and sailed past it. The pirates on their deck cheered as they drew closer, crowding the railing with grappling hooks in hand as the second galley approached.

Runell turned the ship once more, forcing the enemy to adjust their trajectory. The galley was now coming at them head-on, aimed directly towards the middle of the Swift.

Athgar fired off a streak of flame, but it missed the target, landing harmlessly beyond. "Gods!" he yelled in frustration.

The ballista was being turned in his direction, and he concentrated, calling forth his spark. This time, instead of a streak of flame, he set the enemy weapon alight. Flames licked from the wooden arms of the machine, and then the operator jumped back in alarm.

The first galley, still off in the distance, had taken control of the situation with their men clambering down onto the ice and were attempting to free themselves with axes. The second, however, was almost close enough to touch.

Natalia called forth more ice, this time targeting the bow of the nearest galley. They all watched as frost formed where the hull met the water, and then ice starting spreading out. The enemy vessel immediately slowed, letting the Swift pull ahead of them.

Athgar and Natalia ran to the rear of their ship and watched as the galley fell behind. An archer climbed down onto the ice, bow in hand, and lined up a shot. Natalia sent forth shards of ice, striking the man in the chest and knocking him back, leaving a red smear.

The enemy ship floated past, locked in the ice, and Athgar pulled forth more of his magic. Fed by the burning ballista, he called forth thick black smoke to obscure the pirate's vision. The enemy vessel was soon engulfed, making any ranged fire impossible.

The Swift, now clear of the enemy, turned once more to resume its journey.

Captain Runell joined them on the aft deck. "That was well done," he said, "I'm glad they didn't have mages like you."

"It was our pleasure," said Natalia.

"Much as I'm thankful," said the captain, "I'm wondering why you didn't just set the whole ship on fire."

"There are slaves aboard," said Athgar, "I'll not sentence all of them to a fiery death."

Captain Runell nodded his head in understanding, "A good point, and one I'd forgotten. It seems you're well suited to this line of work. You can sail aboard my ship anytime you like."

"Thank you," said Athgar, "I appreciate it."

Brother Cyric came forward to congratulate them. "It seems my skill at arms was not needed this day, I thank the both of you."

"I would have thought you'd be eager to come to grips with them," suggested Athgar.

"No," said Cyric, "though I can fight, I do not take pleasure in taking the life of a man. Your solution was much more...elegant."

CORASSUS

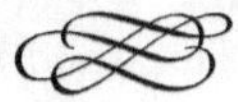

AUTUMN 1103 SR

Athgar gazed across the bay to the fortress that lay beyond.

"Impressive, isn't it?" said Cyric.

"I've never seen anything so large," said Athgar, "but then again, I hadn't seen a city until this year. Tell me, are all castles so large?"

Cyric barked out a laugh, "No, this is one of the largest ones, but you have to realize how many people it holds. There are close to a thousand Temple Knights living there."

"That many?" asked the Therengian. "I had no idea. How am I to find one man among so many?"

"You must take things one step at a time," suggested Cyric. "Get settled into Corassus first, then learn the layout of the city. A plan may come to you in due course, but in the meantime, I shall make some discreet enquiries and see where they lead."

"Thank you," said Athgar, "I appreciate the help. Will you be staying at the fortress?"

"Saints, no," said Cyric, "my place will be at the mission."

"The mission? What's that?"

"It's a large structure down in the poorer section of town. I believe it used to be a place of worship long ago."

"A church?"

"Not to my religion," Cyric continued, "but I believe your people might feel at home there."

"Why would you choose that as a place of operation?"

"It was the only building available in the area. The Brothers of Saint

Mathew tend to the poor and sick, what better place to find them than the slums."

"I don't envy you your job," offered Athgar.

"It is not a job," corrected Cyric, "it's a calling. We are carrying out the will of Saint Mathew."

"I wish you well, and I promise we'll come and visit you once we're settled in."

"I look forward to it," said Cyric. "Where's Natalia?"

"She's helping Lady Arabel. I'm afraid our benefactor had little spare clothing, so Natalia's offered some of hers. I expect they're still altering them."

"They'd best be quick about it," offered the Temple Knight, "we'll be anchoring soon."

"Out here?"

"Oh, yes, only the large merchant houses are allowed space on the wharf. The rest must ferry their cargo and passengers by ship's boat."

"It seems a very unusual situation," observed Athgar.

"You have to understand," said Cyric, "the great merchant houses built the whole dockyard. It's only proper that they should get priority."

"But at the expense of all the others? That hardly seems fair."

"Life is not about fairness," offered Cyric, "in fact, it can often be quite harsh. We must learn to accept whatever comes our way."

"An interesting statement," said Athgar, "and one which, coming from anyone else, I would have taken as insulting, but you actually practice what you preach. I find it strange that we should get along."

"Why so?"

"Well," said Athgar, "I worship the old Gods while you worship the Saints. That, in itself, would suggest otherwise."

"You forget," said Cyric, "that the Saints teach us to get along with our neighbours, living in peace and harmony."

"A notion I admire," said Athgar, "and yet I cannot offer forgiveness for those that attacked my village."

"The Saints will not blame you for that. They understand people far better than you might think. Even the real world must be understood. I know the Church wants peace, but we all feel it inevitable that war will come. The Halvarians crave it, and the Petty Kingdoms are growing frustrated with the great Empire's expansion at their expense."

"How long, do you think, before war breaks out?"

"A year or two, not much more," offered Cyric, "so you should enjoy the peace while it lasts, chances are the next war will engulf the entire continent." He lapsed into silence.

Athgar looked out at the city. It was hard to imagine the scale of war that Cyric was talking about, and he, too, remained silent as he contemplated the concept.

Captain Runell yelled out commands to his crew. They both watched as the ship's skiff was lowered over the side.

"I fear our time together is at an end this day," said Cyric, "for I must get ashore and report to my superiors."

"Aren't we going as well?" asked Athgar.

"Eventually," said Cyric, "but Lady Arabel asked me to deliver a message for her. By the time she's ready to disembark, there should be a carriage waiting for all of you. I believe you were going to stay at her estate?"

"Yes," said Athgar, "why do you ask?"

"I'll need to locate you if I find anything," said Cyric. "In the meantime, give my respects to Natalia. I look forward to seeing you both again sometime soon."

"I will," promised the Therengian.

Cyric made his way to the side of the ship. Athgar watched as the Temple Knight clambered down into the skiff. Moments later, the crew put their backs to the oars, and the little vessel started rowing towards the docks.

Natalia gave the hem one final tug. "That should do, I think."

Lady Arabel looked down, twirling slightly to send the dress spinning. "Excellent," she said, "you've done a marvellous job. It's so nice to get out of that dress I was wearing."

"Shall we go up on deck?" asked Natalia.

"Of course," the lady responded, "no doubt you're eager to see that young man of yours."

Natalia blushed, "Yes, Lady Calderra."

"Well, then," the lady continued, "let us delay no longer."

She made her way to the steps. They were in the aft section of the Swift, much further back than Natalia and Athgar's room. The steps here, were far more gradual, and therefore, easier to climb.

Lady Arabel stepped out onto the deck, pausing a moment to let the warmth of the sun heat her face. Natalia exited shortly thereafter, a smile coming to her lips as she spied Athgar.

"How long have you been up here?" she asked.

"Long enough to say goodbye to Cyric," replied the Therengian. "He sends his regards, but had to report to his superior."

"I'm sorry I missed him," mused Natalia.

"How long ago did he leave?" asked Lady Arabel.

"Some time ago. He's already made the dock, and the skiff is returning."

"Lady Calderra," called out the captain. They all turned at his approach.

"May I say," continued Captain Runell, "that it's been an absolute pleasure having you aboard."

"Thank you, Captain," she replied, "you've been most gracious. I shall remember your kindness."

The captain bowed his head in acknowledgement. "And you two," he said, shifting his gaze to Natalia and Athgar, "we wouldn't have made it if not for your efforts." He handed a small bag to Natalia. "Your fee," he said, "you earned every bit of it. I even added some extra coin, for the Fire Mage."

"You didn't need to do that," objected Athgar.

Captain Runell raised his hand to silence the objection. "No, no, I must insist. I've never seen such bravery before, and I've sailed waters you can only dream about. Good luck to you both, I hope you find what you're looking for."

"Thank you, Captain," said Athgar, extending his hand.

Runell shook it with a firm grip. Natalia moved closer, giving the man a hug. The old sailor blushed but returned it.

"You'll have to excuse me now," he said in a gruff voice, "I've work to do."

They watched him go. No sooner had he crossed the deck than the boatswain called them over. The skiff was ready to be loaded, so they climbed down the side of the Swift, settling in amongst the rowers.

Lady Arabel sat in the bow, looking to the distant shore, but Athgar watched the Swift as they moved across the harbour.

"Are you going to miss it?" asked Natalia.

He turned to look at her, "It was an interesting experience and one I'll not soon forget, but I'll be glad to put my feet back on solid ground. You?"

"I'd be lying if I said no," she confessed, "but I'm looking forward to spending some time alone with you. The ship was a little crowded, after all."

"Agreed," he said, "and they don't have baths."

His statement brought a chuckle from the rowers, and he looked about, suddenly remembering they weren't alone. He blushed furiously, but Natalia just smiled.

They sat in silence the rest of the way, the oars dipping into the cool water of the harbour, but making little noise.

Soon, there was a slight bump as the oars were shipped and then the boatswain leaped to the dock, tying down the little skiff with a rope.

"All secure," the man said. "Would you like a hand, my lady?"

Arabel took the proffered hand and was half lifted, half climbed to the dock. She straightened her dress, looking around, then waved as she saw the approaching carriage.

Athgar jumped onto the dock, then held his hand out for Natalia. She took it, pulling herself up, but kept her hold on him, drawing him into a kiss.

"What was that for?" he asked.

"Do I need a reason to kiss you?" she said. "Now, let's get aboard that carriage, shall we? I can't wait to see Lady Arabel's estate."

The carriage rolled through the city, the wheels clacking as they struck the cobblestones. Natalia and Arabel were deep in conversation, but Athgar's attention was pulled to the streets of the city. They were wide, far wider than Draybourne, and packed with people. As they travelled farther from the docks, the streets narrowed, and he noted more greenery when they entered the wealthier section of town. More than once he saw Temple Knights, their dark grey tabards marking them as Brothers of Saint Cunar. They typically rode about the city on large horses, their armour glinting in the sun. He wanted to shout out at them but realized it would do no good. Somewhere in this city, he thought, the man with the scar waited for him. He had no proof, of course, merely an intuition, but he was convinced of it.

The carriage went through a gate and then rolled to a halt. Two men ran forward, opening the door, a well-dressed servant poking his head inside.

"Lady Arabel," he said, "so nice to see you safely returned to us."

"Thank you, Corban," she said, "it's so good to be home. These are a couple of guests that will be staying with me awhile."

"Very good, Madame," the man replied, stepping back and waiting as Lady Arabel Calderra exited the carriage.

"I think we shall have drinks in the garden," she said.

"Yes, Madame," Corban said, looking around the carriage as if expecting something.

"There's no luggage," said Arabel, "it was lost at sea."

"Lost at sea, Madame? You appear to have had quite the adventure."

"I have indeed," she admitted. "This is Natalia," she said, pointing at the girl, "and this young man is Athgar. He pulled me from the sea."

"Fortunate that he was there, then," the man said. "Shall I show your guests to their rooms?"

"I think drinks are in order first. I'm afraid Captain Runell had an unso-phisticated palette when it came to alcohol. A bottle of our finest, if you will."

"Yes, ma'am," the man said, scurrying into the house.

Athgar and Natalia followed the mistress of the estate through an immense foyer. It was tall, with a balcony looking down upon it, and Athgar wondered why such a large room was necessary.

They exited out the back of the building to an expansive green area, lush with neatly trimmed grass, along with trees to provide shade. There was even an artificial pool here, its clear water standing in stark contrast to the sea they had become used to.

Arabel sat down on a comfortable looking chair, and with a sweep of her arms, indicated they should do likewise.

"Now," she said, "Corban will bring us drinks, and if I know him, a little food. While we're waiting, why don't you tell me what your plans are."

"I was hoping to visit the archives," offered Natalia, the lie coming quickly to her lips.

"Yes, you mentioned that previously. Tell me, what do you hope to find? I know you're looking for family, but I'm not sure how the archives will help you. Is your family powerful?"

"Yes," said Natalia, "the line goes back for hundreds of years. At one time they were quite influential, or so I'm told."

"What's the family name?" the woman asked. "Perhaps I've heard of them?"

Natalia looked uncomfortable, so Athgar spoke. "Sartellian," he said, picking a name from memory.

"Sartellian?" replied Lady Calderra. "Surely you jest, everyone knows that name."

"Natalia was raised in the countryside," offered Athgar, now regretting his choice. "She knows little of such things. What do you know of them? Anything you might be able to offer would be useful."

"The Sartellians are primarily Fire Mages if I'm not mistaken," offered Arabel. "I'm surprised to see a Water Mage among their numbers. I wasn't aware they employed such magic."

"It is rare," said Natalia, now recovered. "I'm more of a distant cousin. Are there any Sartellians here in Corassus?"

"Not that I'm aware of," said Arabel, "though I've been gone for several months. There's certainly none on the ruling council."

Natalia breathed a sigh of relief, and Athgar saw her visibly relax.

"These archives," Athgar said, "are they open to anyone?"

"Oh, yes," the woman replied, "though they demand a deposit for you to conduct research."

"A deposit?"

"Yes," she continued, "to make sure people don't steal anything. It wouldn't be much of an archive if there were nothing left inside."

"Reasonable enough," said Natalia.

"So what will you do," asked Arabel, "once you've visited the archives?"

"That depends on what we find," Natalia responded. She looked around the area, desperate to change the topic, the lie rapidly spinning out of control. "How did you make your wealth?" she asked.

"In shipping," said Arabel. "My ancestors started with a single boat. Over the years, they built a fleet of merchant vessels and then expanded into overland freight. We've been doing it for close to three centuries now."

"And are all the members of the council merchants?" asked Natalia.

"Most," the lady replied, "though at least one is a financier and another is a land baron."

"Is that a noble?" asked Athgar.

Arabel smiled, "No, merely a title. He made his money buying and selling land. He owns most of the farmland outside of the city. What is it you do, aside from rescuing damsels in distress, that is?"

"I'm a bowyer," he explained.

"How quaint," she replied. "What is that, precisely?"

"I make bows," he said, "for hunters and whatnot."

"Oh, yes," she said. "And what about you, Natalia, my dear. What do you do when you're not using magic?"

"I'm a professional mage," she said. "I hire onto boats to make their journeys safer."

"I see," the woman said, "though I might find it more believable if you called them ships."

"She primarily works on the rivers," added Athgar, hastily, "and most of them use the term 'boat'."

"Oh," said Arabel, "I hadn't thought of that. I must apologize, I thought I'd caught you in a lie."

"Apology accepted," said Natalia. "Now, if you don't mind, I think we should get some rest, it's been quite the voyage."

"So soon?" said their host. "We've only just arrived, we haven't even eaten yet."

"Yes, I'm afraid so," said Natalia. "Keeping spells going as we sail is quite taxing."

Athgar stood, "I'll see you to your room, shall I?"

"You mean our room," she corrected.

Athgar blushed.

"Oh," said Lady Arabel, "I hadn't realized you two were married."

"Oh yes," said Natalia, "for some months now, aren't we, my love?"

Athgar struggled not to choke, "Why, yes, my bondmate."

Natalia gave him a strange look. He shrugged, "Are you coming?"

She held out her hand. "Of course," she replied. He took it, walking her back inside the house. A servant met them, leading them to the guest rooms.

Natalia waited until they were alone to speak, "What was that all about?"

"What?" Athgar said, his face a mask of innocence.

"My bondmate? Where did you pull that one from?"

"The Orcs," he said. "Is it not an acceptable term?"

"No, it decidedly is not!" she fumed. "We're trying to avoid any unnecessary complications here. Couldn't you have thought of something better?"

"I'm sorry," he said, "but I have little experience in such matters."

Her face softened, along with her tone. "I know this is difficult, Athgar, but we must try to blend in as much as possible. We can't do that if you're going around using expressions like that. People don't talk that way."

"I would have been more prepared if you had warned me ahead of time," he accused. "Why did you have to say we were married?"

"So we could be housed in the same room. Is it not that way where you come from?"

"No, not really," he replied. "Of course, couples share a dwelling, but men and women don't have to be married to do so."

She looked at him in shock, "Oh, I hadn't realized."

"But," he said, "we aren't married, and we've been cohabiting. Are you ashamed of that?"

"No," she said, "of course not. I suppose I just became caught up in Lady Arabel's world, and I wanted to ensure we would be together."

"We'll always be together," he said. "That, I promise you!"

She sat on the bed, removing her shoes. "So what do we do now? I'm sure she's suspicious of us."

"Easy," he replied, "we rise early and leave the house for the day. Cyric suggested we get used to the layout of the city, that alone will likely take several days. He promised to make some discreet enquiries within the Church."

"Very well," she said. "In the meantime, we'll observe the Cunars. We need some idea of how they operate if we're to fight them."

"I thought you didn't like fighting?" he said.

"I don't," she replied, "but if a fight does come our way, I'd like to be prepared.

"Spoken like a true Therengian," he said.

She smiled, "Thank you, I'll take that as a compliment."

. . .

Natalia pulled back the heavy curtains, letting the early morning sunlight flood the room. A groan escaped the bed, and she looked back to see Athgar, blinking at the sudden brightness.

She moved across the room to sit by his side, her face close to his. "Come along, my love," she said, "it's time we were afoot. We've a whole city to explore, and a lady to avoid."

Athgar grumbled something unintelligible and rolled over. She placed her hand upon him, shaking him lightly. "Athgar," she gently scolded, "we must be off. You can't sleep the day away."

He rolled back to look up into her eyes. He was exhausted and was about to say so, but, seeing her loving gaze upon him, he knew she was right.

"What about food?" he muttered.

"We'll eat once we're clear of the estate," she answered, retrieving his clothes from the floor and tossing them onto the bed, then starting a search for his boots.

He sat up, pulling the tunic over his head, "How long have you been awake?"

"Quite a while," she admitted. "I've been trying to come up with a plan of how we're to proceed."

Athgar rose from the bed, then stooped to draw on his trousers. "The first step's easy," he declared.

"Oh?" Natalia responded. "What is it, then?"

"We go and eat," he replied, "my stomach's growling."

Natalia was now on the floor, looking under the bed. "Where did you put your boots?" she asked.

"On the chair," he said, "right beside the dress you were wearing last night."

"I don't recall wearing it for very long," she said, blushing slightly.

In answer, Athgar held out his hand, helping her rise. He kissed her, intending to continue, but then his stomach made a gurgling noise.

Natalia laughed, "We'd best get you to a tavern, my love, before your stomach wakes the dead." She moved to the chair, plucking the boots from their place of rest and tossing them to Athgar.

The Therengian caught them, then sat on the edge of the bed while he pulled them onto his feet. Moments later, he was standing again, looking in her direction, "All set?"

"One moment," she said, returning to stand in front of him. She ran her fingers through his hair, making it less of a rat's nest. "There we go, you're ready."

"How do we sneak out without alerting the servants?" he asked.

"I've already given it lots of thought," she said, then pointed. "The window."

The Green Serpent was a busy place, packed with early morning merchants, intent on their first drink of the day. Athgar and Natalia made their way into the crowded room to a small table. They placed their orders and then waited as the server scurried off to get their food.

Athgar looked around the room, "Such a busy place this early in the morning, I'm surprised."

"Why," asked Natalia, "didn't they have taverns back in your village?"

"No," he said, "though there was a great hall we would celebrate in."

"What was it called?" she asked.

"The great hall," he replied in all seriousness.

"No, I meant the village," she corrected.

"I know," he said, "I was just jesting."

"Was it very big?"

"Not by the standards of Corassus," he replied. "There were only a hundred or so of us left by the time the attack came."

"You say left, does that mean your people were dying off?"

"Yes," he admitted, "I'm told the village held many more people generations ago."

"What happened? Why the drop in population?"

"Our village had no healers," he said, "not Life Mages, at least. When people became sick or injured, there was little we could do except watch them wither and die."

"Couldn't you have sought outside help?"

"It was not our way," he said. "My people were stubborn in their beliefs. It was forbidden to marry outsiders."

Natalia looked at him in shock, "So your relationship with me..."

"Would have been forbidden, yes," he said. "Though I can see now how ridiculous that rule was. Without outsiders, we were doomed to dwindle, much like our kingdom."

"How awful for you," she commiserated. "Was life harsh?"

"Harsh?" he pondered. "It was just the way of things, I never knew any different. I suppose, looking back, it would be an accurate statement. What was your life like?"

"I was taken to the Volstrum at a very early age," she replied. "I was only ten when I first set foot there, and then I didn't leave until I made my way to Draybourne."

"Ah, yes, the Volstrum. Such a strange name. Didn't you say they trained mages there?"

"Yes," she responded, "though only those that practice the magic of water."

"So really, it was just a school."

"We prefer the term 'Academy', but yes, that would be an accurate description," she said.

"And the family that's seeking you, that's the staff of the academy?"

"Yes," she admitted. "I didn't want to burden you with details when we met, and I didn't really know if I could trust you, so I told you a half-truth."

"Do you trust me now?" he asked.

"With all my heart," she replied.

The server pushed her way through the crowd, depositing two plates before them, along with cups. Natalia had chosen some porridge and fruit, while Athgar's was piled high with meat.

"Now that's what I call a meal," he said, his mouth watering as he grabbed a slice of bacon and popped it in, then swore as he realized how hot it was. He quickly downed the drink the server had brought.

Natalia laughed at his display, "You'd think a Fire Mage, of all people, would be mindful of hot things."

Athgar wiped his mouth with his sleeve, then looked down at Natalia's meagre meal. "Is that what you used to eat at the Volstrum?"

"We had a wide variety of choices," she said, "but I grew accustomed to porridge. Did you have many choices growing up?"

"None, really," he replied. "Food was whatever was available. My whole life was arranged for me, really."

"How so?" she asked.

"I learned my father's trade and was told who I'd marry. My future was decided by others."

"You were engaged?" she asked.

"Yes, why, does that shock you?"

"No, but I just assumed you were...available. I wouldn't have started a relationship with you had I known you were taken."

"I'm not taken," he said. "I was promised at one time, but when I failed at the hunt, she was promised to another."

"Oh, I'm sorry."

"Don't be," he remarked, "it all worked out for the best."

"How so?" she asked.

"I met you!"

"You make it sound like a miracle," said Natalia.

"A miracle? No, but you're the best thing that's ever happened to me,

Natalia. I wouldn't have it any other way. All the trials I've been through have been worthwhile if only to find you."

She blushed. "I've never heard you so verbose," she said.

"Verbose?" he said, stiffening.

"Yes," she defended, "it means full of words. It's a good thing."

"Oh," he said, "sorry, I misunderstood. I'm but a dumb Therengian."

"You are one of the smartest people I know," she said, "you simply haven't had the education of others. Don't think for a moment you're not intelligent."

"I'm sorry," he said, "but back in Draybourne, they don't have much liking for my kind."

"Your kind? You mean Fire Mages?"

"No, I mean Therengians," he said.

"Why is that?" she asked.

"Centuries ago, Therengia was a large kingdom. The modern inhabitants of the region are the descendants of those that defeated us. It's their way of reminding us we are a conquered race. What of yourself? Did you ever suffer?"

"I was brought to the Volstrum as a peasant girl, and they never let me forget it. Low-born, I was called. When I was chosen to be a greater mage, there were many who objected. Only high-born's were supposed to be given that honour."

"What's a greater mage?" asked Athgar.

"Greater mages are those that perform magic in battles. Many people call them battle mages."

"Then what other types are there?

"Lesser mages," she continued. "They are taught to perform more rudimentary spells, but not those associated with battle. Things like creating water or purifying it."

"And so you were selected to be a battle mage, how interesting," he mused. He finally resumed his meal, picking carefully at another piece of bacon, and feeling it for temperature before popping it in his mouth.

"You learn quickly," she chuckled. "It's one of the things I like about you."

He chewed the meat, savouring the flavour, looking about the room as he did so, taking it all in. His gaze halted as he spotted something across the room.

"What's that?" he said, nodding his head in the direction.

She looked to the spot he indicated to see a notice board attached to the wall, just near the entrance, with small pieces of paper nailed to it. In their rush to eat, they had ignored it, but now, there was time to absorb it all.

"It's just a notice board," she replied.

"I don't understand," he said.

"People post notes there. I expect some of them are job opportunities or people trying to make contact with others."

"How do they do that?" he asked. "I don't see anyone standing around asking people for information.

"People leave notes," she said, "and then others can read them later when they have time."

"Oh," he said, blushing slightly as he turned his attention back to his meal.

Natalia, sensing his awkwardness, wouldn't let it rest. "Athgar, can you read?"

"Read?" he said in response. "No, I never learned. There was scant use for it back in Athelwald."

"Athelwald?" she repeated. "I take it that was your village."

"It was," he confirmed, "but no more, thanks to those filthy Cunars!" He hadn't intended to raise his voice, but his temper had gotten the better of him. People all around the room glared at him, a result of his outburst. He lowered his head in shame, staring down at his food.

Natalia reached across the table, placing her hand over his. "It's all right," she soothed, "we'll get to the bottom of this, I promise you."

"Yes," he said, his voice now quieter, "but how? We came all the way to Corassus on a whim, nothing more. I have no proof the Temple Knights are the slavers that attacked my village, only a gut instinct."

"It is a reasonable deduction," she said. "After all, who would dare imper-sonate a Temple Knight?"

"True," he admitted, "but there's no reason they would come to Corassus, is there?"

"I believe that's where you're wrong," said Natalia. "Think of all we've been through on this trip. Do you remember the pirates?"

"Of course," he replied, "I'm not stupid."

"I didn't mean to imply that you are," she retorted, "but think for a minute, what do we know about them?"

"They raid from the cliffs," he said. "What else is there to know?"

"Yes," she agreed, "but they use galleys."

The meaning of her words dawned on him. "Yes," he agreed, "with slaves to man them."

"And they must get those slaves from somewhere," suggested Natalia.

"The Church?" he posed.

"Possibly, though it's only speculation. The big question is, how do we prove it."

"That's easy," he suggested, "we find some of those slaves."

"And how do you suggest we do that?" she asked.

"We liberate them from a pirate ship!"

"We're not equipped to do that," she warned.

"No," Athgar replied, "but I have an idea. My understanding is that the shipping here is controlled by the big merchant companies. If I'm correct in my assumptions, their ships are seldom, if ever, attacked. The brunt of the attacks falls to the independent traders. Perhaps we can convince them to send out an expedition?"

"What makes you so sure the larger companies are complicit in this?" asked Natalia.

"Let's look at this from their point of view. The merchant houses control large numbers of ships. If they weren't involved, surely it would be in their best interest to eliminate the threat? Piracy would hurt all shipping, I would think."

"Maybe we should dig deeper," she suggested. "Perhaps someone at the Archives can tell us when the pirates first appeared?"

"Why would that be important?" Athgar asked. "I would imagine there's been pirates in these waters for centuries."

"Perhaps, but I have a suspicion that isn't the case."

"You're developing instincts," he remarked.

"I learned from the best," she quipped.

"It's a sound idea, but that still leaves us with the problem of where to begin?"

"That's easy," she said.

"It is?"

"Yes, we must visit the Great Archives."

THE ARCHIVES

AUTUMN 1103 SR

The Great Archives were considered to be the most extensive collection of knowledge in the southern kingdoms. Initially housed in a small building, it had grown over the years to become an immense sprawling complex that encompassed over three city blocks. It took the two of them quite some time to decide where to make their enquiries, for there seemed to be little thought put into its growth, and with no apparent central offices in which to make requests, they were at a loss where to start. They eventually settled on the oldest looking entrance, a stone structure with the date 134 SR inscribed over its doors.

They entered into an expansive foyer. Old frescoes decorated the walls while men sat around at tables, each examining a book, scroll, or map. A clerk made himself known as they entered, quickly crossing the distance to greet them.

"May I help you?" he asked.

"Yes," said Natalia, "we are here seeking information."

The man gave her a look of exasperation. "Of course you are," he sullenly replied. "Might you be more specific?"

"My husband has a fascination for pirates," she added. "Have you an expert in such things?"

"Madame," he said, "we have experts on many topics. Yes, as it happens, we do have an expert in your topic of interest, though I must warn you he tends to be difficult to work with."

"And who, precisely, is 'he'?" she asked.

"Tonfer Garul," the man replied.

"A strange name," remarked Natalia.

"For a strange person," the man said, cryptically. "Shall I show you to his area of study?"

"If you would be so kind," she said, opening her purse, "but I believe there's a deposit required?"

The man glanced at her in surprise, and Athgar noted the attention he paid to Natalia's ring.

"For one such as yourself, it is unnecessary," he simply said. "Now, will you follow me, please?"

"Of course," she said, then turned briefly to Athgar. "Ready?"

"Lead on," he added, "I can't wait to meet this Tonfer Garul."

To say that the office was some distance removed from the entrance would be an understatement. They traversed almost the entire length of the structure, then descended stairs to a lower level, continuing on in a most labyrinthine path to reach their destination, a rather old looking door with peeling paint.

"He's directly through there," their guide indicated. "Will that be all?"

"Yes," said Natalia, "thank you."

The man left in a hurry, leaving them to contemplate the door in front of them.

"What do you make of this?" asked Athgar.

"I would say this expert has very few visitors unless I miss my guess."

"I wonder why that is?"

"Well," she mused, "we'll never know if we don't enter."

"Agreed," said Athgar, gripping the doorknob and giving it a twist. The handle creaked, and when he tried to open the door, it seemed stuck. He put some weight into it, and the door finally squeaked open. A dim light flickered somewhere, casting shadows against the wall, but the room itself was filled with shelves that blocked the view to the far wall.

Athgar stepped in, calling out as he went, "Hello? Is anybody there?"

A distant shuffling sound greeted their ears as if someone or something had moved slightly, their boots scraping on the floor.

"Master Garul?" called out Natalia. "Are you here?"

A grunt echoed through the room, and then a voice called out, "Who's there?" in a deep baritone, the sound rough and coarse.

"My name is Athgar, and I'm with Natalia. Are you Tonfer Garul?"

"I am," the voice returned, "but I'm rather busy. Come back later."

"We've come a long way to see you," called out Natalia, "surely you could find time for us? I promise we won't keep you long."

"I'm busy," the voice reiterated.

There was something about the voice that struck a chord with Athgar.

Taking a moment to think it through, he then spoke. *"We come in friendship,"* he said, this time in the Orcish tongue.

"What did you say?" asked Natalia.

In answer, Athgar put his fingers to his lips.

The footsteps drew closer and then a rather bulky figure emerged from behind a bookshelf.

"How do you speak the language of my people?" he said, from beneath a hooded robe.

In answer, Athgar reached into his tunic, pulling the torc from beneath to reveal it.

"Ah," said the Orc, *"now I understand."* He quickly shifted to the common tongue of mankind, "My apologies, Orc friend. What brings you to my humble place of study?"

Natalia looked on in amazement as their host lowered the hood, revealing his green features.

"You're an Orc?" said Natalia, paling slightly.

Athgar took her hand, giving it a squeeze, "It's all right, Natalia, he's friendly. I'm sorry Tonfer, she's never seen an Orc before."

"Quite all right," the scholar replied, "I get that reaction all the time, though visitors seldom come to my domain."

"How is it that an Orc finds himself in these archives?" asked Athgar.

"Life is sometimes a strange collection of chance and circumstance," said Tonfer. He pointed at the torc, "What tribe gave that to you?"

"The Orcs of the Red Hand," said Athgar. "They taught me to harness the flame."

Tonfer bowed slightly, the action looking almost comical in one so bulky. "It is with great honour that I welcome you here. How fares the tribe?"

"Well, the last time I saw them," said Athgar, "and yourself?"

"I manage well enough," the scholar replied, "but where are my manners, come, sit down and I shall fetch us something to drink."

He led them farther into the room. It was clear that this area was in the deeper recesses of the archives, if only because of the shelves that were crammed with documents and books.

"I am afraid you'll have to excuse the mess," the Orc continued. "I am pretty much left to myself down here, and I must admit to being quite lacking in the area of cleanliness." He paused suddenly, turning to face them, "Not to say that I do not bathe, you understand, merely that I lack organizational skills." He turned back to continue his journey.

"Just down here," he pointed farther down the shelves, "is my work area. I have a few chairs around here somewhere." He pushed a stack of books onto the floor, revealing a rather comfortable, though dusty armchair. "There you are," he said, "I knew I'd find it if I moved a few things."

Athgar indicated that Natalia should take the chair while he remained standing.

"Now, what is it you wanted to see me about?" asked Tonfer.

"We're interested in pirates," said Athgar. "We were led to believe you're the expert in such matters."

"I am, among other things," the Orc replied. "Is there something in particular about them you would like to know?"

"We were wondering when the pirates started harassing the shipping in this area?"

"Ah, an interesting subject," the scholar said. "Of course piracy, in general, has been around since the dawn of man, but I assume you are referring to the Pirate Coast, in particular?"

"Yes," said Athgar.

"Let's see," said Tonfer, standing before a table heaped with books and papers. Digging through them, he produced a leather-bound tome that was held together by a thin strap. Undoing it, he opened the book to flip through the pages. "Here it is," he pronounced at last, "the first reported problems occurred about fifty years ago."

"What can you tell us about that time?" asked Natalia.

"According to my research," said the Orc, "they started preying on the merchant houses. The city council of Corassus called on the Church to eliminate the threat, but the Sisters refused, saying it was not within their purview."

"Sisters?" said Athgar. "Are you trying to tell me it was a group of women?"

"The Sisters of Saint Agnes are Temple Knights," the Orc defended, "not lay sisters."

"Then when did the Cunars arrive?" asked Natalia.

"Two years later," said Tonfer. "They were invited by the city council to take over control of the fortress. Of course, they expanded it significantly once they were in residence."

"Where did they come from?" asked Athgar. "Was the temple fleet already here, or did it arrive with them?"

"They were based in Ilea," said the scholar, "and yes, they brought the fleet with them, although they never chased down the pirates. If anything, the pirates grew bolder."

"I'm confused," said Natalia, "if the pirate raids were going on that long ago, where did they get their slaves?"

"What makes you think they had slaves?" asked the Orc.

"We ran across them on the way here," said Natalia. "They used slaves to man the oars."

"Ah," said the Orc, "I see your confusion. Back in those days, they didn't use oared ships. Instead, they used small sailing vessels. The use of galleys came much later."

"How much later?" asked Athgar.

"About forty years ago, around the same time that the great merchants started arming their ships."

"It makes sense, I suppose," offered Natalia. "Given the increase in piracy, it would only make sense to take precautions."

"Perhaps," offered Tonfer, "but I find the whole thing suspicious."

"Why would you say that?" asked Natalia.

"I would have expected the merchant houses to demand the pirates be eradicated by the Temple Knights, wouldn't you?"

"It does seem strange that they didn't take any action," said Natalia.

"What happened to these Sisters you spoke of?" asked Athgar.

"The Sisters of Saint Agnes?" asked the Orc. "Why, the order is still here, though in much smaller numbers. They often work with the Mathewites, among the poor."

"Anything else you can tell us about the pirates?" asked Athgar.

"Yes," replied Tonfer, "after reading through many first-hand accounts, I have noticed a pattern of sorts."

"We know," said Athgar, "they strike when ships are becalmed."

"Yes," agreed the Orc, "but up until forty years ago, the area we now know as the Pirate Coast carried strong and consistent trade winds."

"What could cause that to change?" asked Athgar.

"An Air Mage!" burst out Natalia. "Most likely a very powerful one, at that."

"He would have to be powerful indeed," offered Tonfer. "I've never heard of someone with that sort of magical ability."

"There's another possible explanation," said Natalia, "one which only now occurs to me."

"Which is?" pressed Athgar.

"A linked spell," she said. "I've heard its theoretically possible, but I'm not aware of anyone actually using it."

"What's a linked spell?" asked the Therengian.

"Its a way of linking mages together to perform a more powerful casting."

"How would that work?" asked Athgar.

"Let's put it this way," said Natalia, "you remember the spell I used on the Swift?"

"The favourable seas spell? The one with the currents?"

"Yes, that's the one," she continued. "If you remember, I told you I could move a smaller vessel much faster."

"I remember that," he replied, "but what has that got to do with a link spell?"

"Imagine if I could combine my spell with an identical spell cast by another Water Mage. The result would be even more speed!"

"Does that mean you and I could combine spells?" he asked.

"No," she said, "my understanding is that we'd have to be using the same type of magic, but imagine if a group of Air Mages decided to control the wind?"

"It would make them very dangerous," offered Athgar, "but how common are these mages? I've never seen an Air Mage, have you?"

"I've heard of them," she said, "but no, I've never met one in person. Part of our battle training taught us all about their capabilities, though."

"So, if we could stop these Air Mages..." pondered Athgar.

"We'd eliminate the pirates' advantage," finished Natalia.

"This is exciting news," offered Tonfer Garul. "What will you do now?"

"I suppose we continue with our plan," answered the Therengian.

"Might I enquire what that plan will entail?" said the Orc. "I only ask because I might be interested in assisting."

"I thought you were a scholar?" said Athgar.

"I am," Tonfer replied, "but I'm also a bit of a traveller. I love to enrich my knowledge with first-hand experiences. Don't worry, I can take care of myself."

"Does that include fighting?" asked Natalia.

"Of course," he replied, "I'm still an Orc, after all."

"Well," said Athgar, "you've given us much to think over. If we should be able to arrange an expedition, we'll be sure to let you know."

"Might I suggest," said Tonfer, "that you seek out a vessel called the Zephyr?"

"Is that a merchant?" asked Natalia.

"No," replied the Orc, "it's a pirate hunter."

"A pirate hunter?" said Athgar in surprise. "I didn't know there was such a thing."

"Oh yes," continued the scholar, "the Zephyr was built by some of the lesser merchants. It mostly sits on the beach these days, but they do venture out from time to time trying to track down the pirate vessels."

"It looks as though our luck is changing," said Athgar.

"And if you find these pirates," asked Tonfer, "what do you intend to do with them?"

"It's not the pirates themselves we're looking for," said Natalia, "we're actually trying to track down where their slaves came from."

"Count me in," said the Orc as he ripped a page out of the book and hunted around for a quill.

"What are you doing?" asked Natalia in shock. "You're destroying a book!"

"Don't worry," he said, brandishing the page, "it's empty." Moments later, he sat, writing in a slow and deliberate manner. Finishing his note, he blew on the paper to dry the ink, then handed it to Athgar.

"Here is information on the Zephyr," he said. "Be sure to tell them I sent you. All you need is on that piece of paper. You can send word back to me here if you decide to sail, I won't need much advance notice to be ready."

"Thank you, Tonfer," said Athgar.

"Please," said the Orc, "call me Garul, it is my Orcish name, after all."

THE ZEPHYR

AUTUMN 1103 SR

Leaving the city, they headed westward across the river to travel to their destination. Fortunately, Garul's note was quite detailed, enabling them to find the Zephyr without much difficulty. They walked along the beach, past what appeared to be a small fishing village, the local denizens watching them like hawks. Soon, they discovered the Zephyr, pulled up on the sand in amongst a grouping of ramshackle buildings.

It was easy enough to spot, for it looked more like a longship than a fishing vessel, having no deck to speak of. Instead, wooden seats were affixed directly to the hull, with the oars stacked neatly inside. Athgar walked right up to it, examining the copper plate that bore the ship's name and peering inside, curious of what lay there.

Natalia noticed a group of women watching them and made her way over, her feet digging into the soft sand as she walked, making it all the more difficult.

"Good afternoon," she said in greeting. "I wonder if you might be able to tell me about the Zephyr?"

"What of it?" asked a woman.

"We're looking for its master."

"That would be Zafir," the woman replied. "This time of day, he'd be drinking."

"And where would he drink?" asked the mage.

The woman pointed at a hut some distance down the beach. "Over there," she said, "along with any other man that isn't out fishing."

"Thank you," Natalia said, returning to Athgar.

"You have news of our elusive master?" he asked.

"Yes," she replied, "apparently he likes his drink. He's down the beach a little way."

"Well then," said Athgar, "let's go and pay him a visit, shall we?"

As they approached the door, they could hear words drifting out from within.

"I tell you, she was gorgeous," a voice was saying, "the prettiest thing you ever beheld."

"You're full of stories," said a deeper voice, "I bet you've never seen any of these women you speak of."

"You insult me," said the first. "I've travelled quite extensively and never had a problem acquiring companions."

When Natalia pushed open the door, the conversation abruptly ceased. She saw an older man, with a gaunt-looking face and thin beard, sitting on a small chair while his companion, significantly larger, sat on the floor, nursing a tankard.

"Can we help you?" said the gaunt man.

"We're looking for the captain of the Zephyr," she said.

"Then you've found him," he replied. "Captain Zafir Kopruli, at your service." He stood, a little unsteadily and bowed clumsily. "What, may I ask, is it you want me for?" he said, moving towards her as his eyes roamed over her body. He smiled as she blushed. She stepped to the side, allowing Athgar entry.

"We were told the Zephyr is a pirate hunter," said Natalia.

Captain Kopruli stepped back slightly at the sight of the Therengian. "It was," he said, "though she hasn't sailed in some time."

"Why's that?" she persisted.

"My benefactors have seen fit to withhold their financing," he said.

"Tell them the real reason, Zafir," said his large companion.

"Shut up, Safak," said the captain, "you're not helping matters."

"No tell us," pressed Natalia, "I must insist."

"Well," offered Kopruli, "if you must know, we were unsuccessful in our endeavours."

"Meaning?" she asked.

"Meaning, we never caught any pirates," offered Safak.

"Why is that?" asked Athgar.

"I don't know," replied Zafir. "It was a decent enough idea, and Saints know, we tried our best, but we never managed to locate any."

"Are you trying to tell me that with the entire Pirate Coast at your disposal, you couldn't even find one single pirate?"

"Exactly!" said the captain. "Would you like a drink?"

"No, I don't want a drink!" said Natalia. She turned to Athgar, "It appears we came a long way for nothing."

"Oh, I don't know," he said, a smile creeping across his face. "I think this will work out well for us."

"How can you say that?" she asked. "They've failed to find any pirates."

"That doesn't surprise me," said Athgar. "The pirates obviously put people on the cliffs to watch for targets. If they saw a pirate hunter, they'd surely not come out."

Captain Kopruli sat up straight, suddenly showing a keen interest in the discussion. "What's that you say?"

"I believe I know how they operate," Athgar said, "and I think I know how we can catch them if you're willing to help."

"I'm all ears," said the captain. "We've been trying to get them for years. What do we need to do?"

"Do you still have access to a crew?" asked the Therengian.

"Yes, though it would take a day or two to get them together, why?"

"We'll need some bait, a small merchant vessel to lure them out, and the Zephyr, of course."

"I can arrange that," offered Captain Kopruli. "Now tell me, what's the plan."

"It all hinges on timing," began Athgar.

They left early in the morning, two days later. Natalia and Athgar had managed to avoid Lady Arabel, but she must have been suspicious of them, for they were peppered with questions by the staff. Rendezvousing with the Zephyr before daybreak, they had sailed out into the sea, then headed east, towards the Pirate Coast.

Now, as dawn broke, they sat nestled in a small inlet, their position hidden by the rocky face of a cliff. It had been a tight squeeze, getting the boat inside, for they had to back it up, a process that was quite challenging in the dark. Athgar waited, crouched behind some rocks, staring out to sea while Natalia kept her eyes on the cliffs above.

"The wind is still strong," she said.

"Yes," he agreed, "but the Cormorant should be along shortly. No doubt the wind will die down once they spot it."

"You mean her," Natalia corrected.

"Who?" he asked.

"The Cormorant," she continued. "Ships are referred to as 'she'. They're considered female."

"Why is that?" he asked.

"It dates back to the old Gods," she said, "Akosia was the Goddess of Water."

"She still is," he said, "what of it?"

"In ancient times sailors carved figureheads of her to protect them at sea."

"A strange custom," he remarked, "but where did you learn all this?"

"At the Volstrum," she said, "I'm a Water Mage, remember? We learned all sorts of things connected to the sea. I'm surprised YOU didn't know that custom, I thought you worshipped the old Gods?"

"I do," Athgar replied, "but we seldom pray to the Goddess of the Sea."

"She's actually the Goddess of all water," said Natalia. "I suppose she's like our patron Goddess if you think about it."

"But you don't follow the old Gods, do you?"

"No," she admitted, "but we still understand them. Just because we don't worship the old Gods, doesn't make them wrong."

"I wish the people of Holstead felt that way," said Athgar. "How is it you're so understanding?"

"I've studied magic almost my entire life," she explained, "it's hard to believe there is only one true religion when you're wielding the power of the elements."

"Really? I would have thought the opposite. The Orcs believe it was Hraka that gave the gift of fire magic to them."

"I didn't know they worshipped the old Gods," said Natalia.

"They don't so much worship them as thank them," offered Athgar. "It's actually their ancestors that they venerate, but they are thankful to the Gods for their gifts. I'm not an expert on such things, of course. Perhaps I'll ask Uhdrig about it some time."

"Who's Uhdrig?" she asked.

"She is the shamaness of the Orc tribe I lived with," he said. "A Life Mage, to use the Human term."

"It would be interesting to meet them."

"I'll take you there one day," Athgar promised, "and you can meet Kargen, Shaluhk, and even little Agar if you wish."

"I'd like that," she said.

A bird cry shattered the early morning stillness.

"Someone's hungry," said Natalia. "They want their food."

"That's not a bird," said Athgar, "that was a man."

"Are you sure?"

"Yes," he replied, "it's a signal of some type."

"They must have spotted the Cormorant," she said.

Athgar wet his finger, holding it up to judge the breeze. "The wind's died down, it's time to get ready."

"I can't see their ship yet," warned Natalia.

"I don't suppose we will for some time yet," replied Athgar. "They have the advantage of the heights. You'd best go and let Captain Kopruli know that we'll be moving shortly. You remember the plan?"

"Yes," she replied, "we've gone over it multiple times. How long do you think we have?"

"Not long, I should think, but we must be ready to move quickly if we're to close the distance. I'll keep an eye out here and let you know when I spot them."

She made her way back down to the inlet, leaving the Therengian watching the coastline.

Athgar shifted his feet, full of nervous energy. It was a huge gamble, for the lives of the men on the Cormorant hung in the balance. He silently cursed the great merchant houses of Corassus. If they'd taken it upon themselves to rid the area of pirates, as they should have, then all of this wouldn't be necessary. There would be no need for slaves, and perhaps his own village would not have suffered. He pushed the thought from his head, concentrating instead on the sea.

Athgar spotted the galley soon after, its oars dipping into the water at a slow pace, hugging the coastline to conserve the strength of its rowers. The pirates aboard must be on the lookout for the Cormorant, no doubt warned by their observers on the cliff. He could almost imagine them standing at the railings, peering south for sight of their prize. With a sudden burst of energy from the rowers, the galley sped up. Clearly, they had seen their prey, and Athgar turned south to spot the Cormorant, becalmed, rolling in the gentle sway of the sea.

He looked back to the Zephyr. Captain Kopruli and the others were watching him intensely, their oars at the ready. Natalia sat at the back, while the captain knelt at the bow, his eyes locked on the Therengian. Athgar waved them onward, and the oar strokes began dipping silently into the shallow water, the Zephyr jumping forward. Athgar ran after it, splashing through the knee-deep water. Grabbing the side of the ship, he felt the strong arm of Garul snatch the back of his tunic to haul him aboard.

Athgar flopped to the bottom of the boat as it picked up speed. Sitting up, he spied Natalia readying a spell. Captain Kopruli, seeing deep water to either side, ordered the oars raised and they were carefully stowed on deck. Natalia cast her favourable seas spell, the water to either side of them responding with noticeable effect. As the Zephyr lurched forward unexpectedly, Athgar almost lost his balance.

The captain ordered a course correction, and the man at the tiller made the slight adjustment. They were now moving quickly, much faster than Athgar had thought possible, swiftly bearing down on the pirate galley.

The man on the bow of the galley loaded the ballista, unaware of the Zephyr's approach until someone farther back spotted them. Now alerted, a group of enemy archers started taking up positions by the railing.

Athgar grabbed his bow from the bottom of the Zephyr, having strung it much earlier in preparation. He nocked an arrow and took careful aim, then let loose. It sailed across the distance and struck true, hitting a pirate in the chest. The man staggered back, then fell from sight.

The others aboard the pirate galley let fly with a smattering of arrows. Two fell short while a third overshot, narrowly missing the Orc. Garul roared in defiance, his rich baritone echoing across the water.

The ships were converging quickly. Athgar recognized a look of indecision on the ballista man's face just before the weapon began swivelling towards the Zephyr. Dropping his bow, Athgar let loose with a streak of fire. It was almost impossible to miss at this range, and the shot struck the ballista, flames biting deep. With a bit of good fortune, some of the fire splattered, leaving the weapon's operator patting his arms in a vain attempt to put out the blaze.

Natalia cast again, forming ice on the pirate's oars, slowing their pace as water froze solid beneath them. The enemy vessel turned to the left, their starboard oars frozen while their port side kept rowing, bringing the galley parallel with the Zephyr.

Captain Kopruli moved alongside, his own hull freezing as it met the expanding ice. Natalia gave him a nod, and then the entire crew of the Zephyr exploded into action.

The ice now formed a bridge, and the Zephyr's crew scrambled across it, swarming up the side of the galley. The pirates, surprised by the sudden turn of events, tried to put up a fight, but the fire on the foredeck, along with the ice to their starboard, had already convinced most that this was a hopeless battle. Several dropped their weapons while at least two dove over on the starboard side, hoping to swim to the safety of the shore.

Athgar clambered up the side of the enemy vessel, his axe in hand, only to arrive at an empty railing. With his feet soon on deck, he was scanning across the pirate vessel when an arrow struck near his left foot. He looked up to see a man in the crow's nest, readying another shot. Before Athgar could even begin a spell, ice shards hit the man, sending him tumbling to his death.

Garul was soon beside the Therengian, striking out at a nearby foe. The Orc's axe was blocked by a sword, and then the enemy stabbed forward, causing the scholar to back up slightly. Athgar threw his axe and watched in satisfaction as it took the pirate in the arm. His foe slumped to the deck, clutching the wound, his sword lying untouched nearby, freeing the Orc to move about unhindered.

The fighting was all but over when a movement to the stern drew Athgar's attention. A pirate stood by the aft railing, a lantern in hand and Athgar immediately knew what was about to happen. The Therengian rushed forward, intending to extinguish the flame, but the lantern was tossed through an open deck grating too quickly, and then the pirate charged forward, his blade held high.

Athgar stopped short with the sudden awareness that he was unarmed. In desperation, he called forth flame. It shot from his hands, striking his foe in the head. The pirate staggered back, letting loose a blood-curdling scream while clutching his face, which was now on fire. He tripped on the open grating, following the path of the lantern he had just thrown.

The fighting ceased. Six pirates surrendered, while three more swam for shore, the rest dead or unconscious. Flames began to lick their way up from below, and Athgar cursed as he remembered the lantern. Making his way to the hatch, he peered down, only to be blinded by smoke.

"Abandon ship," yelled Captain Kopruli.

"The slaves!" called out Athgar.

The flames were spreading rapidly now, and Athgar called upon his magic to extinguish the fire that threatened them all, but his power proved insufficient, for the blaze burned on.

The slaves below screamed out in pain and fear. Athgar realized there wasn't much time before they would succumb to a fiery death. Covering his face with his arm, he leaped, dropping below and immediately moving towards the voices. Flames licked at the deck above him, while one rower was already engulfed, his cries of anguish gut-wrenching.

"Athgar!" came a voice from the smoke.

The Therengian staggered towards it, seeing a face loom out of the haze. It was Caladin, a hunter from his village! The young warrior had evidently been taken during the raid last year, and now sat, desperate to be rid of the chains that bound him.

Caladin looked at Athgar, pleading, "You must get us out of here!"

Fire burned up Athgar's sleeve, and although he struggled to cast a spell while choking out the commands, he was able to extinguish it. Turning his attention back to Caladin, the Fire Mage struggled to locate how the man's chains were attached.

"Who brought you here?" Athgar called out, his words almost drowned out by the sound of the roaring fire.

"Temple Knights," the young hunter managed to say, through coughs. "Your sister…" Caladin started, then yelled out in pain as a beam above their heads fell across his legs, flames bursting forth as a rush of air fed it.

Athgar tried to stem the fire with magic, but the air here was rapidly becoming unbreathable, and the mage failed to call forth his power from within. He reached down to pull the chains free, but the metal was hot, searing his skin before he pulled his hands away.

Their screams intensified as Athgar fought to catch his breath in the rapidly growing inferno.

A burnt hand clutched his arm, "She escaped," gasped Caladin, "back in Holstead."

"Who escaped?" Athgar yelled, desperate for an answer.

"Melwyn," the young man said, "she fled east, along with a small group of others."

"What of Ethwyn?" asked Athgar.

"Sold in Corassus," the hunter said, blood bubbling out along with the words. Suddenly, the man's hair burst into flames. Athgar was close to passing out from the heat and smoke that surrounded them.

"Put us out of our misery," Caladin begged, "please!"

Athgar backed up, overwhelmed by the enormity of the request. It took only another scream of pain to make up his mind. He focused, digging deep within himself to release the full extent of his spark. Fire exploded from his hands, pushing him back to strike his head against the side of the hull. The whole world began to spin as he felt himself falling.

With water now swirling around him, he wondered, somewhat absently, if he might have blown a hole in the bottom of the galley. In no time, it was around his waist. He struggled to stand, but his legs wouldn't cooperate, merely laid there unmoving as the water continued to rise. The yelling around him had ceased, no doubt silenced forever by the release of magic, and he knew with certainty that this was his time as well. He would sink to a watery grave, never again to set foot upon land, nor feel the tender caress of Natalia.

He called out her name in anguish, the words cut off as water rose above his head. The embrace of the sea brought terror to his mind as he gasped for breath, and then... he breathed!

Athgar recognized the effect, for it was the same spell of water breathing that was cast upon him when he had rescued Lady Arabel. Desperately trying to quell the panic within, he suddenly felt hands dragging him upward.

His eyes, still stinging from the smoke, couldn't yet focus, but he knew when he surfaced. An arm around his chest held him safe as he floated there, unable to move. It was as if death itself was fighting to claim him, and he almost let it, but then he felt strong arms pulling him aboard the Zephyr.

"We have you," said the deep voice of Garul.

Athgar was gently laid in the bottom of the hull, his eyes facing skyward. Moments later, the dripping face of Natalia loomed over him.

"Athgar," she was calling out in alarm, "can you hear me?"

"I'm here," he managed to spit out.

She lifted his head, crushing him to her chest. "Oh Athgar, you had me so worried. Don't ever do that again!"

"Shouldn't we get the water from his lungs?" asked Garul.

"The spell will have done that," she replied.

"The ship?" asked the Therengian.

"It's gone, I'm afraid," said Garul. "The fire spread quickly, and then it sank. Something must have ruptured."

"It was me," said Athgar, through sobs. "The slaves were chained up. I couldn't save them. I tried, I even burned my hands trying to release their bindings, but I couldn't unchain them."

"What did you do?" asked the Orc.

"I released the spark," the Therengian answered quietly, "all of it."

"You released all your energy?" said Natalia in astonishment. "You're lucky you didn't immolate."

"I had no choice," said Athgar, "I couldn't leave them to burn to death." He looked down to see the marks where his hands had been seared. "I don't feel any pain."

Natalia was examining the wounds, "It's probably shock. We'll get a salve on them as soon as we get back. I'm more concerned about your head wound." She gazed into his eyes, prying them open to see them more clearly. "How's your head?"

"Still a little woozy," he replied.

They lifted him to a seating position, and he peered over the deck. The galley was sinking rapidly in the distance, its bow now the only part left poking out of the water.

"All that effort," said Natalia, "and we are no better off for it."

"Yes we are," said Athgar, through a coughing fit. "Caladin was aboard."

"Who's Caladin?" she asked.

"He was the warrior that was to marry my betrothed. He managed to tell me a few things before he died."

"Such as?"

"My sister, Ethwyn, is alive, or at least she was."
"And the other?" pressed Natalia.
"He confirmed it was the Temple Knights that raided our village."

ON THE RUN

AUTUMN 1103 SR

Athgar stepped out of the Zephyr and into the shallow water, gripping the side of the boat, despite his injured hands, to help haul it ashore. They all collapsed on the sand, soaking in the afternoon sun.

A shadow loomed over the Therengian, blocking out the light. He opened his eyes to see Garul standing over him.

"She is quite resourceful, that woman of yours," the Orc remarked, using his own language.

"Indeed," Athgar replied.

"Do you mind if I offer you some advice?"

"By all means," he replied, *"go ahead."*

"You should bond with her," Garul suggested, *"before someone else does."*

Athgar blushed deeply. *"I'll keep that advice in mind,"* he said, then quickly changed the subject. *"What will you do now?"*

"I will return to the archives," said the Orc, *"I have had enough excitement to last me a while."*

Athgar stood, shaking the sand from his tunic. *"Thank you, Garul, you've been most helpful. I wish you well in your future endeavours."*

"As I to you, Orc friend." He clutched Athgar's hand in a solid grip, then immediately released it as the Therengian groaned in pain. *"Sorry,"* the Orc said, *"I forgot about your burns."*

"Not to worry," said Athgar, *"they will heal soon enough."*

"You should be on your way," suggested Garul. *"May the ancestors look out for you."*

"And may the tribe live on," he replied.

Around him, the crew had risen from their labours and were now removing the prisoners from the boat, a task made more difficult by the rope securing their hands and feet.

"A good job, lads," called out Captain Kopruli. "We might not have saved any slaves, but there's one less pirate ship to trouble us."

"Yes," agreed Safak, "and now we know how to handle their type. With a little luck, our sponsors might cough up some coins."

"What of the prisoners?" asked Natalia. "Will you hand them over to the Temple Knights?"

"No," the captain replied, "we were hired by the independent merchants, it'll be their decision what to do with them."

"But they know about the slaves," Natalia argued.

"I doubt this lot had anything to do with acquiring them," said Kopruli, "they're just the crew, but if we do discover anything of interest, we'll be sure to pass it along."

"Thank you, Captain," said Athgar, "I know it didn't quite work out the way we had hoped, but I managed to get some important information."

"What will you do now?" asked the captain.

"Our journey takes us back into Corassus. We have people to find."

"Good luck with you, then," Captain Kopruli replied.

"And to you," added Natalia.

They walked along the beach, hand in hand, eager to be on their way.

"What's our next step?" she asked.

"Personally, I think we need to get back to the estate and change. I don't know about you, but my tunic has a burned arm, and it stinks like smoke."

In answer, Natalia lifted her arm, smelling her sleeve. Her wrinkled nose told him all he needed to know.

They walked on in silence for a while, soon crossing the bridge that led to the eastern side of the river.

"I could use a bath," she said.

Athgar smiled, looking at her. "Yes," he agreed.

"No," she admonished, "I mean a real bath."

"So do I," he said, a look of indignation crossing his face.

"No, you don't," she accused.

He laughed, releasing a lot of the tension he'd been holding in. "No, I suppose not," he confessed, "but you can't blame me for trying."

"I don't blame you," she said, "I just meant we needed a proper bath FIRST!"

. . .

It didn't take long to reach the city gates, and from there they made their way directly to an herbalist. Natalia was concerned about Athgar's hands. The Therengian had tried to ignore the burns, but the skin was now blistering. They entered the shop to see an elderly woman tending a potted plant.

She looked up as they approached, "Can I help you?"

"Yes," said Natalia, "I wonder if you might have something to help with burns?"

"What kind of burns?" the woman asked.

In answer, Athgar held out his hands, showing his palms.

"That looks painful," the woman remarked. "Give me a moment, and I'll see what I have in stock." She disappeared into a back room, leaving Athgar and Natalia alone.

The Therengian looked around the place, noting the various plants that filled the room.

"I've never seen so much greenery inside a building before," he mused.

"Didn't they have plants back in Athelwald?" she asked.

"Not in someone's house," he replied, "though Skora had an herb garden behind hers. She grew all sorts of odd things."

"Skora?"

"Yes," he continued, "she was an old woman that helped look after us."

His recollection was interrupted by the return of the proprietor. She was carrying a jar of some type of white paste, which she placed on the counter.

"Here we are," she said, "this should help."

"What is it?" asked Athgar.

"It's an ointment made from kingsleaf. It will alleviate the pain and discomfort."

"So it will heal my hands?" he asked.

"No," she countered, "only time or magic will do that, but it will let you carry on with your life as if you weren't burned. Just be careful not to immerse your hands in anything that might wash it off."

Athgar wore a skeptical look, "And you expect me to believe this actually works?"

"Don't just take my word," she added, "try some."

Natalia watched them stare at each other, then grabbed the jar, removing the stopper. She dipped her finger inside, scooping some out.

"Give me your hands," she commanded.

He turned his attention to her, holding his hands palm upward.

Natalia started spreading the ointment over them, rubbing it in as gently as she could.

"How does that feel?" she asked.

"Much better," he said in surprise. He looked to the shopkeeper, "It seems I owe you an apology."

"Not necessary," the woman replied, "but you'll need to pay for the ointment."

"Do you have a smaller container?" asked Natalia. "It's a little awkward walking around town with a jar like that in hand."

"Of course," the owner replied. She moved to a back shelf, scanning its contents before grabbing a smaller pot, then returned to the counter, using a spoon to fill it with ointment.

"That should last you a few days," she announced, "by then you should be well on the way to recovery."

"How much?" asked Natalia.

"Kingsleaf is rare," the shop owner warned, "and even this small sample is expensive."

Natalia dropped some gold coins on the counter. "Will this do?"

The woman looked at them only briefly, then scooped them up. "Consider it paid."

Natalia waited while a cork stopper was affixed to the top of the pot, then picked it up.

"Where to now?" asked Athgar.

"Back to the estate, I think," suggested Natalia. "It would be nice to change, don't you think?"

"Yes," agreed Athgar, "and then, perhaps, some food."

It was but a short trip to Lady Arabel's estate. They were just approaching when suddenly Athgar pulled Natalia off to the side of the road.

"What is it?" she asked.

"Something's wrong," he replied.

"Why?" she asked. "What have you seen?"

"The gate's open," said Athgar. "Lady Arabel usually keeps it closed."

"Perhaps she just has a visitor? She is a rather important person, you know. Why does it matter whether or not she has visitors?"

"We can't just go in the way we are," he said, "it would be a little hard to explain why we're burned and smoky. It might raise suspicions."

"Good point," Natalia agreed. "What if we go in through the window? We got out that way."

"An excellent idea," said Athgar, "but I think I should go in and have a quick look around first."

"Why don't we both go?"

"I'm the quiet one, remember? Unless, of course, you've taken up hunting in your spare time?"

"No, I see your point," she agreed.

"You stay here in the alleyway, it's got a good view of the gate. If you see anything, make a run for it."

"What if you don't come back?" Natalia asked, concern written on her face.

"Don't worry," he replied, "I won't leave you. I'll just have a quick look. If it's safe, I'll come back for you."

"And if it's not safe?"

"Then I'll give up trying to gain entry."

"I suppose that makes sense," she said.

Athgar surveyed the gate before moving forward. Once there, he checked to ensure no one was nearby. A moment later, he was through, edging closer towards the house by moving stealthily from tree to tree.

Soon, he was near enough to see the front door, and he paused, noting the presence of two armed guards. At first, he thought they were merely soldiers, perhaps a couple of hired mercenaries, but when he moved closer, he recognized their grey tabards. These were Cunars!

He thought to rush back to Natalia, to warn her, but then decided he needed more information. With the front door now beyond his reach, he made the decision to make his way to the back, to search for an open window he could use.

The approach was easy enough for one with his talents, and soon, he was looking upon the back of the house. Just as he was about to change his position, two people came out of the rear door. One was clearly Lady Arabel, while the other was a Temple Knight, and they were in the middle of a conversation, their words drifting towards him.

"Are you sure?" the knight asked.

"Quite sure, Brother Septimus," the woman responded. "I saw her ring clearly, though I didn't know its significance at the time."

"And what put you onto her?" asked Brother Septimus.

"Her companion mentioned the Sartellians," she replied. "I knew immediately that something wasn't right!"

"This companion," asked the knight, "can you describe him?"

"Yes, he is young, perhaps in his early twenties, with a scruffy beard and dark brown hair. She referred to him as Athgar, does that sound familiar?"

"It means nothing to me," her companion revealed, "but what's important here is that you've found this Stormwind woman. You know, there's a substantial reward for her capture?"

"I do now," replied Lady Arabel.

"Very well," he said, "we'll keep some of the brethren here until further notice. If these two show up again, we'll take them into custody. I'm sure it won't take long for the Stormwinds to cough up the reward."

"Thank you, Brother Septimus, I'm glad I could be of help."

The Cunar returned to the house, leaving Lady Arabel standing outside. She took a seat and was joined, moments later, by a servant.

"A drink, Madame?" the servant offered.

"Oh, thank you, Corban," she said, accepting the goblet.

Athgar backed up, intent on putting some distance between Lady Arabel and himself. This was staggering news, he thought. Not only were the Cunars responsible for attacking his village, now they were here, looking for Natalia. This Stormwind family had a long reach, it seemed!

He navigated the route back to the gate without any problems but then had to wait as two more Cunars wandered in. They halted, chatting in the lane, confounding Athgar's attempts to leave. He briefly considered climbing the wall, but the iron grate atop made it doubtful he could do so without being spotted. There was nothing he could do but wait, watching as they wandered back and forth. Eventually, they grew tired of their sojourn, making their way up to the house, and Athgar knew his time had finally arrived. He broke for the gate at a run, trying to keep as silent as possible. Soon, he felt the cobblestones beneath his feet and knew he was safe.

Natalia looked relieved as he entered the alley.

"How did it go?" she asked.

"The place is crawling with Cunars," he explained.

"How did they know about us?" she asked.

"I overheard Lady Arabel talking with one of them. She's the one that put them onto our scent. We need to get out of here and find somewhere safe, but where? If the Cunars are looking for us, they'll likely search any inn within the city."

"Brother Cyric?" she suggested.

"Good idea," he responded. "Let's go and find this mission of his."

A man let loose a cry of agony that echoed down the long hall. Brother Cyric bent over him, examining his wound. The man had left a cut untreated, and now gangrene had set in. It would have been a simple treatment, had a Life Mage been available, but alas, the poor had no coins for such care. Instead, they came here, to the mission, run by the generosity of the Order of Saint Mathew.

"How does he look?" asked a robed individual.

"I'm afraid it doesn't look good, Brother Caerwell. There's little we can do for him."

"It is a common enough sight," replied the lay brother, "and the others?"

Cyric rose, beckoning brother Caerwell to follow. "These three," he said with a wave of his hand, "appear malnourished, an easy enough thing to remedy, but those two," again a wave of his hand, "I'm afraid, are not doing as well. This woman has suffered a miscarriage and has bled a lot while this man appears to be the victim of a stabbing. I'm afraid the only thing we can do is make them comfortable and perhaps ease their pain. Their end is, unfortunately, inevitable."

"As it usually is, here in the slums," mused Brother Caerwell. "Tell me, Cyric, why did you come here? You are assigned as an administrator, you could spend your time in leisure at the fortress."

"It is not my way, Brother. I go where Mathew needs me."

"You are a credit to our order," Brother Caerwell remarked. "I wish others were as dedicated."

They were interrupted by a rather short man, his patchy beard covering a pockmarked face. "Brother Cyric?"

"Yes, Brother Joram?"

"You have visitors. I tried to tell them you were busy, but they insisted on seeing you."

"It seems you're popular," offered Brother Caerwell.

"Did they say who they were?" asked Cyric.

"They didn't give their names, but said you'd remember them from the Swift, whatever that is."

"That's the ship I came here on," said Cyric, "and no doubt they are my travelling companions."

"They appear to be in some distress," added Brother Joram.

"How so?" asked Cyric.

"The man had burn marks on his sleeve, and they both smell of smoke. I would suspect they suffered some sort of calamity."

"Thank you, Joram. If you would be so kind as to take them to the library, I shall join them directly."

"Certainly, Brother Cyric," said Joram, "I shall see to it immediately."

"Trouble?" asked Caerwell. "I've heard you have a nose for it."

"I remind you, Brother, that I am a Temple Knight. In addition to helping the poor, it is my duty to protect our assets."

"These people work for the Church?"

"Yes, in a manner of speaking," Cyric replied. "They helped our ship arrive here, despite being attacked at sea."

"Praise be to Saint Mathew for seeing you safely here," said Brother

Caerwell. "That being the case, it is your duty to render assistance, if needed. Shall I prepare beds for them?"

"Let's wait and see what they want," said Cyric. "At this moment, I don't know if they come seeking knowledge or healing."

"Then I shall see to these patients on your behalf," offered Brother Caerwell, "though our supply of kingsleaf is running dangerously low."

"Can we not get more?" he asked.

"I'm afraid there are no funds for it," his colleague replied.

"It is frustrating to see new construction at the fortress when we are so in want of aid," Cyric fumed.

"I am in complete agreement," offered Brother Caerwell, "but there is nothing we can do. I've forwarded requests to the Archprior himself, but little seems to come of it."

"Perhaps, I shall visit him," said Cyric, "and remind him of our responsibilities."

"Would you?" asked Brother Caerwell. "It would mean so much more, coming from a Temple Knight."

"I will see what I can do," confirmed Cyric, "but first I must see to my companions. If you'll excuse me?"

"Of course," said the brother, "I have kept you far too long already."

Cyric bowed respectfully, then made his way down the hallway. At one time it had been the central room of this ancient temple, but now makeshift beds replaced the benches, and the stench of corruption and death permeated the place.

He entered the library, immediately recognizing his acquaintances from the Swift.

"Natalia, Athgar," he greeted, "so good to see you both. I trust you've been well?"

"More or less," said Athgar, "though I'm afraid we've come into a little trouble."

Cyric noted the burn marks on Athgar's tunic, "Are you injured?"

"No," the Therengian replied, "I managed to halt the flame in time."

"He's inhaled a lot of smoke," interrupted Natalia, "I'm worried it has hurt him."

"Let's take a look, shall we?" Cyric offered. "Have a seat, Athgar, and I'll need you to take off your tunic."

"Why?" he asked.

"So I can listen to your lungs."

"Very well," he grumbled, removing his shirt. He sat down, and then Cyric bent over him, placing his ear to Athgar's chest.

"It sounds clear," said the knight. "I rather suspect you heal quickly from smoke inhalation."

"Why is that?" asked Natalia.

"I've read it true of many Fire Mages," replied Cyric. "You're a lucky man. Tell me, what happened to you, the smell of smoke is quite pronounced."

"We attacked a pirate ship," offered Natalia.

"By yourselves?" asked Cyric in astonishment.

"No," said Athgar, "we were aboard a pirate hunter. We were successful, but the enemy set fire to their ship."

"Yes," added Natalia, "and Athgar, here, was caught in the hold when it went down." She moved over to stand beside him, her hand placed gently upon his shoulder, her voice cracking as she spoke, "If I hadn't been there he would have perished. I used a spell to allow him to breathe underwater, then pulled him out. The ship was already submerging by that time."

"This pirate ship," said Cyric, "did it hold any information of value?"

"It confirmed my theory that the Cunars are behind the slavery," said Athgar, "but I'm afraid we have no proof."

"What was the nature of this information? Can it be trusted?" asked Cyric.

"When I boarded their ship, I found slaves manning the oars. One of them was a Therengian, a hunter from my village. He confirmed that Temple Knights were responsible for the attack."

"And where is this witness?"

"I'm afraid we couldn't release him from his shackles, nor anyone else, for that matter."

"By the Saints," uttered Cyric, "what a horrible way to go."

"I made their death quick," said Athgar quietly. "There was no hope for them, so I let out my inner fire. It was a tremendous explosion, I doubt anyone survived."

"Yes," added Natalia, "and it also blew a hole in the hull, that's what sunk it."

"It sounds like it would have burned away to nothing anyway," observed Cyric. "It was regrettable, but at least you're safe."

"We need a place to hide," said Athgar, "at least for a day or two. Lady Arabel is working with the Cunars."

"How do you know?" asked Cyric.

"We went back to her estate. She was waiting there with several Temple Knights. I overheard part of their conversation."

"An unfortunate development," observed Cyric. "We shall have to be careful."

"We?" said Natalia.

"Of course," said Cyric, "I'm a man of my word. I promised I would do what I can, and I intend to keep that promise."

"But the whole Church is against us," she said.

"I doubt it's the whole Church, I suspect, rather, that it is a small minority. The big question will be how many make up that group. If we were to approach the wrong people, it could be trouble. Did you catch anyone's name?"

"Yes, now that you mention it," offered the Therengian. "Someone named Brother Septimus, do you know him?"

"No," admitted Cyric, "but it gives me somewhere to start. In the meantime, we shall put you up here. You'll need a change of clothes, of course. I'm sure we can find something for you."

"And what will you do?" asked Natalia.

"I'm going to go and visit the Archprior of my order and lay out what we know. Don't worry, I won't mention your names."

"And if he refuses to help?" asked Athgar.

"Then I have other options available to me," Cyric said cryptically, "but I must ask you to take no action until you've heard back from me. Can you promise that?"

"Of course," said Natalia.

Cyric looked at Athgar. The Therengian was about to argue the point, but relented, nodding his head.

"Good, then it's settled," the Temple Knight continued.

"When will you see him?" asked Natalia.

"This very evening," said Cyric.

THE ARCHPRIOR

AUTUMN 1103 SR

Cyric pondered his attire for some time before making the trip. As a Temple Knight, he certainly had the right to wear armour during the performance of his duties, but that might be seen as intimidating to the Archprior, and so he chose, instead, to wear the simple cassock and tabard of his order, leaving his armour and weapons behind.

He approached the main barbican, the entryway to the interior of the fortress itself. Two Temple Knights of Saint Cunar watched his approach with considerable interest, the gates behind them closed. However, the large wooden structure had a smaller door inside for individuals to enter.

He paused as he drew closer. "I'm here to see the Archprior," he declared.

"Your name?" the guard asked.

"Brother Cyric."

The guard looked to his companion, who checked a book and nodded his head in agreement, then opened the smaller door.

Cyric ducked as he entered, then followed the path as it turned abruptly left. There were three levels to the great fortress; this, the first, looped around the base of the fortifications so that anyone gaining entry had to withstand fire from its walls to advance to the next gate. The outer ring, as it was called, held nothing but walls and towers, serving mainly to keep outsiders at bay. The towers were manned only by Temple Knights, while still more patrolled the walls between them. It was peacetime, of course, so there were few enough soldiers in sight, but he knew that the entire garrison could be roused in a very short period of time, if needed.

Cyric followed the path, turning down the east side of the fortress to where the harbour gate stood. Its doors were open, and as he approached, he noticed a woman in armour walking through. She had dark brown hair, cut short in a man's style, obviously the better to wear a helmet, though she wore none this day.

"Greetings, Sister," he said as she drew closer.

"And to you, Brother," she replied. "Tell me, what brings a Brother of Saint Mathew here this day? It is rare that we see members of your order."

Cyric halted. "I've come to see the Archprior," he said.

The woman smiled in response, "Then I wish you all the best. I hear he's in a foul mood this day."

"I have heard it said," replied Cyric, "that it is his usual way."

She laughed, "It is refreshing to see one who can joke of such things. These Cunars lack any sense of humour. I'm Sister Morena."

"Brother Cyric," he offered. "Have you been in Corassus long?"

"Several years," she said, "and you?"

"I only just arrived a few days ago," confessed Cyric, "but they've kept me busy."

"Consider yourself lucky," she replied. "The new Cunar commander insists on only using his own men for the defences. It gives us little to do."

"Who is this new commander?" asked Cyric.

"Commander Morvus," replied Sister Morena, "he came here just a month ago."

"I take it he's an energetic sort?"

"He is," confirmed the sister, "but I shan't say more. I wish you luck, Brother Cyric, I have a feeling you'll need it."

"Thank you, I think. Just one more thing," he said, "this Commander Morvus, what does he look like? I should hate to run into him and not give him his due."

"He's a rather tall individual," she replied, "you can't miss him. He has black hair and a distinct scar on his face." She ran a finger down the left side of her face to illustrate.

"Thank you," he said again, "I shall keep an eye out for him."

She continued on her way, and he turned back to the harbour gate, which stood wide open, two Temple Knights standing guard in their distinctive grey tabards. Resuming his walk, he entered, the knights paying him scant notice.

As Cyric passed into the courtyard, the smell of horses drew his attention to the stables on his right where several Temple Knights of Saint Cunar were mounting up, no doubt heading into the city itself to begin their patrol. He gave them a wide berth, moving westward to then turn south towards the inner gate and the Chancellery that lay beyond. He passed by the armoury on his right, the sound of smiths at work echoing through the courtyard, while to his left sat the massive barracks that held all the knights stationed here, save for the sisters. They, alone, were housed past the inner gate. The barracks was a full three stories, its top even higher than the wall it backed onto. This allowed the rooftop to form a place of observation, for it gave a clear view of the harbour below.

The Temple Knights of Saint Mathew were a humble order, with rules to match. It would be unthinkable for a commander of such a force to live in luxury while his brethren slept in small cells, but the Cunars apparently had no such qualms. Their leaders lived in relative splendour, each with an office, living room and bedroom, or so he was lead to believe. Certainly, the officers quarters here appeared extravagant, at least to Cyric's mind.

At the Inner Gate stood two more guards and, upon his approach, he was motioned to halt.

"State your business, Brother," said one of them.

"I am Brother Cyric, Temple Knight of Saint Mathew," he replied. "I am here to see the Archprior of my order."

"Is he expecting you?" asked the guard.

"He is," said Cyric, "I sent word early this morning."

The guard turned to his companion, who referenced a book that sat nearby.

"He's here," replied the other guard, "you can let him through."

"Go in peace, Brother," said the first, "and may the Saints go with you."

"And with you," replied Cyric.

He walked through the archway into the Inner Keep. The area here was smaller than that of where the stables lay but formed the highest point of the fortress. To his right was the chapel, sitting beside the barracks of the Sisters of Saint Agnes, while to his left sat the living quarters for all the ecclesiastic's that worked here.

The chancellery itself was the grandest structure in the fortress, a full three stories in height, much like the barracks, but the ceilings were much higher, making it almost fifty percent taller. This building housed the upper echelons of the Church for the entire bailiwick, and no expense had been spared during its construction. It had massive columns built in a long-ago style, while the roof was covered in copper, the better to protect those below from the ravages of the sea.

Cyric knew all six orders were housed here, and he wondered who would have the honour of guarding this edifice. His question was answered as soon as he entered to see the distinctive blue and white tabards of the Temple Knights of Saint Ansgar standing to either side of the door.

It opened into a large foyer, with a ceiling that reached to the rooftop. Looking up, Cyric saw the mural that decorated the ceiling. He had heard of it, of course, but to see Raphael Durga's masterpiece in person was an experience. Depicting the Saints, all six of them, gathered around the table in Herani, it was called The Pact, an event of significance as they combined their followers into a centralized organization, the precursor to the Church of the Saints.

A cough drew Cyric's attention, and he looked to see a man wearing the white and black livery of Saint Augustine standing in front of him. "Can I help you?" the knight asked.

"Yes, sorry," said Cyric, "I was overcome by the fresco."

The man smiled, "Don't worry, it happens a lot. I've been here for two years, and I still find myself staring at it from time to time."

"The detail is amazing. It must have taken him years to complete."

"Indeed," said his host, "twelve to be exact, but I doubt you came here just to see the painting."

"No," said Cyric, "I've come to see Archprior Legault."

"Of course," the man replied. "I should have realized by your tabard. We seldom see visitors from Saint Mathew, and when we do, it's almost always to see the Archprior. If you'll follow me, I'll show you the way."

Cyric fell into step behind his host. Two massive staircases were visible here, reaching up all the way to the third floor. Taking the one on the right, their feet made almost no noise on the luxurious carpet as they ascended.

His guide stopped at the second floor, pointing down the hallway. "You'll find all the offices of the Mathewites down that way. The Archprior is at the end, and his waiting room is just behind that sentry."

"Thank you," said Cyric, "you've been most helpful."

He waited until the Augustine descended the stairs, taking a moment to think about his coming meeting. He must take care, he reminded himself, for the Archprior was an influential man.

Steeling himself, he walked down the corridor, his sandals slapping on the marble floor. He approached the guard, a Temple Knight of Saint Mathew in full regalia.

"I'm Brother Cyric, here to see the Archprior," he stated. "Is he in?"

"He is," replied the sentinel, who then turned to open the door. "If you'll wait in here, we'll send someone to fetch you when His Grace is ready."

Cyric stepped inside an austere room, with a row of wooden benches along the wall. At one end hung a painting depicting Saint Mathew caring for the sick. As he moved towards it, he decided it was recent, for the dress and armour were far too modern for the time in which the founder of his order lived, but it mattered little for the point of the piece was readily understood.

He sat on the bench, trying to frame his questions in his mind. Athgar had mentioned a Temple Knight with a scar, and it now appeared the very same man was in charge of the fortress itself. How did one casually mention that such a powerful man was evil?

The guard opened the door, "He's ready to see you, Brother."

Cyric rose, following the Temple Knight to the end of the hallway. There, the door opened, and he was ushered inside to stand before a large oaken desk, behind which sat a grey-haired man.

"Archprior Legault," said Cyric, bowing deeply.

"Brother Cyric," the old man replied, "I must admit to some surprise at your request for a meeting. It is my belief you've only just arrived in Corassus."

"It is true, Your Grace," the Temple Knight said, "I arrived less than a week ago."

"I hope all is well at the mission?" asked the Archprior.

"It is, Your Grace, but I fear I have heard tell of something that I thought wise to bring to your attention."

"You have me intrigued," the man said, leaning forward. "Tell me, what is it that vexes you so?"

"I believe that someone in the Church is carrying on illegal activities."

"A very broad statement. Can you be more specific?"

"I have it on good authority that certain individuals have been engaging in the trade of slaves."

"I might remind you, Brother Cyric, that slavery is not illegal in Corassus."

"That might be true," said Cyric, "but it is against Church doctrine."

"Do you propose to lecture me on the rules of the Church?" the Archprior asked.

"No, Your Grace, merely inform you that such behaviour is being carried out."

"This is a shocking accusation, Brother Cyric," said Legault. "Have you any proof?"

"I have reliable witnesses," he replied.

"You must tell me more," the old man said. "How did you come by this information?"

"On occasion," said Cyric, "I have been employed by our order to investigate matters of the Church."

"Surely that is best left to the Brothers of Saint Ansgar," said the Archprior.

"I would agree," offered Cyric, "but when one is not available, the Church must make use of its assets as best it can."

"What is the nature of these investigations?"

"I'm afraid I'm forbidden to talk of such things, Your Grace, but rest assured they were dealt with appropriately."

"I am the Archprior of Saint Mathew! Surely I am fit to hear?"

"I might remind you, Your Grace, that I report to the Grand Master of my order. You are not in my direct line of superiors."

"And yet you come to me for help," Archprior Legault mused.

"It is a matter that concerns us all, not just the brothers of my order."

The old man sat back, interlocking his fingers over his stomach. "Tell me," he finally said, "what details you have. Who is the one you accuse?"

"It appears he is the leader of the Temple Knights of Saint Cunar, Your Grace."

The Archprior's eyes seemed to bulge. "Are you mad, Cyric? You come in here making all sorts of accusations, and now you accuse the local fortress commander of being involved in slavery?"

"I have received confirmation of his acts, Your Grace."

"What kind of confirmation? Have you seen it with your own eyes?"

"No, sir."

"Then who has confirmed it?"

"Independent witnesses," said Cyric.

"Who, precisely are these witnesses?" demanded the Archprior.

"I'd rather not say, Your Grace."

"You'd rather not say," repeated the old man, "and why is that?"

"I fear to do so would be to put them in danger, Your Grace."

"Are these sources reliable?"

"I think so, yes," said Cyric.

"You think so? Tell me, Brother Cyric, how long have you known these people."

"I met them only recently, Your Grace, but in that short time I have come to believe they are honourable and trustworthy individuals."

"So you would take the word of someone you just met over a servant of the Church? I find that most unsettling."

"I take my vows seriously, Your Grace, I cannot stand back and do nothing."

"Are you implying that my vows are any less noble than yours?" bristled the Archprior.

"No, Your Grace," Cyric responded, "merely that I must report what I know to you. It is for you to decide what must be done."

"At last," said the Archprior, "you have reached the crux of the matter. Tell me, what details have you? I shall need names and dates if you have them."

"I shall make all of that available to you, Your Grace."

"Then, I shall expect a full written account. In the meantime, you will speak of this to no one, do you understand? If word got out about this, it would cause dissension in the Church."

"But surely my investigation-"

"Your investigation is under my authority now," said the Archprior. "Do you understand."

"Yes, Your Grace," said Cyric, "of course."

"Good, now you must be on your way back to your mission. You have given me much to think of, Brother."

"Thank you, Your Grace," said Cyric, bowing deeply. He turned, leaving the office of the Archprior, closing the door behind him. As he strode back down the hall, he thought about the Archprior's words. Would he begin an investigation? Cyric thought it unlikely. Archprior Legault appeared more interested in maintaining the status quo than investigating slavery. Perhaps it was time to try another approach.

Cyric reached the stairs, but instead of descending, he walked up to the third floor. If the Order of Saint Mathew was unwilling to investigate, perhaps there were others that might think differently.

THE SEARCH

AUTUMN 1103 SR

"This Archprior Legault," said Athgar, "do you think he'll investigate?"

"I have my doubts," replied Cyric. "He seems more interested in keeping his own position secure. You won't do that if you're asking embarrassing questions."

"So what do we do?" asked Natalia. "If the Church itself is unwilling to investigate, we're at a dead end."

"No!" swore Athgar. "I'll never give up. My people have died or been enslaved by these Temple Knights. They need to pay the price."

"Are you suggesting," asked Natalia, "that we find this man and simply kill him? That wouldn't accomplish anything."

"At least justice would be served," said the Therengian.

"It's not the only option," cautioned Cyric. "While I was in the fortress, I made a discovery."

"What kind of discovery?" asked Athgar.

"It seems," continued Cyric, "that the fortress recently received a new commander. A Cunar, with a scar on his face."

"You've found him!" exclaimed Athgar. "Who is he?"

"His name's Commander Morvus," said Cyric, "but you won't be able to get to him. He's surrounded by hundreds of his men."

"There must be something we can do!" said Athgar. "It's frustrating to think that we've found our prey, only to discover he's untouchable."

"I wouldn't say he's untouchable," said Cyric, "but a direct assault is not the answer."

"Go on," prompted Natalia, "what is it you propose we do?"

"We need proof of his crimes," said Cyric. "He must keep records somewhere."

"Why would he?" asked Natalia. "He'd hardly incriminate himself. Anything of that nature would be dangerous to him."

"Yes," agreed Athgar, "but Brother Cyric is correct. He can't be slaving all by himself. He'd need men to help him, and that means payments to keep their silence."

"I agree," added Cyric, "not to mention contacts with the pirates. That means a record of payments received, dates to meet, and so on."

"Where would he keep that sort of information?" asked Natalia.

"Likely in his office," offered Cyric.

"And where is his office?" she asked.

"In the fortress, right beside the Cunar barracks," said Cyric, "but I don't know for sure which one."

"Can you find out?" Athgar asked.

"It wouldn't be difficult," he replied, "but my presence would be noted."

"Then how do we get into his office?" she asked.

"The bigger question," remarked Cyric, "is how we get you two into the fortress?"

"That's easy," said Athgar, "we dress like members of the Church."

"Easier said than done," said Cyric. "You'd still have to get past the guards at the gates."

"Gates? There's more than one?" asked Athgar.

"Three actually," said Cyric, "but we only need to get you past two of them."

"And if we find the evidence," asked Natalia, "how do we get out again?"

"You won't have to," said Cyric. "As long as you have the proof, we merely have to make sure the right person gets it."

"And who is that right person?" asked Natalia.

"Leave that to me," said Cyric. "Now, how good are you at being stealthy?"

"I thought we were going to go in disguise?" asked Athgar.

"You are," said Cyric, "but once you're in his office, you'll have to avoid detection. No brother or sister of the order would be searching through another's belongings."

"I can be quiet," said Athgar, "and Natalia will stay here. After all, it's my problem, not hers."

"No," said Natalia, defiantly, "we're both going."

"That would increase the chance of being discovered," said the Therengian.

"I'm not letting you go alone. If things go wrong, you'll need my help."

"Very well," he agreed, "but I only do so under objection."

"Duly noted," she said.

"Now," Athgar continued, "you said you had an idea about disguises?"

"Yes," said Cyric, "it will be easy to disguise you, Athgar. All you have to do is dress like a Brother of Saint Mathew. It's Natalia that represents the challenge."

"Do we dress her like a man?" asked Athgar.

"No," said Cyric, "we dress her like a Sister of Saint Agnes. The real trick will be obtaining a suitable outfit for her."

"Can't we get a seamstress to sew one up for us?" asked Natalia.

"No, the cloth used for such outfits is only available in one place, and they would not be willing to risk their lucrative contract with the Church by selling it to others," said Cyric.

"Then where do we get one?" asked Natalia. "Surely you're not proposing we steal one?"

"I don't think it'll come to that," offered Cyric. "I believe I might be able to convince someone to lend us one."

A knock at the door interrupted their conversation. Brother Caerwell poked his head inside.

"We have visitors, Brother Cyric," he said. "A group of Cunar knights under a captain."

"What do they want?" asked Cyric.

"They say they're looking for two fugitives, these two by the sounds of it."

"How did they know we're here?" asked Natalia.

"They talked to Lady Arabel," said Athgar, "and she likely remembered Cyric from the voyage."

"What do we do," she asked, "fight?"

"No," said Cyric, "I'll go and deal with the Cunars. Brother Caerwell, is there someplace these two can hide?"

"There is," the Holy Brother replied, "but we'll have to get you out of the mission first."

"Good," said Cyric, "take them to a place of safety. I'll see if I can buy us some time."

"Good luck, Cyric," said Natalia.

"And to you," the Temple Knight responded.

Brother Caerwell led them down the hallway, past the sick and injured, pausing by an empty alcove.

"This is it," the brother said, pushing against a brick. The action elicited a grating sound, and then the wall pivoted back on a hinge of some sort.

"Go down this corridor," he said. "It'll lead you into the gardens out back, and then you'll have to climb the wall to get outside of the compound. Be careful, they may be expecting you."

"Then where do we go?" asked Athgar.

"There's an inn called the Travellers Rest. It's on the eastern side of town, near the bell tower of Saint Agnes. When you get there, tell them Brother Caerwell sent you. They'll keep you hidden until we can come for you. Now go, you haven't much time."

They entered the tunnel, which sloped downward at a fairly steep angle. With another grating noise, the corridor went completely black as the door was closed.

"I can't see," whispered Natalia.

"Just a moment," said Athgar. He held out his right hand, palm upward, and uttered the words of power. Moments later, a small green flame leaped to life in his hand, illuminating their way. He held out his left hand to Natalia, and she placed hers into his. Moving slowly, they watched the floor lest they trip, trying to remain as quiet as possible.

Hearing footsteps above, they halted, and Athgar extinguished the light while they stood in silence. Natalia edged closer to him, trembling in fear.

Finally, the steps receded, and once more, he brought the flame to life as they advanced, the floor finally levelling out. They must have travelled half a block or more before the corridor ended at the bottom of a ladder, made of metal and cemented into the wall of a circular chamber.

"Where now?" Natalia asked.

Athgar looked at the ladder, "Up there, I suppose. There must be a lever or something at the top."

"I'll go first," offered Natalia.

"Let me," said Athgar, "we might have to fight our way out."

"Then I should go first," she argued, "if you use your magic, you'll light up the whole area. My magic is harder to see."

"Very well," he said, "but I'll be just below you with the flame. After all, you'll need to see what you're doing."

She grabbed the first rung, then took a deep breath. Exhaling slowly, she began the climb. Soon, she was at the top. The handle here looked like it rotated something, so she grabbed it and began turning, finding it remarkably easy to do. The stonework above her started to shift, and then a small strip of the night sky came into view.

"Extinguish the flame," Natalia whispered, "I can see moonlight."

Athgar dispelled the flame and watched as the small strip of the night sky became larger. It was a remarkable feat of engineering, and Athgar wondered who had built such a tunnel. This had been a temple to the old Gods, Cyric had said, and yet surely those that had served the old Gods wouldn't need an escape tunnel!

Natalia climbed out, then looked back down at Athgar. "It's safe," she whispered, "come on."

Up went the Therengian, to emerge into the outdoors, his feet hitting grass as he turned to look back at their exit. It was hidden beneath a statue, made of stone, that had rotated off of its base, revealing the tunnel. The release mechanism was easy to see, and so they activated the lever that moved the statue back to its original position. There was a quiet click, and then the lever vanished into the shoe of the figure.

"The wall," whispered Natalia.

Athgar nodded, moving into the lead. The perimeter of the mission had a brick wall that was slightly taller than his head and covered with ivy. He reached up, grabbing the top, then hauled himself up to peer over its edge, only to see a backstreet, devoid of any light. Silently thanking the Gods, he pulled himself to the top, reaching down to grasp Natalia's hand. She briefly balanced on the wall, and then they both dropped to the other side, disappearing into the inky blackness of the night.

Brother Cyric opened the door to see three Temple Knights before him, each wearing the distinctive grey tabard of their order.

"Is there something I can do for you, Brother?" he asked.

"My name is Brother Septimus," their leader replied. "We have reason to believe you are harbouring fugitives."

"We tend to the sick and poor," offered Cyric, "if one of them is a fugitive, then you are welcome to take him."

"We seek a woman," said the Cunar leader. "She goes by the name of Natalia Stormwind."

"What has she done?" asked Cyric, still blocking the door.

"That is none of your concern," noted Brother Septimus.

"If you wish to gain entry to this mission, then it is my concern," Cyric refuted.

"Stand aside!" demanded Septimus. "We are Temple Knights."

"As am I," said Cyric, seeing the surprise on the man's face.

"Then you know, as well as I, Brother, that we must see justice done."

"You have still not told me what this woman has done, nor have you indicated why you think she is here. Until you have provided that information, I will deny you access to this mission."

"Tread carefully, Brother..."

"Cyric," he responded, "and I walk where others fear to tread. You will answer my questions or be denied access."

"Very well, Brother Cyric," the man responded. "The woman has run away from her family, and they are seeking her safe return. There is a reward posted for her recovery."

"And if this woman does not wish to return to her family?"

"It is of no consequence to us. We are to make sure her family's wishes are met."

"How is it," asked Cyric, "that Temple Knights are being used to retrieve a wayward daughter. Surely you are beneath such things."

"It is at the request of Lady Arabel Calderra. I believe you've met?"

"I have," Cyric admitted, "though I'm at a loss as to why she thinks this woman might be here."

"You travelled with this woman, did you not? Her, and her companion?"

"I did," he confirmed, "what of it?"

"Lady Calderra seems to think you may be harbouring them. What have you to say for yourself?"

Cyric stood back, letting the door open the rest of the way. "You are free to come and look for yourself, Brother Septimus, but I'm confident you won't find them here."

The Cunar stepped forward, pushing his way past. "We shall see, Brother Cyric. If you're found to be harbouring these criminals, you'll stand before a Church tribunal."

"I would welcome it," said Cyric, "for I have nothing to be ashamed of. Can you say the same?"

Brother Septimus turned on him suddenly, glaring at him. "Watch that tongue of yours, Brother, or I shall wipe the smile from your face."

"You are welcome to try, Brother," said Cyric, his face showing no emotion.

The Cunar was quick, but Cyric was faster. Septimus started to draw his sword, but less than half his blade was clear of the scabbard when Cyric struck. The palm of the Mathewite's hand crashed into the man's nose, knocking him off balance and causing blood to pour forth. Cyric followed with a kick to the Cunar's knee, and then his target crumpled to the floor. Before the other knights could react, Cyric leaned down, taking Septimus's blade from the scabbard and holding it at the man's throat.

"Back up," the Mathewite commanded, looking to the other Cunars. They did as he bid, then he turned his attention back to the one on the floor. "This is Holy land," Cyric said, "sanctified by Holy Fathers. If you want to search this mission, you'll need a written request from the Archprior himself. To cross that line is to bring the wrath of the Church down on your head. Do you understand me?"

Septimus nodded, but Cyric recognized the look of hate in his eyes.

"Very well," said Cyric, "then leave this place." He tossed the sword to the floor.

Brother Septimus rose to his feet, his knee in obvious agony as he shuffled forward, then bent to retrieve his sword, keeping his eyes on Cyric the entire time. Scabbarding his blade, he moved past the Temple Knight to exit the mission. "I won't forget this," Septimus swore.

"Good," said Cyric, "neither will I. I look forward to our next encounter."

Brother Septimus limped back into the street, his knights following. Cyric knew they'd be watching the mission, but he hoped he had bought enough time for Athgar and Natalia to escape.

Athgar peered around the corner of the building. In the distance, he could see the Travellers Rest, its interior lit by candles, noise drifting out of the open door.

"Do you see any knights?" whispered Natalia.

"No," he replied, "at least not outside. How do you want to do this?"

"I think it best if we just walk in like regular patrons," she responded.

"We could go around back," he suggested.

"That would be more suspicious," Natalia said. "I think a more direct approach is in order." She stepped out into the street, holding her hand out for him. "Come along," she said, "and relax. We're just two people out for a drink, remember?"

He did as she suggested, then stepped from the shadows. It was an uncomfortable feeling, being out in the open while so many were looking for them, but he was determined to show courage. He took her hand, and together, they moved towards the inn.

Athgar's eyes were scanning the road, on the lookout for danger, but Natalia concentrated on the open door before them. They entered the inn to see a dozen or so patrons, most sitting at tables, chatting amiably, but two were gathered around a board that was attached to the wall, one of them pulling knives from it as they talked.

Natalia and Athgar walked over to the nearest open table and sat down quietly. Moments later, they were approached by a serving girl. "Can I get you something? she asked.

"We're friends of Brother Caerwell," said Natalia, "do you know him?"

"I do," she said, leaning in a little closer. "I take it you'll need lodging?"

"We do," replied Natalia.

"Then follow me," said the girl.

PREPARATION

AUTUMN 1103 SR

Athgar bowed deeply, "And the blessings of the Gods be upon you."

"No," corrected Cyric, "not the Gods, the Saints. You're supposed to be a member of the Brothers of Saint Mathew, remember?"

"I'll never get this straight," he replied.

"You can do this," said Natalia, smiling. "If I can do it, so can you."

"It's nice of you to say," said Athgar, "but it's not so easy, breaking my old habits."

Natalia stood, walking over to him and embraced him. "You need a rest, that's all, you've been going at this all day long."

"I have to get this right," he responded, "or it'll be both our necks in the noose."

"Actually," offered Cyric, "it would be a chopping block, not a noose."

"Truly?" asked Athgar.

"Yes," said Cyric, "the Church is quite clear on such things. Remember, you'll be in the fortress. That's considered Church property, not part of the city. That means Church law will take priority."

"And the penalty for impersonating a member of the Church is...?"

"Beheading," completed Cyric, "but I doubt it'll come to that."

"How can you be so sure?" asked Natalia. "After all, your neck's not in danger."

"I can assure you it is," replied the knight, "perhaps even more so than yours."

"Explain yourself," said Athgar, "I'm not understanding."

"You two can leave once this is over," said Cyric, "while I'll have to remain and explain my actions."

"Fair enough," said Natalia. She kissed Athgar, "There, that's for good luck, now let's try again, shall we?" She sat down, the better to watch him.

"May the blessings of the Saints be upon you," he said, his voice crisp and clear.

"Very good," said Cyric, "you're getting much better at this. Now, you try Natalia, and remember, you're supposed to be dedicated to Saint Agnes. That means you tend to be devoid of emotion when you speak."

"Are you telling me," asked Natalia, "that these women have to show no emotions?"

"Not at all," Cyric revealed, "but they try not to show emotion in public. None of the orders do, actually."

"Why is that?" she asked.

"They want to be taken seriously in the role of warrior monks. In private they're just regular people."

"Who don't have sex!" added Natalia.

Cyric blushed, "Well, that is one of our vows."

"Not at all?" asked Athgar.

"Theoretically," said Cyric, "though there are often those who stray."

"And that includes the women? I'm glad I'm not really one of those."

"So am I," added Athgar.

"Actually," said Cyric, "women are allowed to leave the order at any time to either marry or have children. They can rejoin later if they wish, though they'd have to renounce their marriage."

"And how often does that occur?" asked Natalia. "I would think it rare."

"Not as rare as you might think. I knew a sister once that left to get married. She rejoined years later after her husband died."

"I didn't think you were that old," said Natalia.

Cyric laughed, "I didn't know her when she was a sister the first time, only after she rejoined the order."

"Is it strange for sisters and brothers to travel together?" asked Natalia. "I would think the Church would frown on it. After all, you'd be putting men and women together, something's bound to happen."

"Not at all," said Cyric. "The Sisters of Saint Agnes look after women, while brothers of my order look after the sick and poor, including women, so you can see how their responsibilities overlap. Historically, our two orders have always cooperated, much more so than the others."

Natalia pulled at her dress, a simple cassock of scarlet. Over this, she wore the surcoat of the order. "It's rather a coarse material," she complained. "Can't I wear a nice cotton shift underneath?"

"No," said Cyric, "if anyone were to notice, you'd be recognized as a fake."

"How about you, Athgar," she asked, "is yours any better?"

"I must confess, I agree with you," said the Therengian.

"You'll get used to it," promised Cyric. "It actually gets more comfortable once you stop thinking about it. The material will also soften with use."

"I must say I feel a bit naked without a weapon," said Athgar.

"That's easy enough to fix," said Cyric, "you can carry your axe."

"Are you telling me that brothers can carry weapons?" the Therengian said in surprise.

"The axe is the symbol of our order," Cyric continued, "it's not uncommon for even lay brothers to carry them. Just tuck it into your belt, no one will pay any attention to it."

"I must have left mine on the ship, I'm afraid," Athgar said. "The last time I saw it, it was embedded in a pirate."

"Here," offered Cyric, "take mine. I have a spare back at the mission."

Athgar tucked it into his belt, "That feels much better."

"Good," said Cyric, "now you look every inch the lay brother. Let's go over the plan one more time, shall we? You start, Athgar."

"You and I will approach the barbican as two fellows of Saint Mathew," said the Therengian.

"Brothers," corrected Cyric.

"Yes, that's right," Athgar agreed, "brothers. Natalia will be just behind us."

"Yes," continued Natalia, "close enough to arrive at the same time, but far enough away that I don't look like I'm with you."

"Good," said Cyric. "Now, once we announce ourselves we'll be waved through, I've arranged as much with the Archprior."

"How did you manage that?" asked Athgar.

"I owe him a report," said Cyric.

"Isn't that likely to arouse suspicion?" asked Natalia. "After all, couldn't you have just sent the report?"

"No," defended Cyric. "When I last saw him, I promised a report of some goings-on. It concerns something of great import to the Church that they wouldn't want to get out. Now, back to the plan. What do you do at the gate, Natalia?"

"I tell the guards I'm here to see Mistress Druina," she said, "whoever that is."

"For Saint's sake," uttered Cyric, "how many times do I have to tell you, she's the regional commander of your order."

"You're pushing too hard," said Athgar. "You need to give her more time."

"We don't have more time!" said Cyric. "They're already onto you, and it won't be too long before they are actively searching the streets. If we don't move soon, we'll lose the opportunity."

"If you say so," said Athgar.

"Now," continued Cyric, "what do you do after you tell them about Mistress Druina?"

"I wait," she said. "They'll likely question me about what I'm doing there, and that's when you'll speak up."

"That's correct," said Cyric. "I'll introduce both of us to you, and we shall talk as if there's to be a meeting between the Archpriors of our two orders. You've been called to help with the arrangements."

"And that will get us through the gates?" she asked.

"Undoubtedly," countered Cyric. "Cunars guard the gates, and they're notoriously uninterested in such things. All they like to do is fight."

"And if something goes wrong?" asked Athgar.

"At this stage, you won't be through the gates yet," Cyric explained, "so if things go badly, you can run back into the city, though I'd suggest you unleash your magic."

"Unleash our magic?" asked Natalia. "You mean cast spells at them?"

"Yes," Cyric agreed, "a simple demonstration of your power should be sufficient to convince them not to follow. They'll be caught between their desire to catch you, and the responsibility to report the incident. Given a choice between reporting and being hit by a spell, I'd say their decision should be obvious."

"What about you?" asked Athgar.

"I'll act surprised and talk my way out of it. We'll rendezvous back here if it becomes necessary."

"Are you sure?" asked Natalia. "We don't have to show our faces to the Church again, but the ramifications for you could be severe."

"I've handled worse before," offered Cyric, "but that's an entirely different story."

"All right," said Athgar, "so we make it past the barbican, what's next?"

"We head to the Harbour Gate," said Natalia, "but the guards there won't challenge us."

"Then we continue into the outer courtyard," added Athgar, "and keep our eyes open for the offices."

"Which are?" asked Cyric.

"On our left as we enter," said Athgar. "We're looking for the offices of Commander Morvus."

"That's right," said Cyric, pleased with the results. "And that's where we'll split up so as to avoid suspicion. I'll take up a position by the armoury.

Natalia, you'll enter the dining hall, keeping close to the entrance while Athgar finds the office."

"How will I know which office to look in?" asked Athgar.

"They'll have signs," said Cyric, "and his name will be on a door."

A look of worry crossed the Therengian's face.

"That won't work," interrupted Natalia, thinking quickly. "But I have another idea. Would it be strange for a sister to be looking for a commander of another order?"

"Not if she had a message for him," Cyric responded.

"Good," she continued, "then I'll pretend to be carrying one."

"Someone might want to see it," suggested Athgar.

"Then I'll write one before we leave and carry it with me," she said.

"That makes things too complicated," remarked Cyric, "it's better if Athgar goes in alone. He's less likely to arouse suspicions."

"He can't read," admitted Natalia.

"What?" said Cyric in shock.

"It's true," confessed Athgar. "Back in Athelwald, there was scant reason to learn."

"I wish I'd known that sooner," said Cyric, "but we'll have to take it in stride. Very well, we'll go with your idea, Natalia."

KARSLEV

AUTUMN 1103 SR

Grand Mistress Marakhova Stormwind made her way to the tower, the casting circle within was just what she needed for the task she had in mind. The guards stood at attention as she approached, while a servant opened the door, revealing a circular room, perhaps twenty feet in diameter. In the centre, a circle built into the stone floor inlaid with gold and precious gems caught the light from the windows, causing it to glisten in the mid-day sun.

Standing in the middle was a man, his elaborate green robes trimmed with mystic runes. He bowed gracefully as Marakhova entered, but waited until the door was closed behind her before speaking.

"Grand Mistress," he said, "you honour me with your presence."

"It is you that honour me, Nezerov," she said. "You alone, of all the Sartellians, I can trust with this task. I'm told you've used the spell of recall to travel to Corassus before?"

"I have, Mistress, though I actually use a ring of fire," the man replied.

"Good," she continued, "for that is where I intend you to go."

"It is a long distance," he said, "and I will require rest upon my arrival."

"Understood, Nezerov," she said, "but you should have more than enough time to complete your task."

"And what task might that be, honoured one?"

"You are to seek a woman named Natalia Stormwind," she said. "She has fled the Volstrum and must be punished."

"I see," he said, "and have you any idea where she might be found? Or am I to search the city, block by block."

"Not to worry, Nezerov, we have reports of her whereabouts," said Marakhova.

"And when I find her?"

"It would always be preferable, I'm told, to have her returned to us, but I doubt she'll cooperate."

"And if she cannot be returned?"

"Then," continued Marakhova, "she is to be eliminated. We cannot have rogue members of the family travelling about unsupervised."

"Is this on the orders of the matriarch?" Nezerov asked.

"No, you are under my direct, personal orders," the grand mistress said in reply. "Do you have a problem with that?"

"Of course not," he said, "I merely wished to be clear in my duties. Am I to assume that no one else knows of my assignment?"

"Yes, only you and I are privy to that information, and I want you to keep it that way."

"Then it shall be as you wish. Are there any further details you wish to impart to me before I leave?"

"Yes, Nezerov," she said, "I must warn you that this woman is extremely powerful."

"How powerful?" he asked.

"Likely the most powerful to ever graduate from the Volstrum. You must strike the moment you see her, to do otherwise might give her the advantage."

"Understood," he said. "It shall be as you desire."

She moved closer to him, putting her hands on his arm. "I needn't tell you how important this is, Nezerov. We all stand to profit by her removal, yourself included. Do a good job, and you shall be rewarded. Fail me, and you will incur my wrath."

He smiled, "Then I look forward to my reward."

She stepped back, outside the circle of magic, and nodded, signifying her permission for him to begin his spell.

Nezerov Sartellian placed his arms out to either side, calling forth the power within. The room buzzed with magical energy, the circle of magic coming to life, lighting up like a thousand fireflies. Flames leaped up, blocking Marakhova's view of the Fire Mage, and then they fell again, revealing only an empty centre.

Marakhova smiled, it was all done now; events had been put into motion that would secure her future. She turned from the circle, opening the door herself. The guards stood to attention once more as she exited, her footsteps echoing along the marble floor.

. . .

Flames rose from the circle, all but burning the ceiling above, then fell once more, to reveal Nezerov Sartellian. This room was similar to that in Karslev, but he noticed a distinct smell, the scent of the sea. Even here, beneath the structure, it permeated the air.

He stepped from the circle, making his way to the door. It opened to reveal, not the marble floors of the Volstrum, but the rough stone floor of a subterranean tunnel. Down the tunnel Nezerov went, then up the stairs at the end into an ornately decorated room, filled with comfortable chairs, along with an assortment of drinks, and a small bell. He smiled at a memory from past visits, and then sat, ringing the bell as he did so.

A few moments later, the door opened, and an older, well-dressed man peered in. His thinning grey hair framed a wizened face, and Nezerov struggled but a moment to remember the man's name.

"Virgil Sartellian," said Nezerov at last, "how long has it been?"

"Many years, my friend," the old man replied, "though I go by the name of Jazoc Wright, these days."

"It is good to see you," offered Nezerov, extending his hand out, palm downward.

Virgil's eyes grew wide as he noticed the deep red colour of his visitor's ring. He bowed respectfully. "You have done well for yourself, Lord."

Nezerov smiled at the change in the old man's behaviour. "Tell me, Virgil, how are things in Corassus?"

"They are going well," the older man responded. "I have managed to acquire a seat on the ruling council and have been sending back regular reports of their activities."

"Excellent, then you can tell me all you know about Natalia Stormwind. It was you that alerted the Volstrum, was it not?"

"It was," replied Virgil. "News first came to us by way of another council member, a woman named Arabel Calderra."

"And she knows of our involvement?" asked Nezerov, with a hint of a threat.

"No, Lord, she only thought the woman was acting suspiciously. It seems they became acquainted on the trip to Corassus when the lady was returning from a trip overseas."

"And how did that alert her?"

"Well," continued Virgil, "she demonstrated her power of water on the trip, and later, when Arabel asked her what business she had in Corassus, she claimed to be looking for information about her family. The name Sartellian was mentioned."

"A strange choice of names to drop," remarked Nezerov.

"My thoughts exactly. Lady Calderra reported this information to the

Temple Knights of Saint Cunar, they patrol the streets here. It didn't take me long to hear of it."

"And Natalia Stormwind, was she apprehended?"

"I'm afraid not," said Virgil. "She must have sensed a trap, for she never returned to her lodgings."

"What did you do at that point?"

"The Cunars took it upon themselves to investigate further. Apparently, she was in the company of a man calling himself Athgar."

"That name means nothing to me," said Nezerov.

"He's said to be a Therengian."

"What of it? Is he dangerous?"

"It seems he is capable of using Fire Magic," Virgil explained.

"Surely not," said Nezerov, "we wiped all of them out years ago. Are you sure?"

"We have corroborating witnesses. He demonstrated the use of fire several times during his trip here, and his control was said to be exceptional."

"Meaning?" asked Nezerov.

"Meaning he's been trained by someone proficient in the arts."

"Impossible," said the Fire Mage, "only the family can provide such training."

"And yet, the accounts are quite clear."

"An interesting tale," said Nezerov, "but my objective remains the same, the girl Natalia."

"And the other?" asked Virgil.

"He likely knows her secret and must be silenced. What steps have you taken to find her, so far?"

"We received a tip as to her whereabouts. During their trip to Corassus, they travelled aboard a Temple ship, along with a Mathewite known as Brother Cyric. He had just been assigned to take over the command of a mission his order maintains here in Corassus. Thinking he might be hiding them, we sent a group of knights to search the place, but they came up empty-handed."

"You sent knights?" asked Nezerov. "Where did you get those?"

"Yes, Temple Knights of the Order of Saint Cunar. We have a certain...influence over them."

"How many of these knights know of her connection to the family?"

"Very few," offered Virgil.

"Good, let's keep it that way," said Nezerov. "Who's our man on the inside?"

"A man that goes by the name of Commander Morvus."

"Excellent," said Nezerov, "then after I rest, I shall seek him out. Perhaps he can give me a better idea of what it is we're dealing with here."

INFILTRATION

AUTUMN 1103 SR

The path leading up to the fortress was steep, much more so than Athgar was expecting. He stubbed his toe on a stone and let out a curse, "Gods sakes."

"Saint's sake," Cyric corrected him quietly.

"Why can't you people wear regular boots?" asked the Therengian. "It would be far more comfortable than these things." He looked down at his feet.

"They're called sandals, Athgar," offered Cyric, "and we do wear boots when we're in armour, but today we're travelling as simple lay brothers."

"Still," the Therengian fumed, "it's a poor choice of footwear."

"Oh, I don't know," offered the knight, wiggling his toes, "it helps keep your feet cooler in the summer."

They drew closer to the barbican gate, and Athgar risked a glance over his shoulder, relieved to see Natalia still behind them.

"She's doing fine," said Cyric, "you must learn to trust her."

"I trust her completely," said Athgar, "but that doesn't mean I don't worry about her safety."

"We're almost at the gate," said Cyric. "It's time to start our little act."

"Here goes nothing," offered Athgar.

"Halt," called the guard, his dark grey tabard covering the metal that encased his body.

"Good day," offered Cyric in greeting. "We are here to see the Archprior of Saint Mathew. My name's Brother Cyric, and Brother Mathias, here, is my secretary."

The Cunar turned to his companion, who stood near the doorway, a book sitting nearby. "Brother Cyric to see Archprior Legault," he called out.

The other guard consulted the book, then waved them on.

Cyric took the lead, opening the small door that was within the larger. Behind them, Natalia had just reached the guards.

"Sister Marianne," she said, "to see Mistress Druina of Saint Agnes."

Athgar halted in the doorway, turning back to show a casual interest in the exchange.

"Brother Cadmus," the guard introduced himself, "of the Temple of Saint Cunar. You brighten our day, Sister."

Athgar could sense trouble brewing. He tapped Cyric on the shoulder, causing the Mathewite to turn and watch the developing situation.

"You flatter me, Brother Cadmus," said Natalia. "Tell me, are all Cunars so bold?"

"Better to be bold than a coward," said the guard, "and I'm no coward where women are concerned."

"But surely you've taken a pledge of celibacy," offered Natalia.

"Of course," the man responded, "but one must always tempt oneself to see if they keep their resolve, don't you think?"

"I see," she replied, "this is all about testing your ability to resist temptation. I shall have to mention this to the master of your order, it's a most interesting idea."

The mention of his superior seemed to change the man's attitude. "Well," he fumbled, "you'd best be on your way, Sister... what did you say your name was again?"

"Sister Marianne," she repeated.

"I don't see a Sister Marianne on the list," his companion called from the door.

"Sister Marianne," called out Cyric, "is that you?"

"Why, yes," she replied. "Brother Cyric, so good to see you again."

"I was just talking to Brother Mathias, here, about the meeting between our two Archpriors. I thought I saw your name on the list. Aren't you helping with the arrangements?"

"I am," she replied, "though I fear I'm a last-moment replacement. One of our sisters came down with a fever."

Cyric moved back towards Natalia, "I hope it wasn't the coughing fits again. It spreads so quickly, I'd hate to see others so infected."

Natalia cleared her throat with a cough, "I suspect Mistress Druina neglected to update the list."

Cyric turned to face Brother Cadmus. "I can vouch for her," he said with a practised manner.

"Of course," said the guard, eager to be rid of them.

Cyric indicated that Natalia should lead, and a moment later, they stepped through to meet Athgar.

"That was close," said the Therengian, once they were safely away from the gate. "I thought they'd become suspicious."

"No," said Cyric, "but it appears the Cunar order plays a little loose with the definition of celibacy."

"Can't say I blame them," said Athgar, grinning at Natalia. "After all, it can't be every day that someone so pretty walks up to the gate."

Natalia blushed at the compliment, "Now, now," she said, "that's hardly the way a brother of the cloth should be talking."

"I agree," said Cyric. "Now keep your mind on the business at hand."

"I will," Athgar promised.

They continued up the steep incline that led to the harbour gate. Two more Temple Knights stood watch, but they ignored the trio as they passed through. Moments later, they were in the outer courtyard, pausing to examine the area.

"I'm off to the armoury, just over there," Cyric said, pointing. "You two keep your eyes on the lookout. We're deep into it now, any slip-ups and it'll spell disaster."

Natalia looked over to the barracks, a large, three-storey structure, rectangular in shape, with its back against the fortress wall. Projecting out from either end were two smaller buildings, giving the whole structure the look of a squared-off letter 'C'.

"North or south?" Athgar asked.

"We'll search the southern block first," she said, "less likely to draw attention."

"Why do you say that?" he asked.

"The sun is to the south of us, so there's more shadows to give us cover."

"Good idea," he said, "let's get a move on, shall we?"

They began moving across the open space. One or two knights lounged outside of the barracks, none of them in armour. They were relaxing, nothing more, and, other than a passing glance at the two new visitors, they returned to whatever they were doing.

The block of offices had a small open area in front of it, forming a balcony on the second floor and a stone walkway on the ground. They stepped onto this walkway and were navigating their way down the building when they heard the sound of a door opening and words drifting out.

Looking north, across the open area, to the other block, they saw two men emerge from the entrance to the offices; one wore an elegantly decorated green robe while the other was armoured in full plate, save for his head.

Athgar froze. The scar running down the man's left cheek was the image that was burned into his memory, haunting him at night. The Therengian could not tear his gaze away, and their eyes locked. A yell from the robed man as he spotted Natalia broke Athgar from his inertia.

Nezerov, the green-robed mage, immediately started gesticulating, a streak of fire shooting across the distance. Athgar and Natalia dove, he to the left and she to the right, as fire struck the spot where they had been standing but a moment ago. Hot embers ricocheted off the wall, splashing them both with tiny sparks.

Natalia looked about wildly for cover as the unknown Fire Mage began another incantation, but finding nothing close, she cast a quick spell of her own to protect herself. A floating shield of ice appeared before her just as Nezerov released his magic, shooting flame across the field, searing into the ice, but the shield was sufficient enough, for now, to keep her from harm. Natalia countered with ice shards, and the small frozen spikes lanced out to strike him in the leg. He staggered back, limping slightly before casting anew.

Natalia, finally spotting a low stone wall that surrounded a flower garden, dove for cover. In response, the enemy Fire Mage sent a small spark flying across the courtyard to fall slightly short of her, sinking silently into the ground. A moment later, a snake-like creature emerged, but instead of scales, it had skin like molten lava with bright white glowing eyes. Opening its mouth, it spat, sending a stream of fire directly at her. She ducked as it splashed against the stone.

Athgar rolled back up onto his feet and rushed towards the Cunar commander with little more than revenge on his mind. Ignoring the mage casting at Natalia, the Therengian paused only long enough to conjure a spell, flames shooting from his fingers even as he ran, but in his rush to cast, he had fumbled, releasing only a small fire streak that splashed against the commander's chest, the Temple Knight's thick armour allowing him to merely shrug it off.

Athgar kept charging, reaching for his axe and getting it out just in time to parry the Temple Knight's onslaught, for as Athgar had advanced, Morvus had pulled his sword and stood, waiting. Sparks flew as sword met axe, their weapons locking for an instant, the combatants close enough for Athgar to smell the breath of his enemy. Commander Morvus pressed the attack, using his strength to bear down, but Athgar retaliated by kicking the commander in the shin. Unhurt, but unbalanced by the act, the knight drew back, giving the Therengian some breathing space.

Morvus advanced once more, swinging with his sword, but this time it was not Athgar that he attacked, instead it was his weapon. The axe sailed out of Athgar's hands, leaving him defenceless. There was little the Therengian could do now but dodge, hoping to gain some room to cast.

Natalia shot ice at the fire snake, but as she released the spell, the creature spat, burning her arm and spoiling her aim, the ice hitting the ground and scattering in all directions. She took a quick look around to get her bearings. The area to the west was clear, and she started moving in that direction, intent on finding better cover, but Nezerov threw up a curtain of flame, cutting off her retreat. She was now caught between a wall of flame and the spitting fire creature, with the green-robed mage advancing, his face a mask of rage.

With nothing to lose, Natalia conjured a mist, quickly filling the courtyard and blocking her sight of all but the immediate area.

As soon as Athgar had started running towards the commander, Cyric emerged from the armoury. All around him were shouts of alarm, and the Mathewite ran as fast as he could in the direction of the fight. Before he could help, however, a wall of fire sprang up before him, effectively sealing the combatants within. As a consequence, he was forced to watch, helplessly, as the battle unfolded before him.

Athgar rolled to the side, narrowly escaping the downward slash of the knight commander, but leaving himself prone. Seeing the opportunity, Morvus gave a shout of triumph as he raised his sword overhead, but it was not to be, for just as he started his final attack, a thick mist enveloped them both. The blade swung to Athgar's side, narrowly missing, and then he leaped to his feet, attempting to grapple with his sworn enemy.

Athgar's hands locked onto the commander's forearms, bearing down with all the strength he could muster. There was a titanic struggle as they fought, man versus man, in a test of might, but years of training had given the Temple Knight an advantage, and soon he was, once more, forcing the Therengian to the ground.

———

Natalia moved slowly through the mist until she could make out the fire snake. Without a target, it had started spitting in random directions, no doubt seeking her position. The flames that erupted from the creature's mouth now acted as a beacon. She concentrated on her spell and fired off an ice streak at the summoned beast, striking it dead centre, obliterating it with her magic.

Nezerov Sartellian, not to be outdone, gesticulated again, releasing even more power. A ring of fire appeared around him, expanding outward in a circle, evaporating the mist as it went. Natalia felt the warmth as it passed her position, but it did no damage.

With the mist dissipated, she spotted Athgar and the enemy knight locked in a struggle, but she could tell that Athgar was being overpowered. Calling forth her power once more, she sent a controlled blast their way, taking the Cunar in the arm, failing to penetrate his armour, but causing him to at least release his grip on her companion.

———

Athgar staggered back as Morvus released his hold on the Therengian. The struggle in the mist had somehow reversed their positions, and now Athgar stood, with his back to the open door through which his enemy had so recently emerged. He glanced back at Natalia, and, noting her fight with Nezerov, he chose to fire off a shot at the other Fire Mage, as he had so far been unable to penetrate the armour of his own adversary. Flames streaked from his fingers, hitting the green-robed mage just under the armpit, the man's robes bursting into fire, and knocking him to the side.

Nezerov turned in fury, unleashing a stream of his own fire, striking Athgar full in the chest. The Therengian felt the burning, smelled his flesh bubbling away as he was forced back through the open doorway behind him.

Morvus moved closer, stabbing out with his sword, pressing his advantage.

Natalia saw the flames drive Athgar back and cried out in alarm. This mage was killing him and must be stopped! Heedless to her own danger, she pointed her hands at her opponent, unleashing all the power she could. This time, she completely opened herself. There was a strange sensation as if water was being channelled through her, pulling her inside out as it rushed across the distance like a giant wave, to strike Nezerov.

At first, only frost began to appear on his clothes, and then it turned to ice, but still, her power poured forth, no longer subject to her control. Her hands went numb, small ice crystals forming on them, while her foe iced up even more. Soon, he was frozen solid, and she finally dropped to her knees in exhaustion, the taste of blood in her mouth. A cracking noise reached her ears, and she looked up in fascination as the ice began to slew off of him, then fascination turned to horror as the mage's entire body fractured, falling to the ground like so much broken pottery. Natalia collapsed, accompanied by the sound of breaking glass.

***

With the death of Nezerov, the wall of fire ceased to exist. Cyric rushed forward, eager to be of assistance, only to see Natalia, slumped on the ground, but no sign of the Therengian. The brother rushed towards her fallen body, the earth around her stained red with blood.

"Natalia," he called out, "can you hear me?"

Lifting her head, he was distraught to see blood pouring from her ears and mouth.

All around him, people were finally reacting, released from the spectacle of the fight. Temple Knights rushed from the barracks, their weapons held ready.

***

Athgar fell back, blood pouring from his wound. He was burned, in pain, and struggling to stay conscious.

Commander Morvus stood in the doorway, blocking his exit. "Who are you?" the Temple Knight demanded.

"You burned my village!" roared Athgar. "You left me for dead in a burning hut."

"Did I?" Morvus remarked. "I don't remember, but I should have made sure you were dead when I took the rest of your people away."

Athgar backed farther into the room, placing himself behind a desk, desperate to put some space between them.

"Do you think that will help you?" Morvus declared. "I shall enjoy killing you!"

"I may die," said Athgar, "but I'll take you with me."

"With what?" his opponent said. "You have nothing left."

Athgar closed his eyes, digging deep for his spark.

Commander Morvus watched intently, mistaking his actions. "Go ahead, pray to your old Gods. It will do you no good."

Athgar released his power. One moment it was a simple office, the next, smoke began emanating from every piece of wood, then flames erupted, sucking the very air from their lungs. The Temple Knight dropped to his knees, struggling to breathe as thick black smoke engulfed the room.

Athgar sprinted for the door, but instead of exiting, he closed it, placing his back against it.

Commander Morvus crawled across the room, moving towards the exit, his sword slicing erratically through the air. It cut across Athgar's stomach, and blood gushed forth, staining the floor red. Athgar remained standing, and the Temple Knight watched in horror as even more words of magic fell from the Therengian's mouth.

Morvus was sweating profusely now, his armour heating up all around him. He yelled in pain as the padding beneath started to smoulder. The commander struggled to rise from his knees, just as Athgar released all the energy he had remaining. A beam above them splintered into a thousand pieces as a burst of fire destroyed it, and then the ceiling came crashing down, burying the Cunar in burning rubble.

Athgar slid to the floor, his back still leaning against the door. The screams of Morvus grew more intense as the fire consumed him and then, went quiet. Only the roar of the fire could be heard as the Therengian finally passed out.

***

Cyric was lifting Natalia's head, looking for wounds, when the sound of an explosion seized his attention. Looking up to see the windows blow out of the northern offices, he watched as flames rose in abundance. In that instance, he knew, without a doubt, that Athgar must be somewhere inside.

The fire was spreading rapidly now, consuming all it touched. Cyric noticed a group of Temple Knights trying, in vain, to stem the spread of the flames, their backs bent to the task of hefting buckets of water.

As the offices burned, a sign caught his eye. It read 'Commander Morvus', and even as the edges began to char, he knew what must be done.

Cyric gently lay Natalia back down on the ground, then rushed towards the burning building.

He grabbed the door, intent on opening it, the handle almost too hot to hold. The Mathewite put his shoulder to the task, his weight behind it, but it only moved slightly. Smoke poured from the opening, but Cyric spotted something. An arm! Bracing again, he pushed even harder, the door moving only a handspan or two, but enough that he could squeeze his bulk through the opening as he held his breath.

The entire room was ablaze, the heat attacking him in a tremendous wave. Smoke stung his eyes, and his lungs cried out in protest, but then he saw the Therengian, jammed against the door. Cyric pulled Athgar to the side, allowing the door to open fully, then grabbed him beneath the arms, pulling the unconscious man out into the open.

He let go, leaving Athgar lying in the courtyard as his own legs gave way. Footsteps came closer, and Brother Cyric looked up to see himself surrounded by Temple Knights of Saint Cunar.

CELLS

AUTUMN 1103 SR

Athgar opened his eyes as he felt someone press a damp cloth to his forehead. Natalia bent over him, concern written on her face.

"Where are we?" he asked, the words croaking in his smoke-ravaged throat.

"In a cell," she replied. "We've been placed under arrest."

He tried to shift his position slightly but was wracked with pain.

"Stay still," she soothed, "you've been badly injured. I've bound your wound as best as I can, but there's little I can do for your burns."

"I killed him," he said.

"Yes, you did," she agreed, "but I fear it will do little for our present condition. We now sit, condemned to death for killing a temple commander."

"You can escape," he said.

"You're in no shape to move," said Natalia, "let alone try to escape."

"You can use your magic to save yourself," he pressed, "you're more than capable."

"No, I've used up all my power and then some. I'm afraid I'll not be casting for some time."

"Then use your name," he demanded. "Your family has influence, they wouldn't dare hurt a Stormwind."

Natalia looked at him in shock. "How do you know my family name?"

"I overheard them at Lady Arabel's," he confessed. "It didn't take me long to piece everything else together. I've seen how powerful you are, and you told me early on that your family was looking for you. Tell the Church who you are, and they're sure to let you go."

"No," she said, "they'd take me back to the Volstrum."

"But at least you'd be alive."

"I won't leave you!" she swore.

"I killed one of their commanders," he said, "they'll hang me."

"Then we'll hang together," she said, tears coming to her eyes. "I never really had a life until I met you. You accepted me for who I am, not my name. I love you, and I won't stand by and watch you die, for part of me would die with you. Better to surrender a full life than linger with half of one." She leaned forward, kissing him tenderly. "You are my heart, Athgar," she whispered.

"And you, mine," he choked out.

Their moment together was interrupted when they heard raised voices outside the barred window.

"What's that?" asked Athgar.

"The hangman, most likely," she said.

"No," said Athgar, "Brother Cyric said they prefer beheadings, remember? At least death will be quick."

The door to the jail was thrown wide open, and two men wearing plate armour entered. Their blue surcoats were emblazoned with a white sun, making the prisoners wonder who these knights might be.

One stayed by the door while the other came closer to their cell, unlocking it.

"Come with us," the man ordered.

Athgar staggered to his feet with Natalia's help. She led the way, Athgar leaning heavily on her shoulder as they left the cell, watched intently by their new visitors. The sun was high in the sky, the warmth pleasant on their skin as they exited the building to be met by Brother Cyric, flanked by men in the same blue and white surcoats. The Mathewite moved forward, embracing them both.

"Brother Cyric?" said Athgar.

Cyric backed up, tears clearly visible on his face. "I'm so glad you're both alive," he said.

"I don't understand," said Natalia, "are we not under arrest?"

"No," answered Cyric, "and we have a Life Mage on the way."

"Who are these people?" asked the Therengian.

"Let me introduce Brother Renaldo of the Temple of Saint Ansgar. These are his men," he swept his arms wide to indicate the blue and white-clad knights.

"Saint Ansgar?" said Athgar.

"Yes," said Cyric, "the order was formed to investigate corruption and the like within the Church itself. When I took my concerns to the Archprior, he was less than enthusiastic about looking into them, so I decided my best course of action was to contact Brother Renaldo here. Members of his order can be found throughout the kingdom, in virtually every major city. They have broad powers to carry out their duties, and no one is immune from their questions. When I told them of my suspicions, they launched an immediate investigation."

"So all this was for naught?" said Athgar.

"No," said Cyric, "you have revealed the duplicity of Commander Morvus, and for that, the Church will be eternally grateful. They have rounded up his colleagues. The rest of the order has been cooperating fully."

"And that Fire Mage," asked Natalia, "who was he?"

"We were hoping you could shed some light on that," said Brother Renaldo.

"He must have been a Sartellian," offered Athgar, looking to his companion. "He definitely recognized you."

"True, and he certainly knew how to wield fire," admitted Natalia, "and yet I thought they wanted me alive. He didn't appear interested in catching me."

"Perhaps somebody wants you silenced?" suggested Cyric.

"But why?" she asked. "I'm nothing but a peasant girl."

"We may never know," said Cyric, "but you'll have to watch your back from now on. He may not have been working alone."

"I'll look after her," promised Athgar.

"We'll look after each other," corrected Natalia. She took his hand, holding it gently. "What of the slaves?"

"The Cunar slavery ring is broken," said Brother Renaldo, "and I have no doubt that without Commander Morvus, the Church will order the temple fleet to eradicate the pirates that have plagued the coast for so long. They'll likely attack them from land and sea, hoping to rescue as many slaves as they can to make amends for allowing this tragedy to take place under their very noses. The Pirate Coast will also no longer bear that name."

"So that's it?" said Athgar. "We're free to go?"

"You're in no shape to go anywhere just yet," warned Natalia.

"Agreed," said Cyric. "Let us heal you first, my friend, then fit you out with horses and supplies, or would you rather take a ship somewhere?"

"No, thank you," said Athgar, rather hurriedly, "I'll keep my feet on solid ground for a while if you don't mind."

"What about you?" asked Natalia. "Surely the Archprior won't look kindly on you going behind his back?"

"I'm sure he won't," the temple knight admitted, "so I sent a letter to the

Grand Master of my order asking him to move me elsewhere to avoid any repercussions."

"And you think he'll do it?" asked Athgar.

Cyric smiled, "Let's just say the Grand Master and I have an understanding. He sends me places, and I keep an eye on things for him."

"I thought you said that was the job for the Brothers of Saint Ansgar?" said Natalia.

"I'm not referring to internal matters," said Cyric, "but there are many things outside of the Church that merits further investigation. Don't worry, I'll have plenty to keep me busy."

Athgar shifted his feet, then swayed.

"I think we'd best get him a seat," said Natalia.

"Agreed," said Cyric, "and let him rest while we wait for the healer.

Sometime later, the healer arrived, an elderly Life Mage wearing a rather stylish, but tattered robe. He kept muttering to himself as he looked over the Therengian's wounds, then stepped back in shock as he finally took notice of Athgar's grey eyes.

"This man is a Therengian!" he announced.

"What of it?" asked Cyric.

"He's a heathen! They all worship the old Gods," the man proclaimed.

"He is an ally of the Church," declared Cyric, his voice patient.

"This is most unusual," the healer persisted. "These heathens are known to worship the old Gods. Who knows what strange rites he has been a part of?"

"Then I'd suggest you heal him, the better to be gone from his sight," offered Natalia.

"Why is he wearing the cassock of your order?" the mage pressed.

"As I said," Cyric repeated, "he's an ally of the Church. Can you tell a man's beliefs by the colour of his eyes alone?"

The Life Mage, much humbled by the rebuke, went quiet for a moment. "No," he finally admitted, "I suppose not."

"Good," said Cyric, "then how about you heal this man?"

"Very well," the healer relented. He held his hands in front of his face, speaking the words of power. When his fingers began to glow bright orange, he touched Athgar's shoulder, the light transferring into the Therengian's body. It lingered at the site of his wounds, then slowly dissipated, revealing fresh, unblemished skin.

"It is done," the Life Mage said, "though he will be weak for some time."

"Thank you," said Cyric. "Brother Renaldo will see to your payment."

The healer nodded, "Thank you, and may the blessings of the Saints be upon you."

"And you," added Cyric.

He waited till the man was out of earshot, fumbling in his cassock for something. Moments later, he fished out a purse.

"Here," he said, handing it to Natalia.

"What's this?" she asked.

"A gift from the Church," said Cyric, "to help you on your way."

She peered inside to see the coins within. "We can't accept this," she protested.

"Nonsense," replied Cyric, "it's the least we could do after the mess you uncovered here. Consider it payment for not speaking of this matter."

"Ah, I see," said Athgar, "the Church wants this hushed up."

"Fine by me," said Natalia, "I don't have any problem with it."

"Nor do I, I suppose," said Athgar.

Cyric looked across the open area to the stables beyond. Three horses were being brought out, already saddled. "These are for you," he said.

"Three horses?" asked Natalia.

"Two actually," said Cyric, "the last is for me. I'm going to escort you out of the city."

"But I can't ride," objected Athgar.

"Nor can I," added Natalia.

"It's not that difficult," soothed Cyric, "and these horses are old and know their business."

"You're giving them to us?" asked Athgar in surprise.

"Yes," Cyric replied, "to do with as you wish."

"But why horses?" asked Natalia. "Why not send us by coach?"

"That's simple," said Athgar. "Coaches are easy to locate and have to keep to the roads. With horses, we can go cross country, making it much harder to be followed."

"You learn quickly," said Cyric.

Cyric pulled himself into the saddle, sitting comfortably while others moved to help his friends mount. Athgar looked extremely uncomfortable in the saddle while Natalia appeared quite pleased with herself.

"My rear end is not going to like this," the Therengian complained.

"Nor mine, if the truth be told," responded Natalia. "I wish they'd taught us riding at the Volstrum."

"I thought they had," offered Athgar, "you look so comfortable sitting there. It suits you."

"It's purely show, I promise you," she replied.

"Now that you're done here," said Cyric, "where will you go?"

"North," said Athgar with some determination. "There are rumours of survivors who've escaped from the slavers. We'll seek them out if we can."

"And if you can't find them?" asked Cyric.

"Then we'll go wherever we need to, to keep Natalia safe."

"Come along then," said Cyric, "it's time we were going. You'll want to be well out of the city by dark." He urged his horse forward, the other two following along behind him.

They made their way through the outer keep, where rescuers still picked through the fire-ravaged barracks, searching for survivors.

Athgar looked past the Temple Knights, to the smouldering wreck of the building in the background. "Fate is strange," he said at last, "my journey to here began in ashes, and now, it ends the same way."

"No," corrected Natalia, "it's our journey, and it has only just begun."

EPILOGUE

AUTUMN 1103 SR

S tanislav Voronsky shifted in the dirty straw, his eyes staring into darkness. Time in this filthy prison no longer had any meaning, merely stretching on forever, neither day nor night, an eternity with no chance of escape.

Distant footsteps drew his attention. Someone was approaching, he thought, is this to be my final day? They halted outside the door to his cell, and then a voice spoke out, loud and clear.

"Unlock this door," a woman said, "then leave us."

Stanislav heard a key inserted into the lock, and then the tumblers creaked as the door was unfastened. Someone entered, but it took some time for his eyes to adjust as the torchlight from the hallway flooded into his tiny cell.

His visitor waved a hand, and a small globe of light appeared, almost blinding him. The mage hunter shielded his eyes until they adjusted to the change and then stared in surprise as he recognized his visitor.

He struggled to his feet. "Matriarch," he said, his legs shaking with the strain.

"Sit, Stanislav," commanded Illiana Stormwind. "We have things to discuss, you and I."

He lowered himself back to the damp straw, keeping his eyes on her.

"It was Marakhova that put you here," said the matriarch, "was it not?"

"It was," he said, "I was accused of plotting against the family."

She stared at him a moment as if sizing him up, then turned slightly, pointing at the doorway and uttering a spell. Moments later, a thick wall of ice blocked all egress from the room.

"There," she said, "now we can talk in private."

"Why are you here, Matriarch?"

"To make you an offer," she replied.

"I'm listening," he said.

"I will release you," she continued, "and in exchange, I want you to do something for me."

He saw a chance at redemption, but then wondered what the cost might be. "Very well," he finally agreed, "it seems I have little choice."

"I will provide you with funds," she said. "I want you to travel the continent."

"For what purpose?" he asked.

"I want you to find Natalia."

"I won't bring her back here," he swore.

"Nor would I expect you to," she said, surprising him. "I want you to find her and keep her safe."

"I don't understand?" he said. "Why would you do that?"

"I'm an old woman," she confessed, "and have outlived most of my own family. Did I ever tell you the story of my son, Antonov?"

"No," he said, "but I fail to see what he has to do with any of this."

"He was a powerful Fire Mage," she continued, ignoring his comment, "but he fell into disgrace after visiting the estate of Baron Rozinsky."

Stanislav's eyes lit up, this was indeed something of interest. "The same baron," he said, "that Natalia's mother was indentured to?"

"The very same," she replied. "My son died later that same year, immolated attempting to cast a powerful spell. He never knew that he left a child behind."

"Natalia is your granddaughter!" exclaimed Stanislav.

"She is," Illiana confirmed.

"But why this plan? Surely you'd want her by your side?"

"I don't have much time left in this world," she continued, "and my enemies would attempt to use her against me. I would have her free from such interference. When I pass on to the Afterlife, I want assurances that Natalia will remain free of the family's influence."

"Then I accept," said Stanislav. "And on my honour, I will protect her."

———

CONTINUE THE SERIES WITH EMBERS: BOOK TWO

REVIEW ASHES

If you liked *Ashes,* then *Servant of the Crown,* the first book in the *Heir to the Crown* series awaits.

START SERVANT OF THE CROWN

CAST OF CHARACTERS

ORCS

Agar - Youngling, son of Shaluhk and Kargen, Red Hand Tribe
Artoch - Master of flame, Red Hand Tribe
Durgash - Hunter, Red Hand Tribe
Gorlag - Chieftain of the Orcs of the Red Hand
Kargen - Chieftain, bondmate to Shaluhk, Red Hand Tribe
Khorsune - Hunter, Red Hand Tribe
Laruhk - Hunter, brother to Shaluhk, Red Hand Tribe
Shaluhk - Shamaness, bondmate to Kargen
Tonfer Garul - Scholar at the great archives in Corassus
Uhdrig - Shamaness, Red Hand Tribe Shaluhk

THERENGIANS

Athgar - Fire Mage, main character
Caladin - Hunter, betrothed to Melwyn
Ethwyn - Sister to Athgar
Melwyn - Athgar's ex-betrothed
Rothgar (Deceased) - father to Athgar
Skora - Old woman

THE FAMILY/THE VOLSTRUM

Alexi Sartellian (Deceased) - Son of Ivan and Svetlana, founders of the Family
Antonov Stormwind (Deceased) - Son of Illiana Stormwind, Dagor Sartellian
Dagor Sartellian - Fire mage and agent of the family
Dominique Stormwind - Water Mage, instructor at the Volstrum
Galina - Water Mage, student of the Volstrum
Gregori Stormwind - Water Mage, instructor at the Volstrum
Helene Sartellian (Deceased) - Fire Mage, mother of Katrin
Illiana Stormwind - Matriarch of the Stormwinds
Ilya Stormwind - Water Mage, instructor at the Volstrum
Ivan Sartellian (Deceased) - Founder of the family, married to Svetlana Stormwind
Katrin - Water Mage, student of the Volstrum
Kelvin Stormwind - Water Mage, instructor at the Volstrum

Kolyak Stormwind - Fire Mage, father of Katrin
Lydia - Water Mage, student of the Volstrum
Marakhova Stormwind - Grand Mistress of the Volstrum
Matias - Water Mage, student of the Volstrum
Mikhail Stormwind - Water Mage, student of the Volstrum
Natalia Stormwind - Water Mage, student of the Volstrum, main character
Nezerov Sartellian (Deceased) - Fire Mage
Nina Stormwind - Water Mage, instructor at the Volstrum
Oksana - Water Mage, student of the Volstrum
Pyotr - Water Mage, student of the Volstrum
Svetlana - Water Mage, student of the Volstrum
Svetlana Stormwind (Deceased) - Founder of the family, married to Ivan Sartellian
Tatiana Stormwind - Water Mage, instructor at the Volstrum
Terekhova Stormwind
Vasily - Water Mage, student of the Volstrum
Virgil Sartellian (Jazoc Wright) - Fire Mage, ruling council of Corassus
Voltana Stormwind - Water Mage, instructor at the Volstrum
Yana - Water Mage, student of the Volstrum

The Church

Ambrose - Lay brother of Saint Mathew
Cadmus - Temple Knight of Saint Mathew
Caerwell - Lay brother of Saint Mathew
Cyric - Temple Knight of Saint Mathew
Druina - Regional Commander of Temple Knights of Saint Agnes
Joram - Lay brother of Saint Mathew
Joram - Lay brother of Saint Mathew
Legault - Archprior of Saint Mathew
Marianne - Name used by Natalia, Sister of Saint Agnes
Mathias - Lay brother of Saint Mathew
Morena - Temple Knight of Saint Agnes
Morvus - Commander, Temple Knight of Saint Cunar
Renaldo - Lay brother of Saint Mathew
Septimus - Temple Knight of Saint Mathew

Others

Akosia - Goddess of Water
Andre - Magehunter
Arabel Calderra - Baroness, City Council member of Corassus

Corban - Servant of Lady Calderra
Harnen Runell - Captain of the Swift, a merchant ship out of Ilea
Howe - Captain of the Marianne, a river boat
Hraka - God of Fire
Nikolai - Member of Stanislav's team
Redblade - Human hero from the east
Rozinsky - Baron in Ruzhina
Safak - Sailor of the Zephyr
Stanislav Voronksy - Magehunter
Viktor (Deceased)- Member of Stanislav's team
Vladimir Kurzak - Bounty Hunter
Zafir Kopruli - Captain of the Zephyr

PLACES

Athelwald (Destroyed) - Old village near Ord-Kurgad, birthplace of Athgar
Caerhaven - Capital, Duchy of Krieghoff
Corassus - City State, Coast of Shimmering Sea
Cragmore - Village in the Duchy of Holstead
Draybourne - Capital of the Duchy of Holstead
Grazburg - Foreign kingdom, possible posting for Natalia
Halvarian Empire - East of Petty Kingdoms
Herani - Holy City, birthplace of Humanity
Holstead - Duchy in the Petty Kingdoms
Ilea - City State
Karslev - City, capital of Ruzhina
Korascajan - Sartellian Fire Mage Academy
Krieghoff - Duchy, West of Holstead
Ord-Kurgad - Orc Village, Red Hand Tribe
The Traveller's Rest - Inn in Corassus
Therengia - Ancient Kingdom destroyed centuries ago
Volstrum - Stormwind Water Mage Academy, city of Karslev

THINGS

Drake - Inn in Draybourne
Green Leaves - Inn in Draybourne
Magerite - Gem that shows the potential of Mages
Rygaurs - Flying creatures
Swift - Ship on the Great Sea
Zephyr - small boat, pirate hunter

A FEW WORDS FROM PAUL

When I started writing Ashes, I knew I wanted to tell the story of an extraordinary pair of mages. Though roughly the same age, they are from entirely different backgrounds, his the rustic life of a small, backward village, hers one of relative privilege amongst the most powerful mages on the continent. Each is naïve in their own way, but together they form a formidable partnership, one which makes them both stronger.

Along the way, they meet others, such as Brother Cyric. His devotion to the church helps introduce the Church of the Saints, an archaic, confusing organization that is showing signs of crumbling. Athgar and Natalia's story is far from over, as you will see in book 2 of the series, Embers. Brother Cyric, meanwhile, still his own issues to deal with, and these will be explored at a later date in a new series of books!

I must, of course, thank all the wonderful people that helped bring this story to fruition. It was a long road, made longer by all the background detail I had to develop to bring this new story to fruition. Once again, a big thank you to Christie Kramberger, for creating the cover art.

I would also thank the following people for their insightful input and support during this process:

Brad Aitken, Jeffrey Parker, Stephen Brown, Rachel Deibler, Tim James, Mark Tracy, Phyllis Simpson, Don Hinkley, James McGinnis, David Clark, Kathy Brown, Stuart Rae, and Diana 'Dee' Lundgren.

As before, my biggest thanks must go to my wife, Carol Bennett, without who's tireless efforts this book would not have reached print.

Finally, I thank my readers. I originally started writing because I felt I had stories to tell, and you, the readers, have responded with enthusiasm and glee, encouraging me to write even more.

EMBERS - THE FROZEN FLAMES: BOOK 2

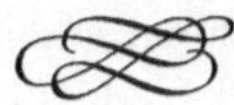

CHAPTER ONE - MORNING

Winter 1104 SR*
(Saints Reckoning)

Athgar opened his eyes to see the sleeping form of Natalia beside him, her bare leg laying across him, poking out from beneath the blanket. In the cold morning air, his breath frosted, and he looked over at the fireplace to see nothing but embers, their expected glow all but extinguished.

Calling on his inner spark, he pointed, and moments later, a small fire burst to life, its flames desperately trying to ignite the burned remains. It wouldn't last long, he knew, probably only long enough for him to rise from his bed and place more logs to fuel it, but to do that, he must first extricate himself from Natalia's limbs. He gently lifted her leg, deftly rolling out from beneath her and paused, making sure he hadn't disturbed her slumber.

Athgar stood, pulling a cloak from the back of a nearby chair and wrapped it around his shoulders. The chill was starting to wane, the magical flames driving it from the room, but he knew it wouldn't last. He moved to the fireplace, placing more logs, and waited, entranced by the fire as it slowly danced its way across the wood. The heat warmed him as he crouched, deep in thought. As a wielder of fire, he had learned to control this destructive force of nature, and yet the Orcs had taught him the importance of respecting it. As the flames grew, his mind wandered to more recent events.

After their encounter with the Fire Mage in the great port of Corassus, they knew they couldn't remain there. Thanks to Brother Cyric, they had been given horses, but their lack of riding skills and the cold weather had worn them both out. They had left the city with no clear destination but had finally found refuge here, in Ostermund, a little village in the foothills of the Grey Spires Mountains. It was far removed from the great cities of the Petty Kingdoms, and, he hoped, beyond the reach of Natalia's family.

"Athgar," Natalia called out, "what are you doing?"

He turned his attention back to her. "I'm just warming the place up," he explained. "The fire had burned down, and it was getting chilly."

"Come back to bed," she urged, "and I'll keep you warm."

He smiled as he moved towards the bed where she had rolled onto her back, her dark hair framing her pale face as she looked up at him.

"Well," she said, "what are you waiting for?"

"Can't a fellow admire his mate?" he asked, his face breaking into a grin.

"Is that what I am?" she said in mock seriousness. "Athgar's mate?"

"Oh, you're much more than that," he explained.

"Then come to bed and show me," she invited.

Athgar threw off his robe and climbed into the bed, pulling the covers around them as he snuggled up closer to her, and then she suddenly called out in protest.

"Your feet are cold!" she declared, shrieking in laughter.

"Then let's warm them up together!"

Some time later, Natalia awoke to the room still lit by the fire, filled with its warmth. She lay on her side, with Athgar snuggled up behind her. Deftly removing his arm, she climbed out from beneath his embrace to stand beside the bed and gaze down at him, taking in his youthful appearance. He was brown-haired, like most Therengians, with the patchy beard typical of a twenty-year-old, and she longed to look into his grey eyes, the mark of his race. She could stare into them for hours, she decided, content just to be with him.

Tearing her gaze away from the bed, she moved instead to the window, where the glass was frosted over, evidence of the winter that had descended upon them. Scraping away the frost, she gazed out upon the vista before her. Off in the distance, she could make out the peaks of the Grey Spires, not the biggest mountain range on the Continent, but undoubtedly impressive to one that had never seen such terrain up close.

Natalia longed to stay here, in Athgar's embrace, and spend a lifetime together in peace, but she knew it was not to be. Ever since her escape from the Volstrum, she had become a wanted woman, destined to be forever on the run from the family. They weren't her real family, of course, for she had been born a mere peasant girl, but when her magical potential had manifested early, she had been whisked away to be trained as a Water Mage and inducted into the Stormwind-Sartellian family. Once she completed her training, she had become the first-ever low-born to be inducted into the family as a battle mage, but then they had made known their intentions; she was to be bred with a Fire Mage to produce a powerful offspring.

Looking back down at the bed, she suddenly became keenly aware of the strange twist of fate that had led her to Athgar, or more accurately, he to her. She had balked at the thought of a forced coupling with an unknown Fire Mage, and yet here she was, doing the very thing she had fled from.

Athgar shifted slightly in his sleep, bringing a smile to her lips. He was no ordinary Fire Mage, she knew, for the Orcs had taught him a disciplined way of controlling his powers, rather than the full-strength magic expected of a Volstrum graduate.

Natalia turned her attention back to the window, staring off at the distant peaks to the north. Somewhere, beyond those mountains, lay Karslev, and the Volstrum. Was there any place that was free from their influence? She involuntarily shivered.

"Nervous?" Athgar's reassuring voice broke through her thoughts. He had risen from the bed, and she saw his reflection in the glass as he walked up and placed his arms around her.

"Not with you here," she replied. "You make me feel safe."

"Then what is it?"

"How long will we have to be on the run?" she asked.

"It depends," he responded. "How long will the family keep looking for you?"

"They'll never give up!" she admitted.

"Then we'll keep running forever," he promised. "We'll do whatever it takes to keep you safe."

"I can't ask that of you," she said. "You deserve a chance to live, to raise a family."

"Nonsense," he argued, "I am living. It's you that brought joy to my life. We'll see this through to the end, even if we have to destroy the entire family ourselves. In any case, we're safe here."

"How can you say that?" she asked.

"We've been here for almost two weeks with no sign of the family," he explained.

"But what of your own people?" she asked. "And you still have to find your sister, Ethwyn. I'm only getting in the way."

"No," he insisted, "you're not. If they've survived this long, they're still alive, and they'll likely remain that way. Our job right now is to keep you safe. The search for Ethwyn and the other Therengians will have to wait. I'm sure the Gods will understand."

She turned to face him, his arms still around her. "Do you really think the Gods take an interest in such things?"

"I suppose I do," he remarked. "Can't you say the same thing for your Saints?"

"An interesting thought," she responded, "and one to which I've never given much reflection. I've never considered myself to be very religious. I suppose that's common for mages."

"So you consider us meeting a chance encounter?" he asked.

"I'd say fortuitous," she confessed, "why? Are you suggesting your Gods brought us together?"

"I'm not saying anything, I'm just glad that we met, whatever the circumstances."

"Me too," she said, "but maybe it's time we moved on?"

"To where?" he asked. "We're already at the edge of the known world, where else can we go?"

"I don't know," she replied, "likely nowhere is safe for long. I'm not sure what to do."

He moved his face closer to hers, kissing her tenderly. At that precise moment, his stomach growled, and she burst into laughter.

"It appears it's time to eat," she said.

He blushed, "So it is!"

"Come along then," she urged, "let's get some clothes on and see what's for breakfast.

Continue reading Embers

ABOUT THE AUTHOR

Paul J Bennett (b. 1961) emigrated from England to Canada in 1967. His father served in the British Royal Navy, and his mother worked for the BBC in London. As a young man, Paul followed in his father's footsteps, joining the Canadian Armed Forces in 1983. He is married to Carol Bennett and has three daughters who are all creative in their own right.

Paul's interest in writing started in his teen years when he discovered the roleplaying game, Dungeons & Dragons (D & D). What attracted him to this new hobby was the creativity it required; the need to create realms, worlds and adventures that pulled the gamers in to his stories.

In his 30's, Paul started to dabble in designing his own roleplaying system, using the Peninsular War in Portugal as his backdrop. His regular gaming group were willing victims, er, participants in helping to playtest this new system. A few years later, he added additional settings to his game, including Science Fiction, Post-Apocalyptic, World War II, and the all-important Fantasy Realm where his stories take place.

The beginnings of his first book 'Servant to the Crown' originated over five years ago when he began a new fantasy campaign. For the world that the Kingdom of Merceria is in, he ran his adventures like a TV show, with seasons that each had twelve episodes, and an overarching plot. When the campaign ended, he knew all the characters, what they had to accomplish, what needed to happen to move the plot along, and it was this that inspired to sit down to write his first novel.

Paul now has four series based in his fantasy world of Eiddenwerthe and is looking forward to sharing many more books with his readers over the coming years.

Member of:
    Alliance of Independent Authors (ALLI)
    Science Fiction Writers of America (SFWA)

www.ingramcontent.com/pod-product-compliance
Lightning Source LLC
Chambersburg PA
CBHW061621190726
48288CB00007B/2415